The Careless Word

Catriona King

Discover us online:
www.crookedcatpublishing.com

Join us on facebook:
www.facebook.com/crookedcatpublishing

Tweet a photo of yourself holding
this book to **@crookedcatbooks**
and something nice will happen.

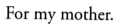

For my mother.

About the Author

Catriona King trained as a doctor and a police Forensic Medical examiner in London, where she worked for many years. She worked closely with the Metropolitan Police on several occasions. In recent years, she has returned to live in Belfast.

She has written since childhood; fiction, fact and reporting. 'The Careless Word' is the eighth novel in the Craig Crime Series. Book nine in the Craig Crime Series, 'The History Suite', will be released in spring 2015, book ten, 'The Sixth Estate' is currently in edits.

Acknowledgements

My thanks to Northern Ireland for providing the inspiration for my books.

I would like to thank Crooked Cat Publishing for being so unfailingly supportive and cheerful.

My thanks to Andrew Angel as editor, and thanks to Leondra Clarke, owner of 'Forever Bridal', Belfast.

And I would like to thank all of the police officers that I have ever worked with, anywhere, for their unfailing professionalism, wit and compassion.

Catriona King
Belfast, January 2015

Also by Catriona King

The Craig Crime Series

A Limited Justice
The Grass Tattoo
The Visitor
The Waiting Room
The Broken Shore
The Slowest Cut
The Coercion Key
The Careless Word
The History Suite
The Sixth Estate

Discover more at: **www.catrionakingbooks.com**
Engage with the author: **catriona_books@yahoo.co.uk**

The Careless Word

Chapter One

Belfast. Thursday 17th July 2014. 2 p.m.

The smoke cleared as the young man gazed around him, stunned in the near silence and caged-in by the debris that was all that remained of the small, quaint shop. Only a faint ringing in his ears and the ache in his head made it seem real.

Once-tall wooden shelves lay splintered on the floor and the books they'd held hid shredded and singed in what remained of corners, or floated as solitary pages across his view. In his shock the boy reached out to grasp one. He checked himself, dropping his hand to his side and shaking his head hard. Not to relieve the dull, high cadences of tinnitus, but in disbelief that he was still alive.

Surrounding him were bodies with their limbs heat-charred and locked forever in a pose, or lying feet from their owner beside the remnants of some other corpse. A dying man's voice gasped one word; "Why?" His eyes begging for an answer to the destruction before it stole his life.

The young man gazed down vaguely, wiping blood from a cut on his hand. He turned the question over in his mind. "Why?" Why indeed? But his was a different why. Not why had this happened but why had he survived?

***

Docklands Coordinated Crime Unit. The Murder Squad. 3.30 p.m.

"Of course, you realise what this means?"

Liam Cullen threw his question across the squad-room expecting immediate attention and was sadly disappointed by the lack of reply. He cast a disgusted look around, seeking proof that he was being deliberately ignored. Except that he wasn't. Only the team's analyst, Davy Walsh, was present and he was busy; tapping at his computer, hunched over it like a man half his size and three times his age. Liam clambered to his feet and strode across to stand beside the young Emo, then he repeated the question again in his booming bass.

Davy recoiled from the noise, pressing both hands against his ears. "Ow! W…What the hell, Liam?"

"What the hell what, son? Don't you mean where the hell? As in, where the hell are all the people who're supposed to work in this place?"

Davy leapt to his feet in a mock-challenge. He stood half-a-head shorter than Liam's six-feet-six frame and fifty percent lighter, but the fifty percent that was left was solid, lean muscle, built up by his marathon training with the local head pathologist, John Winter. Liam snorted at the younger man's display of bravado and waved a hand around the room.

"So? Where are they then?"

"Nicky and Annette took a long lunch to s…shop for w… wedding outfits. Jake's at the dentist and the boss is…"

Davy turned to scan the room, so fast that his long dark mane whipped round and caught Liam across the face. As Liam spat out a mouthful of hair and began a 'short back and sides' lecture, the double-doors of the squad-room slid open and the tall shape of Marc Craig strolled onto the floor. Davy pointed and finished his sentence as if Liam hadn't interrupted. "… there."

He sat down triumphantly and tossed his hair deliberately to display its length, knowing that it irritated the hell out of the old-style cop. It was one reason why he would never join the police, that and his desire to stay alive. Craig smiled at the interaction as he wandered across the room. He grabbed a chair beside Davy's desk and beckoned Liam to sit, then he unbuttoned his well-cut jacket and shot them both a grin.

"OK, let me guess. Liam, you're bored and looking for attention, and Davy, you're deliberately not playing ball?"

Liam pretended to be offended. "Don't take me for granted, boss. You don't know everything that makes me tick."

Craig's grin widened. "And you learned that phrase from Danni."

Liam was about to launch into a speech about what a good husband he was to the mother of his two children when Craig continued. "OK, Nicky and Annette will be back at four; they're buying their outfits for John's wedding." He scanned the other men's faces. "That just leaves us three, so I'm going to give you a choice."

"Of w...what?" Davy's light stammer on 's' and 'w' had the effect of making his every sentence sound excited or vulnerable, and the vulnerability was fading with the years.

"Of whether we take a case or not."

Liam raised an eyebrow sceptically. "Yeh, right. Like you're ever going to walk away from a case."

Craig shrugged. "We're flying to Barbados for John and Natalie's wedding on the 30th, so taking on a case that we mightn't have time to finish would be a bad idea."

"And letting a perp get away would be a worse one." Liam leaned forward eagerly. "What's the story?"

Craig frowned for a moment before he spoke. "It's a strange one; and yes, before you say it, I know that they all are. But this one really is. I'm not even sure that it's a case for us, but..."

Liam opened his mouth to speak but Davy interjected before he could. "But s...something in your gut's telling you that it is."

Liam threw him a look of chagrin as Craig nodded. "That's exactly it. It mightn't be targeted murder per se, but I think it is. I'd like to wait until Annette and Nicky get back before I outline things. Meanwhile..." He turned to Liam. "What happened to that new constable you promised me?"

"You mean Delia Anderson?" Liam shook his head. "She decided to do her Masters in Criminology instead. Fancies herself as a future Chief Constable."

"Good for her. So who does that leave us with?"

Liam shrugged. "No-one, unless you want to cast the net wider? I could speak to Andy White in Portstewart and see if anyone up there fancies a move to the big smoke. And there's always Vice; they might have someone who wants out of the swamp of porn and drugs."

Craig laughed. "As opposed to the blood and corpses of murder." He thought for a moment and then nodded. "Actually, that's not a bad idea, Liam. Have a word with Andy, and Aidan Hughes down in Vice. I'll try Counterterrorism."

The sound of high heels clicking and female laughter in the corridor alerted them to the fact that Nicky Morris, Craig's P.A., and Annette McElroy, the team's Detective Inspector, were back. Craig gave a wry smile as he noticed Liam straighten up and smooth back his short, sandy hair, knowing that it was for Nicky's benefit. Their long-running office flirtation was the source of many jokes. They were both married and it would never come to anything but it gave everyone else a laugh.

He gave a second smile as he saw the number of shopping bags that the women were carrying. After ten minutes of displaying the day's purchases Craig interrupted the party mood.

"Sorry, everyone, but we need to get back to work."

Annette was instantly alert. "Who and where, sir?"

Craig beckoned them to gather round then he perched on a desk while Nicky busied herself making coffee before joining them with her notepad and pen.

"OK. A bomb exploded this afternoon in the centre of Belfast."

Liam lurched forward. "Dissidents!"

Craig waved him back. "Was that a question or an

assertion?" He continued without waiting for a reply. "Whichever it was, they haven't claimed it and we know that the dissidents usually do." His lip curled in disgust. "God forbid someone else might steal their glory."

Annette interrupted. "They might still claim it. What time did it happen? "

"Two o'clock this afternoon. And you're right, Annette, they might, but my instinct says not."

"Sir."

It was said in a husky voice and everyone turned towards Nicky. Liam scanned her pencil skirt, starched white shirt and patent heels with a smile. Her fashion choices were always eclectic but today's outfit was a triumph of 1950s office chic.

"You been watching 'Mad Men' again, Nicky?"

Nicky tossed her pony-tail haughtily and Craig saw the beginnings of a blush on Liam's cheek; firmly put in his place with a glance. Craig waved her on.

"Well, I was just wondering… what was blown up? It could tell us who did it."

Craig smiled. "Well done. That's exactly the right question. It was a shop, a bookshop in Smithfield to be precise."

Liam snorted. "Porn-shop then."

Annette shot him a look of disgust and Craig raised a warning eyebrow, knowing that Liam's mouth had no filter. But he knew where he was coming from. Smithfield was one of Belfast's oldest areas and its reputation in the 19th and 20th Centuries had been mixed to say the least. Filled with colourful characters; the poverty and over populated tenements had bred disorder. The Smithfield of nowadays was different. Urban living had become the vogue and apartments and hotels ruled the city-centre. Smithfield's thriving market had bred some of the city's most successful entrepreneurs, but Liam was right; 'adult' shops were still a very real feature there.

"It was a rare bookshop called Papyrus. Mostly rare books and first editions, with the occasional modern prize-winner thrown in."

"You mean like that Snooker prize?"

Craig laughed so hard he almost choked. "You mean the Booker Prize, Liam, and yes, exactly like that."

Davy interrupted the exchange. "But w…why would dissidents blow up a bookshop, chief? It's hardly their usual target."

"That's why I don't think it was dissidents, Davy. They haven't claimed it and it's not their usual fare."

Annette cut in quietly. "Who was killed? Someone must have been or we wouldn't be discussing it."

Craig nodded. "More than one, unfortunately. At least three people were in the shop when the bomb exploded. Only one survived, a young man; he's injured."

"At least three?"

"The amount of human debris points to more."

Nicky shuddered. "A bookshop…"

Craig turned, waiting for her to continue. She crossed her legs primly at the ankle, completing the picture of '50s glam.

"Well, it's just… Why would someone target a bookshop? Because the owner owed them money?"

"OK, good, let's carry through Nicky's theme. What do we have in the way of motives?"

Davy interjected. "Revenge."

Craig dragged a flip-chart across to the group, writing up the words as they were shouted out. After two minutes the page was covered with ideas; money, love, revenge, fraud, religion and more, including the inevitable reference to the bomb's timing, during Northern Ireland's traditionally loyalist 'Twelfth fortnight'. Dissident republican involvement seemed a real possibility.

Craig squinted at the chart and then wrote the ages of the known dead in one corner. Both the identifiable victims were men; one over sixty and one in his forties. The only survivor was a twenty-year-old, identified as Fintan Delaney by his credit card. Craig tapped his marker against Delaney's age.

"Why was he there?"

Liam was puzzled by the question. "I don't understand, boss. Why not? It's a free country; anyone any age can visit a bookshop." He snorted. "Mind you, I don't understand it myself. Boring places."

Annette rolled her eyes. "You prefer comics, I suppose."

Liam reared up. "They're called graphic novels and there's no…"

Craig waved them to be quiet. "OK, perhaps a better question would have been, why did the boy survive? But before we get to that, we need to decide if we're taking the case. We're flying out on the 30th, so we'll need to have it wrapped up by then. I want a show of hands. All in favour of taking it…"

Every hand in the group rose. Annette's quickly, displaying her eagerness and ambition, and Nicky raised her pen elegantly adjusting her fake horn-rimmed glasses on the way past. Liam raised one finger casually, as befitted a jaded man of the world, with Davy mimicking him in a display of hero-worship. Craig had noticed that the displays were smaller and shorter now compared to when Davy had first joined the team. Their little boy was growing up.

"OK. That's settled then, we'll take it. I'll OK it with Counter-Terrorism. Right, the division of labour. Depending on how many people died there may have been five or six victims in the explosion."

"Here, you just said …"

"However many people were there plus the shop. We have to treat the shop itself as a target. Someone could have wanted it destroyed, perhaps even the owner for the insurance money."

Annette leaned forward. "Or planning permission, sir. Maybe the shop was in someone's way. There are lots of new housing developments in the city-centre, and now we're coming out of recession the building trade is picking up again."

Craig nodded. "Everyone; that's exactly the way I want you

to think. Look at every possible angle for each of the victims." He tapped the list of men's ages for emphasis and then threw his marker onto a desk. "Right, I'm off to the lab to see if John can help us with the I.D.s. Liam; you, Annette and I will split the victims between us until Jake's back. I'll take the survivor. Davy, I want you to start digging into background on the shop. Everything you can find; history, past owners, finance, insurance. Look at the area around it and see if there's anything there as well."

Liam cut in. "Aidan Hughes can help with what's what in Smithfield. Vice knows the place like the back of their hands, especially the gentlemen's clubs."

He guffawed loudly and Craig shot him another warning look. Liam made a show of being ashamed, remembering that he was a D.C.I. now and supposed to be politically correct, but Craig knew the jokes would ramp up as soon as he was out the door.

He nodded at the flipchart. "Nicky, type that up and get it to everyone, please, then call bomb disposal and say we'll meet them at the shop after five." He turned towards the doors then changed his mind and turned back again. "Liam, you're with me."

Then he was across the floor and in the lift with Liam scrambling to keep up.

Chapter Two

The Lab. 5 p.m.

The Saintfield Road based Science Park that housed Dr John Winter's pathology lab was basking in the late July sunshine. When Craig and Liam pushed their way through the PVC doors into John's normally dark, Moulin Rouge themed lab, they were stunned to see the sunshine had hit the walls there as well.

The previously rose coloured walls were now a shade of bright yellow, and the heavy oak cabinets that had housed Winter's collection of antique medical instruments and artefacts from around the world, had been replaced by ones made of stainless steel and glass that gleamed in the fluorescent light. The old-fashioned views of the Folies Bergère and Montmartre had gone and in their place hung black and white Banksy prints. The final touch, or insult depending on your point of view, were several vases of yellow flowers dotted around. It was like your favourite aunt suddenly having a face-lift; a bad one.

John Winter stood amidst his new décor wearing a hesitant smile as Liam's once-stunned horror at the lab's old Rue Morgue ambience was replaced now by gawping disbelief at its violation. Craig knew he was about to say something rude on both their behalves and Liam didn't disappoint.

"Who the hell did this? It's like Ikea on Ecstasy!"

Craig stifled a laugh then stifled it harder as John's face fell.

"Natalie chose it." He set his jaw defiantly. "And I like it!"

Liam opened his mouth to contribute another interior

design review and Craig swiftly intervened.

"It's very… sunny."

John's face fell even further. He gazed first at his long-time friend and then around the room, as if seeing it for the first time. His voice held a defeated tone. "It's awful, isn't it?"

Craig tactfully said nothing but Liam nodded vigorously and inhaled to speak again. John continued before he could.

"Natalie likes yellow and she said the place was dull." He turned dolefully to Craig. "Did you think it was dull?"

"Nope. I thought it was calm and academic; a bit like an old library."

John shrugged, realising that he'd let himself be pressured into the wrong decision. Craig patted him on the shoulder.

"I know Natalie meant well, but if you want my advice, change it back. It'll send the message that you're going to stick to your guns. Marriage isn't a dictatorship, John."

Liam made a martyred face. "Tell that to Danni."

Craig laughed. "You're the least hen-pecked man I know, Liam. So forget the sympathy." He gestured at the walls. "Tell Mary you want it re-painted."

Mary McCarthy was the long-suffering manager of the labs, who'd been given the thankless task of keeping the pathology and forensic teams on-budget by Stormont. Something that she singularly failed to achieve.

"You can get your old cabinets and pictures out of storage and have it back to normal in a few days." Craig headed for John's small office. "Now, let's get to work. Put the coffee on and give us an update on the bodies."

John strode towards his office assertively, more certain of his ground. He removed a slim folder from the top drawer of his desk and spread out four pages bearing the post-mortem header, starting to report in a solemn voice.

"I'm sorry to say it but these are going to be fairly useless, at least for the next few days."

Liam gestured at the pages. "How so, Doc? We already know

the two intact bodies were men, surely there must be something to I.D. them by."

John fixed Liam with a sceptical stare. There would have been an excuse for Craig asking the question; he'd spent fifteen years policing in London and only returned to Northern Ireland in 2008, ten years after the Good Friday Agreement had been signed and peace had started to reign. But Liam had worked in Northern Ireland all through the Troubles; these weren't the first bomb victims that he'd seen.

"I wasn't talking about the intact bodies, Liam. Do you have amnesia?"

Liam railed in irritation. "No, I bloody don't. I picked enough of my mates' body parts off the ground to know what the scene must have looked like. But there's always something to give an I.D."

John nodded, accepting that he was right. He smiled apologetically.

"Sorry, my bad. I'm stressed about the wedding and to be honest I haven't seen a lot of blast victims so it's a nasty one even for me."

Liam nodded in realisation. Most of the explosions in Northern Ireland had been thirty years earlier, while Craig and Winter were still at school. Liam assumed his role as Dad of the group, smiling wisely at them with the benefit of thirty-one years as a cop.

"No problem, Doc. I've seen a lot more bomb debris, human and otherwise, than you or the boss. It's a dubious privilege, trust me." He waved a freckled hand towards the papers. "What did you find?"

John started to report. "I have two mainly intact bodies downstairs but the C.S.I.s also gathered parts of more. We have remnants of limbs torn away in the explosion and small fragments of bone. My guess is that whoever the bones belonged to was standing closest to the bomb when it went off." He took a gulp of coffee and carried on. "The two intact bodies were male, one around early forties, and one older; probably in his sixties somewhere. I haven't started their P.M.s yet." He made a face. "That's tomorrow morning's joy."

Craig interrupted. "Is there any way to I.D. them, John? Teeth, prints…"

John nodded. "Yes, those two should be fairly easy. Des is working them up now." He glanced at the phone. "I'll call him down in a minute."

He paused and took off his glasses, rubbing his green eyes hard. They all knew it was a distraction technique. It wasn't his eyes John was rubbing; it was the images of the dead bodies that he was trying to erase. Craig prompted the pathologist gently.

"The others, John?"

Winter nodded slowly. "Yes… the others. They were probably male as well." He turned to Liam and a note of incredulity entered his voice. "How did you do it, Liam? For all those years? How did you see those things and not go mad, especially when it was your friends who'd been killed?"

Liam's normally open face clouded and he shook his head. When he finally spoke his deep voice was sad.

"It was another time, Doc and we were all running on a hamster wheel. Every day brought a new explosion that had to be cleared up, and the only way to get through it was not to think. Not to think that the thing you were picking up from the street was actually part of someone with a name. "He swallowed hard. "It was easy enough when the bits looked like nothing, but…"

Craig interjected, saving his deputy. "When they looked human, it was something else."

Liam nodded. "Especially when you knew the owner's name."

John asked the question that he knew Craig wanted to ask but didn't really want to hear the answer to. "What did you do to cope, Liam?"

Liam was gazing through the small room's window, back into

the past. He started at the question.

"Me? I drank, Doc. A lot. The police club was one of the few places where we could socialise safely, so there were a lot of heavy drinkers around." He smiled wryly. "Nowadays you'd call them alcoholics. Sport as well; I kicked the hell out of a ball every chance I got."

"And the others?"

"Aye, well. They went to hell their own way. Booze, affairs, drugs; you name it and someone was doing it."

Craig nodded. They already knew from a recent case in Portstewart that the affairs hadn't all been confined within the ranks. Melanie Trainor, an Assistant Chief Constable, had 'crossed the floor' and had an affair with a republican terrorist. He was sure that she hadn't been the only one. War made strange bedfellows.

Craig decided it was time to deal with the present, before the faraway look in Liam's eyes dragged him down the rabbit hole into the '80s.

"OK. Today's explosion. Two intact victims and judging by your four pages, two not so. How did you reach the conclusion that all the victims were male, John?"

John brightened up and tapped the file. "With the intact victims there were characteristics, with the others it was the shoes. It's surprising how resilient shoes are. Clothing gets shredded in a blast almost instantly but shoe leather lives to tell the tale. All the shoes we found were flat lace-ups so at the moment we're assuming that they all belonged to men, although one pair is pretty small, a size seven. We found four different types, so four victims; two bodies still intact. The interesting thing is Fintan Delaney, the young man who survived. He was practically untouched. Just a few cuts and bruises."

Liam nodded. "We used to see that with people just outside the blast radius."

John shook his head. "Not this time, Liam. The back of the

shop and the whole yard behind it was damaged, so he was well within the bomb's radius when it went off."

"How's he still breathing then?"

John gave a small smile. "Bookshelves. We think there were some between him and the blast. They were made of teak, one of the strongest woods there is, so they protected him. You'll see when you get to the site, but we think the bomb was planted at the back of the shop. Delaney was standing near the front door and the bookshelves were in between."

Craig whistled. "Lucky boy. He's at St Mary's. We'll head up there after we check out the scene." He grinned. "I can tell Natalie you're changing your lab back to its former glory while we're there, if you like."

Natalie Ingrams, John's fiancée, was a consultant surgeon at St Mary's Healthcare Trust and a five-feet-tall bundle of energy and fun. 'Dynamic' didn't do her justice but Craig couldn't think of another word. Natalie was the best thing that had ever happened to his quiet friend, but she liked her own way, and whether by cajoling, orders or blackmail, she usually managed to get it.

John shook his head hastily. "Let me tell her when I'm ready. Natalie doesn't like to be thwarted."

Something dawned on Liam. "By any chance is Nat having yellow flowers at the wedding?"

John nodded innocently. "Yes, actually. They're called Poinciana; the Pride of Barbados. They're the National flower of the island. But how did you know?"

"It explains the colour of your walls."

While John recovered from the fact that his lab had become a yellow wedding accessory, Craig lifted the phone. It was answered in two rings by Dr Des Marsham, up on the fifth floor. Des was Head of Forensic Science and he and John made a formidable team.

"Des' place."

Craig laughed. "Hi Des, could you come down to John's

office and bring anything you have on the explosion. Liam's here as well."

Within two minutes the ever-widening figure of Des Marsham entered the room, his face adorned by an immoderate amount of hair. Liam was first with a wisecrack.

"You look more like Santa Claus every time I see you, Des. Eating for two?"

Marsham thrust his abdomen forward challengingly. "Go on. Punch it."

Liam guffawed. "I'd knock you into next week."

"Do it."

"OK, you asked for it."

Liam drew his arm back and punched Des' stomach for all he was worth. Craig winced at the thud that followed but Des didn't even flinch, just came back with a caustic. "Is that all you've got?" He patted his abdomen and then took a seat before Liam decided to have a second shot. "Muscle, pure muscle. I'm taking part in a strongest man competition in a few months and I've been training. What you see in front of you, gentlemen, is a man at the peak of his powers."

Craig interjected dryly. "Is the facial hair a sign of something too?"

Des stroked his newly regrown beard. "Virility. All the competitors have beards."

Liam jumped in, quick as a flash. "I bet your virility's not getting much of a work-out with that fuzz. Annie hated your beard last time."

Craig raised a hand to still the banter. "OK. Entertaining as all of this is, Liam and I have a scene to get to." He turned towards the champion weight-lifter. "Des, I know it's early days, but do you have anything for us yet?"

"As it happens, yes. I've managed to I.D. one of the bodies from dental records, and the first returns from the C.S.I.s show that the bomb was set under a bookshelf at the very back of the shop."

Craig interrupted. "Any idea what types of books were kept there?"

Des looked at him curiously. "Why?"

Craig shook his head and waved him on.

"OK. The answer to your question is no, not yet. We found remnants of signs indicating topics like history and politics, but they were blown all over the place so we've no idea which area of the shop they referred to. Your best bet on getting the layout is the owner's wife, although she may be too upset to help. Her husband is the body we've just I.D.ed."

Craig nodded. Piecing together the shop pre-blast was going to be a challenge; he just hoped that there was a floor plan somewhere.

"What was his name?"

"Jules Robinson. He was sixty-eight. Davy can find out more for you, but initial checks show that he'd owned the shop since 1995."

"What sort of place was it?"

Des answered Liam's question in exaggerated tones. "It sold books, Liam. Ones without pictures."

Liam rolled his eyes. "Very funny. But you're too late; Annette's already cracked that joke. I meant did the shop have a specific theme?"

John interjected. "It's a valid question, but as far as we know, no. It was antiquarian and held some valuable first editions, but in terms of their subject matter, we don't have a clue beyond the signs Des mentioned."

Des chipped in. "The question is why the hell would someone blow up a shop full of fusty old tomes? There must have been something crooked going on behind the scenes."

Craig nodded. "That's what we aim to find out. Anything else?"

Des nodded. "Yes, actually there is and it's a bit strange. Something was found amongst the bomb debris."

Craig leaned forward eagerly. "In the shop generally, or in

the bomb itself?"

"Right in the centre of the bomb. Army bomb disposal are gathering everything they can, hoping to get the bomber's signature, but they sent me the images of the debris because they'd never seen anything like it before."

Des reached for a folder that no-one had noticed him carrying and distributed the photocopies inside. There was silence for a moment as they all stared at the sheets. Amidst the charred wires and metal remnants lay the unmistakable outline of scrollwork, set in a rectangular shape.

Craig spoke first. "It's a photo-frame."

The others peered at the image and acknowledged that he was right.

"Who the hell puts a photograph inside a bomb? You'd have to hate someone a lot to blow up their picture."

Craig shook his head. "Or the opposite. You could be saying 'I did this for you'. If you hated someone you'd make them the victim of the bomb, not use the bomb to celebrate them. We'll find out for sure when we see who was in the photo." He turned to Des. "Was there anything that could have been a picture found nearby, Des?"

Des shrugged. "That was all they sent through. You'll have to ask the army."

Craig leapt to his feet, beckoning Liam to do the same. "That's exactly what we're going to do."

Chapter Three

5 p.m.

Katy Stevens wrinkled her forehead at the dress in front of her, struggling hard not to show her dismay. It was a blancmange of yellow taffeta, with yards of frills down one side. Natalie Ingrams watched her best friend's face through a lens of excitement.

"Isn't it gorgeous? You'll be carrying a posy of Poinciana as well; they're the flower of the island. It's almost identical to my dress, except mine is white of course."

She grinned broadly and danced around the room, holding Katy's bridesmaid's dress in front of her. When Natalie slowed down, Katy took a deep breath and motioned her best friend to take a seat; rifling through her medical training to find the section headed 'breaking bad news'. She prayed that she was equal to the task. If she wasn't then she'd be spending Natalie's wedding dressed as a giant fruit.

"It's... lovely, Natalie. Very pretty. But..."

Natalie's face fell and Katy felt instantly guilty. She fought her need to confess that she was trying to change Natalie's mind because the dress was hideous, and convinced herself that it was impractical instead. She could beat herself up for the lie later.

"It's just... I checked the temperature on the island, so that I knew what to pack, and it's going to be in the eighties for the whole two weeks. If you wear taffeta, you're going to be par-boiled." She produced the piéce de resistance. "You'll be bright red in all your photos!"

Katy convinced herself that it was for the greater good. The wedding photos would haunt Natalie for years, not to mention making her look like a giant grapefruit. Natalie's small face fell further as she considered, then her expression brightened and Katy could see logic beginning to trump desire.

"Eighty degrees? Are you sure?"

Katy nodded, setting her blond waves flying. "Positive, I wanted to know what sun factor to bring."

Natalie pondered for a moment longer and Katy could see every thought reflected on her face. She interjected cautiously.

"Have you paid for the dresses yet?"

Natalie shook her head. "No. They're off the peg. On approval for a week, from that bridal shop in the city-centre. You know, the one called 'Never leave me.' "

Katy nodded. She knew the shop and from what she'd seen of the dresses it sold, it would be more a case of 'Bye-bye' than 'Never leave me' for most bridegrooms. She reached into her U.N. peacekeeper's toolkit and made a tentative suggestion.

"What if…"

Natalie blue eyes swivelled round like a hawk. "What if what?"

"Well… the ceremony's being held on the beach. Yes?"

Natalie nodded suspiciously. "Yes… so?"

"So it's going to be absolutely roasting and do you really want to spend the happiest day of your life feeling like a cooked chicken?"

"But…"

Katy pushed on. "Because I know a shop where we can find something absolutely perfect for you. Light and floaty, a dress that will suit you to a tee." And one for her too, she hoped.

Natalie's tone was sceptical; she'd trailed round a dozen shops already. "Really?"

Katy fixed an earnest expression on her face, keeping an image of Craig gazing admiringly at her in her bridesmaid's dress firmly in her sights.

"Yes, really. It's called 'Forever Bridal'; I know the lady who runs it and she's lovely. Look, what do you have to lose? 'Never leave me' is going nowhere so you always have that option. Let's just go and have a look. If you don't like any of the dresses then you've lost nothing."

Natalie considered the suggestion and finally uttered a grudging "Well…"

It was the opening Katy needed. She phoned 'Forever Bridal' to book an appointment, praying that it had both their sizes in stock.

***

Gresham Street, Smithfield. 5.30 p.m.

Craig stood in the doorway of the erstwhile bookshop and scanned the debris in silence. All that was left of 'Papyrus' was a heap of paper and wood partially swept into one corner by the army forensics team, and the remnants of shattered shelving gripping the walls for dear life.

The bookshop had been small; cosy, Craig imagined the owner had called it, with leaded-glass windows onto Gresham Street and a musty old-book smell that had survived the blast. He could just make out the remnants of a wooden banquette on one side, where prospective buyers would have been encouraged to sit and browse amidst the dusty quiet. Shreds of dark-red leather lay in the corner revealing the banquette's past covering, and shards of smooth brown wood lay everywhere, its joists and grooves saying that it had once formed bookshelves that stood tall and strong, supporting the written word. It was the sort of shop that Craig loved and had often longed for, as a place to spend the endless hours waiting while girlfriends shopped in town.

Liam watched his boss, smiling quietly and reading his thoughts. He'd longed for a place to hide when Danni dragged him into the city-centre too, but his ideal venue had beer on tap and a football match on the box. He broke the shrine's silence reluctantly, but one of them had to or they'd be there all night.

"They fairly hammered it, didn't they?"

Craig dragged his eyes away from an aged leather-bound volume with barely three pages left inside, wondering whose first effort it had been. He stared at Liam in the fading afternoon light.

"The shop might have been incidental. A casualty of war."

Liam glanced at him curiously. "You mean they were after the people? I thought you said earlier…"

Craig nodded, remembering what he'd said. "I've reconsidered. If you just want to destroy a building, you do it when it's empty. This was aimed at someone or something in the shop."

Liam's curiosity turned to puzzle. "But if it's one man you're after, why kill everyone else in the process? Bit indiscriminate, wasn't it?"

Craig glanced up sharply. "Good point. One man could have been taken out anywhere; at home or perhaps even shot in the street. It would have been a lot less messy than this. You know what that means?"

Liam didn't know but decided on a well-worn bluff. "Aye." The word implied knowledge without the need to elaborate.

"It means that either they were after more than one person who was in the shop, or there was something in the shop that they wanted to destroy as well. They were after both man and thing."

Craig's assertion was greeted with a sceptical snort.

"Who kills for a pile of old books? A mad librarian?"

Craig gave a small smile. "I know it sounds unlikely, but books can be very valuable, Liam. There was one sold in the '90s for thirty million dollars; a 15th Century Da Vinci Codex. Collectors will pay a lot."

Liam gave a low whistle. "More money than sense."

Craig continued his train of thought. "Maybe they would even pay to stop a book falling into someone else's hands." He considered for a moment and then shrugged. "This is all speculation until Davy and Des give us more."

Craig took the single step down from Papyrus' doorway and began to move slowly around the room, stopping occasionally to peer at some small pile at his feet. Liam did the same without any idea what he was looking for, holding his nose to block out the smell of burnt wood and flesh.

Suddenly a shape appeared from the gloom at the back of the shop. Liam stepped back quickly, his hand reaching instinctively for his gun. Craig waved him down. The shape was a light-green suited bomb disposal officer, searching for the final remnants of whatever had caused the blast.

"Thanks for agreeing to meet us." Craig noted the man's rank and added. "Captain…?"

"Smith. But it's Kenneth, Ken, please."

Smith shook Craig's hand then removed the mask obscuring his face. The face that appeared was in its early thirties; its grin said that the man found something amusing. He nodded towards Liam, making his blond fringe flop across his brow.

"Your mate's a bit jumpy, isn't he?"

Craig smiled and introduced Liam, adding. "He's seen a few too many bombs in his time."

Smith grinned again and shook Liam's hand. "Veteran of the Troubles, then. Brilliant experience for bomb disposal. I missed all that."

Liam gave a wry smile. "Your miss was your mercy, lad. They were grim times." He nodded towards the back of the room. "Bomb planted back there, was it?"

Smith nodded enthusiastically. "Yes. It packed quite a punch. Simple design; basic Semtex and a timer. For some reason they used an old pocket watch for that; it's pretty bashed up but it did the trick. Anyone nearby was a goner."

Craig interjected. "One man wasn't."

Smith nodded. "Yes, we're not quite sure how Delaney escaped. " He kicked some shards of wood at his feet. "The bookshelves might have saved him, we're not sure yet. My boss is trying to get hold of the floor plan to work out the logistics."

"So are we." Craig glanced around the shop. "Can you talk us through what you've got so far?"

Smith nodded eagerly and walked towards the front door. "Give me a minute to get out of this clobber and I'll be with you."

One minute later he re-appeared, clad in khaki trousers and T-shirt. He was lean and fit with the year round tan of the well-travelled; although in Smith's case Craig was certain he'd holidayed in Iraq and Afghanistan, not Barbados and the South of France. Smith's blond hair was as long as regulations would allow and Craig could just make-out a small hole in his earlobe, where an earring was worn on his days off. He smiled to himself, knowing the young officer was just his younger sister's type, not that Lucia was ever likely to meet him.

"Right then."

Smith's crisp English tones focused them on their task and they walked slowly towards the back of the shop. He hunkered down, pointing at a pile of glass and dust beside the back wall, close to what was left of a small doorway. Craig joined him while Liam decided to take their word for it. Hunkering down with his bad back might mean that he wouldn't straighten up again for a week.

The bomb disposal officer lifted a pen from his trouser pocket and spread the dust, revealing a clear area underneath.

"You'll notice that the floor around here and most of the walls have been damaged, but this area is clear. That's because it's where the bomb was sitting. The blast went up and out from the centre, leaving the area directly beneath it clear." He nodded at the doorway behind them. "That door led to the loo and staff-room. They've been wrecked but not quite as badly as the shop itself, so we reckon that door was closed when things kicked off. There was no-one in there but if there had been they might have survived as well."

Craig interrupted. "Dr Marsham, our Head of Forensic Science, said there was some sort of frame found in the bomb debris."

Smith nodded so hard Liam thought his fringe was going to concuss him. His voice echoed its excitement.

"Yes. It's brilliant. We think it's made of titanium, really rare and really hard, that's why it survived the blast semi-intact. It has scrollwork down the sides and a glass front. That splintered in the heat of course, but there were remnants of a photograph underneath."

Craig cut in urgently. "Titanium? Who makes a photo-frame out of that? Unless they wanted it to survive the blast because whatever it held was important. Could you make out an image? Where are the frame and photo now?"

"At our labs. It'll take the tech people a while to work out what it was. "

Craig's voice was stern. "It needs to be in our labs. Have the frame remnants sent over to Dr Marsham please. And whatever's left of the watch."

Liam knew a battle for ownership of the forensics was about to begin. He'd done this dance with the military before. He attempted a joke to lighten the mood. "I've heard of nail bombs, but never one with a photo and an old watch."

No-one laughed. Instead Smith leapt to his feet and for one minute Liam thought he was going to salute. Instead he snapped out. "Yes, sir. Right away. I'll speak to Major James."

Craig waved the younger man down. "When we've left will be time enough. It's just important that we don't lose the evidence. You understand."

Smith exhaled noisily, relieved that he wasn't in trouble. "Yes, sir."

Smith spent the next ten minutes moving slowly around the room, pointing out scorch marks and wood and paper debris that Craig knew represented thousands of pounds of valuable books. Every so often they paused at an area of red and pictured the dead body that had lain there, or the detached body part that had caused a smear. Finally the tour was finished and the three men emerged onto Gresham Street. Smith stretched out his hand to shake.

"I'll speak to Major James immediately, sir."

"That will be fine, Captain. Now, go and enjoy whatever's left of your evening and we'll try to do the same."

As Smith climbed into the waiting armoured car Liam squinted at Craig. "Did you mean that about us going to enjoy our evening? 'Cos if you did, I could just get home in time to watch the footie and you could head to your folks early."

Craig thought of his mother Mirella's three-line whip for Friday night family dinner, happy to defer the experience for a while. She'd moved it to Thursday this week because Katy was coming with him for the first time and she was on-call for most of the weekend. Craig knew an evening of scrutiny lay ahead of them and he was eager to defer it as long as he could.

Craig smiled at Liam, knowing that they had opposing agendas. "No, I didn't mean it. We're heading for St Mary's to interview our survivor."

Liam shook his head in defeat, knowing that another hour of questioning lay ahead before home. He just hoped that Danni remembered to tape the match.

Chapter Four

St Mary's Healthcare Trust. 6.30 p.m.

St Mary's main building just off the M2 was familiar territory for the police. Every young constable visited its Emergency Department more often that they wanted to, whether to take statements from doctors, accompany prisoners who needed examined, or to break up a brawl at the weekend. It used to be only weekend nights that fights broke out, but with the drinking culture in the UK, practically every night in the ED was party-time now. Some hospitals in England even had dedicated police; they were called so often. Was it any wonder that so many police officers married hospital staff?

It was a trap that Craig had resisted falling into throughout his career; partly because he'd dated an actress for nine years and partly because it was mostly the junior ranks that lived in the ED. He'd finally succumbed to the siren call of the health service three months before, when he'd started dating Katy Stevens, a consultant physician. They'd met on a case but it was only John's engagement to Katy's best friend Natalie that had caused them to see each other again.

As Craig walked down St Mary's main corridor deep in thought, Liam was having thoughts of his own, mainly that if he never saw the inside of a hospital again he'd be a happy man. He'd been there too often over the previous two years, once during a case involving patients' murders and twice more as a patient himself, first poisoned and then shot at by perps. He didn't fancy his luck again.

After a minute's walking Craig turned sharp left down a corridor that led to the well-lit ED. Their survivor was in a side-room on its admissions ward, with a P.C. standing guard outside. Craig nodded the young constable off for coffee and pushed at the room's half-open door. They were greeted by the sight of a jet-haired young man whose skin was almost as pale as his sheets. His eyes were closed as they entered and they stayed closed, giving no acknowledgement that anyone had entered the room.

Craig halted several feet from the bed and scrutinised Fintan Delaney, gathering information from everything he saw; even the man's lack of response. There was nothing on the bedside table except the obligatory water, and a menu card waiting to be completed for the next day. Liam lifted it idly, wondering when seared salmon had become health service fare.

Craig's eyes scanned the young man's narrow face, seeing everything. Delaney was handsome, even a man could see that, and young; he looked even younger than his reported twenty years. His eyes could be brown, green or blue, black hair with any of those was common on these shores; Craig's own blue eyes were testament to that. But something made Craig veer towards brown and something about the young man's features reminded him of Andy White, a D.C.I. from Dungiven in the North-West. Without asking a question or hearing a word, Craig knew the boy was from Derry or somewhere close by.

While Craig scrutinised the patient, Liam did the same to his boss, smiling to himself. He knew exactly what Craig was doing; it was a technique that they all learned. Distant information mining or end-of-the-bed diagnosis in health, so Natalie had told him during a drunken debate at her engagement bash. The art of divining information about a person without them saying a single word.

When Craig had learned as much as he could in silence he lifted a metal chart noisily from the end of the bed, watching the patient for some response. A faint flicker of the young man's eyelids said that he'd heard.

The chart was headed 'Fintan Delaney'; a good Irish name. It went with his colouring, typical of the dark Irish of the North-West. 'La Trinidad Valencera', a ship of the Spanish Armada, had wrecked in Kinnagoe Bay in Donegal in 1588. Generations of Spanish-Irish blood and looks had been the local result.

Craig continued reading Delaney's notes. Date of birth, first of May 1994, address, The Prehen Estate, Derry/ Londonderry in the North-West. He'd guessed correctly. He patted himself mentally on the back as Liam watched the whole proceedings with a smirk. Finally, when Craig had learned all he could from the chart, he spoke.

"Mr Delaney."

The boy's lids flickered again but remained stubbornly closed.

"I'm Superintendent Craig and this is D.C.I. Cullen. Can we have a word?"

Again, nothing. It left Craig with a dilemma. Was this a man in shock? After all, he'd almost been blown to buggery. Or was this someone who didn't like the police? Craig gave a wry smile. Hard though it was to believe for all those who knew and loved them, he knew that the police weren't popular with the whole world.

Or was it option number three; did Delaney have something to hide? Was that why he was playing deaf? The only way to find out was to ask a professional. Craig nodded Liam to stay in the room and walked into the corridor, following the sound of voices to the nurses' station. A woman was hunched over the desk reading and didn't hear him approach. Craig coughed and she looked up; he could tell from her age and badge that she was a student.

"I'm Superintendent Craig. Could I speak to the doctor caring for Mr Delaney, please?"

The girl startled at the sound of his rank and Craig sighed inwardly, wondering when he'd become the bogey-man. He made a note to ask Katy why people always reacted that way to the police and then he smiled again, as unthreateningly he could. The girl raced off down the corridor, returning a moment later with a male doctor in tow. He looked almost as young as she did and Craig laughed at the reversed stereotype; who said old age began when the policemen started looking young?

The young man extended his hand formally. "I'm Dr Hinton. Mr Delaney is my patient."

Craig indicated a row of chairs and sat down. "I wonder if you can help me. You probably know Mr Delaney was the sole survivor of an explosion this afternoon and, as such, he's a valuable witness. Could you tell me if he's fit to be questioned? At the moment he seems unable or unwilling to respond."

Hinton blinked furiously and reached into his pocket, withdrawing a tiny notebook, not unlike the ones that P.C.s used. He flicked quickly through its pages until he reached one headed 'Fintan Delaney'. Craig tried reading the medical shorthand upside down but gave up at the third acronym. Hinton moved his head across the page as he read, flicking back to the left side periodically, like the carriage of an old typewriter. Finally he made a satisfied sound and closed the notebook, then he stared at Craig and began reciting from rote.

"Mr Delaney hasn't spoken since he was brought in this afternoon at three o'clock. He's been examined by a neurologist, Dr O'Neill, and her opinion is that there's no physical damage, except cuts and bruises, but that the shock of what Mr Delaney experienced has rendered him mute."

Craig interrupted. He'd seen post-traumatic responses before. What he needed to know was how long it was going to last.

"When is he likely to recover, doctor?"

The junior doctor shrugged, not rudely but in bewilderment. "To be honest I don't know. Dr O'Neill said it could be days or weeks, and she couldn't tell how much was involuntary and how much was Mr Delaney simply clamming up. There's no way of telling at the moment."

And short of torture, which wasn't a sanctioned interview technique, they would probably never find out; although Craig was sure that Liam would be keen to try. He had a sudden thought.

"Has Mr Delaney opened his eyes at all since he was brought in?"

Hinton flicked through his pages again then nodded. "He co-operated with all the visual field tests, so he would've had to. But he definitely hasn't spoken."

Craig nodded and rose to his feet. "How long do you intend to keep him here?"

Hinton clambered to his feet, keen to even up the status. "He'll be moved to the Neuro ward as soon as they get a free bed, but how long for will be up to Dr O'Neill. She'll do a ward round tomorrow at ten-thirty and decide then."

Craig nodded and took out a card, scribbling his mobile number on the back.

"Mr Delaney may have been the target of the explosion which means that his life could be at risk. We won't know for some time, so we'll be leaving an officer here to guard him. Could you please ensure my card gets to Dr O'Neill and say that I'll drop by tomorrow morning to speak to her?"

With that Craig headed back to Delaney's room. As he went to enter he was greeted by an obstacle; Liam had found a chair and was sitting against the door. Craig's entrance tipped him forward.

"What the hell?"

Craig turned swiftly towards the bed, just in time to see Fintan Delaney's eyes fly open at the noise. He shut them tightly again, so tightly that they wrinkled like a man's twenty years his senior, and Craig knew Delaney was keeping his eyes shut deliberately because they were the police. He crossed to the bed and leaned in close to Delaney's ear, speaking loudly enough for Liam to hear him across the room.

"Mr Delaney, I know you can hear us and I know that you can see; I've spoken to your doctor."

The only response was a further tightening of Delaney's eyelids. Craig continued.

"You've been in an explosion and you were the only survivor. Four people died, so we'll need to speak to you, no matter how long it takes. I'm leaving an officer outside your door and I'll be back tomorrow to speak to your consultant. I realise that you've been through a trauma but we need your help."

More silence. Liam joined Craig at the bedside and spoke in a stage whisper. The loudness of his voice was enough to make Delaney wince.

"Do you want me to have a go, boss? I'll get him to open his eyes."

The threat was clear and Craig smiled, knowing that Liam was trying to provoke a response. He did. Delaney's previously still hands gripped the bed cover like a life-belt. A few hours of undiluted Liam and Delaney would definitely speak, if he didn't die of shock first. Tempted as he was Craig decided against it. He leaned in again.

"D.C.I. Cullen and I will be back tomorrow morning. Let the officer outside know when you're ready to talk."

Craig turned on his heel, beckoning Liam to follow and they exited the room in a deliberate show of noise. Fifty feet down the corridor Liam spoke.

"Either he's in shock or he's guilty of something, boss."

Craig nodded. His suspicious mind said guilty, but of what? Planting a bomb and then waiting there until it went off? Not the dissidents' style and other terrorists did suicide bombing much more efficiently. If Fintan Delaney had meant to kill himself in the blast then he'd failed abysmally.

Possible explanations flew around Craig's head until he settled on what he knew. Only two things were certain. Delaney knew more about the explosion than he was telling them, and it wouldn't be long before he would talk.

***

Holywood. Tom and Mirella Craig's home. 10 p.m.

Lucia Craig glanced at her mother's back as she stood at the cooker, then she caught her big brother's eye and made a face, staring at her nose until her eyes crossed and making both Craig and Katy laugh. The first two courses of the meal had passed easily enough in chat and pleasantries, but they all knew that Mirella was gearing up for the main event; to grill Katy on everything from her background and parentage to her views on children, education and, most importantly of all to Mirella, music.

Mirella had been a professional pianist all her adult life, touring prestigious concert halls for years before finally retiring, to play for charity and practice every day. It was during a tour that she'd met Craig's father, when they'd been in the same conference centre in Venice. She'd left her home in Rome to be with him and brought up both her children to be musical and play instruments; Craig the piano and Lucia the violin. But she'd been horrified by her scientist husband's preference for technology over music, and her son's testosterone driven adolescent abandonment of music to run around a football pitch. Craig had started playing occasionally again, but he would never practice often enough to please his Mum, just as in Mirella's eyes no woman would ever be good enough for her son.

Tom Craig watched as his wife turned from her Aga and drew breath for her first interrogation of the night, then he glanced quickly at his son and made his move. The worst Mirella could do was huff with him, and he could get past that by puffing his GTN spray and holding his chest in mock-pain. Having a heart attack wasn't an experience he'd like to repeat, but the one he'd had the year before had got him out of plenty of scrapes since.

Tom Craig's baritone reached the air before Mirella's Italian-English could. "So Katy, Marc tells me you're a physician at St Mary's? Do you enjoy it?"

Katy spotted Mirella's quick scowl at her husband, immediately knowing what she'd had planned. She answered his cue gratefully, starting a ten minute round table discussion on medicine and science that everyone genuinely enjoyed. As it reached its natural conclusion over pudding Mirella drew breath again, squinting at her husband as if daring him to speak. He didn't but Lucia did, launching into a Q and A about Natalie and John's wedding that lasted through coffee and relocation to the living room. This time it was Craig who headed his mother off at the pass, recounting the painting of John's laboratory with jokes that even she laughed at, although they could all see that her good humour was starting to fray. Craig felt vaguely guilty about blocking her every attempt to question Katy but a quick glance from his father said not to; he knew exactly what was on Mirella's list.

At eleven o'clock Craig noticed Katy starting to fade and he grabbed at the opening, retrieving her coat from the hall. As they were leaving Katy smiled at Mirella and said.

"Ringraziamento per il pasto meraviglioso, la signora Craig. La linguine era incredibile, come era tutto. Spero di rivederti presto" (Thank-you for the wonderful meal, Mrs Craig. The linguine was amazing, as was everything. I hope to see you again soon.)

Everyone gawped, including Craig, but Mirella beamed from ear to ear, answering Katy in an effusive flood of her native tongue, that said everything from "You're very welcome, please come again" to "would you like the recipe?"

As she kissed Katy goodbye they all heard the subtext that said she'd passed Mirella's first test. When the front door had closed behind them Craig turned to face his girlfriend and smiled. "That was very sweet of you. Did you learn that sentence just for tonight?"

To his surprise Katy shook her head. "No. I said it on the spur of the moment. I learned Italian at night class a few years ago. I'm not great but I can get by."

Craig wrapped his arms around her waist. "There's a lot I don't know about you, isn't there, Dr Stevens?"

She smiled mischievously. "More than you'll ever find out, Signore Craig."

Craig bent down and kissed her tenderly, picturing two uninterrupted weeks of kissing her under a Caribbean sky, then he took her hand and led the way to the car.

"What's the hurry, Marc?"

Craig smiled. "I think it's about time I taught you the Italian for romance."

Chapter Five

The small side-room was bright and clean and smelled of a nameless combination of detergent and summer. The sheets on the bed were starched to near-board stiffness and the pale cotton cover was sterile and threadbare, its salad days long gone. Fintan Delaney lay very still, listening to the chatter of nurses in the corridor, and the sharp, delft clatter of breakfast being served. Every so often soft footsteps would halt outside his door without entering, their owner giggling softly with his uniformed guard instead.

Guard. That's what he called him because that's what the police officer was. There to prevent him leaving, without any proof that he'd done anything wrong. His freedom curtailed, guilty until proven innocent, in a Lewis Carroll skewing of the justice system; the law through a looking glass.

The young man scanned the room urgently for an escape route as frustration at his lack of words overcame him. He couldn't speak; but why not? Shock was the doctor's diagnosis, guilt the policeman's the night before. He didn't know the answer because he couldn't remember a thing. Not about what had brought him to hospital and not about his life in the years before. They'd even had to tell him his name, gleaned from a bankcard found in his clothes.

The desire to be free suddenly overwhelmed him and he knew that if he couldn't achieve it physically then spiritually would have to do. Slipping from the pristine bed he searched

37

the room for some way to end his short life. Delaney seized a sharp metal bolt that formed part of his bedside locker, wrenching it from its moorings. With his mind racing he laid its sharp edge against his vulnerable inner wrist. He halted suddenly, surprised at the feeling of revulsion that the action provoked. Was he a religious man? It sounded right. It would explain his hesitation; if he was Christian then suicide must be against his code.

Delaney slumped defeated against the white linen of his bed, his pallor making them seem as one, then he dropped the bolt to the floor, knowing that the noise would bring his watchdog running in. With that single action he knew that he'd given up his search for a way to end his life, resigning himself instead to hours of questions that he couldn't answer and days or years spent in limbo, unable to remember a thing.

***

Docklands Coordinated Crime Unit. 8 a.m.

Liam raked his close-cut sandy hair as hard as its limited volume would allow. He envied Craig his thick hair, not for any desire to look like a matinee idol but for the sheer pleasure of a dramatic gesture now and then. Raking three inches of hair looked much more effective than raking half-an-inch of sandy scrub, and he bet that it made a head massage a whole different experience as well.

Craig squinted across the desk at his deputy, wondering why Liam was staring so hard at his head. He shrugged; who knew what went through Liam's mind. Usually football, beer and women, except when they were on a case, then Liam's sharp insights sometimes surprised even him. Just then the double-doors to the floor swung open and a wave of noise hit them both. High volume chatter from Nicky's loud laughter mingled with Davy's and Annette's more subdued tones. Nicky's husky voice carried furthest. "All I'm saying is that yellow and white is a nice colour scheme."

Craig raised his eyes to heaven. Liam had obviously told them about the makeover at John's lab. He's had enough of the interior design discussion at dinner the night before, now he had to hear it all again at work. Davy laughed.

"There's a difference between a bit of yellow in the bride's bouquet and painting your husband's whole lab to fit in w… with the theme! Besides, yellow's a girl's colour."

Annette raised an eyebrow. "Now there you've lost me, Davy. I agreed with you up to the point where you started allocating colours a sex!"

Craig rose so that he appeared from behind Liam's filing cabinet and the small group smiled sheepishly, all except Nicky who was undeterred. Her husky voice echoed through the room, even more audible because of the other's sudden silence.

"Barbados' national flower is called Poinciana. It comes in lots of colours; red, orange and yellow. So I think yellow and white will be lovely."

Craig smiled. "If you don't mind looking like a giant blancmange, according to Katy." He waved them all to take a seat and Nicky put the coffee on to perk.

"OK. That's enough wedding talk, at least until Liam and I leave. We're heading to St Mary's to see the consultant after her ward-round but I wanted to catch you all first and start things rolling." He indicated Liam. "Liam will update you on the explosion site, I'll bring you up-to-date with the lab findings. Then we'll both tell you about our visit to the hospital last night."

He nodded Liam on and mimicked drinking a cup of coffee to Nicky. As she brought it over Craig saw that a lemon biscuit accompanied it. He smiled, knowing that they were doomed to be wedding themed for the next two weeks.

Liam sniffed loudly before starting. In the absence of hair to rake it was the most fitting detective gesture he could think of.

It implied knowledge that no-one else held and a slightly jaded view of life; well it did on the TV anyway, to Annette it seemed to imply something else.

"Are you getting a cold, Liam? I've some Lemsip in my desk."

Craig smiled to himself, knowing that Annette had just ruined Liam's big moment but not sure if she'd done it deliberately or not. The beatific smile on her face gave no clues. Before Liam could remonstrate Craig waved him on.

"Aye, well, the scene. Basically the place was blown to buggery. It was a one- roomed shop with a wee staff area and toilet off the back leading out to a yard. As far as we could make out the room had free-standing bookshelves, as well as the ones around the walls." He was interrupted by Nicky handing him a mug and a slice of yellow and white Battenberg. He took a deep slurp of coffee and continued, eyeing the cake as he did. "What was left of the bookshelves was on the floor, brushed to one side by the army forensic lads." He added hastily. "After our C.S.I.s had done their stuff of course. It was mostly wood shards and paper, ripped to bits." He snorted. "If those books were worth a fortune, they aren't any more."

Davy interrupted unexpectedly, with a faraway look in his eyes. "I bought my Dad a first edition from there the year before he died. It w…was beautiful. Leather bound with a gold embossed title."

Craig saw Liam about to speak and caught his eye, silencing his response. It was the first time Davy had ever mentioned his parents and it was a sign of something; after almost three years on the team he felt safe enough to confide in them. They knew very little about Davy, except that he was exceptionally bright and Queen's University kept asking him back to do his doctorate. Craig knew they would lose him to research someday; it was only a matter of when. But they knew nothing more except that the young Emo was desperately shy, something that his stutter had signposted from the start. Craig's asked the question quietly.

"When was that, Davy?"

Davy glanced up, surprised, as if he'd intended to say the words only to himself; then he smiled. "Four years ago. He w… was… w…was…"

Craig knew from Davy's increased stuttering that the next words were painful for him to say. He leaned forward encouragingly.

"It w…was a car accident. On the Lisburn Road."

"I'm sorry, Davy. We didn't know."

Davy smiled and Craig knew he was remembering his father in happier times. "My Dad loved books; he was a Professor of Literature. I bought it for him with my first month's s…salary."

He suddenly sat up very straight and Craig knew it signified the end of the confidence. Davy waved Liam on before he could and Liam picked up the conversation and ran with it for ten minutes, accurately describing the scene and the location of the bomb. He mimicked Ken Smith's pukka English accent perfectly, making everyone laugh. Craig wondered idly when someone would start calling mimicry racism; the powers that be shifted their politically correct goalposts every day. They'd probably get him for imitating his mother's broken Italian-English soon.

Finally Liam finished and Craig decided to add to the lightened mood with a vivid description of John's lab that Liam couldn't help but embellish.

"It was like being inside a giant sherbet lemon! The Doc thought he'd no choice."

Craig cut in. "It'll be back to normal by Monday, but no-one's to mention that to Natalie. OK?"

He scanned their faces until he was sure that the innocent expressions weren't concealing mischievous intent, thinking how fed-up he got having to be the grown-up all the time.

"OK, back to work. According to John there were five people in the shop. Two bodies were found intact but badly burnt. They would have been standing further away from the bomb

41

than the two others, with the sole survivor, Fintan Delaney, standing furthest away, behind the bookshelves. That's what protected him."

Annette cut in. "So he was standing near the front door?"

Craig nodded. "There were free-standing bookshelves between the back door and the front. They provided sufficient cover from the blast."

Liam interjected. "Delaney's not small so they must have been nearly ceiling height."

"How do you work that out?"

"Well, otherwise Delaney's top half would have been exposed to the explosion, whether he was standing by the front door or not. If they'd been waist-high jobbies the blast would have gone clean over the top of them, so only the lad's legs would have been saved. There's hardly a mark on him so he must have been shielded head to toe."

Craig nodded. The shop must have been laid out with six-feet-plus bookshelves front to back to avoid killing the young man. Liam continued.

"And if he was by the front door it stands to reason he'd just entered the shop or was just leaving."

Davy had been tapping his pen quietly against the desk but now the volume suddenly increased. Craig turned towards him.

"Yes, Davy?"

Davy had been so deep in thought he jumped at the sound of his name.

"W…Well… this is just a thought, but if you owned a shop that s…sold expensive books, things that are easily stolen and carried out of the shop, and you had high bookshelves preventing a clear view…"

Annette finished the question, smiling. "How could you see shoplifters?"

Davy nodded, setting his long hair flying. Liam had a fleeting thought that he would rake his hair all day if he owned that. He parked his follicular envy and answered before anyone else could.

"CCTV."

Davy and Annette squinted at him menacingly for stealing their thunder and Craig jumped in like the good boss he was.

"Well done Davy, good call. There had to be CCTV in the shop or books would have been stolen every day."

"There was one of those scanner things by the door as well, boss. You know, like they have in clothes shops."

Annette nodded. Liam was referring to the shop exit gates that set off an alarm during thefts. "That means the books must have been tagged."

Davy looked puzzled. "W…Why would they have needed both? If they had tags then why have CCTV?"

Craig thought for a moment before answering. "Some books might have been too valuable to tag, and they would have needed to watch for people removing the tags or just defacing books."

Nicky's husky voice rang across the room. Even though she was ten feet away at her desk she missed nothing.

"What sort of eejit defaces books? If I ever caught our Jonny…"

Craig turned to face her. "Jonny values his life too much." Nicky's twelve-year-old son was one of the best behaved kids he'd ever met, more from fear of his mother's wrath than instinct he suspected. He just hoped that Nicky didn't keep the reins on too tight, but then in the paramilitary dominated area she lived in she probably needed to more than most.

"Anyway, there've been plenty of book-destroyers in history, Nicky, the Nazis for instance. Let's accept that the shop would have had security measures and start looking for them."

Craig continued with the forensics and then updated them on their survivor. "Liam and I are going back to the hospital later, to see what we can find out. Annette, dig further into the CCTV please and pay a visit to Papyrus. I'd value your opinion of the scene, just in case we missed something."

He turned to Davy. He was examining his hair for split ends. Before Craig could comment, Davy showed that he'd been listening attentively. "I'm looking into each of the victims' backgrounds in detail, including the s…survivor."

"Great, and give Des a call on the forensics as well, please." Craig paused and a rueful expression crossed his face. "Don't ask me why but I think the army's going to be difficult about the details of the bomb."

Liam nodded. "They always are. Mind you, that young lad Smith seemed friendly enough."

"That young lad is about thirty-five, Liam, and yes, he was friendly, but his boss might be a different kettle of fish." Craig squinted at his deputy. "Besides, when did you get so fond of army officers? You've never had a good word to say about them until now."

Liam nodded. He'd crossed swords with the military plenty of times during the Troubles. Some of them had thought their jurisdiction included the whole country and they'd wrangled to take the lead in the investigation of every blast. If he had respect for them it came from their willingness to defuse bombs; that bit he'd been very happy to leave them with.

"Aye, that's true. They can be a bolshie lot."

Liam grinned pointedly at Craig and everyone knew he was thinking about Julia McNulty, Craig's ex. She was a D.I. up in Limavady now but she'd been an army captain for years and the hierarchical manner had never left her.

"But they know their stuff on bombs, right enough. They were usually able to give us a name, just by looking at the way the device was rigged."

"Good, let's hope they can this time. Davy, on the off-chance that they're less than generous with information, I still need to know everything that the army knows about our blast. "

"I have a contact at the barracks. I'll try him."

"Good. Let me know if you get anything. I'll arrange a meeting with Major James as well. I also need a copy of the shop's floor plan, its ownership history and everything you can find on its stock. Also the finances of all the victims."

"W…What are you thinking of?"

Craig shook his head slowly. "I'm not sure yet, but there was a reason that shop was targeted and it can only be to do with one of the victims, the shop, its contents, or some other history we don't know about. Smithfield might be OK now, but the area has had a variable past."

Annette nodded. She remembered going there to collect her children's school uniforms and the number of shops with blacked-out windows and furtive looking men outside had been substantial even then.

Liam yawned widely, wishing he'd gone to bed instead of sitting up till two a.m. watching his recorded football match.

"You thinking protection racket, boss?"

Craig shrugged. "Maybe, or maybe something else. We'll find out when we start digging." He sprang to his feet, preparing to leave, then stopped suddenly and scanned the room. "Jake's still off with his root canal?"

"Aye. He should have stayed away from the dentist, that's what I do. Brush and pray and you'll be all right."

"Not everyone has your faith in God."

"Danni does the praying for me. I just brush."

Craig resisted making a crack. "When are we expecting Jake back?"

Annette smiled apologetically. "I thought it was going to be today or Monday, but it seems I was wrong. Jake's partner called me last night saying he was in agony. He's got an infection so he's likely to be off for the best part of next week."

Craig made up his mind. "OK. Then we definitely need another pair of hands. Liam, chase up Aidan Hughes, and all of you get onto the other squads and see if anyone fancies a secondment to us, just for this case. We'll recruit more formally after John's wedding."

He resumed his exit, beckoning Liam to follow and yelling

"briefings at eight and four o'clock each day unless I say not" as they left.

***

Pakistan. 12 p.m. local time

Jennifer Weston gazed across the high yellow grass, made brittle and pale by the sun. Her blue eyes turned silver in the high midday light and she wondered where her lover was now; somewhere much better than this if what she'd heard was true. She thought of his dark-brown eyes and white unblemished skin, remembering how cool it had felt to touch; like stepping into a refreshing lake to escape the heat of the midday sun. He had been sweet, sweeter than any fruit she'd ever tasted, his innocent faith making him seem much younger than his years.

How long had it been since they'd first met? Only twenty months, outside the student's union in Belfast. Belfast; so far away now and yet part of both their roots. She thought of him in his student uniform of jeans and T-shirt, eager and ready to learn in his new, exciting world. He'd viewed everything un-cynically and showed all the signs that would make him easy to snare.

And her... her what? What had she been? A visitor to her old college, steeped in knowledge that hadn't come from any degree and seeking a willing pupil. She'd spotted his vulnerability quickly and moved to separate him from the crowd, making him hers and owning him from then on. It had been so easy.

So easy to impress him with her knowledge, wrap her ideals around his and then twist them into one thread. So easy to do to him what had already been done to her. To seduce him, physically and emotionally, until he was clay waiting to be moulded by her hands. Clay that would eventually become a weapon.

***

St Mary's. 11 a.m.

By the time Craig and Liam arrived at the ED the white-coated consultant and her students were disappearing into the distance like a migrating flock. Craig dispatched Liam to ask when Dr O'Neill would be free to talk then he nodded hello to the P.C. by the side-room and pushed open the door.

Fintan Delaney was lying with his eyes closed, just as he had been the evening before, his pallor even stronger now than then. Could pallor be stronger? Craig asked and answered the question yes; Delaney's skin was so pale that if he hadn't been squeezing his eyes so tightly Craig would have sworn that he was dead.

He walked to the side of the bed and stared down at the boy, wondering if he had ever looked so young. He had of course; they all had once. When did it change; gradually or in incremental steps? Looking twenty for ten years and then overnight an older man, as if time had chased and caught up with them at some finish line. Craig's reverie was broken by a twitch of Delaney's hand. He looked on as the young man stilled it deliberately and then lay frozen, like a child who hoped that if they closed their eyes and didn't move they wouldn't be seen. Craig's warm voice broke the silence.

"Mr Delaney, I know that you can hear me."

More silence and another twitch. Craig wondered if a touch would constitute assault and decided to take the risk. He rested his long tanned fingers on Delaney's forearm knowing that the boy would feel the pressure and react. Delaney didn't disappoint him. He jerked his arm away to avoid a further contact and in doing so he pulled his hand straight into Craig's.

What the boy did next surprised Craig. Instead of pulling his hand away again he let it rest there, touching Craig's as if he was seeking comfort, or giving up the fight. Whichever it was it was

47

accompanied by hesitantly opening eyes. Brown eyes, just as Craig had guessed. His name was Fintan Delaney and he had black hair and brown eyes. The rest would come.

Chapter Six

The Lab. 11.30 a.m.

John Winter gazed around his lab and smiled. It had taken Craig and Liam to make him see what had happened but only five minutes after they'd gone for him to assert himself. Mary had responded quickly to his call the day before and a squad of painters and movers had been in overnight. Now his once-yellow walls were restored to their former glory and his dark-wood display cases were back in their rightful place. His lab looked like his inner sanctum again, instead of a tier of Natalie's wedding cake.

John corrected himself quickly. His and Natalie's wedding cake, although it often felt like hers alone. That was partly his fault. Once they'd set the date he'd been happy to hand planning the wedding over to her, partly from laziness and disinterest and partly because he hadn't a clue what to do. He'd never understood why women got so worked up over a single day. All he wanted was to be married to her, not to have a party for the whole world. He'd also handed things over because he knew that was what Natalie wanted; to spend months fussing over colour schemes and details with her mother and Katy, and then to appear on the day, serene and beautiful, as if she hadn't been running around like a headless chicken for months.

John poured himself a coffee and bit into a day-old scone, thanking God that they'd decided to get married abroad. They'd have people there that they knew and cared about, instead of thirty anonymous cousins and uncles who he'd never met.

There would be sun, sea and hopefully the other 's' as well, and it had still worked out cheaper than a marquee on the Ingrams' lawn, not to mention hiring a castle for the day like some people did!

The soon-to-be married pathologist allowed himself a moment imagining his wedding night in a luxury beach-hut, with the scent of flowers and the sea mingling in the night's warm breeze, then he turned his thoughts back to the case Craig had given him and enthusiastically returned to work.

***

St Mary's.

By the time Liam re-joined them Craig and Fintan Delaney were sitting eye-to-eye, staring at each other. Craig held a pen and notepad in his hand and Delaney a pen in his. The pad's top page was covered with two different styles of handwriting. Craig's clear, elegant, half-print and a larger, rounder hand than belonged to someone young. Liam crossed the room noisily and grabbed the only remaining chair, sitting beside Craig and squinting suspiciously at their charge. After a moment's more scribbling Craig set the pen down and beckoned Liam outside.

"He can't speak."

Liam scratched his chin and nodded. "Aye. That's what the Doc said. Says she'll be down for a chat in a minute. She's on her last patient."

Craig held up the pad and Liam read it quickly. The gist of the Q and A was that Fintan Delaney remembered nothing about himself or his life. He only knew his name because the nurse had told him. He wanted to speak, but every time he opened his mouth only air emerged, or, at a push, a dry grunt.

Liam sniffed. "Do you believe him?"

Craig hesitated for a moment and then nodded. "Yes. And no. He knows that something bad happened and I think he

50

feels bad about it. That could mean he's actually guilty of something, or just feeling guilty because he survived."

Just then they were joined by a slim, white-coated woman whose perfectly coiffed hair and air of confidence said consultant louder than any badge. Craig thought about Nigel Murdock, a corrupt surgeon that they'd encountered on a previous case. He'd been arrogant and rude but this woman extended her hand to Craig and smiled warmly, underlining the fact that not all doctors were the same.

"Superintendent Craig?"

"Yes. Thank-you for agreeing to talk to us, Dr O'Neill. I know your relationship with Mr Delaney is confidential, but anything that you can tell us would be helpful."

Janet O'Neill nodded and went to open the side-room door. "Just give me a moment." With that she disappeared, to reappear two minutes later with a smile.

"I've obtained Mr Delaney's written consent to discuss his case with you. Please follow me."

They walked to a small office and she waved them towards two seats, then she started speaking immediately.

"Mr Delaney has global retrograde amnesia. He remembers nothing about his life before today, not even his own name."

Liam interrupted. "How do you know he's not faking it?"

O'Neill raised an eyebrow. "Thirty years of experience, Mr Cullen."

Craig gave Liam a glance that said 'wait' and nodded the consultant on.

O'Neill steepled her fingers and stared at them in turn. "It's quite common after trauma for the patient to have no memory of the incident itself, or of the few days before. Retrograde amnesia. It's due to shock, particularly if there's been a head injury. Often those memories never return; lost days. But global amnesia like this is much rarer."

She paused and Craig leapt into the gap. "In your experience what does that mean? Survivor guilt, trauma, or shutting out memories of responsibility for the event?"

O'Neill gave a small smile. "Any or all of those, Superintendent. I believe that when Mr Delaney was found he was standing in the room filled with dead people, only two of whom even resembled people at all. That's a horrific sight, even for someone experienced like us, never mind a twenty-year-old. Added to that Mr Delaney was temporarily deaf from the blast and probably couldn't believe that he hadn't died as well."

"So he could simply be traumatised by what he saw and by the fact that he survived, without there being any culpability?"

The consultant nodded. "He could. Or he could have planted the bomb. I've seen people go into complete denial when they see the results of what they've done."

Liam cut in. "How long are you going to keep him in?"

"At least a week I should say. We have to ensure that he doesn't suffer any delayed reaction, physically or emotionally. He was caught in quite an explosion."

Or he caused one.

Janet O' Neill leaned forward. "In the meantime, can I ask your help with finding his family? He's anxious to find out more about himself and familiar faces can sometimes help with that."

Craig nodded and rose to his feet. "We'll do that. In the meantime I'd like another quick chat with Mr Delaney, and on the off-chance that he is guilty, we'll be leaving an officer here for the rest of his stay."

***

Forever Bridal. Upper Lisburn Road, Belfast. 4 p.m.

Katy yawned exaggeratedly and pointed at the time, watching as Natalie twirled around in her fifth dress of the day. There was no question about it; everything in the shop was exquisite. Each dress was a triumph of silk or lace, chosen with experience by Leondra, the shop's owner, on one of her buying trips abroad. Anything Natalie chose would be exponential improvement on the taffeta puffball she'd shown her the day before.

Natalie disappeared into the changing room, shooting Katy a sheepish grin and holding up one finger to signify that she had a final dress to try on. Somehow Katy doubted it would be the last but she smiled benignly at her friend. It wasn't every day someone got married and it was a new experience to see Natalie behaving girlishly, or wearing anything much besides her surgical scrubs. Katy was pleased for her, but she also knew that the situation would have comic value for years to come.

Katy had just picked up a copy of the Ulster Bazaar and started to flick though its glossy pages when a loud squeal came from the dressing room. She jumped up, certain that Natalie had ripped something expensive then Natalie suddenly reappeared in an exquisite dress. Her eyes sparkled and her skin had taken on a glow that made it seem airbrushed. Katy had never seen her look so pretty and it was easy to see why. Wrapped around her petite form was a wedding dress so beautiful that it brought tears to Katy's eyes.

Soft folds of silky white fabric fell like a waterfall from one shoulder, held there with by an elegant silver clasp. They reached the floor and continued the analogy, spreading out behind Natalie in a fluid train, long enough to announce the importance of the occasion but short enough not to swamp her tiny frame. Katy gasped as Natalie walked slowly to the mirror and turned, showing that the dress was just as beautiful from the back. She nodded for permission to touch the silk. It was cobweb light and cool and Katy pictured her friend walking towards John wearing it, with her long dark curls flowing down her back. The effect would be stunning.

Natalie gazed at herself in the mirror, wearing a shocked expression. She smoothed down the fabric and glanced at her friend with a hopeful question in her eyes. Katy smiled and just then Leondra produced a matching bridesmaid's dress in the creamiest lemon that they had ever seen. Natalie would have her yellow and white wedding and they would both look lovely while she did.

***

Saturday. 7.30 a.m.

Davy was at work uncharacteristically early. He was already yawning at his desk when Craig arrived, having managed to slip through the morning traffic around St George's Market before it built up. St George's was a Belfast landmark; the last surviving Victorian covered market in Belfast, built in 1890. Its stalls traded in everything from gourmet food to art.

Craig threw his suit jacket in his small office and strolled out onto the floor, holding a percolator aloft in invitation. Davy nodded and loped across to Nicky's desk to meet his boss. Nicky's desk was a strange place; an unofficial village square where people hung out. The street corner that they'd all frequented as teenagers, knowing that it was the place to see and be seen if you were cool. It was where things happened first; phones rang offering exciting new cases and printers spat out the, literally, hot news. Nicky's percolator held ever-bubbling coffee and her desk drawers were an Aladdin's cave of sweet things. Above all Nicky's desk was beside Craig's office, the epicentre of the squad, where the coolest kid, the Fonz himself, hung out.

This morning Nicky's desk was just the nearest coffee stop and the two men watched bleary-eyed as the brown liquid bubbled, until Craig finally deemed it fit to drink and poured them both a mug. He perched on the edge of the desk and considered Davy carefully; he saw his team members every day but he didn't often look at them.

Davy had always been tall, well at least in the three years he'd been on the squad, but he seemed to have grown recently. His once reed-thin frame was broader and more adult and his almost pretty aquiline features were morphing into more masculine good looks. Craig knew Davy hadn't even noticed; unless something had a code or cipher on it he ignored it completely. Craig completed his scrutiny, skimming past Davy's shoulder-length hair and stopping at the tiredness of his face. Dark shadows had settled under his eyes like gathering storm clouds and Craig had noticed enough to know that they hadn't been there the day before.

He smiled kindly. "Couldn't sleep?"

Davy nodded slowly as if unsure how much to say. Craig said it for him.

"It was the book you gave your father, wasn't it?"

Davy nodded and at that moment Craig was ashamed of how little he knew about his staff. He knew that Davy had been dating Maggie Clarke, a journalist he'd met on a case, for almost two years and he vaguely remembered a mention of a sister, but beyond that nothing. He knew he'd failed on the team part of his job but once he was focused on a case everything else ceased to exist, a point that every woman he'd been involved with had pointed out.

His voice softened. "Do you miss him a lot?" Hoping it would be enough to make Davy talk. It was. Davy nodded again, throwing his dark hair across his face. Craig wondered if being concealed somehow made it easier to speak.

"It's funny, but w…when he died, I thought about him every day. And now…."

Craig smiled. "Now it's only occasionally. That's normal Davy. No-one can keep up that level of grief forever; you couldn't live."

Davy's voice dropped so low that Craig could barely hear it. "I know you're right, but…"

"He was a Professor of Literature, wasn't he?"

"Yes. Early twentieth century w…writers mainly; Yeats, S…

Shaw, Dylan Thomas… The book I gave him was a collection of Yeats' works."

"Think like a wise man but communicate in the language of the people."

Davy smiled. "That was one of his favourite lines. He used to read it to me w…when I was a kid." He glanced away quickly. "I think he w…was disappointed that I preferred s…science."

Craig shook his head and then realised Davy wasn't looking. His voice became firm. "There is no way you disappointed your father, Davy. All parents want their children to love what they love. God knows if my Mum had her way I'd be playing the piano in some concert hall, not chasing criminals. But sometimes they love you more precisely because you're different from them." Davy stared at him. "Your father would have seen your gift and known that you had to explore it. He'd have been proud when you got your Masters."

Davy grinned and the expression made him look like a kid again. "That's w…what my Mum says. She says he would have loved that Emmie read English at Uni and that I was helping to s…solve crimes. Dad used to read crime novels all the time."

Emmie; short for Emily or Amelia? He would get Nicky to check. Craig tucked the name away for future reference and was just about to ask Davy more about his father when a sudden vibrating of the floor said that Liam had arrived. His voice blasted across the squad-room like a town crier's.

"Here, what's happening? How come you two are in so early?"

Craig turned, with a deadpan expression. "We've been working all night and we've cracked the case, so we're leaving you to do the paperwork while we head to the pub."

Annette and Nicky entered just in time to hear Liam's roar.

"What? That's not right, boss. I know you wanted this put to bed before the wedding, but solving it yourself isn't on."

Craig raised his eyes to heaven, incredulous that Liam had believed him.

"We haven't even started. We just got in early."

Nicky's husky voice cut in. "Did I hear the word wedding? Has anyone decided what they're wearing yet?"

She threw her handbag on her chair and stared pointedly at Craig perched on her desk, waving him away with a manicured hand. Today's nail varnish colour was bubble-gum pink, to match her rather disturbing outfit of ankle socks and wide 1950s skirt. All that was missing was John Travolta and they could have been on the set of 'Grease'.

"Go away, all of you. You're untidying my desk." She scanned her terrain and then squinted at Craig. "And who touched my percolator?"

Craig took the hint and moved everyone down the floor, miming coffee pleadingly as he left.

"Right. Let's get started. Liam's right on one thing. We need this done and dusted before John's big day, hopefully well before it; the last thing I want is to be flying to the Caribbean exhausted. I've a best man's speech to give."

They sat by Davy's desk; far enough away not to annoy Nicky but close enough to smell the coffee perking when it did. As Craig opened his mouth to begin, Liam across him in a self-satisfied tone.

"I've found us someone."

Annette got his meaning first. "How? You were working all day yesterday."

Liam tapped his nose; the universal sign of 'I'm bloody clever and you don't need to know'. Annette was wishing she'd never asked when Craig made it clear that he did need to know.

"I presume you're referring to an officer joining us? And yes, how, Liam? Did the name come to you in your dreams?"

Liam sniffed knowingly. "As a matter of fact it did. I woke up this morning with the idea and a call ten minutes ago sorted it."

Annette snorted. "I bet whoever you phoned this early on a Saturday was overjoyed."

Craig nipped the exchange in the bud. "OK, Liam. Who and how?"

"Aidan Hughes in Vice. I didn't need to wake him 'cos those boys never sleep; too many late nights staking out brothels."

Craig shot him a quizzical look. "You mean Aidan wants to work with us? He's a bit senior."

Nicky arrived with the coffee and Liam took an enormous slurp, giving Craig a look that said he was daft.

"No, not Aidan. He has a wee lassie on the squad and I remembered him saying she was finding Vice rough going. It seems she's a 'laydee' and the filthy world of sex and drugs is not to Madam's liking." Liam extended his little finger like a Victorian Duchess. It looked like a sausage appearing from his mug.

Craig smiled at the reference to 'Little Britain'. "Does this laydee have a name, by any chance?"

Davy leapt in. "Flower of Victorian womanhood?"

"Don't encourage him, Davy." He turned back to Liam. "Well?"

"Her name's Carmen McGregor. She's Scottish, from the posh part of Edinburgh. Anyway, Aidan says she's bright and keen to learn."

Craig raised an eyebrow. "What's the catch?"

Liam bit into a digestive and shook his head. "What do you mean?"

"Come off it. You know Aidan as well as I do; do you really think he'd let such a gem go without a fight, unless he wanted shot of her? "

Nicky had stopped typing and was craning her neck to listen and Annette wore an expression that said 'please God, don't let her be difficult.'

Liam popped the last crumbs of biscuit in his mouth and was just reaching for a second when Craig's gimlet gaze halted him. He leaned back in his chair and shrugged, conceding.

"Aye, well… Apparently she's a bit challenging."

Craig raked his hair and Annette mouthed "Oh, God."

"Challenging how?"

Liam was about to play for time when four pairs of eyes warned him not to.

"Well… She's a bit mouthy, thinks she knows it all. And apparently she got a crush on one of Aidan's lads and followed him around." He saw Craig's head begin to shake and added hastily. "But she's got a first class degree in something and she works her ass off. And it's only for two weeks and then we can give her back."

Craig thought for a moment and then dragged his hand down his face in a gesture of defeat. He looked directly at Annette. In Jake's absence she would be the person with most contact with a new junior. If she didn't want Carmen McGregor to join them then she wouldn't. Annette read Craig's mind and thought for a moment before she spoke.

"OK, here's the deal. Until Jake's back Liam and I share responsibility for her equally."

Liam lurched forward, scattering crumbs all over the floor. "Here now, I'm a D.C.I."

"I don't care if you're the Pope, those are my terms."

"Ach, boss."

Craig ignored his whine. "Carry on, Annette."

"If she's lippy we need your permission to rein her in then and there, sir, not have to refer her back to you."

"Agreed. Is that it?" Craig knew that it wasn't.

"And Davy has to let her shadow him sometimes so that we get a break."

Davy had only been half-listening, reckoning that a new detective was the business of the police-officers in the room, not him. He'd left a programme running on one of his computers and had been craning his neck to see how far it had progressed when he heard his name mentioned and turned back hurriedly to the group.

"W…What?"

Craig knew he hadn't been listening so he summarised. "Annette wants the new girl to be able to sit with you sometimes, to learn what you do."

Davy shook his head with a vehemence that surprised them all. "No. W…What I do is… is complex. I need peace and quiet." He finished with a veiled threat. "That's if you w…want results."

Craig did want results so he was on Davy's side. "Sorry, Annette. But you, Liam and Jake, when he's back, will have to split the load. Davy's off limits, and before you ever think about it, so am I. It's up to you. So, do you want Constable McGregor with all her foibles or not?"

There was a Mexican standoff for a moment then Annette's shoulders slumped and they had their new member of staff.

"OK, good. Liam, call Aidan and say yes, but only from this Monday until we leave for the wedding. Now let's get back to the case. Liam, update us on the bomb then I'll do the hospital. Davy, it looks like you're waiting for something to come through on your screen?"

"Yes. Hopefully I'll have the victims' details s…soon. Well, the I.D.ed ones."

"Excellent." Craig waved Liam on to start.

Liam spent ten minutes running through the army's preliminary report on the explosion then he paused for breath, took a swig of cold coffee and gave Nicky a look so pathetic that Annette started to play an imaginary violin. Nicky took the hint and as they were waiting for fresh drinks Liam handed out some pages; copies of the army's summary.

Craig read for a moment then nodded, realising that he needed to pay a visit to the local base.

"As you can see, boss, they've kept it as vague as buggery. 'Timed device with Semtex explosive.' No details on the bomb's signature or hint of where it might have come from."

Just as a painting was signed by the artist on the canvas and a composer printed their name clearly at the top of each page, so every bomb bore a signature. Not signed with words of course, no matter how proud they were of their destructive creations few bombers were willing to lead the forces of law and order directly to their door. But each bomb was signed by its chemical composition and the structure of the device, and the military world-wide could read the signatures as clearly as a name. Craig tapped the page in front of him.

"They haven't said it was anonymous."

Liam was about to answer when Annette cut in. "They haven't said anything, sir. Surely that means that they just don't know?"

Craig shook his head tiredly. "I wish it did, Annette. But their lack of elaboration speaks volumes. The army knows who exactly made this or they can find out; they just don't want us to."

"Aye. That's what I thought. I asked but they just fobbed me off. You'll have to go and see that Major James yourself."

Craig nodded in resignation, knowing that he'd be stonewalled all the way. He'd try the polite approach but if Major James tried to obstruct his investigation then he'd go over his head. Just then an air-raid siren's whine came from the direction of Davy's desk and he raced over excitedly and started typing on some keys. Liam frowned in irritation.

"I asked you to tone that noise down."

Davy ignored him and two minutes later they had new sheets in their hands and Davy started to report.

"Right. W…We have I.D.s on three of the bomb victims. Fintan Delaney, the s…survivor, Jules Robinson, the shop owner, and a third man; Barry McGovern, a forty-two-year-old businessman who often browsed in the s…shop."

Craig interjected. "Leave Delaney till the end, Davy. Tell us about McGovern first."

Davy nodded. "OK. Barry McGovern. An accountant w… working at Roulston's in North Street. He's been there for ten years, before that he w…worked in London. Nothing very

61

exciting about his life. Married, with three children aged three to thirteen."

Annette groaned. "Poor kids."

Davy nodded and continued. "Wife, Maria. S…She's an event's organiser for a children's charity called 'The Belfast Buzz'"

Liam cut in. "Here. Isn't that the one Lucia used to work for?"

Craig nodded. "Years ago. She might know Maria McGovern. I'll ask." He waved Davy on.

"I'm getting McGovern's financial details and phone and computer dumps now, but s…so far there's nothing nasty."

Annette interrupted with an annoyed look on her face. "Why are we getting all that? Are we treating everyone as a suspect, even if they died?"

Craig shot her a sceptical look. "We have to, Annette, you know that. Even if it's only to rule them out. What's the problem?"

Annette shook her head, setting her sensible brown bob flying. Craig smiled inwardly at her flat shoes and prim suit. Annette had never dressed casually but nowadays it seemed she was dressing as if someone was assessing whether she was suitable senior officer material. He knew she was ambitious and getting more so but she didn't need to carry it that far.

Gone were the days when women had to hide their attractiveness to be taken seriously; feminism was in its third wave. Well, that's what Lucia and Katy told him if he asked how they walked all day in five-inch-heels.

Annette's Maghera tones dragged Craig back from his thoughts. "Well, it's just… hasn't the wife suffered enough already without her husband being treated like a suspect?"

Craig shook his head. "This is behind the scenes work, Annette, and if you're worried I'll let you interview Mrs McGovern. OK?"

Annette nodded, mollified, and Davy picked up his report.

"The s…shop-owner Jules Robinson is more interesting. He was a civil servant, then ten years ago he bought the shop outright w…with cash."

"Retirement money?"

"Maybe, but I can't find any s…sign of where it came from and retirement funds would normally be paid into a bank account, w…wouldn't they? Maybe it was dodgy money?"

Craig laughed. "So young and yet so cynical. It's probably perfectly innocent but follow it up anyway. Dig into every corner of Robinson's finances; personal and business. Anything on his family?"

Davy shrugged. "Wife, Sarah, s…seventy-two."

Liam grinned. "Here. Old Jules was a toy-boy."

Annette snorted. "And if he'd been some sad old man with a ponytail and a twenty-year-old on his arm you'd have said 'good on him'. It might interest you to know that in forty-eight percent of marriages the woman is the same age or older than the man."

The way she said it made Craig expect a "So there" to follow. It did, from Nicky. Her husky voice grew louder as she approached the group with more biscuits.

"Good on her. I hope I'm dating a fifty-year-old when I'm eighty. Joan Collins is an example to us all." She deposited the digestives with a haughty sniff and left.

Craig waved the chatter down. "OK, everyone. I know we're all de-mob happy about John's wedding but let's focus, please."

Davy focused. "The Robinsons led a quiet life. No children, just a cat and dog. They seemed to put everything into the s… shop. Mrs Robinson helped out there."

Craig leaned forward urgently. "Find out how often, Davy, and if she was expected to be there on Thursday. Any changes in her routine, flag it up to me. We need to know if she could have been a possible target."

"W…Will do. Do you want to take over for Fintan Delaney?"

Craig nodded then started reporting on his two encounters with Delaney and his belief that the youth's amnesia was genuine. "He can't even remember his own name. The consultant called it global amnesia and said the sooner we find Delaney's family the sooner his memory might return."

Davy waved for attention. "I've found them. He has parents, John and Bronagh, and two younger brothers, Dermot and Liam."

Liam sniffed proudly. "Great name. Did you know that Liam was William in Irish?"

Craig laughed. "So we can start calling you Billy?"

"Not if you want an answer."

Craig signalled Davy to continue. "Fintan is at Queen's studying P.P.E.; Politics, Philosophy and Economics. He's just finished his s…second year. Did OK in his exams."

Annette interrupted. "What does he do apart from study?"

"Like attending 'bomb-making for beginners', you mean?"

Liam guffawed loudly. "Nice one, son."

Annette shot Davy a 'don't be cheeky' look. "No, I didn't. I meant most university students join societies and clubs. What did Delaney join?"

Davy smiled, conceding. "You're right. He's in the drama s… society and chess club."

Craig interrupted. "Not much terrorist activity going on there. OK, Davy, dig into his politics and his family's. Include all family members and do a wide search for gang connections and terrorist offences. You know the drill." Craig checked the time and stood-up. "Right. There's plenty for everyone to do and we have two more dead victims still to I.D. John's working on that. Liam, go and see Sarah Robinson. Annette, can you visit Barry McGovern's wife, please. Davy, can you and Liam pull any traffic cameras and CCTV around the shop for the hours before and after the blast. I'm going to the army base and then onto the lab."

He swung round to see Nicky sitting with her pen and

notepad poised. "Nick, can you arrange for Fintan Delaney's parents to be brought to the relatives' room downstairs for about three p.m., or I can meet them at the hospital if they prefer." He headed for his office to lift his jacket. "And get Major James' office on the phone and say that I'm on my way to the base. I should be there by ten o'clock."

Suddenly Craig felt someone staring at him and he turned to see the small group still in place.

"Did I forget something?"

Annette beckoned him back and Nicky joined them. Their faces were solemn and Craig wondered what he'd done wrong.

Annette spoke first. "Sir, we have something every important to ask you and your reply is a matter of life and death."

Craig's eyes widened and for a moment he was worried, then he saw Nicky giggle and he knew what was coming next. "You want to know what to get John and Natalie as a wedding present."

Craig shook his head and headed for the double-doors. "I have absolutely no idea. What John likes Natalie will hate and vice versa, so the best of luck with that."

Chapter Seven

10 a.m.

The British Army base was set high in the Craigantlet Hills, near the small town of Holywood, home to Tom and Mirella Craig. The setting was picturesque, overlooking countryside whose hills gave a new meaning to the word 'rolling'. They pitched and veered unexpectedly at angles that were unfeasibly steep, only to level off suddenly to reveal a green vista that stretched for miles. It was that suddenness that made Craig love the area; he had since done he was a boy. He remembered running up and down the slopes with his gang of friends and playing hide and seek in the long, dry grass. He'd hiked the miles from home just to play there, even though there were flatter spaces closer by; but none of them held the mystery of grass that he was small enough to hide in and the chance of finding a gully that no-one had discovered before.

But the Army hadn't chosen the location for its beauty; it had far more practical considerations. The base was positioned far enough from Holywood's urban build-up to bestow privacy, and high enough above it so that the only neighbours who could have spied on them were the MLAs at Stormont, and even they would have needed an astronomer's telescope. As Craig drove up the narrow mud track to the reinforced, barbed-wire topped gate he wondered whether what happened there would bear scrutiny any better than what happened in Parliament Buildings would, although undoubtedly it involved younger, fitter men.

After the theatre of name checking and badge flashing at the small gate-post, the wide, high gates opened inwards to reveal a dusty road that ended at a large building a mile further on. Modern houses lined the road and between them lay small commons, with young children running to and fro, playing the games that Craig and his friends had played thirty-five years before outside the gate. Children would always be children, playing whenever they got the chance.

Five minutes of driving at the base's speed-limited pace brought Craig to a gravelled courtyard outside the large building; double-fronted, made of granite and named by a small signpost as the Officers' Mess. A young squaddie appeared and pointed Craig to a parking space. He left his Audi and strode towards the Mess' oak front door, knowing exactly what he would find behind. Long, polished corridors and high-ceilinged, brightly-lit rooms, adorned with the badges and emblems of yesteryear. Portraits of long dead warriors would hang on every wall, alongside mottos that reinforced the honour and love of duty that was the army's stock in trade.

Suddenly a young officer emerged from a doorway, wearing a casual uniform of T-shirt and combat trews. Craig wondered why everything about the army was green; green uniforms, green jeeps and tanks, even green metal guns. He was sure it gave camouflage in the jungle, but not in colourfully populated urban streets.

His reverie was broken by the sight of the man's cheerful grin and he recognised him as the captain he'd met two days before. Ken Smith greeted him warmly, extending his hand to shake.

"Superintendent Craig. Good to see you again."

He sounded as if he really meant it and Craig thought that he probably did; it would be his senior officer who was less pleased.

Craig shook hands and nodded around the corridor. "Nice Mess"; he smiled at the oxymoron.

Smith shrugged. "It's OK. To be honest they all look the

same after a while." He dropped his voice confidingly. "I think they make them identical to fool us that we're always at home, regardless of which shithole they post us to."

Before Craig could reply Smith waved him into a large anteroom. It was filled with high-backed, deep-buttoned armchairs set around a large, unlit fire. The portion of the room's walls that wasn't covered in wainscot was lined with shelves of books. Smith motioned Craig to take a seat.

"Coffee?"

Craig nodded, wondering where it would come from. A moment later a white-coated member of the catering staff gave him his answer. He set down a tray laid with a silver coffee-pot, cups and biscuits then retreated diplomatically, leaving Smith to be mother and pour. As he did so Craig glanced around the room, wondering how the army justified luxury like this. Smith read his mind.

"If you take people away from their life and family and offer the likelihood they'll be killed, the least you can do is feed them well."

They drank coffee and chatted for five minutes then Craig put down his cup and cut to the chase.

"Major James isn't going to see me, is he?"

Smith blushed and swallowed the biscuit he had in his mouth. "No, he is. I mean, yes he is. He's just been delayed."

Craig shot him a sceptical look. "You mean he's on the phone checking how much he's allowed to tell me."

Smith gave a weak smile. "Something like that. The bomb's…"

His sentence was aborted by sharp footsteps behind them and a well-bred baritone slicing through the air. "Captain Smith." The words were innocuous but their tone carried a clear warning not to say any more.

Smith snapped to his feet before Craig had time to turn. When he did he saw Smith standing, arm raised and hand pinned sharply to his forehead. The word "Sir" said that a senior officer had entered the room and as Craig rose he could see the source of Smith's nerves.

An older man than both of them was standing in the doorway. He was six-feet-five if he was an inch, making Craig wish that he'd brought Liam along. The old soldier's fatigues were so crisply pressed that each irregular green smudge in the fabric's pattern looked as if it was an affront and should tidy its edges immediately and conform. Each button shone and each scrap of leather: boots, belt and cane, was buffed until it gleamed. But what impressed Craig most was the beret set precariously on the man's greying head. It hung there, plumped perfectly and angled steeply with the certainty of a mountain goat, defying gravity to do its worst.

Craig took in the details in a second and then settled his gaze on the man's face. To say that it was craggy didn't do it justice. Craggy applied to ranges of bare rock, all sharp edges and protuberances, but they paled into a vista of smooth concrete compared to this. Each feature on the man's face was exaggeratedly large and each crevice overly deep, the skin a battered, ruddy mahogany that screamed of years of sun exposure overseas. No-one was born looking that extreme; life and the elements had left their mark. Craig knew instantly that the man welcomed the rugged effect, for the fear and respect that it would make others feel.

Craig broke the silence. "Major James." It wasn't a question.

James nodded and entered the room, shaking Craig's extended hand in a surprisingly throwaway manner. It was almost rude, except that James was too well-bred for that. Smith stepped back, ushering his boss into the circle of chairs then he poured everyone fresh coffee as Craig and James sat in silence sizing each other up. Smith retook his seat mutely and Craig knew what was coming next. Major James and he would converse and Smith would listen; the rules of rank rendering him mute unless invited to speak. Craig smiled inwardly, trying to imagine Liam behaving that way.

For a moment Stephen James said nothing, merely stared at Craig. Craig knew the stare was supposed to make him nervous; it didn't, it merely amused him instead. It was a tactic criminals employed to try to unnerve their interrogators, especially if they were inexperienced. It wouldn't work on him but he could imagine its effect on a raw recruit. His thoughts flew suddenly to Julia McNulty. She'd been unhappy in the army and if James was typical of her senior officers then he could understand why.

Craig decided he'd had enough of standing on ceremony. It was eleven o'clock and he had other things to do.

"So, Major James. Two things. The forensics that your team collected and the bomb itself. What can you tell me?"

From the corner of his eye Craig could see Smith's eyebrows shoot up in surprise that he'd taken the lead. James squinted, knowing that he held no rank over Craig and had to rely on body language to give the impression that he did. Craig ignored the squint and repeated his question.

The standoff ended a few seconds later when James nodded Smith to lift the wall-phone. It was the signal for a young woman to enter the room. She was younger than twenty, although her tightly wound bun, drab outfit and flat, laced shoes did their best to make her look like a maiden aunt. Craig strained to imagine the glamorous Julia dressed that way and gave up; Julia was a woman who wouldn't be easily parted from her high-heels.

The girl carried a buff-coloured file that she handed to James without a word, then she turned briskly and left the room. James began reading in a monotonous tone.

"The forensics revealed that the device was situated at the back of the shop and the blast radius was approximately twenty feet. The unidentifiable victims would have been standing nearest to the device when it exploded, the other deceased were within the radius but not shielded by any substantial obstacle. The sole survivor was by the shop's front door, furthest away from the device and shielded by five high bookshelves that we believe were almost the width of the shop. They saved him from certain death."

Craig already knew it all but he smiled politely. James glanced up from the file. "There is more forensic detail that we have sent to your pathologist this morning."

Craig nodded. "Thank-you; it will help us piece together the scene. And the explosive device itself?"

Smith tensed visibly and averted his eyes from his superior's face, as if he was waiting for him to roar. Stephen James merely shrugged and tapped the page. "It's in here. Standard Semtex-based device with a crude timer; five kilos of Semtex. Nothing exciting."

Craig persisted. "We both know that bomb makers have a signature, Major; so who signed this one?"

James shook his head. "It's no-one that we know."

Craig snapped back. "You mean it's not a dissident?"

"If it is then they have a new bomb maker on their staff. The signature doesn't match any of the devices in Northern Ireland in the past ten years."

Craig raked his hair, thinking. If it wasn't a known dissident they could be at a dead end early in the game. He thought of something and re-framed his question.

"Does it match any signatures from the past fifty years?"

James' face cracked slightly and from his subordinate's decrease in tension Craig realised that it was probably what passed for a smile.

"Very good, Superintendent. The answer is we're checking that at the moment. Quite a few of the records sit with MI5, or in archives in London, so it will take us a few days. I'll let you know as soon as we do."

Craig nodded, slightly mollified but not satisfied yet. "And the other metal found on the bomb? The scrollwork and the watch?"

James shook his head. "I confess that we're at a loss there. The scrollwork was titanium, not part of the bomb material, and it was far too ornate to be useful. I've never seen anything like it. The watch was an 18th Century pocket watch, quite valuable I imagine. It acted as the timer. But why they didn't use a modern digital device I have no idea."

Craig scrutinised the major's face and could see he was telling the truth; he hadn't a clue. Craig decided to share their speculations in the spirit of entente cordiale.

"You know there were glass fragments near the bomb site."

James sat forward, more interested now. "Yes, but they could have come from a window or cabinet."

Craig shook his head. "No. There were no glass cabinets in the shop as far as we know and any windows were at the front of the shop. Flying glass from those would have blown outwards or been halted by the bookshelves and never reached the area round the bomb. Besides, the glass was much finer than either of those sources could explain. We…"

He hesitated for a moment and then shrugged; they were all on the same side, and even if James thought that rivalry helped to build teams, he didn't.

"We thought that it might have come from a picture frame; the titanium scrollwork forming the frame. In fact it was Captain Smith who first suggested as much."

Craig smiled as Smith blushed. James turned sharply towards the young officer.

"Why is this the first I'm hearing of your suggestion, Captain Smith?"

Smith stammered wildly, reminding Craig of Davy when he'd first joined the squad.

"I…I…We…We didn't like to bother you with it, sir. It was only a wild idea."

James set his jaw. "Well, wild idea or no, you should have told me." He sniffed grudgingly. "In either case it seems you may have been right. Well done."

Smith's blush deepened and a look of pride covered his face. "Yes, sir. Thank-you, sir."

He was about to say something else when Craig cut in, calculating that anything more Smith said would irritate James and it was better for him to quit while he was ahead.

"If it was a photograph, the question is of whom and why was it attached to the bomb?"

The question was rhetorical. Craig knew that he and John would speculate much more creatively than the stolid James ever could. James' silence said he was right so Craig tried another tack.

"Captain Smith, you mentioned that there was the remnant of a photograph in the scrollwork and you were giving it to your tech people. Any progress on that?"

Smith shook his head, avoiding James' eyes and gazing directly at Craig. "I've sent it to our lab in London and they're piecing it together now. Would you like whatever we have?"

Craig nodded but his eyes said Smith should already know the answer; the full forensics should have been with them by now. "It would help if you could send it over to Dr Marsham and also to Davy Walsh, our analyst. He can do amazing things with images."

Craig felt James about to object and he realised why Smith hadn't confided about the picture to his boss. Craig continued before James had time to block the idea. "We all want to find whoever did this and the photograph could be a clue to that. Thank-you for working closely with us on this, Major. Captain Smith has been most helpful."

Before James could counter Craig glanced at his watch and rose, extending his hand.

"I'm sorry but I must go. I have another meeting. Thank-you for your help, Major." He turned to Smith. "And thank you, Captain. Perhaps you would show me out?"

Smith grabbed at the request eagerly and before Stephen James could say anything more they were out of the anteroom and halfway down the hall, under the stern gaze of heroes from the past. As they emerged into the morning sunshine Smith gave a loud laugh that Craig knew had been bottled up for the past half-hour.

"I'm glad that's over. He's a tough old stick but you handled him well. Thanks for that."

Craig smiled. "He reminds me of a boss I once had, although James seems more reasonable." His mind flew back to 'Teflon' Terry Harrison and he thanked God that he wasn't his problem anymore. Julia was stuck with Harrison now in Limavady.

They crunched across the gravel to the Audi and Craig paused before he got in. "That bomb signature info is interesting. If it's definitely not one of the dissidents, what are the odds that it's some old bomber harking back to his glory days? But if it is why destroy a bookshop?"

Smith frowned. "The odds I can help with, by finding the signature if it's out there, but you're on your own with the bookshop bit."

Craig climbed into the car and wound down the window as Smith talked on.

"I promise I'll get everything we discussed over to your lab and analyst; James will have to stop blocking it now. And I'm happy to stay as involved as you like in the case." Smith cast a look towards the Mess. "To be honest there's bugger all else for us to do here at the moment. Most people are on leave before deployment and I'm bored rigid, so if you need a spare pair of hands…"

Craig smiled. "How would Major James feel about that?"

Smith shrugged. "I think he'd be glad. I'm driving him mad at the moment, asking for work that he doesn't have to give me."

Craig thought for a moment and then nodded briskly. "Fine. We could do with the help for the next few weeks. I'll clear it with my Chief Constable and Major James and come Monday you can work with us as army liaison on the case. There's just one thing…"

Richard leaned in eagerly. "Yes? Anything you need."

"I need you in a dark suit. All this green is giving me a headache."

***

Donegall Street, Belfast. 12 p.m.

Liam parked his car in the quiet city-centre street, scanning both sides for some sign of a dwelling. This was the address he had for the Robinsons, but there seemed to be nothing here except tall, red-brick terraces housing business and restaurants, and aging churches sandwiched between them trying to make God's voice heard. He re-checked the note Nicky had given him, smiling as her exaggerated calligraphy leapt off the page. It was theatrical, just like everything about her; from her ever-changing clothes to her hair. Liam allowed himself a moment's musing about what it might be like if they were a couple, hastily adding the caveat 'if his wife and Nicky's husband hadn't met them first'. It allowed him to muse guilt-free and the result was bliss. Marriage to Nicky would be one long roller coaster of banter and laughter, not to mention the sex.

The appearance of St Xavier's Church in the periphery of his vision cut Liam's daydream short. At heart he was still an altar boy, steeped in religious guilt. Imagining a relationship with Nicky was as far as he would ever go and he would never swop Danni for the chance, but even imagining it this close to a church made him want to confess his sins. With his fantasy firmly packed away he returned to the task in hand and rechecked the address.

Just then he noticed a small white house set back fifty feet from the road, hidden between a takeaway and a charity shop. He smiled to himself; Jules Robinson had owned a quirky bookshop so it was fitting that he'd lived in a quirky house. As Liam approached the house's front door he saw just how quirky it was.

A small patch of garden sat behind a white wooden fence, recently painted if the smell was any sign. There, dotted in a random pattern across the grass was a selection of garden gnomes; more than Liam had ever seen before. They played the violin, fished and laughed all over the place, with red, round cheeks and ample stomachs to match. There were gnomes of every race and sex and Liam wondered dryly if they crossed the political divide as well. One particularly large one sat in a corner holding a pair of binoculars; a sign round its neck said 'Gnome CCTV'. Liam guffawed and then caught himself, remembering that he was there to speak to a widow; but a widow with a sense of humour if the garden was anything to go by.

He reached the house's cheerful red front door in two strides, composed his face into a sombre mask and raised his hand to knock. Before his fist fell the door opened and a small, round woman in her seventies who could have been the gnomes' sister, beckoned him inside.

Liam reached for his badge. "Mrs Robinson, I'm D.C.I…"

But the woman had already turned and was halfway down the hall, motioning Liam to keep up. Her voice was quiet but cheerful.

"Cullen. I know; your office rang. My name's Sadie and we're in the kitchen."

She bustled into a small, warm kitchen, which boasted an open fire despite the summer day. For a moment she worked in silence, putting out a plate of warm scones and a large pot of tea, glancing at Liam's large hands before eschewing the china cups for larger mugs. She placed a pot of jam on the table and nodded Liam to sit. As the tea brewed Sadie Robinson began to talk.

"Help yourself, Inspector. There's plenty here."

Liam opened his mouth to speak but she ignored him and continued in a brisk tone.

"Right, now. You're wearing your sad face because I'm a

widow now. Some little sod blew up my husband and destroyed our shop. The shop is insured, my Jules is gone and nothing on God's good earth can ever bring him back." She raised her eyes to heaven mid-diatribe. "God rest his soul. I'll pray for him every day of my life and anyway, I know that he's still here with me. But no amount of sad faces will make me feel any better or worse, so smile, let's have a nice cup of tea and then you can ask me whatever you've come to ask."

With that she sat down on a small, cushioned chair and started to pour the tea. Liam smiled quietly in admiration. This was why he loved old people; he always had since he'd been a kid and spent summers at his grandparent's farm, exploring the fields all day and coming home every evening to a feast not unlike this. Old people were calm, with none of the histrionics of teenagers or women of his own age. They'd seen it all, felt it all, not only worn the T-shirt but probably designed and printed it as well. They didn't overreact when you told them things; just shed a silent tear, much as he imagined Sadie Robinson had done when she'd been told that her husband was dead. He was dead but she was still alive; that was her gift and her trial until she could join her Jules. And by the sounds of it she already had inside her head.

They slurped and munched in silence for five minutes until Liam finally broke the quiet.

"Nice gnomes."

The old woman beamed from ear to ear and started to tell him how the gnome garden had come to be; she and Jules had been great travellers and each gnome was a souvenir of one of their trips.

"Where did you get the CCTV one? It's brilliant."

Sadie smiled, twinkling her already twinkly brown eyes. "That's Frederick, after my father. We got him in New York. Jules has cousins there."

Liam was touched by her use of the present tense then he remembered that she believed her husband was still around.

Sadie read his thoughts and smiled.

"I know you think I'm doolally, Inspector, but Jules is still here. I knew the second that he died, even though I was here at home. Two o'clock on Thursday afternoon. I felt him leave."

Liam didn't think she was doolally at all; he'd heard things like that said many times before by the relatives of victims. He'd even felt it himself once or twice with close mates killed while they were on patrol, and his Mum had known the moment his father had died in an accident in the fields. Sadie elaborated enthusiastically.

"You know how when you walk into a room, even in the dark, you can sense if someone is there? Not because you can see them or even hear them breathe, but because you just sense their presence. Well that's what happens when someone dies, except in reverse; it's as if they've suddenly left the room. Even if you see can their body you just can't sense them anymore."

Liam lifted another scone and spread butter on it, nodding his elderly hostess on.

"Jules and I were happy for forty years; that's more than a lot of people ever get. He bought Papyrus in 1995 after retiring from the RUC."

Liam's ears pricked up. Jules Robinson had been a police officer! Davy had said he'd been a civil servant, but that was a euphemism a lot of policemen in Northern Ireland used when they were asked what they did. It made it harder for terrorists to I.D. them. Had Robinsons' police career been a motive for the bombing? Sadie read his mind.

"It might have been why Jules was killed, Mr Cullen, although we'd never had any threats. But there were other reasons why people might have wanted him gone."

Liam leaned forward urgently. "Why? What had he done?"

Sadie smiled mysteriously. "Jules did plenty of things in his life, good and bad, but it wasn't what he did that I was referring to."

At that moment she touched the tea-pot and made a face,

tutted "it's cold" then rose to re-boil the kettle. After the tea ceremony was completed to her satisfaction she retook her seat and started again.

"I don't know how much you know about Smithfield, Inspector, but let's just say that it's a varied area. There are plenty of respectable business people there but there are plenty of others who see it as their private playground."

Liam's curiosity was piqued. "In what way?"

Sadie sniffed disapprovingly. "They'd like it to be like Soho in London used to be; all naked girls, porn-shops and drugs. The places that are already there are bad enough, we certainly don't need any more."

"So, what? They wanted you out, or they wanted you to pay protection money?"

Sadie sipped her tea and nodded. "Both. They charged Jules protection every month just to trade; I don't know how much."

Liam interrupted. "Do you know who?"

She wrinkled her nose as if there was a bad smell. "I know who all right and I'll gladly give you their names. But they wouldn't have wanted the shop destroyed or they'd have lost their income."

Liam shook his head thoughtfully. "Unless your husband refused to pay them?"

It was Sadie's turn to shake her head. "Jules wouldn't have done that. He loved the shop and he'd got over being angry about the extortion years ago. No, he paid them and I don't think they destroyed the shop, but I'll give you their names and perhaps you can stop them doing it to others."

"So if it wasn't the protection racket, why else? You said someone wanted you out of the shop?"

Sadie nodded. "Not just us, all the shops on that row."

"Developers?"

"You've got it in one. So called progress."

She waved a hand around and Liam realised that she was indicating Smithfield, not the room they were in. "Belfast is starting to grow again, now that we're almost out of the recession. That means that a lot of apartment developments that had stalled for years are restarting and others are being planned. Jules was offered a lot of money to sell the shop."

Liam nodded. It was a fair assessment of what happened once money started to flow. "Who's the developer?"

"A company called SNI. They first approached Jules last summer. They made him a fair offer but he said no. We thought that was the end of it, then the two shops beside us were sold one after another. That only left us at one end of the terrace and the convenience store at the other. We heard last weekend that they were leaving as well."

"That only left your bookshop in the developer's way."

Sadie nodded and bit into a scone. "They want to build new apartments. A 'boutique' development they call it. Apartments, a gym, swimming pool; the whole shebang." Her face fell and for a moment Liam thought she was going to cry. "They'll get their way now that the shop has gone."

Liam nodded kindly but he was thinking of other things. In one conversation Sadie Robinson had added three potential motives and suspects to their list; SNI the developers, the extortionists and someone who might have wanted Jules Robinson dead because of his past life in the RUC. The case was beginning to look unsolvable before the wedding. Liam parked his doubts and focused, gazing across the table at the woman whose life he knew had just been destroyed, no matter how brave she was trying to be about it. He spoke in the softest voice that he possessed.

"Do you have any family, Mrs Robinson?"

Sadie Robinson shook her head sadly and then sighed. "We had no children. God didn't bless us that way. I have a sister in England, but…"

Liam cut in. "I think you should go and stay with her for a while, at least until we get this sorted out."

Sadie's brown eyes widened. "You do? You think that I might

be at risk?"

Liam shook his head. "It's unlikely, but until we're certain who did this, I'd rather that you were safe."

She smiled, pleased that someone cared. She patted Liam on the cheek as if he was her son. "I'll do it, Mr Cullen, if you promise me one thing."

"What?"

"That you'll come and take tea with me another day."

Liam nodded. Not out of politeness and not to make her go to her sisters, but because he meant it. Sadie Robinson had just made a new friend.

Chapter Eight

The Lab. 1 p.m.

John was in his outer office arranging his newly reinstated cabinets when Craig arrived, and from the prints and paintings leaning against the wall Craig knew what his next task was going to be. He stood in the doorway and considered his best friend for a moment. John looked happy, happier than Craig had seen him in… well, ever really.

John had been a solitary only child when they'd met at grammar school; small and thin for his age and wearing glasses. He hadn't exactly been bullied but he'd spent every lunchtime alone, reading a book or working on experiments in the lab. Everyone had thought he was doing it to suck up to the teachers but the years had proved them very wrong. What had started as childhood curiosity had become John's way of life.

Craig had been curious about the quiet boy from the start. He was an uber-fit jock who played every sport at school and most of them to Captaincy. But he was something else as well; he'd been raised by educated parents and his grades were always good. It had set him apart from some of his more Neanderthal teammates who'd used brute force and ignorance to carve a path through life. That and his half-Italian parentage had isolated him at times and he'd recognised the same loneliness in John. It had driven him to make the first move towards friendship, and once past the awkward first conversations they'd become inseparable, bonded by a wicked sense of humour.

Their friendship had weathered the years, through his time in

London and years of emotional purdah after his split from Camille. Through the loss of both John's parents and Mirella's unofficial adoption of him as her second son. Now here they were, preparing for John's wedding and solving crimes like some latter-day Holmes and Watson, although Craig often wondered who was who.

John saw Craig watching and knew what he was thinking, but a moment's sentimentality was all that either of them could bear so he held up an antique stethoscope and broke the mood.

"Are you going to stand there all day doing nothing, or are you going to give me a hand with this?"

'This' was the task of putting John's antique medical devices back in their rightful places and Craig joined in, talking as he worked.

"Any joy on the other bodies yet?"

John was staring at a small metal device that looked as if its use had been some form of torture. He replied without looking at Craig.

"Give me a chance. You've got McGovern's and Robinson's I.D.; isn't that enough to go on with?"

Craig shrugged. It was something but it was never enough.

"Liam's interviewing Mrs Robinson at the moment and Annette's at the McGovern's, but that still leaves us with two unknowns. Can't you get something from the remains?"

John shook his head and motioned Craig to pass him a scalpel bearing a small tag. Craig read it before he handed it over; 'Auschwitz 1945.' He shuddered as he realised that the implement had probably killed hundreds.

"Hell John, what do you want this stuff for?"

"It might be horrific but it's important. To remind us never again."

John placed the artefact firmly inside a cabinet and answered Craig's original question.

"To get something from the remains we'd have to find recognisable prints and so far all we have is one thumb. Des is printing it as we speak, so I'm hopeful we'll get a match on one more victim soon. We're depending on DNA alone for the final victim, always hoping we can isolate it from a possible five DNAs in the shop. We'll do our best but you need to prepare yourself for us never finding out who they were."

Craig interrupted. "Davy and Liam are working on the CCTV and traffic cameras. If we can find an image of them entering the shop that might be enough."

John's reply was instant. "Unless they left by the back door." He gave Craig a baleful look. "We might be looking for a missing person appeal."

Craig's face fell. He hated TV appeals; they were sad and desperate and although they sometimes yielded information they were a dreadful way for a family to discover that their loved one had gone. He grasped at the final straw.

"I don't suppose there's any chance that you're wrong?"

John raised an eyebrow. "About what?"

"That there were five people in the shop. Couldn't there just have been four? Delaney, McGovern, Robinson and the owner of the thumb?"

John shook his head and set down the antique pill bottle he was holding. "Not unless one of them was morbidly obese. There was too much flesh for just one unknown victim. Army forensics agrees with me."

Craig screwed up his face at the image then conceded, changing the subject quickly before John started to explain exactly why the amount of flesh was too much.

"I've just been to the army base."

John headed for his office with Craig in tow. He switched on the percolator and took a seat before asking the question.

"And?"

"Captain Smith is being helpful; in fact he's going to join us as liaison for the next two weeks if I can wrangle it. He's bored and we need the help if we're to get everything wrapped up in time for the wedding."

At the word wedding John smiled; he was a man going willingly up the aisle. Craig continued.

"Major James on the other hand is an old sod. It was like pulling teeth getting information from him."

"But you did."

Craig smiled. "Yes. They agree Delaney survived because he was by the front door and the bookshelves shielded him. They've sent the bomb signature off to be looked at but it doesn't match any recent dissident attempts so that just leaves the past fifty years' efforts to compare against."

John interrupted in a sceptical tone. "Or this is a first-time bomber who isn't known to anyone."

Craig raked his hair. "Don't even think that. We need a break."

The percolator signalled the coffee was ready and there was a brief pause before the conversation restarted.

John speculated thoughtfully. "OK, let's just say that the bomber's someone from Northern Ireland's delightful past, then what?"

"Then we follow it where that leads, but my money says that it won't be. There's something about this explosion and the target that feels all wrong."

John smiled. "More wrong than an explosion normally feels?"

Craig sipped his coffee for a moment before answering. "OK, why a bookshop? And if you wanted the large crowd of people that you could find in a retail outlet, then why a small antique bookshop? Why not one of the big high-street chains? God knows there are enough of them around." He shook his head. "No. This is personal."

"To the bookshop?"

"Or to its owner. Perhaps even to a particular customer."

Suddenly Craig grabbed for his mobile and pressed Liam's name, mouthing at John. "Liam may have got something from the owner's wife."

The phone was answered quickly and Craig set it on the desk, pressing speaker. It wasn't necessary; Liam's voice was so loud that they could have heard his words without the help.

"Hi, boss. What's up?"

Craig leaned towards the phone. "I'm at the lab, Liam, and John and I are talking about motives for bombing Papyrus. Did Mrs Robinson suggest anything in the way of motive?"

Liam smiled to himself. He liked having information that no-one else had, even if only for ten minutes; it allowed him to impart wisdom to the masses. In the split second Liam hesitated Craig read his mind and added. "And before you make us drag it out of you admiringly, don't bother. I'm not in the mood."

Liam harrumphed loudly and launched into a shorter than planned summary. He finished with. "So basically it's because Robinson was in the RUC, because of the local protection racket, or because SNI developers wanted him out of the shop. Take your pick. They were all out to get him."

Craig let out a low whistle and Liam felt more appreciated. "Good work, Liam. Thanks. Where are you heading now?"

"Off to have a look through Robinson's RUC record to see if anything stands out. I'll see you back at the ranch."

With that Liam cut the call and Craig knew it was his way of saying he was annoyed at his shortened exposition. John nodded.

"Well, there's your list of motives, Marc. Take your pick."

Craig shook his head. "Maybe… or maybe there's something else. One of those might explain some things but none of them feels one hundred percent right." John went to speak and Craig raised a hand. "Before you ask, no, I don't know why I feel that, I just do. Call it instinct."

"Or delusion."

They both smiled. They had a long running debate about logic versus instinct with John always erring on the logic side. He was an empirical scientist and had been all his life; if it couldn't be measured and replicated then it simply didn't exist.

Craig agreed, up to a point, and it was at that point that his instinct and 'sense' of things took over, and their methods of crime solving diverged. John didn't know where Craig's instinct came from, perhaps his romantic side, but either way he'd seen him pull an answer out of the vapour of ideas and be correct. John decided it was time to change the subject.

"Katy's took Natalie to some new wedding shop yesterday."

Craig smiled. "Yes, she said they were planning it. She was hoping they'd come up with something spectacular."

It was John's turn to smile. "Something that wasn't bright yellow taffeta, you mean."

They laughed for a moment then Craig gestured towards the outer lab. "Glad to see it back to its subdued glory."

"Not half as glad as I am. Yellow might be fine for one day but I was starting to need sunglasses to venture outside. Now all I have to do is tell Natalie it's been changed back."

***

Karachi, Pakistan. 9 a.m. local time

Jennifer Weston cast a last look down the runway and then walked briskly towards the plane, adjusting her neat uniform. She didn't like it, but needs must when she had a job to do. As she gripped the metal stair-way to the Boeing 747 she was joined by three women of varying ages, identically clad. She listened to their chatter, pretending to be interested, but all she was interested in was reaching her goal.

A red-haired girl was the most vocal. Her broad Dublin accent rang through the air, echoing the others' thoughts. "Who's the captain today?"

A woman with short hair, nearing the end of her career, answered. "Groggins." She rolled her eyes and the others groaned.

"Gropey Groggins… God help us. Right then, we're drawing

lots to see who serves the cockpit. Last time I went in there he put his hand right up my skirt. "

Jennifer smiled as if she was listening, but in reality her mind was 4,000 miles and 13 hours away. The job was a means to an end, like so many others she did; an occasional front for her real work in life. Work she needed to ensure hadn't been compromised by the stupidity of the man at her destination.

As the plane soared into the air she caught a last glimpse of the strong Eastern sun and said a silent prayer that she would return to see it again.

***

Belfast. 3 p.m.

Annette slipped off her flat shoes and rubbed her instep, soothing the hot ache as best she could. She'd never suffered this much pain when she wore heels, but she wanted to be taken seriously for promotion and flat shoes said serious officer so, no pain no gain. She slipped her shoes back on and rechecked the address, glancing at the neat semi-detached house she was parked outside. This was it, the McGovern residence. She braced herself for the emotional encounter she knew was coming and left the car, walking down the path to the house and wishing that it was longer. Anything to defer the moment when she had to see three children cry.

The McGovern's house was unremarkable; an off-white, pebble-dashed semi, like so many others in Belfast. Its small front garden had been neglected until the grass was patchy and beige, and the flower border had died and turned to scrub. Annette pictured three small children doing their worst and a father who'd given up worrying about the garden until they were grown. Barry McGovern would never have to worry about it again.

As Annette adjusted her jacket and raised her hand to knock, the front door opened a crack and a sullen-looking girl appeared. The McGovern's eldest; thirteen-year-old Kathleen. The girl stared at Annette with hostile eyes and Annette gazed back with sympathy in hers. How could this child possibly understand that the father she loved had been blown apart for something that was probably nothing to do with him? Just an ordinary man on an ordinary day, standing in a bookshop reading a book.

As she gazed into the girl's blue eyes a sob caught unexpectedly in Annette's throat. She swallowed it down, thinking again how much she admired Liam. She never told him but her awe at his work during the Troubles was enormous. How many times had Liam stood on a doorstep like this, about to talk to someone whose love and life had been ripped apart by a bomb? How had he coped? With alcohol? Definitely. And with a sense of humour as well. By growing bitter? No, she didn't think so. Liam was irritating and politically incorrect, and at times his inappropriate banter drove her mad, but he was never really hard.

In the split second it took the thoughts to race through Annette's mind a woman joined the young girl by the door. She opened the small crack wider and beckoned Annette in, ushering her through to a warm back room. Annette's sob subsided during the journey but it threatened again when she saw who else was there. A determined looking boy of around eight was seated at the table, his arms folded and his chin jutting up as if he was the new man of the house. A tiny girl, a toddler, was playing at his feet and as Annette entered the boy reached down and pulled her protectively onto his knee.

Maria McGovern motioned Annette politely to a seat and disappeared for a moment, returning with a ready-prepared tray of tea and cake. She broke the silence as she poured, in a voice so soft that Annette had to strain to hear.

"You'll have to forgive the children, Inspector. Their only other encounter with the police was on Thursday when…"

The young widow's voice tailed off and she dropped her head, hiding her face behind her long fair hair. Annette leaned forward, seeking her eyes. She smiled into them sympathetically, encouraging Maria McGovern to sit down, then she took over the conversation, smiling at each of the children in turn.

"I'm sorrier than I can say about your husband, your father. It's a terrible, terrible thing that has happened to you. But I'm not here with more bad news; I'm here to ask for your help."

On her last few words Annette directed a smile at the boy, making him feel as if he was in charge. His high voice cut through the air.

"You have to get them. The men that did it to my dad."

Annette nodded. "Yes, we do. But we need your help." She scanned the faces in front of her. The girl's no less hostile than before and the baby's and mother's lost and confused. "We need all your help. Please. Anything that you can tell me about your father, his love of books, why he went to the shop that day, did anyone ever threaten him? Anything you know might help."

She turned back to Maria McGovern and repeated her plea. "Anything, Mrs McGovern, no matter how trivial it seems."

Maria McGovern nodded and started talking, with her children joining in, and an hour later Annette left the house with a list of speculations and memories, and one possible solid lead.

Chapter Nine

Docklands. 4 p.m.

"Everyone gather round, please. Nicky, can you take notes; we need to get this into some sort of order."

Nicky lifted her notepad and perched on a chair beside her boss, just like a secretary from sixty years before. Liam wheeled himself over on his desk chair and Davy did the same, while Annette tutted disapprovingly at the tracks they'd left on the carpeted floor.

"I'll do a brief intro, then Davy; I'd like to hear anything you've found, followed by Liam and Annette. Then we'll open it up. OK?"

Craig was answered by a series of nods and slurps.

"I've had two meetings today. At the army base and at the lab with John. A quick summary is that Captain Ken Smith of The Swords Regiment will be acting as liaison for us and working out of the squad here from Monday." He glanced at Nicky. "Can you find him a desk please, Nick and get all the passes etc. sorted out."

Nicky nodded and smiled. Craig knew immediately what her smile was about. "Yes, he's youngish and yes, he's probably good looking, although Liam can tell you more about that sort of thing. He had a serious case of hair envy."

Liam had just taken a gulp of tea and he almost spat it out in surprise. "I did not!" He wiped down the front of his jacket then uttered a grudging. "Smith's all right looking, I suppose, although why I'd be expected to know I'm..."

"You're being wound up."

Liam's eyes widened in realisation. "Oh, right. Nice one."

Craig carried on. "OK. Smith told us that the bomb was basic Semtex with a timer; they used an old pocket watch for that, probably 18th Century, no idea why. The signature doesn't match anything they've seen from the dissidents in the past ten years. They're checking it against the whole Troubles' database now, so let's hope that they get a hit."

"Or not, boss. I'd rather this wasn't some sad old scrote from the 'war' having their death rattle, if you don't mind."

"So would I, Liam. But better that than a completely unknown bomber who we'll never find. Smith also said that the scrollwork that they found attached to the bomb was, as they thought, a photo-frame. They found a fragment of an image in it which they're reconstructing now." Craig glanced at Davy; he was scribbling furiously on the back of a page.

"Something important, Davy?"

Davy looked up and realised that all eyes were on him. "Actually yes. I'm w...writing a programme for pulling the image out of a photograph." He grinned cheekily. "You were going to s...say that next, weren't you? That Captain Smith was going to send the image across for me to look at as well?"

Craig laughed, both at Davy's genius and his cheek. The genius had been there from the beginning but the cheek was relatively new and it still surprised him.

"That's exactly what I was going to say. Captain Smith said he would send it over to Des. But he said that days ago and he was prevented." He glanced at the time; ten-past-four. "If it's not here soon give Smith a call. And can you and Des check the watch fragments they found in the bomb. It seems strange they used it instead of a modern timer. It must have some significance."

Craig took a quick gulp of coffee then carried on, updating them on his conversation with John. "John seems convinced that the volume of remains they found indicates two more dead but he's only found the thumb of one. Hopefully we'll get an I.D. off that."

Davy interrupted. "We already have."

Craig's eyebrows shot up. "Already? Brilliant work. I'll hand over to you on that in a minute. OK, that means that we now have three dead victims identified and one that we're still clueless on. It could have been a man of any age, perhaps even a woman; all the shoes were flat lace-ups but one was only a size seven.

Nicky sniffed. "A woman with big feet."

Craig ignored her. "Hopefully CCTV will give us something, or Fintan Delaney will if he regains his memory." He turned to Davy. "Right. Over to you, Davy. What have you found?"

Davy turned over the sheet he'd been scribbling on and started to report.

"There w…were a couple of traffic cameras in the street outside the shop so we're pulling those images, but I'm having a hard time getting any joy because it's the w…weekend. I'll try again on Monday. The shop's interior CCTV might yield something as well. Des says that the back-door to the s…shop was shut but not locked, s…so it's unlikely that the bomber left that way but not impossible."

Liam cut in. "That's if he left at all, lad. He might have blown himself up. It wouldn't be the first time."

Craig raked his hair thoughtfully. Idiot or suicide bomber? "By accident or on purpose, Liam?"

"Aye well, that's the million dollar question, isn't it? There were idiots during the Troubles who blew themselves up with their bombs and they definitely didn't mean to, but there are plenty of people nowadays who'll deliberately kill themselves for a cause."

Davy asked the question that was on everyone else's lips. "Muslims?"

Craig shrugged. "It's very unlikely in Belfast, but we can't rule anything out until we get the bomb signature."

He waved Davy on before the briefing turned into a debate on world politics.

"OK. I s…started checking on the victims. First, the new I.D. from the thumbprint. W…We struck gold there."

Annette frowned. "In what way?"

"W…Well, first it belongs to a known paramilitary, albeit retired, and secondly it was a w…woman. Sharon Greer, member of the UKF. They're loyalist paramilitaries."

Liam lurched forward. "You're sure, lad?"

"Positive."

Liam whistled so loudly that Nicky held her ears. "Well, I'll be buggered. Sharpy Greer! We looked everywhere for her but she dropped out of sight after the Good Friday Agreement in '98."

Craig interrupted Liam's trip down memory lane. "The UKF's a new one on me. Who was Sharon Greer and what had she done?"

Liam was still reminiscing. "Sharon 'Sharpy' Greer was a real bad bitch, if you'll pardon my French. Hard as nails and twice as bad as the men. She was married to David Greer, head of the UKF. They were a loyalist splinter group that worked on the fringes of the Troubles, mostly making a profit from them, but they also carried out targeted attacks on Catholics. David Greer was a bastard but Sharpy was even worse. She tortured men before her hubbie killed them and by all accounts she got off on it."

Nicky's husky voice cut in. "Rose West and Myra Hindley. When you get a bad woman she's ten times as bad as a man."

Liam gestured at the menacing way she was waving her pen. "Remind me not to hack you off." He warmed to his theme. "Anyway, Sharpy was wanted for everything you can think off. Wounding, shooting…"

"Bombs?"

Craig's question brought Liam down to earth with a bump. He shook his head grudgingly. "No, no I don't think so. Davy?"

Davy shook his head. "I've got her record here and it's as Liam s…says. No bombs."

Annette ventured an opinion. "It could just be coincidence, sir. She could just have been a book lover in for a browse."

Craig smiled at her determination to believe the best of everyone. "She could have been but somehow I doubt it, Annette." Something occurred to him. "Liam, the protection racket in Smithfield. Any word on who runs it yet? "

Liam shook his head. "Not yet, but I like how you're thinking, boss. Ex-paramilitaries turned extortionists."

Annette broke in, annoyed. "What protection racket?"

"Sorry Annette, we haven't got to that bit yet. Let Davy finish first."

Davy re-started with a look that said they weren't to interrupt. "OK, S…Sharon Greer's our fourth victim. There'll be more on her when I get it. Barry McGovern was a forty-two-year-old accountant married to Maria, thirty-eight. They had three children: thirteen-year-old Kathleen, eight-year-old Darren and three-year-old Petra. McGovern looks clean s…so far, not even a parking ticket. He was however a member of four libraries, so we have a pretty s…solid history of book loving there. Then there's Jules Robinson, the shop's owner. Owned Papyrus since 1995, before that he was in the RUC. Married to Sarah, no children. No financial problems so far, no criminal offences, good reputation in the book world; he's a member of the RBDA; the rare book dealers' association."

Liam interrupted, much to Davy's annoyance. "I'll tell you more on him in a minute."

Annette joined in, competing. "And me too, on the McGoverns."

Craig waved them down and turned back to Davy. He was frowning. "W…When you two are reporting I'm going to interrupt every two minutes and see how you like it!"

The culprits grinned apologetically and he carried on. "I checked and S…Sarah Robinson only worked in the shop

Monday to W...Wednesday each week, that's why she wasn't there when it blew up."

Craig nodded. The bombers may or may not have known that; either way Sadie Robinson's had had a narrow escape. Davy continued.

"Fintan Delaney. Twenty years old, s...studying P.P.E. at Queen's. There are no terrorist, gang or political connections in his family anywhere. He hasn't been involved in any marches, riots or s...student protests. He hasn't even attended political debates."

Craig interrupted. "Isn't that a bit unusual for a politics student?"

"That's exactly w...what I thought so I phoned around some of his class mates. They all said that Fintan was a nice guy who preferred to spend his free time working for the church."

"Which church?"

"Catholic mainly, but he also did some work for the Ecumenical Missions, working with Methodists and Presbyterians. His parents are members of an ecumenical congregation and Fintan went to an integrated school. There doesn't s...seem to be any bigotry or affiliation with republican causes. Quite the opposite, both parents canvassed for Alliance at the last election."

Liam let out a low whistle and Davy turned sharply. "Do you have s...something that you'd like to say, Liam?"

Liam's freckled face took on a look of saintly innocence. "Who me? I would never interrupt."

Davy rolled his eyes. "Oh go on, spit it out."

"I was just going to say that Delaney seems to be an example of the post-Troubles generation who don't want to repeat their parent's mistakes. They bend over backwards to integrate."

Craig raised an eyebrow. "And that's a bad thing?"

"I didn't say that it was a bad thing. Actually it's a very good thing and it was just an observation." Liam's voice became huffy. "I can say things without being sarcastic you know."

Craig smiled. "Only occasionally. Carry on Davy."

"W…Well, the only other things about Delaney are that he's a member of a book-club, so it's very possible that he was just in the shop to browse. He also took a trip to Pakistan last year."

"To do what?"

"Charity work. He was there for six weeks helping to rebuild a village."

Craig nodded. Lucia had done something similar in Chile when she was a student but not from any sense of religion, more for humanitarianism.

"OK. That's great, Davy. Everyone top up your coffee then we'll move on to Liam and Annette."

As they were refreshing their drinks another thought hit Craig. "Davy, did Delaney have a girlfriend?"

Davy looked blank for a moment and Liam jumped in. "You know, a girlfriend, those nice soft things that keep you warm on a winter's night."

The remark was greeted by howls of indignation from Annette and a caustic "you make us sound like duvets" from Nicky. Craig waved the impending furore into silence and turned back to Davy. He was nodding.

"Yes he did. At school, a girl called Hanna Weir. They split up before Delaney went to Queen's."

Craig nodded. "Check her out. And Nicky, tell Delaney's parents that I still need to speak to them; we keep missing each other. OK Liam, you have the floor, and everyone else, feel free to interrupt him at any time."

Liam pretended to be offended but spoilt it with a grin. He launched into a description of Sadie Robinson's garden gnomes that made them all laugh. As the laughter subsided he described her accepting approach to her husband's death.

"I've seen it before but every time I see it, it impresses me. Some people have a real faith in what comes next."

Annette nodded thoughtfully. "I saw patients like that when I was a nurse. They would be given terrible news and accept it with a nod, and they were always so nice. I asked one lady who'd been told she had only six months to live how she could be so calm. She just smiled and said that there was something better after this. "

Liam shrugged his shoulders "Well whatever it is, Sadie believes it, and she made great cake as well." He laughed, breaking the solemn mood, and went on to outline Sadie Robinson's theories about her husband's death. "There were three pretty good reasons to target Jules Robinson, if that's who the bombers were aiming for. He was in the way of a property developer, he was paying protection money and we don't know if he'd come up short on that, although his wife said she didn't think so. And last but not least he was an ex-cop. RUC no less, not the most popular police force in the world and I say that being a past member of it."

Davy chipped in. "Bet that didn't help its popularity."

Liam made a wounded face. "I'm hurt that you could say a thing like that, lad."

Craig watched as Davy blushed and tried to backpedal, stammering that it had only been a joke. After a few seconds Liam let out a loud guffaw, chalking a one-all score in the air.

"That'll teach you to play with the big boys."

Craig shook his head and waved Liam on.

"Aye, anyway. We have three possible motives to check out for Jules. Mrs Robinson thought the RUC link was the least likely. They'd never had threats from any direction, although given the fact it was a bomb that killed him we can't rule it out."

Craig interjected. "Which could in itself be a double bluff."

"Right. It pays to have a warped mind in this job." Liam pushed another biscuit into his mouth and chewed loudly for a moment before continuing. "So that leaves us with the protection racket. We need to pursue that, especially now that bits of Sharpy Greer have been found in the wreckage."

Craig shook his head; something didn't fit. If you were

involved in extorting money from a business why blow it up, unless it was seriously in arrears? And why blow it up with yourself inside? Liam read his mind.

"I agree boss, but they wouldn't be the first muppets to kill themselves as they planted a bomb."

Craig ran with the idea. "OK, let's just say the bomb was planted by whoever was extorting money from Jules Robinson. If it was the UKF and Greer was still aligned with them, then either they employed an idiot to set the charge, or there's a rival gang running protection in the area."

He thought of the Russian gang they'd encountered two years earlier and turned quickly to Davy. "Davy, get on to Captain Smith and ask them to widen the bomb signature search to include devices planted by international groups. Liam, get onto Vice and nail down who's running protection in Smithfield."

"Will do. OK, so that leaves us with who's behind door number three; the developers." Liam ran through the information that Sadie had given him then scanned the group's faces for ideas. "That's the one Sadie thinks is the most likely and blowing up the shop would definitely have saved them demolition costs. The company's called SNI."

Annette looked thoughtful and Craig motioned her to speak. "Well, it's just… If you're a reputable developer then surely you'd try every legal recourse to get the shop before you did something like this? Throw money at the Robinsons; offer to relocate the business, anything but blow people up."

Craig played devil's advocate. "And if you're a disreputable developer?"

Annette bit her lip for a moment and then shook her head. "No, I still don't get it. If you're a crooked developer you'd know that the first people we would look at would be you."

Liam leaned in to interrupt but Annette held up her hand to stop him. "Don't get me wrong, Liam, we have to explore all of these avenues but my feeling is that there's something less obvious going on here."

"Like what?"

Annette glanced at Craig and he nodded her on to report. She covered the generalities of her visit to the McGovern's, rushing through the details of three small children clinging to their Mum. Seeing it had been bad enough, she didn't need to relive the experience. When Craig signalled to interrupt she was grateful.

"I checked. Lucia never met Mrs McGovern at The Belfast Buzz. Lucia left just before she started."

Annette nodded and turned to the subject Maria McGovern had raised just before she left.

"Barry McGovern was an avid reader, had been ever since he was a boy. We know he was a member of four libraries and his wife showed me his book collection. He only had a few but they were all first editions."

Craig cut in. "Any particular subject area?"

"History mostly and a few on philosophy. Anyway McGovern belonged to some private internet chat-rooms."

Liam's booming voice drowned out her next words. "Oh aye, one of those, was he?"

Nicky wrinkled her nose in distaste and tapped Liam's hand sharply with her pen. She wanted to throw it at him but she still remembered his howls when she'd done it once before.

Annette frowned and continued. "Rare book internet chat-rooms. McGovern told his wife he'd heard a rumour that Jules Robinson was getting in a rare first edition in last week, so rare that an online bidding war was likely to ensue. He went to Papyrus hoping that he might get a glimpse."

Craig raked his hair; it gelled with a feeling he'd had. "So this might be about a rare book that some collector wanted. Badly enough to kill for it?"

Annette shrugged. "I don't know sir, but it's another theory. Some of those big collectors are nutcases; recluses who have collections worth millions."

"Granted, but blowing up the shop would have destroyed the book as well. Unless…"

Davy finished Craig's thoughts. "Unless they s…stole the book and used the explosion to cover the theft." He let out a long whistle, surprising them. Whistles were Liam's stock in trade but it seemed he had a competitor.

Craig dragged a white board over then wrote up their theories so far in a list: RUC, developers, protection gangs and now a rare book. He tapped the list for a moment as if he was going to add something and then dismissed the idea as too far left of field. He'd keep it to himself for now. He checked the wall clock and then allocated the tasks.

"OK. Davy, get into the chat-rooms and see what's there, also, check into the UKF. See how active they are at the moment and whether there's any word of Sharpy Greer still being involved."

He turned to Liam. "Vice, Liam."

"Yes please."

The retort was so quick that even Craig laughed. "It wasn't an offer, it was an order. Get onto Aidan Hughes and find out who's running the girls and drugs in Smithfield; they'll be running protection as well. Also ask Geoff Hamill about gangs and dig into Jules Robinson's RUC record. Who had he banged-up, who hated him enough to kill him; you know the form. Go beyond what's on the page, please. Use your contacts to get the gossip. OK?"

Liam rubbed his hands in glee. It was the perfect excuse for a few beers with his old mates. Craig moved on to Annette.

"Annette, I want you to chase down all the developers involved in Smithfield, the legal and illegal ones, particularly SNI. Find out who's interested in the area and don't confine your search to developers based in the UK. There's foreign money coming into Northern Ireland now and they all want to make a fast buck. When you've gathered the information I don't want you interviewing any of them alone. If Jake's not back then take Captain Smith with you."

Craig stopped abruptly, remembering something. He turned towards Liam accusingly. "Where's my new staff member? You were supposed to get on to Aidan about her."

Liam's eyes widened in astonishment. "Here, give me a chance, boss. I've been a bit busy."

"Well, make that your first priority tomorrow please. We're running short-handed and everyone wants this case done and dusted before the 30th." He scanned the row of faces then wrapped up. "I'll take Fintan Delaney and chase victim number five with John. I'm working up something else as well, but it's too early to discuss it yet."

Craig glanced at his watch. It was after five o'clock. "OK, for anyone who isn't heading home the drinks are on me. I'll see you in The James Bar in five. Everyone else, we'll brief an hour later tomorrow at nine, just as a Sunday treat."

Chapter Ten

Dublin Airport. 6.p.m.

The large jet disgorged its load of passengers and Jennifer Weston stayed behind with the other crew to tidy up, gathering the lost mobiles and discarded newspapers for reclaiming or the bin. After an hour she waved goodbye and stepped down from the plane, heading for her hotel and a thirty-six hour turnaround. It was tight but it was all the time she needed, to pay the visit she needed to pay and then disappear without anyone picking up her trail.

Weston tutted to herself as she entered her hotel room; she hated loose ends and right now they had a big one. As she sank into the warm bubble bath she decided on her outfit for the following day. It had to be right to blend in, but not so perfect that it would look out of place. And above all it had to be suitable for a visit to a sick friend.

***

Sunday. 5 a.m.

Craig slipped quietly out of bed and wandered into the living room, his thoughts preoccupied with the case. Katy was sleeping and he didn't want to wake her; a doctor on-call got little enough sleep, even when they were consultants. He stood by the window, staring out at the brightening morning sky. The air was humid, more humid than he remembered Northern

Ireland being; the people who dismissed global warming as nonsense were definitely wrong.

Craig glanced back at the tightly shut bedroom door and smiled, tempted to return and disturb his pretty girlfriend's sleep. But they hadn't closed their eyes until two o'clock, so wrapped-up in their still new lovemaking that time not spent locked together seemed like a waste. He would let her sleep; her bleep would go off soon enough.

He sat down in his well-worn armchair and sipped thoughtfully at some juice, trying to organise his thoughts about the case. They had plenty of leads to follow, so why did none of them feel quite right? Why not go for the obvious and say that Delaney or a developer did it? Or was he so needful of a puzzle to solve that a quick closure didn't satisfy him anymore? Perhaps. He started to sift through the things they knew and quickly arrived at the gaps.

Fintan Delaney, the blast's only survivor had no memory of the event. So what? It was perfectly feasible that Delaney had survived because he was standing farthest away, shielded by bookcases that he couldn't possibly have designed. Delaney had no history of anything except good works and his family was the same, so why couldn't he quite believe it? Was he becoming a cynic? Craig smiled as soon he asked himself the question. Becoming? Or was his disbelief his gut's way of telling him that something didn't fit?

Then there was the fifth body; who was it and would they ever know? The body had been completely vaporised which meant that they must have been closest to the blast. The bomber? Perhaps they'd get lucky and catch a break from the CCTV, but he wouldn't hold his breath. He hoped John could extract DNA from the shapeless tissue and made up his mind to check the next day. Craig caught himself; the next day was already here.

He gazed at the sun rising in the distance and thought about John and Natalie, smiling at the party that was to come. It would be amazing, because Natalie was such a livewire and because everyone was so happy for them both. That and the sun, sand, sex and cocktails in Barbados would ensure a good time for everyone. Except... Craig thought about Annette and the fragile state that her marriage was in. Her husband Pete had been unfaithful the summer before, citing the stresses of Annette's job and her long hours spent at work. Ostensibly she'd forgiven him and they were trying to patch it up, except... Annette's ambition had trebled since the incident and he could see her becoming more detached. Perhaps the wedding would bring them closer, or perhaps it would only underline what they'd once had and lost.

Craig shook his head and turned to the final thread of the case. Rare books. Davy was working on it now and if there was anything to find he would. But something was niggling at the back of his mind, so far back that he couldn't see it yet. It was like an intruder lurking in the shadows, always there but never showing their face. Craig shrugged; he'd travelled this road before. The answer would appear when he least expected it and hours spent chasing wouldn't speed it up.

He hadn't seen the bedroom door opening or heard Katy's soft footsteps cross the room, but he felt her warm kiss on the back of his neck. He reached around and pulled her onto his knee, returning the kiss with a passion that he'd never felt before. Yes, he'd been in love with Julia and Camille, they were both fascinating, beautiful women in their different ways, but he loved Katy as well as being in love. It wasn't her prettiness, although that was substantial, and it wasn't her ability as a doctor, no matter how impressive it was. He loved her for her kindness and the way that she always put others first; patients, friends, family, him. He'd never liked a woman quite as much as he liked her and as he carried her back to bed, the feeling worried him more than anything had ever worried him before.

***

105

St Mary's. 7 a.m.

Morning pale rays of sunlight stretched across the hospital room to touch Fintan Delaney's small, starched bed. Bright enough to make him visible, but not so bright that they seeped between his lashes and told his confused brain to wake. It would be a pleasant way to waken, before murmured voices in the corridor or the metallic clash of instruments reminded him of where he was. But it wouldn't be his awakening that day.

Outside in the long, quiet hallway the lights remained dimmed, awaiting the nurses' handover that would tell the morning routine to start. A young constable guarded the side-room, arm's folded and perched on a hard plastic chair, determined to be vigilant, as he had been all night. But his unfailing alertness was no match for a professional who said they needed to enter and check a pulse, especially if they showed their I.D.

The white door opened quietly and the young woman slipped inside, scanning the room for the man she'd come to see. As her vision adjusted, Delaney turned fitfully in his sleep until he faced her, his eyes still closed tight. The woman froze for a moment, until he settled into his new position still sleeping and she was safe to approach the bed.

Jennifer Weston gazed at her young lover, wanting to stroke his thick black hair and trace his full mouth with her finger and then her lips. For a moment she hesitated in her task, remembering long, warm nights spent wrapped in his arms and a love that had strengthened by the day. Did he really have to die; did it help them in any way? She already knew the answer. Her feelings for Fintan were strong, but not as strong as for the man who'd groomed her, and what they worked for was stronger than them all.

Before her feelings could prevent what she knew had to be done, she slipped the syringe from her pocket and slid the needle into her lover's I.V. Delaney's eyelids flickered and opened and what he saw shocked him then brought the first hint of recognition that he'd felt in days. He gazed into her blue eyes and mouthed a word that only she would understand; Salerno. It confirmed that she'd been justified in her task. Fintan knew everything and soon he would betray them to the police.

Jennifer Weston smiled tearfully at the man she loved and held his hand as he began his departure from this world. Then she scribbled on his chart and turned in the churchlike silence of the morning, to leave the room and the hospital as easily as she came.

***

Docklands. Sunday. 9 a.m.

"OK, this is going to be quick. I've had a few thoughts."

Liam groaned deliberately loudly and it had the desired effect. Craig raised an eyebrow then laughed at his disrespect and the others joined in. All except Davy; he was leaning back in his chair staring at the ceiling, as if it held information that no-one else could see. Craig could hear his brain working from where he sat.

"Penny for them, Davy?"

Annette chipped in, applying her pale pink lipstick discreetly behind a mirror at her desk. Nicky's bright red gloss wasn't nearly as discreet.

"I think it's a pound nowadays."

Whatever Davy's thoughts could be bought for he wasn't ready to share them. He shook his head then leapt from his chair and sauntered across to where Craig sat, with a cockiness that said he was onto something. They'd find out when he was ready.

Craig turned to the small group. "Right, I'll keep this short and sweet. Liam, get that constable from Vice here today please.

107

I want her in place when Captain Smith arrives tomorrow." He turned towards Nicky, just in time to catch her mouthing something at Annette.

"Am I going to have to pay for your thoughts as well, Nick?"

Nicky shook her pony-tailed head. "No, I'm a cheap date. I was just wondering if we could commandeer part of Inspector Miller's floor-space."

She pointed past Liam's desk to a small corner of the squad-room that was rarely used. For good reason. It was windowless and cold, even when the rest of the floor was warm.

Craig made a face. "It's pretty unwelcoming, considering that they're both coming to help us. Don't we have anywhere better?"

Nicky swept her arm in an arc, like an estate agent showing a house. "If you can find somewhere else, be my guest. That's the only space I can see and Inspector Miller might not even let us have that."

Craig had known Bob Miller for years. He was an amiable looking man whose personality backed up the theory that people's exterior reflected what lay inside. He was barely five-feet-six inches tall and almost as wide; if the police had had an annual fitness test, Bob would have failed it several hundred donuts ago. His face had a ruddy complexion that said he lived outdoors, which he did; spending each weekend roaming the Glens of Antrim with his dogs and kids, doubtless singing 'Fa-la-ri' as he walked. No-one had ever seen Bob lose his temper, or even heard him raise his voice.

Craig smiled reassuringly at Nicky. "Bob will be as good as gold. Give him a call at home today, Nicky. But wait until lunchtime, please. He'll be up Slemish Mountain this morning."

Liam squinted at his watch and then at Craig, with a 'you've got to be kidding' expression.

"He leads the local scout troop. They go there every Sunday."

"All that exercise doesn't seem to affect his waistline."

Craig ignored the comment. "If Bob says we can have the space, which he will, then get it sorted today please. Get a couple of desks, chairs…"

Nicky sniffed. "I know what to do, sir."

"Sorry. Of course you do. Do something to brighten the place up a bit as well, please. Flowers or plants, whatever you like; I'll pay."

Craig turned back to the group. "Right. As I said, this will be quick. I've been thinking about a few things. First the unidentified fifth person; Davy, can you get on to John and Des and see how quickly they can identify DNA from the tissue they found. "

"There's likely to be two types, chief. Possibly five if the others bled a lot."

Craig sighed, knowing it could take a while. "Try anyway, please." He turned to Liam and Annette. "You two, get Carmen in today and brief her. I want her up to speed ASAP. I'll see her today or tomorrow, whenever I can. Liam, when you're chasing the protection rackets today; be careful. We all know who these guys are linked with and how much they hate the police. Annette, do as much of the developers' search as you can on your desk-top. If you need to be on the street before Captain Smith arrives tomorrow then take Liam with you, please."

Annette protested loudly. "That's unreasonable, sir. If you don't mind me saying so."

Craig raised an eyebrow as she carried on.

"I'm quite capable of looking after myself and most of them will be no more than fat estate agents."

Craig raised a hand to quiet her. "But one of them might not be, Annette, if they've already blown up a shop."

Annette was undeterred. "I saved your lives three months ago." She was referring to a shoot-out on a case when she'd saved both Craig's and Liam's lives. She smiled smugly at the memory. "Maybe Liam should have me along for protection."

Craig stifled a laugh and conceded, but only partly. "I know you can take care of yourself, Annette, but you had a gun then and you're not carrying this time. In hand-to-hand combat you're still no match for most men, not unless you've learned a martial art in the past few months?"

Annette went to protest then shook her head grudgingly.

"OK then, my order stands. Take someone with you to the interviews." He swung round to face Liam, catching the end of his grin. "And you needn't look so smug. Annette saved your life last time. I don't want you taking risks with the gangs either. Wear your vest please."

Craig ignored the inevitable groan that followed and carried on. "OK, Liam's going to bring in our new team member Carmen and then pay a visit to the protection gang. Annette's going to be here doing background work on the developer, and then she and Liam can pay them a visit." He stood up. "Davy, Nicky; you both know what you're doing. I'm going back to the hospital to see Delaney, then I'll be at the lab if you need me."

Craig headed for the main doors then stopped as the phone rang on Nicky's desk. A call this early on a Sunday was never going to be good news.

"Murder Squad. Can I help you?"

The room felt silent as everyone saw the expression on her face. Before Nicky dropped the receiver Craig knew what exactly she was going to say.

"Fintan Delaney's dead, sir."

By the word 'dead' he was halfway out the door.

Chapter Eleven

10 a.m.

By the time Craig reached the hospital Jennifer Weston was on the train back to Dublin, preparing to gather her uniform and belongings for her return flight to Pakistan. She gazed through the train's pollen-smeared window and sobbed as she thought of the man she'd just killed.

Fintan had been different from the other men she knew; kind and uncynical, only ever wanting to help. It had led to his death. She wished that she'd never met him, just let him walk by in the student's union that day. But something about his soft eyes and shy smile had made her stare, a stare that he'd felt and returned. What had she seen; gullibility or someone she could love? Probably both, but whatever it had been from that moment his fate had been sealed.

They'd been inseparable, just two young people in love, doing the usual romantic things. Long walks and cool swims, first in Belfast and then under a warm Pakistan sun. They'd made love tentatively at first, her sensing that it was his first time; until the pupil had become the teacher and he'd aroused her in ways that she'd never known before.

Jennifer sobbed before she could stop herself and glanced quickly around the carriage to see who might have overheard, but there was only a young couple there, both deaf to the world. Their heads were nodding in sleep and their bodies were intertwined, as if they were travelling home from some romantic night. The sight of them made her sob harder; she'd loved Fintan like that, really loved him. Oh God, what had she done?

How many times had she wished that she was just an ordinary girl, as Fintan had first thought she was? Young, free and doing good works. But she wasn't and the works she planned on doing were a different world's version of good.

To the others, Fintan had just been another asset that they could use, so they did. When he'd survived the explosion her orders had been clear; go to Belfast, finish the job and keep the movement safe. The movement. She wanted to spit the word on the floor but it was too deeply ingrained; seared on her heart since she'd been an undergraduate. She'd had to choose; her personal feelings or the greater good. Jennifer cast a final look at the young lovers and then sighed and turned her eyes towards the countryside. The greater good; it would win every time.

***

St Mary's. 10 a.m.

Craig raced down the bright, white corridor, forcing his way through the crowd of nurses and police. As he pushed open the door of the side-room the sight that greeted him was even worse than he had feared. A dark-haired woman lay prostrate across the bed, crying racking tears. A stern-faced man, ashen but upright stood beside her, gazing down at the body of his dead son. Fintan Delaney lay unseeing amidst his parents' grief, oblivious to the world that he'd just left.

Craig halted at the door, torn between his pity for the couple and his desire to shout "get out"; every forensic trace of Delaney's killer would have gone by the time the C.S.I.s got there. Because if there was one thing that Craig was sure of, it was that this was no normal hospital death; Fintan Delaney had been murdered.

Craig backed out of the room quietly and spoke to the

nearest officer; a middle-aged sergeant who he recognised. He was an affable Cork man called Joe Rice who punctuated his sentences with the word 'so', in the character of his home county. He and Craig always got on well but today there was no preamble and Craig's tone was very far from warm.

"Why wasn't this room sealed off, Joe?"

Rice stared at Craig, bewildered, as if the idea hadn't occurred to him. "It's a hospital death, sir. Why would we have done that, so?"

Craig's jaw dropped in astonishment at the man's stupidity and then he realised that he was the stupid one. As far as St Mary's knew they were guarding Fintan Delaney because he might be a criminal or a witness. No-one, including him, had thought of Delaney as a potential victim who could be targeted.

"Do it now, please."

As Rice cleared the side-room Craig's mind raced with possibilities. Had Delaney been the real target of the bomb all along? Should he have foreseen that whoever had planted it would have come back to kill Delaney, or any survivor? Was there something that he'd missed? No, they had no reason to believe that Fintan Delaney had been the main target, everything pointed to it being something to do with Jules Robinson or his shop. Delaney's record was clean; if anything he was a model citizen and it was too early to have disproved that. Craig berated himself for a minute about things that he couldn't possibly have predicted, then he berated himself for not posting more guards outside Delaney's room.

Suddenly something occurred to him. Where had the guard been when Delaney had been killed? He looked sharply at Joe Rice. "Who was posted here last night?"

Rice indicated a brown-haired young man three feet away. He was wearing a look of surprise. Craig beckoned him over, dialling his temper down a notch.

"What's your name, Constable?"

The P.C. stumbled over his words. "Con...Constable

McCormick, sir."

His nervousness softened Craig's heart slightly, but not enough; he had a dead witness and a dead end in his case. Craig's voice was cold. "Where were you last night?"

McCormick's eyes widened. "H…Here, sir."

He pointed hastily at a chair outside the side-room's door.

"For how long?"

McCormick looked at Joe Rice pleadingly, seeking support. Craig repeated the question. "How long, Constable McCormick?"

"All night, sir. I came on at ten p.m. and never moved."

"Did you fall asleep?"

McCormick was indignant and it made him forget his nerves. "No, I didn't. You can ask anyone who passed by, or ask the nurses who were in and out of the room." He folded his arms defiantly. "It was like a revolving door, there were so many of them in and out."

Craig thought for a moment and then turned on his heel, barking "Stay there. We haven't finished" at the young man. He strode to the nurse's station and waited impatiently while a pleasant looking woman finished her telephone call, itching to cut her off.

"Can I help you?" The woman's tone said that she wasn't impressed at the chaos and her demeanour said that the ward was definitely hers.

"Sister?"

The woman nodded. "Sister McHenry."

Craig extended his hand and she took it, surprised; relatives rarely shook her hand. Craig flicked open his warrant card.

"Superintendent Craig. I'd like to ask a few questions about the nursing care Mr Delaney received last night."

The sister sighed, resigning herself to the chaos lasting another while. "What would you like to know?"

"How many times nurses were scheduled to enter his room."

She reached for a small flipchart and ran her finger down a

114

list of names. "Mr Delaney was on two-hourly observations because of his head injury. A nurse would have checked on him every two hours during the night. At one a.m., three and so on until nine this morning. That was when he was found dead."

Craig's heart sank; the P.C. had been telling the truth and he would have had no reason to prevent the nurses' access to the room. Craig had a thought. His gaze shot towards the ceiling and then back to the nurse.

"Are there CCTV cameras on this floor, Sister?"

"Yes. I'll show you."

One minute later Craig knew the position of each camera on the floor and in the stairwell outside. He nodded his thanks then said the words that were guaranteed to make any ward-manager's heart sink.

"I'm sorry, Sister, but this is a crime scene. I need the whole floor sealed off until further notice. A forensic team will be here soon."

Craig ignored her widening eyes and made a series of calls, then he headed back to Delaney's room. Jordan McCormick tensed as the senior officer approached but Craig's apologetic smile said that he had nothing to be worried about.

"I owe you an apology, Constable McCormick. The sister has confirmed that Mr Delaney was on nurse observations throughout the night." He paused to give the young man a chance to say something, good or bad, but McCormick's shoulders merely slumped in relief.

"OK, I need your help. This is a crime scene. I'm going to talk to Mr and Mrs Delaney and in the next ten minutes the C.S.I.s will arrive to work up the room. We'll need your help to I.D. the nurses who entered the room last night. Can you do that?"

McCormick nodded. "I checked every badge and they were OK, honestly. I remember what they all looked like."

Craig's eyes widened. Either one of the badges had been a fake or they were looking for a real nurse.

"OK. Good. In the meantime, clear the floor of anyone who isn't police, seal off this corridor and impound last night's CCTV tape from the ward. The sister's been informed and she's making arrangements to move the other patients elsewhere. Is everything clear?"

McCormick looked like he might faint. "He was murdered?"

Craig nodded. "I'm certain he was. The post-mortem will confirm it. Delaney was on the mend, there was no reason for him to suddenly deteriorate and it's just too damn convenient." He glanced towards the side-room door. "OK, let's get to work. And Constable McCormick..."

"Yes, sir."

"Apologies again. You did your job."

***

Docklands. 11 a.m.

There weren't many things in life that Liam Cullen admitted challenged him, after all, he'd dealt with bombs and bullets during the Troubles and long before that he'd shoed horses and birthed cows on his granny's farm. That was enough challenge for fifty twelve-year-olds. No, he wasn't easily fazed by life and he wasn't easily deterred, but the five-feet-five, thirty-something woman standing in front of him could prove to be his nemesis yet.

Liam stared down at Carmen McGregor and then back at Aidan Hughes, wondering how he'd managed to get sold such a pup. Not that there was obviously wrong with McGregor, if anything she was a looker. Petite, with fine features and the brightest blue eyes that Liam had ever seen, topped by a heavy fall of copper hair that he sincerely hoped she would tie back on a job. Nope, if looks were the criteria then they'd struck gold for two weeks; it was when McGregor opened her mouth that the fireworks began. She'd been sniping since Liam had arrived and he had a headache worse than a hangover now.

Liam glared at Aidan and received a look of feigned innocence in reply that Liam recognised as usually belonging to him. He nodded towards Hughes' office and they entered it, with Carmen scowling at their backs. Once behind the firmly closed door Liam let rip.

"Too ladylike for Vice my ass, and 'she had a crush on a colleague', complete bollocks! You just wanted rid of her. Thanks for this, Aidan. I'll do the same for you someday. How the hell am I going to explain this to the boss?"

Hughes perched on the edge of his veneered desk and grinned. He rearranged his long limbs to get comfortable, as best he could in a tiny office hosting two men over six-feet-four, and then he waved Liam to calm down.

"Ah, now, don't get yourself in an uproar. Just tell Marc it was my fault and he'll be as good as gold."

Craig had known Aidan Hughes at school and too late Liam remembered his warnings about Hughes' warped sense of humour.

"Only if I tape her mouth shut for a fortnight!"

Hughes waved Liam to a seat and poured two coffees that were a while past their perk-by date. His next words held an indignant tone.

"You only have her for two weeks, Cullen, then you're off to Bali-Hi or wherever, for John's splicing. Pity me; I have her all year round, and her tongue hasn't blunted any in the past six months."

He held out a packet of Jammy Dodgers and Liam seized one grudgingly, like a man doing him a favour by deigning to partake. Hughes kept talking.

"Look. McGregor's a good officer, works her socks off and she even has moments of real inspiration; she's just a bit… blunt."

"Blunt! She nearly chewed my face off when I asked why she'd been christened Carmen. I just wondered if she had

Spanish blood!"

Hughes raised an eyebrow sceptically. "Don't kid a kidder, Cullen. You were about to launch into a chorus of 'Agadoo' and she knew it. Anyway, all she said was that her Mum chose it 'cos she loved opera."

"Those might have been her words but her look could've killed." Liam palmed his face and groaned. "The boss has just got Jake knocked into shape and everything peaceful and now I chuck 'Hand-grenade McGregor' into the mix."

Hughes drained his cup cheerfully then he stood up and headed for the door. "Aye, well, that's your problem. I'm just looking forward to peace and quiet for two weeks. I'll have the hand-grenade back soon enough."

They re-entered the Vice Squad's main office to see Carmen McGregor with a notebook in her hand. She was scribbling frantically and Aidan whispered to Liam under his breath.

"That's your list of transgressions so far. It'll get a lot longer, trust me."

He loped to the main door and pulled it open wide, smiling from ear to ear. "Bye, now, you two. Have fun and I'll see you in a fortnight. If anyone feels the urge to call me before then, please don't."

***

A third pencil flew past Davy's ear and landed on the floor beside him and finally he looked up resignedly from his screen. He would get nothing done until he'd answered whatever query Annette had, so he might as well get it over with. He'd just flicked his screen to the Planning Office's database, preparing to talk about developers, when Annette's question took him totally by surprise.

"What are you wearing at the wedding?"

Davy stared at her as if she was insane while Nicky perked up at her desk. He took so long to answer that Nicky decided to fill the gap. She crossed the floor in the prim manner she thought was in keeping with her chosen '50s outfit of the day and started.

"I'm bringing every summer dress I own, so I can choose on the day. Gary's wearing a linen suit."

Annette nodded. Linen seemed wise given the likely heat. Except… "Linen creases, Nicky. You'll spend all day following him around with an iron."

Nicky snorted in a decidedly un-fifties manner. "He'll be doing his own ironing. I'm there for a holiday and if I don't come back with a tan, I'll kill him."

She turned towards Davy and repeated Annette's question. Davy's normal fashion sense ran to dark T-shirts and a pair of black-washed jeans. The idea of him dressed in anything else was hard to imagine, although with his looks he'd have to work hard to look anything but good.

Davy shrugged. He hadn't a clue about clothes and he didn't really care, but he knew that Maggie would have other ideas.

"No idea. Maggie will sort it out."

Nicky raised her eyes to heaven. "I bet that phrase is repeated in every house in Belfast at least once a week." She sighed theatrically, with a faraway look in her eye. "Why can't Northern Irish men be more like the Italians or French? They always look so… suave."

Annette smiled. "I think it's something to do with their freckles and pale skin. A tan improves everyone." She tapped her chin thoughtfully with the only pencil that she hadn't thrown. "I don't know what to get for Pete. He's a hard shape to dress."

They fell silent as an image of Pete McElroy sprang to mind. He was a P.E. teacher so he was fit and slim enough, but he was so flat-footed that he walked like a duck and he had an unfortunate tendency to place his feet at ten-to-two. His habit of folding his arms tightly across his chest at all times was another problem. Nicky assumed it was part of being a teacher and exercising disapproval but it would play hell with a linen suit.

"Not linen, it'll be creased before he takes his seat."

Annette nodded. "No, not linen. But what does that really leave for men? Lightweight summer…"

Her fashion discourse was cut short by the sight of Craig striding into the squad-room with a look like hell on his face. Davy thanked God for the rescue and turned quickly back to his work. Craig strode past them and into his office, slamming the half-glass door behind him with a bang. After a moment exchanging looks with Annette, Nicky bravely knocked on the door.

"Yes?"

They all heard the same pissed-off yes, what was different was their responses. Annette sat upright nosily, Davy hid behind his screens and Nicky pressed hard on the door handle and marched straight in. She stood in front of Craig's desk, hands on her hips in a 'what's your problem?' gesture. A gesture completely wasted as his back was towards her. He was gazing through his window at the river and swearing quietly under his breath. He turned sullenly to his P.A.

"Yes, Nicky? And before you start complaining about my bad manners, Fintan Delaney was murdered."

Nicky went to open her mouth then she closed it again, widening her eyes instead. Craig was about to give her the details when he thought better of it and ushered her out onto the floor, calling the others to take a seat. If he was going to tell one person he might as well tell them all.

He leaned back against a desk and sighed. "Fintan Delaney is dead and I'm positive that it was murder. The C.S.I.s are at the hospital now; they're pulling the CCTV for the whole floor and the constable who was guarding Delaney is I.D.ing everyone who entered his room last night. When forensics have finished Delaney's body will go to John; I'll head to the lab later." He raked his hair so hard he was almost pulling at the roots. "OK;

comments or questions?"

Annette spoke first. "Do you think Delaney was the original target? And that's why they went back to get him?"

Craig shrugged. "Perhaps, or perhaps he had something to do with the bombing and they're cleaning house."

Nicky interjected. "How can you be sure that he was murdered? I mean, he did have a head injury."

"Yes he did, but he was improving, and his observations were all recorded as normal. The last time they were recorded was at seven a.m. and they were fine. The P.M. will tell us why but he died sometime after seven o'clock."

Davy screwed up his face.

"What's on your mind, Davy?"

"W....Well, it's just that if people were going in and out of the room then we'll s...see his killer on the CCTV."

Craig decided to test him. "Which could be useful, unless they wore a disguise."

Davy shook his head. "It can't have been an obvious one or the officer on the door w...would have twigged."

Craig nodded Davy was quick. "You're right. Delaney was on two-hour nurse observations so the killer either dressed as a nurse or actually was one."

"Do you think they were a clean-skin, sir?"

Nicky frowned at Annette. "What's a clean-skin?"

Davy leapt in. "S...Someone with no rap sheet. Not known to law enforcement."

Craig smiled at Davy's excitement; he loved anything to do with the covert. "Not necessarily. The constable was a rookie; he wouldn't have recognised even a known crook. But even if you're right, Annette, and they are clean to us, that doesn't mean that they won't be wanted somewhere." He straightened up. "Davy, get onto Joe Rice over at St Mary's. Tell him to upload the floor's CCTV to you, then run all the faces please; first against the hospital database, then against the DVLA and passport office. You know the rest."

"Fine, but s…shouldn't I just run the last person in the room before Delaney was found; they must have been the killer."

Craig shook his head. "Only if whatever they used to kill him was fast-acting. If it was me I'd have used something with a delayed onset. It would kill him a few hours after I'd left and give me time to get away."

Annette smiled; she'd have never thought of that. Craig continued.

"The tox-screen will tell us what killed Delaney but it won't tell us why." Craig turned to leave the floor then he turned back.

"Davy, make that I.D. your first priority, when you find the face that doesn't belong in the hospital get it to every port and airport on the island. They may try to skip the country and if so they've probably already gone, but it's worth a shot." He glanced at his watch. "OK, we're briefing at four, so focus on whatever you were doing and let's see what we can get before then. I'm heading back to the hospital."

***

Liam glanced at the woman seated beside him and for one moment he thought about just dumping her in the squad-room and leaving Nicky to sort her out, then the part of him that enjoyed a challenge kicked in. That and the part that knew he'd get the blame for bringing a mouthy constable on board to disrupt the team. He turned the key in his old Ford's ignition and raked the gearstick into reverse.

"Buckle up, constable. I drive fast."

Carmen Mc Gregor winced at the crunching gears then said her first words in ten minutes, in a Scottish accent so lilting it sounded like mood music and almost disguised her sarcastic intent.

"Don't you mean buckle up because if you drive anything like you change gears we'll both be dead soon?"

Liam hit back immediately. "With a mouth like that I'm surprised you aren't already!"

He raked the car into neutral and jerked on the handbrake, leaving the Ford's rear-end protruding from the parking space. Then he unbuckled his belt and turned as dramatically as he could in the confined space. The tone in his voice was unambiguously pissed off.

"Now listen to me, Little Miss Mouthy. You might be used to Vice, where everyone is so politically correct that they'll let you say anything in case you cry sexism, but you aren't working in Vice now. This is the Murder Squad and we have serious crap to deal with every day. That means pressure to get results and stress from the top. The last thing we need is more shit from inside the team. Do you understand me?"

McGregor folded her arms defiantly and said nothing, so Liam raised his voice just a notch. In the small space it transformed his already loud bass into a roar and his passenger howled "Ow!" and clamped her small hands over her ears. Liam was undeterred. He leaned forward and stared into McGregor's sky-blue eyes, signalling her to remove her hands.

"Do you understand?"

Carmen nodded grudgingly and Liam carried on. "Now, the Super's a nice man and he worries about things like people's feelings; unlike me. He likes to run a happy team, so it'll take him longer to say these things to you. But make no mistake, if you piss him off enough he will. Then he'll chuck you back in the pool with all the other little constables. I, on the other hand, don't give a monkey's about your feelings, or why you're such a grumpy cow. Maybe someone stole your ice-cream when you were a toddler, or you didn't get invited to the school dance; I. Don't. Care. You have two choices. You can be nice and work hard, get on with everyone for the next two weeks and leave with a good reference, or you can behave as you obviously do normally; mouthing off and acting like the world owes you a break. In which case I'll make your life hell and eventually Superintendent Craig will give you the push."

Liam raised his voice again to underline the point, watching amused as his companion recoiled at the sound.

"Well? Which is it to be?"

Carmen glared at Liam with real hatred in her eyes and he knew she wasn't used to anyone standing up to her. He wondered in passing why she was so angry with life, after all, she seemed to have everything going for her, and then he decided that he didn't care. Not his problem.

While Liam was carrying out his analysis, the woman seated next to him was calculating her best way to go. Marc Craig obviously liked to keep the peace, that made him a wimp in her book; but even wimps had power. She could behave however she liked, last one week and wreck her name forever in the force, or she could bite her tongue and count down the days until she'd be back in Vice. Carman decided on the latter and contorted her lips into a false smile.

"I'll play nice with the other girls and boys."

Her words were dripping with sarcasm and Liam knew she didn't mean them, but he'd take whatever he could get. His headache was blinding after just ten minutes of arguing with her. He decided on one last gift to himself.

"Sir."

Carmen gave him a puzzled look. "What?"

"I'll play nice with the other girls and boys, sir."

Liam folded his arms, indicating that they were going nowhere until she said the words, so after a moment's defiant silence Carmen capitulated, in a tone so saccharin sweet that Liam could feel his teeth beginning to rot. As he drove out onto Pilot Street he knew that she was already plotting her revenge.

Chapter Twelve

Dublin. 1 p.m.

Jennifer Weston completed the flight safety briefing and strapped herself in for the steep ascent, relieved that she was home and dry. The mission had been successfully completed; they'd achieved their goal and the only man who could have incriminated them was dead.

She gazed around the small galley and thought of Fintan and his crooked smile. He'd just been the wrong man in the wrong place all those months ago. She was sorry that he'd had to die, and she was sorry that she'd had to lose her chance at a healthy love, instead of her addiction to Fareed. But Fintan's death would serve a higher cause and they'd been bred for sacrifice. Her sacrifice was that she would never see her family again.

***

Belfast. 1 p.m.

Liam drove for ten minutes in silence, down Queen's Road and past the iconic Titanic Belfast building, until finally, when the new apartments and office blocks that signalled the city's inward investment were behind them, he pulled off the road onto a patch of wasteland. Its only occupants were seagulls, signalling how close they were to Belfast Lough. They were everywhere. Perching on the old fence-posts that said something more than pebbles and remnants of piping had once stood here, and in the air above them, circling in patterns so seemingly random that it was only scientists who could prove that they weren't. They surrounded the car like curious children, cawing and flapping for attention and food as the car's five minute immobility turned into fifteen and Carmen finally spoke.

"Are we waiting for someone, or did you just come here for the nice view?"

Liam tutted at her sarcasm and raised a warning eyebrow, but he had to admit that she was right about the view. The vista that stretched in front of them was impressive. The lough's industrial Belfast shore had given way to clear water, unobstructed by people or boats of any sort. It stretched in front of them for miles until, just as the next logical step was to transform into open sea, it was fringed by a shore so green that it belonged to a different place. It was. It was Bangor; home to boats, regattas and other rural pleasures that Belfast's inhabitants drove out of town to see, and the few who made their lives there enjoyed every day.

Finally, when he'd drunk in the view for long enough, Liam answered the question. "We're here to meet someone. He has information that I want."

Carmen sat forward eagerly and Liam was certain he saw a smile in her eyes. Well, well, so that's what it took to make Little Miss Mouthy happy.

"Is this about the protection racket you mentioned? Are they loyalist paramilitaries?"

Liam sniffed knowingly. "They might be, indeed they might. But don't you know there are no paramilitaries anymore, only misunderstood ex-combatants? We have peace nowadays."

He was about to wink conspiratorially then thought better of it; she would probably call it sexist. Liam sighed heavily, knowing that he was looking at two weeks of watching his back. He was about to say something else when the sound of a badly out-of-tune engine made him turn. A battered silver Nissan had pulled onto the wasteland and was driving slowly towards them.

Liam watched it in his rear-view mirror with a smile. He knew who the driver was but that didn't stop his hand resting on his gun; you never knew who might be hiding in the back seat.

The car drew-up parallel fifty feet away and the decade's old rattling finally stopped. The driver sat immobile, except for turning his head, and Liam caught the unmistakable visage of Tommy Hill. Hill was well known to the police for his loyalist exploits during the Troubles. He'd served ten of a twenty-year stretch for shooting four people on their way home from a wedding. He'd climbed calmly onto their mini-bus, killing three men and the driver as they tried to escape through the windows and past him to the door. It had earned him 'urban hero' status amongst his paramilitary pals and twenty years in prison, but he'd been granted early release under the Good Friday Agreement, despite widespread protest. The squad's last big encounter with him had been after the murder of his daughter, Evie, the year before. Hill had been left with a baby grand-daughter, Ella, and was a supposedly changed man.

After a five minute stand-off the two men emerged from their cars simultaneously, as if it was part of a well-rehearsed dance. Carmen went to unfasten her seat-belt but a sharp shake of Liam's head said 'stay' louder than any word. The men stared at each other across the wasteland gap for a moment until Liam spoke.

"'Bout ye, Tommy? How's life?"

Tommy Hill was half Liam's size, with a face like a warning against excess. Carmen craned her neck until she could make out the tattoos on his neck and arms. She wished that she had her camera; the scene would have made a brilliant clip for an urban noir. Tommy answered the question in a smoke-worn voice that was intent on being hard and cool, but betrayed that he didn't actually hate the D.C.I.

"Aye, aye, not bad."

Liam took the first step to close the gap, talking as he went. "And Ella? She must be getting big?"

Hill's craggy face cracked at the mention of his granddaughter. "She's walkin' nye."

He reached a tattooed hand inside his jacket and Liam's finger twitched on his gun, but all that emerged was a family snap. They were face-to-face now and Hill handed it to Liam. The picture showed a well-to-do couple; Ella's other grandparents, the Reverend and Mrs Kerr, and Tommy looking uncomfortable in a suit and tie with a beautiful baby girl perched on his knee. Hill stretched out a worn, brown finger to touch the print, smiling proudly. "That's her christening. She's a bonny lass."

Liam relaxed and smiled, taking a genuine interest. Hill's granddaughter had been born not long after his son Rory, but in much sadder circumstances. The old lag was staying out of trouble for her sake; that and the fact that most of his gang was still banged up in Maghaberry.

The niceties over, Tommy lit a cigarette and blew the smoke into the clear summer air. "OK, Ghost." It was a half-affectionate nickname; Liam's extreme pallor, regardless of the season, had earned him the moniker from Hill long before. "What can I do for ye?" He nodded towards Liam's Ford. "An' who's the weeman?"

"Someone I'm showing the ropes to; no-one to bother you." Liam paused while Hill took a last, long drag of his cigarette, then he flicked the live butt into the lough and nodded Liam on.

"I need to know about the protection rackets running in Smithfield these days. Is it just your side or are the republicans taking a cut?"

Hill laughed unexpectedly and Liam heard an undertone of pride. "Those dickheads? Away on with ye. They cudn't organise a piss-up in a brewery these days." He smiled maliciously. "It's all ar lads. One hundred and ten percent." He squinted up at Liam, shielding his small eyes from the sun. "Why? Ar they givin' ye problems, officer?"

Liam didn't miss the optimism in his tone. Tommy mightn't be active these days but he still liked to hear someone from the loyalist side was giving the peelers grief.

"Aye, aye, you're all real hard men. Sorry to disappoint you, Tommy, but they're not giving me any problems; I just need to find out which one of your muppets is running things there nowadays. So which three letter acronym stating with 'U' is it this week?"

Tommy yawned loudly at Liam's disrespect. After a moment's silence that proved to him he was in charge, he rasped.

"Four letters, actually. Used to be the UKF but it's the UKUF nye."

Liam's eyebrows shot up. UKUF? It sounded like it should be a swear word. What did it stand for? Tommy answered his unvoiced question.

"UK Ulster Force." He smiled proudly. "It's brilliant, isn't it? Does exactly what it says on the tin. There'll be no United Ireland shite while they're around."

Liam was curious. Sharpy Greer had been matriarch of the UKF for years, so had there been a gang war? Liam asked the question and Tommy laughed for an overly long time, irritating the hell out of him. Finally Liam had had enough.

"Aye, very funny. Just answer the bloody question, Tommy."

Tommy raised a chastising finger. "Temper, temper, Ghost. I'll answer ye. I'm just surprised that ye didn't know the UKF and UKUF was the same thing. They changed their name after that flag disgrace at the City Hall. Takin' down our flag; the scum."

The flag dispute had started in December 2012 after a vote by Belfast City Council limited the days the previously permanent Union flag could be flown from Belfast City Hall. It was the catalyst for a campaign of loyalist street protests in which over one hundred police officers were injured and almost seven hundred people were reported or charged.

Tommy lit another cigarette and took a long drag.

"So is Sharpy Greer still the boss then?"

The question caught Tommy unawares and he coughed so hard that Liam was waiting for his lungs to appear. Eventually Hill gasped out "No weeman's the boss of anything. The very idea."

It was semantics. Sharpy Greer might not have been the boss on paper but her husband had been, and everyone knew that she'd ruled Davy Greer with a rod of iron.

Liam gestured in irritation "You know what I mean. Davy might have been named boss but Sharpy had him pussy-whipped years before he died."

Tommy's coughing tailed off. "If ye mean is the UKUF the same as the UKF, then yes. They're the only wans operating in Smithfield. But the son Zac's the crown prince now. "

Liam didn't care about their names, he cared about their business. "So... they run protection. What else? Drugs? Girls? Counterfeiting scams?"

Tommy shook his head. "No way ye're gettin' that from me, Ghost. I've said enough. Nye, what about what yer doin' for me?"

Liam had expected the question and he'd come prepared. He reached into his pocket, gratified to see Tommy tense just as he had earlier. Liam withdrew a sheet of paper and handed it to his companion then he watched as Tommy read the words that were going to change his life. A small smile lit up his wizened face and a minute later Hill drove away and Liam strolled back to his car.

Carmen turned her eyes quickly back to the lough, reluctant to give Liam the pleasure of seeing she'd been curious. They were halfway back to Docklands when she cracked.

"Well? What was that about? He was obviously an old crim. What did you give him?"

Liam said nothing, just gave what he liked to think of as his enigmatic smile, although Danni said it just looked like he had indigestion. Carmen clammed up, determined not to ask again.

They were out of the car and in the C.C.U. lift by the time she caved in again.

"Are you going to tell me what that was about or not?"

Liam shook his head, enjoying winding her up. "You'll hear it at the briefing, just like everyone else." He stared down at the feisty constable. "Now… in a minute we're going to enter the squad-room. Everyone will be nice to you because they don't know what a pain in the ass you are yet. Remember what I said. Be nice and it'll go fine for you; be your normal irritating self and it won't." Liam's voice cooled. "Am I clear, Constable McGregor?"

Carmen glared defiantly at him through two floors before capitulating, and as they walked into the squad-room, they both plastered on a smile.

***

2.30 p.m.

By two o'clock Craig had spoken to everyone who knew anything about Fintan Delaney. From his grieving parents who thought they knew their son best, and probably in many ways they did but not enough to explain what had happened in the past few days. Through to the consultant neurologist and Sister McHenry, who were adamant that Delaney had been on the mend and nothing medical could have caused his death. A touch too adamant if recent news reports on the UK's hospitals were anything to go by, but Craig knew that they were probably right.

That just left the forensics, P.C. McCormick and John to give him some explanation for the death of a healthy twenty-year-old man. Craig went to think in the ward office they'd been allocated for their investigation, he didn't have time to think about anything before Joe Rice and Jordan McCormick clattered into the room. The constable's face dropped when he

131

saw Craig then he cheered up again as he remembered he had good news.

"We think we have them."

Craig leaned forward urgently. "You're sure?"

McCormick nodded and launched into the process of elimination they'd used on the CCTV.

"We showed Sister McHenry the footage and she was able to identify everyone on the tape as a female nurse she knew, except for one man. He entered Delaney's room about two hours before he died and no-one seems to know who he was."

"Did you see him at the time?"

McCormick nodded sheepishly. "Yes. He was wearing a nurse's uniform and he showed me I.D. like the rest. We had quite a chat as well." He nodded towards the door. "I've just done a composite with the sketch artist."

Craig's heart sank. Whoever the man had been he wasn't their killer, he'd lay money on it. No killer would stand and talk to a policeman long enough to have his face recalled. The man would turn out to be a nurse that the sister didn't know.

Craig shook his head. "He's not our man. Check and see. He'll have come from another ward to cover the night shift. That's why the sister didn't recognise him."

But it told Craig something. "Our killer was a woman." He sprang to his feet. "Where's the tape?"

McCormick's wary expression said he thought he was in trouble again so Craig smiled reassuringly. "Good work, constable, but the man you spoke to was innocent. Our killer was one of the female nurses that Sister McHenry recognised." He turned to Joe Rice. "Set up somewhere to view the film and get the sister there, please."

Five minutes later they were in Mary McHenry's office watching the tape. McCormick handed Craig the name of their male suspect. Just as Craig had suspected, he was innocent; a nurse sent from another ward to provide night cover. As each female nurse's face appeared on the CCTV tape, Craig signalled to stop and asked McHenry her name and background. When the tape reached 7.a.m. Craig said a sharp "stop" and peered closely at the screen. He turned to the sister.

"Who is this?"

McHenry squinted at the woman's face. "That's Jenny. Jenny Weston." She smiled warmly. "She's a lovely girl; kind to the patients as well as being very bright."

Craig didn't have time for sentiment. Something about Weston's demeanour as she left Delaney's room told him that they had their girl. "How bright?"

McHenry looked puzzled for a moment then she shrugged. "She got a degree in some subject I can't remember before she decided to do nursing. She said it was religious faith that drove her to help people." She paused before continuing. "To be honest, I'm surprised to see her on the tape; the agency must have sent her over."

"Isn't she one of your usual night nurses?"

"Oh, no." She widened her eyes suddenly, aghast. "Oh, I'm terribly sorry. Is that what the constable thought when I said I knew her? I do know her but Jenny hasn't worked with us for ages. She went abroad about a year ago. I didn't even know that she was back until I saw her on the tape."

Craig's heart sank. Abroad. That was all they needed, an international dimension. He'd had his fill of that in cases the year before. He smiled tightly.

"Don't worry. Everything will be fine." They ran through the remainder of the tape then Craig rose, signalling that the meeting was at an end. "We'll get the ward re-opened as soon as possible, Sister. Constable McCormick will let you know when."

McCormick ushered the sister from the room and Craig grabbed his mobile and hit dial. Nicky answered immediately.

"Nicky, put me on to Davy please."

Nicky transferred the call then turned her attention back to the desks she was arranging for their new guests. Davy answered cheerfully.

"Yes, chief."

"The hospital CCTV footage. Pull it up, will you?"

"I'm looking at it now."

"Good. Fast forward to around seven o'clock and you'll see a woman that the ward sister has just identified as Jenny Weston. What have you got on her?"

Davy smiled. He'd already got Weston on his list of possible suspects, but then he had the benefit of her background checks. How had Craig known? He decided that now wasn't the time to ask and started reporting.

"Jennifer Louise W...Weston. Aged twenty-five. Born in Newtownards to Melanie and Geoff, both teachers. She had a pretty uneventful life until she w...went to Queen's. She studied Theology and was a member of quite a few debating groups and cliques. Graduated in 2010 then trained as a nurse before going to work abroad a year ago."

Craig punched the air. She was their killer; he could feel it in his bones. "Davy. Focus on the groups and cliques for me and also the exact subjects she studied. And I want to know exactly where abroad."

"You think she's involved in some s...sect, chief?"

"I think she's involved in something that got Fintan Delaney killed."

***

The Lab. 3.10 p.m.

Craig had slumped in a chair in John's office ten minutes earlier, with no greeting beyond a grunt. He'd said nothing for the whole ten minutes, despite John's banter about the wedding and two coffees so strong that they would have shocked anyone else into gabbling by now. Finally John had had enough. He slammed his file shut, cursing the fact that paper didn't make a satisfying bang.

"You know, much as you're decorative to look at, well that's what Natalie says and who am I to argue, a conversation would be nice, Marc. Even the odd 'yes' or a laugh at one of my jokes would be enough." John's cultured tones grew artificially loud, as if he was speaking to someone who didn't speak English. "Anything to stop me thinking that I'd hired a statue for company would do it."

He leaned over and waved a hand so close to Craig's face that it clipped him on the nose. Craig's howl of indignation was the first noise he'd made for almost a quarter of an hour.

"Ow! What did you do that for?"

"Halleluiah! It speaks!" John retook his seat. "I did it because, great as it is to have your company, unless you want something specific I have work to get on with. So?"

"So what?"

John gave an exasperated sigh.

"So what do you want, Marc? I have things to do, like finish the post-mortem on your man Delaney."

Craig thought for a moment then rose and headed for the door. John shrugged a goodbye and turned back to his file. After a moment he realised that Craig was waiting for him, so with an exaggerated sigh John followed him to the dissection room. Fintan Delaney's body lay shrouded on the centre table, flanked by two others covered with the charred remnants of two human beings. Craig finally spoke.

"I've been thinking…"

"He speaks! Thank God for that. I thought someone had found your off-switch."

Craig ignored him with the rudeness of thirty years of friendship.

"…about two things. The fourth bomb victim and Delaney's cause of death."

He updated John on what they knew of the two intact victims; Jules Robinson and Barry McGovern, outlining the

135

theories of protection rackets, ambitious developers and Robinson's history in the RUC.

"That brings us to Sharpy Greer..."

"Who?"

Craig realised that John hadn't spoken to Liam or Davy so he updated him on their third body. John whistled. "Well, well, shades of the Troubles."

Craig shrugged. "It's a pity we couldn't work out how many thugs just joined in the Troubles because they were criminals, and how many actually believed they had a cause."

"I imagine the numbers who've stayed involved in crime since The Good Friday Agreement should provide your answer."

"True. OK, Liam and Annette are following up the leads, so that leaves us with bomb victim number four." Craig stared intently at his friend. "OK, first, are you positive that there was a fourth victim, John?"

John's fine-boned face creased into a smile. "Unless one of the others had three hands, then yes."

Craig's eyes widened. "You found another hand? Can we get a print?"

John shook his head apologetically." Sorry, Marc. When I said three hands, I meant my idea of a hand, like the scaphoid bones. There was nothing that we could fingerprint. Frankly there was no intact skin at all."

Craig was undeterred. "But you can get DNA, can't you?"

"From the scaphoid?"

"It's worth a shot, isn't it?"

John made a face, thinking. "OK... yes, I might be able to get it, but you'll have to find something to match it against. I've always said that a world-wide DNA database..."

Craig cut in before John climbed onto his favourite hobby-horse. "If we get any images from the shop's CCTV, then we might have a shot at finding someone to match." Craig smiled for the first time since he'd arrived at the lab. "Excellent."

John smiled as well but for a different reason; amusement.

Craig didn't need an answer to be happy; he just needed the hope of one. Craig continued.

"Right, so that brings us to Fintan Delaney. We think he was killed by a woman." Craig had a thought. "Actually, how would you and Des fancy coming to the four o'clock briefing tomorrow. You should have the forensics by then."

John smiled. "Nice to know we're being invited for our charm. I'll check with Des but that should be fine. OK, Fintan Delaney."

"Yes?"

"It's too early to have a definitive cause of death. I can tell you that he was healthy and there was nothing obvious that would have killed him."

Craig nodded towards the shrouded body. "Have you opened his head yet?"

John rolled his eyes at the lay-man terminology. "I have performed craniotomy and examined his brain; yes. And no, there was nothing there that could have killed him. Whatever was causing Delaney's amnesia it wasn't physical. Shock from the explosion I should think, but it's a moot point now. But he definitely didn't die from any physical after effect of the bomb. I haven't finished swabbing the body but I'll stick my neck out and say yes, someone murdered him."

"Poison?"

"Chemical of some sort. It's unlikely that his killer woke him up to make him swallow it, so it was probably inserted through his I.V. Des can tell you more after he's examined the giving set."

Craig knew it was a Sunday and that Delaney had only been on John's table for a few hours but he thought he'd push his luck.

"Type of chemical?"

John laughed. "Now you're really chancing your arm. There's no way the tox-screen will be back until tomorrow lunchtime earliest. You'll just have to wait. Although…"

Craig smiled. John never liked to disappoint. "I can tell you what it wasn't. And Des may have pulled a print from somewhere around the bed. That might give you a name."

Craig shook his head. "We already have one; Jennifer Weston. The ward Sister I.D.ed her from the tape."

"A nurse?"

Craig nodded. He caught sight of the time on the wall clock and turned to leave. "Sorry John, I have a briefing to get to. Thanks for all that." He halted at the door and turned back. "By the way, what wasn't it?"

"What?"

"The poison that killed Delaney."

John walked towards him enthusiastically. "Well, there was no scent of bitter almonds, so it definitely wasn't cyanide, and there was no sign of haemolysis so that rules arsenic out. I could go on for hours."

Craig was sure of it so he waved goodbye quickly and headed for his car.

Chapter Thirteen

UKUF Headquarters: Garvan's Bookmakers.
East Belfast. 3.30 p.m.

The door to the small back room banged open and a slight young man entered with a scowl on his face. The expression was tinged with anxiety but Bryn McIlveen was fighting hard not to let it show. Anger scored points in his gang; anxiety and fear never would. His words staccato-ed out in a broken tenor.

"Has anywan seen Sharpy?"

The two men in the room ignored him and sorted slowly through their poker cards. One held his so close to his chest that he could only view them with an exaggerated sloping of his head. It made him look like he was about to head-butt his competitor. Eventually he barked "two", signalling the swop of two fresh cards for his own.

McIlveen croaked again. "Sharpy. Has anywan seen her?"

The close-chested man turned slowly, barely lifting his eyes from the game. "Missing yer squeeze, are ye?"

The young man's face turned red and he clenched his fists. "Fuck you. I'm jest askin' 'cos no-one's seen her fer three days."

The card dealer glanced up with curiosity in his eyes, paying attention at last. "Have ye asked Zac?"

The boy shook his head. "I was afeard to. He's pissed aff about sumthin' as usual. Ye ask him."

The man rose, revealing two arms covered in tattoos, with a red, white and blue 'UKUF' the largest of them all. He slipped his cards untrustingly into his pocket and nodded his opponent to do the same, then he walked past the boy and knocked hesitantly on an inner door, opening it on a high-pitched "come in."

The man's walk altered as he entered the room, into a subconscious display of deference. His arrogant dander became quiet steps and his previously squared shoulders hunched into a slope. If anyone had seen the stripling who greeted him they would have wondered why, but what Zac Greer lacked in physical prepossession he made up for in cruelty and guile.

The tattooed man stood with his head bowed until a single word gave him permission to look up.

"Well?"

Zac Greer lounged behind his desk in a high-backed leather chair that swung slightly as he moved. He was young; younger than the young man who had started the disruption and too young some said to wield the influence that he did. But that was mere conjecture because Zac had held it for as long as he could breathe. He was the son of David and Sharon Greer, Sharpy to her friends and enemies alike, and he'd inherited his father's crown upon his death. Zac Greer had been groomed to rule from the day that he could walk. Men may have muttered in corners about his right but genetics won out every time.

The tattooed man gabbled out words like "Sharpy" and "no-wan's seen her since Thursday last" and in moments Zac had the full story. He loved his mother but they didn't live in each other's pockets; he ran the whores and drugs and left the protection side to her. It wasn't unusual for them not to see each other for days so he hadn't even noticed that she was gone.

Zac's annoyance at missing something turned to fury and in a second he was across his desk; his short, wiry frame standing too close to the larger man and the contrast between his designer clothes and the other's bargain-basement T-shirt and jeans impossible to miss. He yelled at the older man.

"What d'ya mean she's not been seen? Since when?"

"I… I don't know, boss." The man glanced hopefully towards

the door. "It was young McIlveen what noticed."

Greer dropped his tenor voice to a baritone growl. "Fetch him in, and get everyone together. I want to know who was supposed to be guarding my Ma."

The man was out the door and back ten seconds later with Bryn McIlveen. A minute of interrogation revealed that he'd last seen Sharpy on Thursday morning when she'd said that she was heading into town. She'd said she would bring back cakes but she hadn't re-appeared. He'd thought nothing of it, knowing her tendency to disappear, but it was three days now and that was way too long.

Zac Greer glared at the gawky teenager who'd had the temerity to notice what he'd missed. His fury wasn't displaced guilt; the emotion was completely alien to him, bred out of him before he could walk. His fury was based on a firm belief that he knew everything, and anyone who proved that he didn't was at risk.

The sound of men's voices in the corridor made Zac break his glare and storm outside. A dozen men were standing there and their murmured words ceased abruptly as he appeared. The crown prince scanned their faces then he beckoned McIlveen. He pointed to one man. He was slim and small with skin so dark that the others called him by a racial epithet; his given name was Robbie Long.

"Long. You were guarding my Ma last Thursday. Where is she?"

Robbie Long froze where he was standing. His eyes widened and the men close-by could read the thoughts rushing across his face. What had happened to Sharpy? What had he done wrong? And most important of all; what was Zac going to do to him?

Long suddenly realised he was expected to give an answer and he gasped one out so breathlessly that only Zac and the tattooed man beside him could hear.

"Sharpy made me drap her off at Castle Court centre an' leave; I wasn't wanted. She said she was goin' shoppin' then hud a meeting. No-one else was to know about it. Honest to God, Zac, she tawl me to piss off."

Zac's eyes narrowed, not in concern for his mother but at the idea that she'd been up to something he didn't know about.

"Who was she meetin'?"

Long shook his head so hard that the tattooed man winced, knowing that it must hurt. But if Robbie Long thought the strength of his gesture would save his bacon he was wrong. Zac repeated three questions relentlessly. 'Who, where and when?' He asked them in different voices of different strengths accompanied by a punch or slap, until finally Robbie Long fell to his knees, unable to take any more. Finally he squeezed out. "Sharpy said she'd kill me if I tawl anyone."

Zac bent down and pushed his face close to the man's. "I'll kill you if you don't."

Long's shoulders slumped and he nodded. "She was meeting sumwan about thon bookshop. You know, the weird wan in Smithfield. She said he was goin' to pay her a lot for sumthin'"

Zac Greer recoiled at the words. The bookshop was gone, blown apart; it had been all over the news. He hadn't paid much attention; after all it hadn't been their handiwork. Until today he'd had no reason to give it a second thought, but now…

He grabbed Robbie Long by the throat. "Where? Where was they meetin'?"

Long raised his eyes pleadingly, already knowing that it was a futile task; there was no sympathy in Zac to be begged. "I don't know, Zac. That's all she tawl me." He scrambled furiously for something that might save him. "I think they was meetin' in Castle Court."

Zac relaxed imperceptibly; his Ma had been in Castle Court, streets away from the bomb, but that didn't change Long's betrayal. Zac turned his back to the crowd and whispered something in the tattooed man's ear, then he re-entered his office, leaving Long to be dragged screaming to a near-death beating in an alleyway.

Anyone watching might have mistaken Zac's sombre face and quiet strides for concern, anyone who didn't know him that was. He wasn't worried, he was thinking; thinking about the pot of money that someone had been prepared to pay his mother for something, and her betrayal in keeping the details from him. But even more than that he was contemplating what to do on her return and planning her overthrow. He rehearsed his coronation speech in his head. 'The Queen is gone. Long live the King'.

***

Docklands. 4 p.m.

Liam shot Carmen McGregor a look that everyone missed, everyone that was except Nicky. She'd shaken hands with their temporary constable as soon as she'd arrived, ignoring Liam's raised eyebrow as she did. Raised not because Nicky wasn't normally polite, but because shaking people's hands wasn't usually her thing. But Nicky had felt the tension between Liam and the red-haired secondee as soon as they'd entered the floor, and shaking hands would tell her much more than a smile and hello.

She was right. Carmen McGregor's handshake was over-firm, almost stubbornly so, and she'd held Nicky's gaze defiantly as they shook. There was no smile in McGregor's eyes, just a pissed-off gaze that said Liam and she had had words at some point in the day. Nicky had released the woman's hand and offered her a coffee. It was accepted with barely a nod; no thanks and no smile. As Carmen McGregor had turned towards her indicated desk Nicky'd given her the once over. Mid-thirties or slightly less and extremely pretty in a porcelain-doll-like way; although she tried to hide it under a shapeless suit and an unkempt, Boho hairstyle that did her no favours at all.

Nicky also knew McGregor was angry, so angry that it had been palpable in a five second handshake. She would lay odds on that she was mouthy with it, except that Liam would have jumped all over that.

Nicky poured the coffee for the briefing, nodding to herself and stifling a smile. She knew exactly what was wrong with Carmen McGregor and it was eminently curable.

Just then Craig entered the squad-room and walked towards his lively P.A., just catching the tail-end of her smile. It was a knowing smile that said Nicky had information no-one else had and he knew she would tell him when she thought he ought to know. He nodded hopefully at the coffee.

"Is that for us, Nick?"

Nicky pursed her lips primly, as befitted her fifties theme, and shot him a sceptical look. "Is it ever not?"

Craig smiled and turned to face the room. He spotted Carmen and approached her immediately with an open hand.

"Welcome to the team, Constable McGregor. I'm Superintendent Craig. I hope you'll enjoy your time with us."

Carmen was caught off balance; literally and metaphorically. She'd been kneeling to fix a drawer handle when Craig approached, and her shock at the sight of him coupled with her rush to shake his hand had made her fall flat on the floor. Liam gave a loud guffaw and Craig rushed forward to help her. Carmen was torn between shooting Liam a look that would kill and gabbling "thank-you" to her new boss.

As she scrambled onto her chair Carmen admitted to herself that she was shocked. She'd heard that Craig was good looking but she hadn't expected this; he looked like a matinée idol! He wasn't her type; she preferred blonds, but he was a shock nonetheless. Still, behind his charm he was probably a bastard, a wimp or a bully, that was her usual experience of men. Nicky viewed the interaction from a distance, smiling again and ticking off the list that she'd made in her head. She'd diagnosed Carmen McGregor correctly, now she just had to formulate a treatment plan.

Craig nodded towards his guffawing deputy. "No doubt Liam's been showing you the ropes with his usual delicacy?"

Carmen couldn't help but smile at the words, and at Liam's indignant face.

"Here now, I've been as good as gold, boss."

"I'm sure."

Craig grabbed a chair and sat down near Nicky's desk. "Right, everyone. Gather round please. It's a Sunday and we all have homes to go to, so let's make this short and sweet."

When everyone was seated Nicky appeared with a box of cream cakes. Craig raised an eyebrow as she spread them primly on a plate.

"It's Sunday afternoon tea. A new tradition."

Liam reached a hand out to grab an éclair and Nicky rapped it with a spoon, making Carmen smile again.

Nicky's tone was firm. "Good manners are an old tradition. So wait."

Craig carried on. "Everyone, I'd like to introduce you to Constable Carmen McGregor who's joining us from the Vice Squad for a couple of weeks."

A chorus of 'Hi' and 'Hello' came and went as Craig continued. "Carmen is one of two people seconded to us for a fortnight. The second person is Captain Ken Smith, one of the bomb disposal team. He'll join us tomorrow and also hopefully Jake will be back. We'll need everyone we can get to wrap this case up by the 30th. It's a tricky one and getting trickier by the day."

Liam nodded and bit into the éclair that Nicky had finally given him permission to take.

"OK. I'm going to update you then I'll hand over to Davy, Annette and Liam in turn."

Craig started reporting, first of all on Fintan Delaney's death, then on the woman they'd seen on the CCTV; Jennifer Weston. He brushed past the shock of the people who didn't already know and nodded at Davy to chip in. Davy scratched his head for a moment before starting. It was a gesture that said 'I'm puzzled', not about the findings but about what they meant.

"Fintan Delaney died s…sometime this morning, best estimates from witnesses and Dr W…Winter say around seven a.m. Dr Winter is adamant that it was murder; there's nothing on the P.M. that s…says natural causes, but there's nothing that gives an obvious cause of death either. No knife or bullet w…wounds, so we're probably looking at poison."

Craig cut in. "The tox-screen will be back by tomorrow lunchtime. Until then John has no idea what the poison was. Des is working on the method of introduction."

Davy nodded. "Poison w…would make sense. Jennifer Weston was dressed in a light nurse's uniform and poison is all that could have been easily concealed." He reached over to his desk and lifted a folder, distributing the sheets inside. "You'll see three s…sheets; the top two are the ward CCTV pictures of W…Weston entering and leaving Delaney's room and all the data we have on her to date."

Liam let out a low "Hmmm…"

Craig took the bait. "OK, shoot, Liam."

"Well… she's made no attempt to hide her face from the camera. In fact she actually turned towards it, like she was taking a selfie."

Annette cut in. "She doesn't care if we I.D. her."

Liam nodded. "And you know what that means."

Carmen watched the interchange curiously. Craig's team were so familiar with each other that they almost spoke in shorthand. It was impressive.

Craig answered Liam. "She's already out of the country."

"Aye and somewhere that we can't touch her as well."

Craig nodded glumly. It was unlikely they'd never see Jennifer Weston again, but that didn't mean they wouldn't have a damn good try. He turned back to what they could tackle right away.

"Davy?"

Davy had listened to the exchange calmly, knowing that Craig never veered too far from the point.

"OK. The point is that w…we believe Weston killed Fintan Delaney and perhaps her method will give us some more clues about her. Now we need to find out why s…she killed him." He tapped a finger on Weston's biography. "Weston and Delaney both went to Queen's but she'd left by the time Delaney arrived. She studied Theology and we know that Delaney w…was heavily involved with his faith, so I'm checking if they were in any religious groups together, but the university office is closed today."

Annette interrupted. "If Weston went abroad after her nurse training, do we know where?"

Davy shook his head. "Not s…so far. I'm running the airline passenger databases but I think the quickest w…way to find out is to ask her family." He nodded at his page. "Their details are on there."

Davy paused for a moment, considering whether he'd finished with Jennifer Weston. A barely perceptible shrug said that he had. He turned to page three of his hand-out.

"OK. This is the most up-to-date info on the forensics from Papyrus. Three of the blast victims have been identified and Fintan Delaney was, until this morning, the only s…survivor. The fourth bomb victim is so far unknown but Dr Winter is working on the DNA and I'm hoping to get the s…street and traffic-cam info through tomorrow, so we should be able to see who entered and left the shop that day."

Liam leaned forward. "I've some stuff on Sharpy."

Craig waved him back. "Let Davy finish first."

Davy smiled so smugly that it had the subtext of him sticking out his tongue, then he realised that he had actually finished. He scrambled for something more to say to thwart Liam's inevitable satisfied smile. "And I'm getting Fintan Delaney's laptop and phone tomorrow."

Craig nodded. He hadn't thought of it but he was glad that Davy had. Something occurred to him. "Hold on, Davy; where are they coming from? We didn't get a warrant for Delaney's house."

Davy grabbed a piece of paper from his desk and handed it to Craig. It was headed with a regimental crest.

"Captain Smith got it after the explosion. Apparently it's normal procedure when there's a bomb. Everyone, even a survivor, is s…suspect."

Annette nodded. "Especially the only survivor, I imagine."

Craig frowned, unsure of either the legality of the army warrant or its jurisdiction. "Did the army search the house, Davy?"

"Not in any depth as far as I know, just lifted the computer. Delaney's phone was already at St Mary's. The w…warrant covers a search and all the contents." He stared at Craig. "Do you w…want me to leave it, chief?"

Craig stared hard at the paper. He wanted to know what was on Fintan Delaney's computer as much as anyone; it probably held clues to what had got him killed, but he didn't want dodgy procedure messing up their case in court. After a moment he nodded.

"Leave it until I check this with the lawyers. I spoke to Delaney's parents and they seemed happy for us to look at anything in his flat, they just want his murder solved." He set the warrant down. "I'll get them to sign something then we won't need this. But good thinking anyway. I'm pretty sure you'll get the phone and laptop contents tomorrow either way. Anything else?"

"That's me finished." Davy was about to hand over when he remembered something else. "Oh, yes. Hanna W…Weir, Delaney's old girlfriend. She's clean. S…She's at Uni in London and engaged."

He sat back and Craig waved Annette on while he thought of the army's arrogance. They weren't content with just dealing with the bomb; they'd almost messed up his murder investigation as well.

Annette handed out a single sheet. "I know it doesn't look like much but it's taken me hours of land searches and calls to Company House to narrow things to this. The company developing that part of Smithfield is called SNI Property Holdings. Don't ask me what the SNI stands for, because trust me, I've searched everywhere."

Liam cut in. "The N.I. must be Northern Ireland."

"Thanks, Einstein. I'd already worked that bit out. It's the' S' that's a mystery. Anyway, the parent company has holdings in the UK, Republic of Ireland, Italy, Australia and elsewhere."

Craig interrupted. "Where elsewhere?"

"China mostly and some in the Middle East. Their modus operandi is to find an area they want to develop and aggressively target the existing tenants until they leave. They offer money and perks and if that doesn't work they make life so difficult that people move."

"Have they ever destroyed a property before, Annette?"

Annette shook her head firmly. "Never. That brings me onto my next point. I don't think they had anything to do with the explosion. They've intimidated and bought people out, but none of their target properties in any country has ever been bombed."

Craig shrugged. "Perhaps they'd never encountered anyone as stubborn as Jules Robinson. He sounds like he gave a new meaning to the word thran. Either way, we need to dig deeper."

Davy whispered to Liam. "W…What's thran mean? I've never heard of it."

Liam leaned back, totally ruining Davy's attempt at covertness, then he explained in a loud voice, like a teacher lecturing a particularly dim student.

"Thran means awkward, stubborn or pig-headed."

Davy smirked. "So basically the boss was describing you."

Craig stared at them. "Pay attention, you two."

He waved Annette on and she covered her research into SNI, ending with a puzzled frown. "That's all I could find, except that their solicitor in Belfast is someone we all know; James Trimble."

Liam lurched forward. "James Trimble who did all the UKF's defence work?"

"The same. He's been working with SNI since 2012."

Craig nodded. It made sense. If the UKF's solicitor acted for the company that had wanted Jules Robinson's shop then it was likely that Sharpy Greer had been in contact with SNI. If she was inspecting SNI's future purchase it would explain why she'd been in Papyrus. It also made it unlikely that either the UKF or SNI had planted the bomb. Craig perused the group's faces as they all reached the same conclusion; all except Liam. He checked that Annette had finished and nodded Liam on.

"Aye, well; Sharpy... I met with an old mucker of ours earlier today; Tommy Hill."

Craig raised an eyebrow, not in disapproval but in curiosity. "How is Tommy these days?"

"Keeping his nose clean by all accounts. Full of the joys of the baby. He even showed me her photo." Liam smiled, thinking of his baby son. "She's bonny, right enough, and the Kerrs have had her christened; that's what the photo was. Anyway, the old lag seems to be keeping his nose clean for her sake."

Craig interrupted. "That and the fact that half his gang are still locked up in Maghaberry."

"Aye, that's helping too. Anyway, it seems that the UKF have had a name change."

"To?"

"UKUF. I can't keep saying 'the' UKUF; it's way too grand for that bunch. Anyhow UKUF stands for UK Ulster Force. Seems they changed their name after the flag fiasco at the City Hall, just for emphasis."

"I'm guessing Tommy didn't say fiasco."

"Nope. He called it a disgrace. Anyhow. Sharpy was still ruling them with a rod of iron, helped by her son Zac."

Craig startled. Zac Greer would still have been at school. "Look into that, Liam. Zac can't be sixteen yet."

"Alexander the Great w…was sixteen when he became regent."

Craig glanced at Davy sceptically. "Zac is no Greek hero, trust me. He's got a juvenile record as long as your arm."

Liam dragged the spotlight back to himself. "Aye well. Whoever UKUF's boss is, Tommy confirmed they're running protection in Smithfield. I tried to get him to tell me about their other activities but no joy."

Craig nodded. So Sharon Greer had been at Papyrus inspecting her protection interest, and probably casing it for the SNI takeover. She'd just picked the wrong day to do it.

"By the way, boss. I gave Tommy what we discussed last week."

"Good. Hopefully it will keep him out of trouble."

Annette looked quizzically at the two men. "What did you give him?"

Liam tapped the side of his nose conspiratorially and Annette decided that to ask any more would give him too much importance. She would find out some other way.

"I was planning a visit to UKUF tomorrow, boss. What do you think?"

"Take Jake with you please, or if he's not back take some uniforms. The paramilitaries on both sides hate us. And remember, we haven't notified the next of kin about Sharon Greer's death yet, so the boy won't know."

Liam nodded and handed back to Craig to sum up. Some threads were coming together and others were unravelling. Sadie Robinson's story about protection was true, as were her words about the developers. UKUF was extorting money from Papyrus, and probably all of the businesses in the area, so there would have been no percentage it in for them to blow the bookshop up. And unless Zac Greer had suddenly decided to stage a coup, he certainly wouldn't have destroyed the shop with his own mother inside; it was too like a plot from ancient Rome, even for them. Who would have benefited from blowing-up the shop, as opposed to a well-ordered demolition? Craig threw the question out there.

"OK, who wanted the shop gone?"

"The developers."

"UKUF?"

"Someone who hated Jules Robinson."

The suggestions came thick and fast and Craig sifted through them.

"OK, not UKUF unless Zac wanted his mother dead. Liam, check that out tomorrow. Someone who hated Jules Robinson is a possibility, but they could just have easily hated one of the other victims. We need more background on all of them to rule that out, including how often did each of them visit the shop and was it regular enough to tie it to that specific day? Everyone, get on that, please. We know that Fintan Delaney was a target, but was he the original target of the explosion?"

"Bit of a blunt way to kill him, blowing up a whole s... shop."

Craig nodded. Davy was right. The niggle that had been there for days suddenly returned to annoy him. He couldn't work out what it was yet, but he knew that it wasn't something they were already working on.

"Demolishing the shop was part of the plan for SNI, albeit not in quite such an explosive way."

"But knocking it down served their purpose, sir. It didn't serve anyone else's."

"True, Annette, but if SNI was working with UKUF then they would hardly have destroyed the shop with Sharon Greer inside."

Liam interjected eagerly. "Unless they'd got the message that Zac wanted rid of his Mum so he could take over the empire."

Craig considered for a moment. They'd gone past detective work into the realm of speculation. It was always a risk but sometimes they struck gold. If Zac was involved they needed facts to prove it.

"OK, that brings us to background again. Liam, follow up on UKUF. Annette, go and meet the boss of SNI. Davy, you'll have your hands full with the background checks and Delaney's computer and phones. I'm going to his flat tomorrow to see if there's anything there, then I want to interview James Trimble."

"Here or at High Street, sir?"

Craig was taken aback by Nicky's words; she'd been so quiet he'd almost forgotten she was there.

"Good point, Nicky and I think you're right, High Street will put Trimble on the spot. It'll make a pleasant change from him doing it to one of us. Invite him to join me there tomorrow afternoon. The timing is up to you." Craig stood up. "Right. It's almost five o'clock on a Sunday and you all have a life outside this place. So go and live it and we'll brief tomorrow morning at eight o'clock."

Nicky waited until the group had dispersed and then glanced across the floor, to where Carmen was making no moves to leave. She watched as the constable rummaged in her handbag with an intense look on her face, as if its contents were desperately important. The others grabbed their coats and headed for the exit, hurrying home to their partners and kids. She was eager to do the same but she had a theory to prove. She hung back, well out of Carmen's eye-line and watched as she glanced up occasionally to check if everyone else had gone.

Craig walked past his sparky P.A. and turned to see where her eyes were fixed. Nicky glanced at him meaningfully then back at the new member of the team. Craig beckoned her into his office. "What do you think?"

"I think she's spikey and Liam's been giving her a hard time for it; rightly, probably. But it's why she's spikey that's interesting. I think she's lonely, sir."

Craig's raised an eyebrow. "On what basis?"

"Well, look at her. It's a Sunday evening and she doesn't have any work to do yet, yet she's hanging around here pretending to look in her bag for something until she thinks that everyone's gone."

"And?"

"She looks so sad." Nicky folded her arms in a way that brooked no argument. "She's lonely."

She stared pointedly at Craig's wall clock and her message was clear. Craig nodded and they walked out of the office together and across to Carmen's temporary desk. Craig spoke first.

"We didn't get a chance to talk, Carmen, so how about that chat now?"

Carman's blue eyes lit up before she realised how nerdy such eagerness must look. She glanced away, feigning cool. "But it's a Sunday evening, sir. Haven't you got better things to do?"

Craig shook his head. "Nicky and I were just heading over to The James Bar for a drink. Let's chat there." He glanced at Nicky. "OK?"

"More than OK. Gary's taken Jonny, that's my twelve year old, to his granny's. They won't be back until seven."

"That's settled then. We'll leave in five minutes."

Craig turned on his heel quickly, but not so quickly that he didn't see the happy look in Carmen's eyes. Nicky was right; she was lonely. But a drink was only a temporary solution. Craig shook his head and smiled, knowing that this was only step one of whatever plan Nicky was hatching. If he knew one thing about his kind P.A. it was that she wouldn't be happy until their new detective constable was.

Chapter Fourteen

Karachi. 9 p.m. local time

By the time the long plane journey ended Jenny Weston had convinced herself that she'd done the right thing. The explosion had destroyed one part of their problem and her terminating Fintan had dealt with the rest. She'd foolishly allowed herself to develop feelings for the boy; it was self-indulgent and had almost threatened their mission. Fareed had been right to send her to finish the job; it had brought her focus back.

As she disembarked the plane, the last thing she expected to see was the head of their operation in the arrival's lounge. Fareed nodded at her and then towards the exit, his message clear; follow me. It could only mean one thing; that somehow their mission had failed. Perhaps Fintan was still alive? She shook her head. No, he was definitely dead. But whatever had happened their mission wasn't over yet.

***

Docklands. Monday. 11 a.m.

"Nicky, what time am I meeting Trimble?"

"Two o'clock. Is anyone going with you?"

Craig cast a look around the squad-room. Annette and Liam were out and Jake was off the scene for at least another week. That left Davy and Carmen. Carmen had been pleasant enough company in the pub the evening before, although her tendency to quote facts in a 'did you know' way was vaguely annoying. But with Jake gone she was all they had. Craig remembered something and frowned.

"What happened to Ken Smith? He was supposed to have been here at nine o'clock."

Nicky smiled. "He phoned through. He'll be here at one. Something about Major James insisting that he takes some parade."

Craig nodded, unsurprised at Stephen James' need to assert his power; it had been written all over the man when they'd met. He pondered James' ploy for a moment. He'd never understood the military's thing about parades; the need to line everyone up and have them bellow out their name. It was like school. Craig smiled, imagining what would happen if he tried it on his team. Nicky read his mind and shook her head.

"OK, Carmen can come with me to High Street. The way we're going for staff we're lucky to have her."

Craig re-entered his office, casting a longing look at Nicky's percolator on the way.

"You want coffee and not to be disturbed for an hour. Right?"

"Right. Unless it's John."

She lifted a pile of files and pressed them into his hand. "Since you've got a free hour these need your signature for court, and I've some more letters to bring in."

Craig closed the office door firmly behind him and sat down in his chair, swivelling it round so that his back was to the door. He stared out at the glinting summer river, forgetting the files he'd just set on his desk, and started to search for the itch that was scratching at the back of his brain.

Why would a developer blow up a property when they knew it was going to draw unwelcome attention? SNI had never done it before. And if they had decided to do it, then why not at night when the place was empty? It would have served the same aim; to destroy the property. The Robinsons were elderly and unlikely to want to rebuild. They would have got the insurance money, sold SNI the land and everyone would have been happy enough.

And if Sharon Greer was working with SNI then why would they kill her? Why would UKUF? Even if Zac Greer wanted his mother out of the way, and they had no proof that he did, there were easier ways that wouldn't start the cops snooping into their affairs. Craig shook his head. No; none of it made sense. Unless…

The office door was tapped quietly and Craig said "come in". A moment later he was holding a strong coffee and staring at a pair of seagulls on his windowsill. His thoughts returned to the case.

Unless what? Unless whoever had planted the bomb had wanted to kill everyone in the shop as well as destroy it. No, too random. Not everyone in the shop, just someone. The logical answer was that Fintan Delaney had been the target all along and that's why they'd come back to finish him off, but there were things that pointed away from him. First his age; how many enemies could someone have made by the age of twenty, especially enemies this vicious? And there must have been other places where they could have killed him more easily; his student digs for a start. And if Delaney was the target then why allow him to be in the most protected position in the shop when the bomb went off? Surely they would have arranged for him to be right on top of it. Craig shook his head in frustration and turned back to the other victims.

So Sharon Greer was at Papyrus inspecting her empire and Barry McGovern was a regular visitor. How regular? Regular enough to say with certainty that he would have been in Papyrus on a Thursday afternoon, or was he just there at the wrong time? More questions to ask. That left Jules Robinson who was there every day, but if he'd been the target, with or without his shop, then why not blow it up when he was alone, opening or closing up? And what about their unidentified victim; who was he? Craig hoped fervently that if John managed to extract his DNA it was on a database somewhere. He lifted the phone to the lab and John answered in three rings.

"Did you get it?"

John raised an eyebrow and considered lecturing Craig on his conversational skills. Instead he answered in kind.

"Running the database now."

"Brilliant! Get it over to Davy as and when."

"I'll see you at four."

Craig dropped the phone, forgiving his own rudeness; John was just as bad when he was fixed on an idea. They had their bomb victim's DNA and soon they would have a name. Even Craig knew that his optimism was touching; if their victim wasn't on a database he might be John Doe forever.

Craig sipped his cooling coffee and turned back to the niggle that had kept him awake half the night. He reached hard for the elusive idea as it disappeared, first down one rabbit hole and then down the next. Finally he had it cornered in the darkness. What if it hadn't been Papyrus or a particular person that the bomber had wanted to destroy, but something else? But what?

A concept? A brand? No, too intangible. Suddenly the rabbit-hole's light flickered on and Craig could see the answer clearly; it was something he'd already thought of and dismissed. A book. What if they really had bombed Papyrus to get rid of a book, or books? What if Jules Robinson had found a valuable book that someone had wanted? Or wanted to destroy? But why? For its worth? A collector trying to maintain their own rare book's value; a value that only held true if you owned the only copy?

Craig was out the door and across to Davy before Nicky had time to turn.

"Davy!"

Davy raised his eyes calmly, quite used to Craig's eureka moments. Carmen on the other hand was not. She gawped at the speed that he crossed the room; Aidan Hughes had barely moved beyond a stroll.

"Yes, chief?"

"Books."

Davy nodded and tapped on the screen to his right. A document appeared and Craig grinned.

"Is that Jules Robinson's inventory?"

"Yup. All except whatever he'd ordered in the past two w… weeks."

"Damn."

"Don't w…worry. I'm going through the order books his w…wife gave me and following up a few other leads."

Craig nodded. "Print me a copy of that list and keep me up to speed with anything you get."

A moment later Craig was holding twenty hot pages and heading back to his room.

***

1 p.m.

Davy swung between his three computer screens and frowned as he tried to link the traffic-cam views and street CCTV around Papyrus with what was left of the feed from inside the shop. He was tapping so frequently on his keyboards that it was irritating. Eventually Nicky had had enough and she rose to tell him just as an athletic looking man entered the squad. From his confident stride and upright posture Nicky guessed military. Ken Smith's clean-shaven smile backed her supposition up.

"Ken Smith to see Superintendent Craig."

A small frisson of excitement made Nicky brush back her already smooth ponytail, then she reminded herself that she was married and reluctantly accepted that someone else would have to benefit from Smith's charm. As she turned to show him into Craig's office she had a mischievous thought. She knocked

Craig's door once and opened it, ushering the captain in.

"Captain Smith, sir. I'll bring fresh coffee."

Craig rose and the two men shook hands. Nicky returned quickly with coffee and biscuits then left the door open just a crack, knowing that any information she gleaned would aid her plan. Craig poured the coffees, talking as he did.

"We're glad to have you, Captain Smith."

"Ken. I can't go around being called Captain."

Craig smiled. "Fine. Well, we're glad to have you, as I said. Jake McLean our sergeant is off sick, and we have a new member of staff seconded to us from Vice, just for two weeks. That just leaves five core team members. Nicky, who you've already met. Just remember that she owns this floor and you'll be fine. D.C.I. Liam Cullen, who you met at the explosion site. Detective Inspector Annette McElroy; she and Liam are both out on enquiries, and Davy Walsh our analyst, who I'll introduce you to in a moment. We also work very closely with the Northern Ireland Forensic labs and our lead pathologist and forensic scientist are coming to the briefing at four o'clock."

"Who's the other secondee?"

Craig suddenly remembered Carmen and nodded. "Ah yes, sorry. That's Detective Constable Carmen McGregor; she's outside now." Craig glanced at his watch. "Sorry to rush you but Carmen and I are interviewing at High Street Station at two. We often use the rooms there for interviews. I'll introduce you to anyone who's here now and Nicky has prepared a pack with up-to-date findings for you to read before the briefing." Craig glanced at the percolator. "Top your coffee up and follow me."

A moment later they were standing in front of Davy's desk, listening to him swear beneath his breath as his eyes darted back and forth between three screens. Smith gazed at him with an amused expression until eventually Craig coughed and Davy registered that they were standing there. He sighed dramatically, launching into a rant about street cameras until Craig's sideways glance at Smith drew him to a halt; he'd been so focused that he'd hadn't noticed they had a guest. Davy sprang to his feet and nodded hello. Smith nodded hello back. He considered shaking hands then realised that the gesture was too old-fashioned for the young Emo.

"Davy, this is Captain Smith; Ken. He's joining us for two weeks as military liaison."

Smith interjected. "And general dogsbody. I'm happy to help in any way I can."

"Good. Davy's your man for cameras, computers, phones and links with Dr Marsham in forensics. For pretty much everything really."

Nicky chipped in. "Everything that I don't do."

Craig smiled. "Like Nicky said. OK, Davy, Ken's going to remain here and get up to speed for the next few hours. Give him any help you can, please."

Davy nodded eagerly. "I'd love to talk to you about bomb s...signatures."

"Sure. Give me time to read the briefing pack then I'm all yours."

Before the two men disappeared into a discussion about wires and chemicals Craig steered Smith towards the empty desk that Nicky had set up.

"This will be your home for two weeks; let Nicky know if you need anything."

He was just about to head back to his office when he caught Davy's eyes signalling towards Carmen. He'd forgotten all about her! Craig's horror at his bad manners was mitigated only by the fact that she was so new. He covered his mistake by turning smoothly towards Carmen's desk, set diagonally opposite Smith's own.

"Captain Ken Smith, let me introduce you to Detective Constable Carmen McGregor."

Craig completely missed the colour rising in Smith's cheeks as Carmen rose to shake his hand.

"Carmen McGregor."

"Ken Smith."

Smith lingered a second too long on his handshake and both Davy and Nicky read the situation in a glance. Nicky smiled to herself. She'd been planning to match-make the newbies since Smith had walked onto the floor, but now that he was so obviously attracted to Carmen, it would be even easier. Carmen's disinterested expression made her think again.

Carmen's happiness at being invited to the pub the evening before had underlined her social isolation and Smith's obvious attraction to her seemed like the answer to a maiden's prayer. So why wasn't she sending out interested vibes?

The secondees settled back to their desks and Craig strolled back to his office, throwing. "We're leaving in twenty minutes, Carmen" behind him as he did. He re-entered his office, completely missing the direction of Nicky's continued gaze. Davy didn't. He loped over to her desk and perched beside her.

"Are you planning w…what I think you are?"

Nicky turned briskly towards her screen. "What are you talking about?"

Davy squinted at her. "You know w…what. You're planning to match-make those two."

Nicky thrust out her chin stubbornly. "What if I am? I think they'd make a great pair."

Davy's voice rose an octave in indignation. "W…Well first, I'm not sure Carmen agrees with you and s…secondly, how come when Maggie and I were getting together you tried to s… sabotage it at every turn, but this time you're setting it up?"

Nicky was outraged. "I did not try to sabotage it!"

"Oh yes you did. You told me she was too old for me and that I couldn't possibly date a journalist because she would try to s…snoop on our cases!"

Maggie was a journalist at The Belfast Chronicle and five years older than Davy. In Nicky's opinion she'd been far too sophisticated for the twenty-five-year-old Davy when they'd met, although she liked her now.

Nicky was about to deny everything then she thought for a moment and laughed instead, making Davy even more irate. She raised her elegant hands in surrender.

"OK, OK. I admit that I was protective of you and I was wrong; Maggie's lovely."

"You can tell her that at the w…wedding. She's still terrified of you."

Nicky was about to say "really?" but she stored the fact away for future use instead. It was no bad thing to have people a little afraid of you; it stopped them taking liberties. The old expression 'Keep in with the bad for the good will do you no harm' held more than a grain of truth. Nicky smiled.

"I'll tell her, I promise. But that's not the point. You needed protection, Carmen doesn't; she needs a boyfriend." She placed her hands firmly on her keyboard, signalling a return to work, and muttered determinedly under her breath. "And whether she likes it or not that's exactly what she's going to get."

Chapter Fifteen

East Belfast. 1.30 p.m.

Liam pushed his way through the crowd of severely over and underweight men milling outside the terraced row of shops, and entered Garvan's Bookmakers and Turf Accountants, musing that the place should have had a health warning above the door, or at least a sign saying 'Abandon all hope, ye who enter here'.

He'd never understood gambling, the logic of putting your hard-earned money on the back of some uncontrollable four-legged animal or the turn of a playing card, knowing from the off that the odds were against you, completely passed him by. Gambling was a pastime for the rich with money to burn, he would rather spend his on something he could hold, drink or eat. Danni insisted on doing the lottery each week, regardless of what he said, convinced that someday her numbers would come up, a hope inspired and confirmed by the odd time she won ten pounds. Liam smiled, thinking about his tiny wife. He could lift two of her without breaking a sweat but she was the boss of him without a doubt.

The door opened inwards, giving a warning buzz to anyone who was interested, with each of the shop's inhabitants taking a different message from the sound. The desperate men yelling at the TV horse race would welcome any new entrant as a friend; someone who understood the thrill of the chase or the toss of a coin, not knowing that Liam was not so secretly pitying them all. To the men behind the bullet-proof glass at the back of the dingy room the buzz meant something else entirely. It shouted 'mug' or 'eejit' or 'here comes another one', ready to put his money in their hands and wave goodbye to his life. Well they could think again. The only thing Liam would be putting near their hands was a pair of cuffs.

Even without the door's buzz Liam would never have gone unnoticed in the small, cold space. His six-feet-six inches made sure of that. He'd stopped trying to be inconspicuous once puberty had hit and he'd started to tower above his friends. Instead he'd embraced his larger-than-life body by developing a larger-than-life personality and voice to match.

In two strides he was at the glass rapping on it hard and bellowing "shop". A weasel-faced youth with bad skin appeared on the other side.

"For fuck's sake leave us sum windee, wud ye! What di ye want? The one-thirty's already on."

Liam frowned for a moment, puzzled by what he meant, then he realised the boy was referring to the race running on TV. The confidence of knowing there was a land-rover full of Tactical Support cops outside made Liam display his badge. Its effect was startling. The weasel-faced youth paled, making his spots look even worse and the crowd of men watching the race quietened and thinned, exiting the shop in a buzzer symphony. Liam saw the youth's hand reach beneath the desk, and even though he knew no gunshot could penetrate the glass he moved his own to his Glock in response. He needn't have bothered, the boy was merely pressing an intercom and the burly man who appeared beside him a moment later told Liam who'd been on the other end. Liam gave a loud guffaw.

"As I live and breathe. Rory McCrae! I thought you were still in Maghaberry."

McCrae was one of Tommy Hill's crew and news of his release was an omission Liam would be taking up with Tommy another time.

McCrae sniffed; the product of years of smoking and bad

adenoids. "Got out in June. Good behaviour. What do you want, Ghost?"

Liam shook his head exaggeratedly at the use of his nickname. "Tut, tut. Don't you mean, what do you want Detective Chief Inspector, sir?"

McCrae growled. "Fuck away af."

Liam tutted again as if he was the etiquette master at a boarding school then he leaned in towards the glass, beckoning McCrae forward. When the wary henchman had moved close enough Liam banged his fist hard on the glass, deafening his foe.

"Ow! You big fucker."

Liam's action had the desired effect. McCrae stormed out and Liam wedged the door open with his foot. He was inside and heading for the shop's back room without skipping a beat. Liam slid out his gun and kicked at the thin wooden door, ignoring McCrae's indignant shouts.

"Armed police. Put your weapons down."

The sight that greeted him was exactly as expected. A small group of men were hunched over a table, sorting piles of notes into twenties and tens and smoking so heavily that the room was filled with a nicotine mist. Beyond the table lay another door; the one that Liam really wanted.

He waved his Glock in the men's shocked faces, grinning cheerfully. "As you were, lads. Oh, and if any of you budding heroes are thinking of reaching for your gun, there's a truckload of armed cops outside."

Liam backed himself into the corner and kicked hard at the inner door, shouting the warning again. One glance inside told him he needn't have bothered. Sitting in one corner of a small, plush office was a teenage boy flicking a remote at a TV screen. Zac Greer glanced up when Liam entered and beckoned him to a seat with the insouciance of a Napoleon.

"Fancy a drink, officer?" He glossed over Liam's absent reply. "No? Well then, grab a pew."

The boy yelled through the door. "McIlveen, take some cold drinks out to the lads in the land-rover. They must be hot."

Liam stifled a smile, imagining the TSG commander's face. He stared down at the lad, shaking his head at his head-to-toe designer gear and an arrogance so ingrained that it would take a decade of therapy to reverse its delusional effect.

"I take it you're Zac Greer?"

Zac inclined his head regally and again waved Liam towards a chair. Liam sat, not out of any sense of deference but because he could do with the rest. He kept his gun firmly in sight and nodded towards the door, trying to handle the situation the way that he thought Craig would. There was no question that the lad was a scrote and probably a murdering one, but they'd not long identified his mother's dead body so he deserved some sympathy. He had no idea what Sharon Greer's relationship had been like with her son, apart from the rumours of palace coups, so he needed to play this softly.

"My boss would like you to answer a few questions. How would that be?"

Greer considered for a moment and then shrugged, revealing his youth with his next question. "Do I get to ride in the land-rover?"

Liam was taken aback for a moment then he nodded. "OK. We're heading to High Street Station."

Greer stood and Liam smiled at his too-long trousers as he sauntered past him to the door. Zac yelled out an instruction. "McCrae. Get Trimble to meet me at High Street. I'll be a couple of hours."

Liam's smile deepened. Greer would get a surprise when he saw his solicitor was already there.

***

Paris. 2 p.m. local time

167

The wide Parisian boulevards were almost deserted, with barely a car traversing them. The usual stream of chic business people had been replaced by scores of badly dressed foreign tourists. They carried guide books and cameras and filled the dry summer air with shouts of "stand there while I take a shot" and "smile."

Every accent of English could be heard, combining with Spanish and Asian languages to create a dialect soup. It made the few Parisians who hadn't quit the summer city for somewhere cooler, scowl and shake their heads.

Alain Berger was scowling as well, except in his case the expression wasn't because of the tourists. He had bigger poissons to fry. He clutched his attaché case closer to his chest and hurried through the narrow streets of the 3rd arrondissement, in the Marais. After five minutes of rushing he stopped outside a small café and peered through its grimy windows to see who was inside. It was empty apart from a single shape behind the counter. Berger exhaled softly in relief and pushed open the low glass door.

The light inside the coffee-house was dim, made dimmer by the dark Moroccan wood that lined its walls, but Berger could make out the tall man drying glasses; the man that he had come to see.

"Monsieur Augustin?"

The man turned, revealing his substantial girth; it was struggling for freedom through a white apron and being unsuccessfully restrained. Augustin's scowl matched Berger's own of five minutes earlier.

"Oui. Who asks?"

Berger rushed forward eagerly, extending his hand. "My name is Alain Berger. I have what your client wants."

Augustin glanced around for invisible eavesdroppers then he strode to the front door and locked it, drawing down the blind. He waved Berger irritably to a seat.

"Where did you get my name? And what do you mean by

my client?"

Berger smiled; he'd forgotten he was a stranger to the man.

"Apologies. I mean the gentleman in Geneva. I read of his desire online."

Augustin feigned ignorance for a moment before his curiosity won. "Where online? How did you come by the merchandise?"

Berger smiled, feeling comfortable for the first time that day. He answered the second question. "It was a challenge. Especially after what happened in Ireland last week."

"Ireland?"

"Oui. The north; Belfast." Berger frowned and shook his head. "It became very messy."

Augustin nodded. "Then you are wise to take precautions." He shot Berger a questioning look. "Where is it?"

For a moment Berger pretended he didn't understand. Then he laughed. "I cannot tell you that. It is far too dangerous." He opened his attaché case and withdrew a document "Here is the paperwork. Please have your client verify it. Then we will meet again."

He rose quickly and headed for the door, leaving Augustin to gaze at the file. Before Berger could exit Augustin spoke again. "They."

Berger turned, unsure that he'd heard correctly and fervently hoping that he hadn't. "What did you say?"

"They. It is not 'he' who is my client but 'they'."

A group. Berger's heart sank, knowing that their chances of surviving the transaction alive had just been severely reduced. The more people who knew about the deal the more chances of a leak and all their deaths. What had happened in Belfast five days before was proof of that.

***

High Street Station. 2.30 p.m.

Craig raked his dark hair, exasperated by the man in front of him. James Trimble smiled at the effect he was having. Causing exasperation was one of his best techniques. It had resulted in a constable punching him once; the man hadn't been in uniform for long after that.

While Jimmy Trimble's university classmates had been studying Tort and Contract Law, he'd spent hours in front of a mirror rearranging his features into a mask of this or that, trying to work out which expressions best produced the effects he desired. He'd decided long ago to leave oratory to the barristers; after all, they were basically show-offs who loved strutting their stuff in court. You could spot the budding barristers from the first day in undergrad; how many of them were frustrated thespians was anyone's guess. No, he'd leave the long speeches to the Oliviers of the courtroom; his skill in defending his clients lay in what he didn't say. If he was good enough at that then they'd never see inside of a court.

Carmen watched the men from the small, dark viewing room behind the mirror, unsure if Craig's exasperated gesture was for effect, or whether he really was fed up with the smug brief. A voice from the darkness answered her.

"The Super's playing him."

Carmen swung round sharply towards the man who'd been silent since they'd entered twenty minutes earlier. Jack Harris smiled at her brittleness. If she stayed in the Murder Squad it would wear down naturally, and if not then it would be her cross to bear. Jack unfolded his arms and rose, walking across to the glass. He nodded his head towards Craig.

"He looks annoyed, doesn't he?"

Carmen nodded, giving the elderly sergeant a quizzical look.

"Well he's not, but he knows Trimble wants him to be, so he's giving it to him."

Jack gazed at the young woman and shook his head, not, as

Carmen thought, at their conversation or her obvious inexperience, but in puzzlement. How had such a bonny lass, because that's what she was, ever developed such a prickly shell?

Nicky had phoned to brief him during the ten minutes it had taken Craig and Carmen to walk from Pilot Street to his station's reception desk, but even if she hadn't he would have spotted what ailed Constable McGregor straightaway. She was lonely, desperately lonely. It was written all over her in big letters, letters etched by her family being far away in Edinburgh and made deeper by her lack of social circle here. The etching had made her curl into herself like a child who wished that someone would give her a hug, but was cloaked in a coat of spikes so sharp that no-one would dare approach.

Jack had seen it before, too many times; in perps and victims and relatives. He'd felt it himself when he was young and posted to a faraway station, he even felt it now on the occasional day. They were all alone in this world and they were all alone inside their heads, but the company of others sometimes made the solitude easier to bear.

As Jack was thinking his thoughts Carmen was waiting to be enlightened about Craig's technique, so he obliged. He pulled a chair up to the window and waved a hand at Craig.

"OK. Perps fall into many categories but solicitors only have three. First you have the ordinary, decent solicitors who want to do the best for their client, whether they're guilty or not. Because they believe that's their job, or in some cases their vocation. Right?"

Carmen nodded. She'd thought all solicitors were like that so what were the other categories? Jack folded his arms on his stomach and continued, warming to his theme.

"Then you have number two; the crusaders. The ones who want to change the law and the world and really believe that they can. They come in here with books full of arguments, most of it labelled 'Human Rights'. "

Carmen went to protest and Jack held up a hand to stop her.

171

"Let me finish please, constable."

The appellation reminded Carmen that detective she may be, but in terms of rank the man's beside her was higher than hers.

"Human Rights are all well and good, and like it says, everybody human should have them, but the crusaders forget that victims have Human Rights as well. Now don't get me wrong, some laws need to be changed and some have been, thanks to campaigning lawyers and people who complain. But some laws don't, and trying to say that the law is wrong just to get your client off doesn't wash. But crusaders try it all the same and it gives all of us more work, not to mention earache listening to them."

Carmen waited until he'd finished and then cast a look through the glass. Craig had stopped looking exasperated and was giving Trimble what for. She knew Craig was asking about links between Trimble's two clients; UKUF and SNI. She wanted to turn on the microphone and listen but Jack continued with his third category.

"Now category number three is the one that Mr Trimble falls in."

Carmen dragged her eyes from Craig and asked the question that she knew she was supposed to ask. "And that is?"

"Ah well, now. Mr Trimble is what you'd call a player." He caught Carmen's narrowing eyes and clarified hurriedly. "I mean player in the legal sense, not in any other way."

The coldness of her gaze gave Jack more information. Carmen wasn't just homesick, she'd been hurt by a man, perhaps by more than one. A 'player' who'd messed her about. He'd tell Nicky later; it might affect her match-making plans.

Carmen's interest was piqued now and she listened with only the occasional glance at Craig. He was lounging back in his chair and James Trimble was leaning forward across the desk, gesticulating and mouthing some words that she couldn't hear. She didn't need to hear; it was clear that Trimble was feeling defensive. Whatever Craig had hit him with had worked. She turned to Jack.

"What do you mean?"

"OK. Take Mr Trimble for instance. He only takes certain clients; criminals. Not ordinary folk who find themselves being treated like criminals for a while, until it's clear that they are or not, but career criminals. Some of them wear tattoos signposting it and some of them wear nice suits, but their stench is still the same."

Carmen interrupted. "So he never has an innocent client?"

Jack shrugged. "They might be innocent of the odd thing, but not of most. Trimble knows that going in and he doesn't care. His job is to get them off and he's good at it. Either he'll find a procedural error that some rookie P.C. has made, or he'll cite misconduct by the custody staff, cruelty or some other tripe. You know the sort of stuff."

Carmen nodded. She'd seen a bit of it in Scotland, but the legal system there was as tight as a drum.

"I'd say he gets about twenty percent off on that. Then he'll turn to the Human Rights and Equality stuff."

"Does he know his law?"

Jack smiled tightly. "Oh, yes. He knows it even better than some of the crusaders. Make no mistake about it; Trimble's a bright boy. The difference between him and the other bunch is that he doesn't give a monkey's about Human Rights, he just uses the words to spring the crooks."

He stared through the glass and smiled as Craig leaned forward, nose-to-nose now with his foe. Sweat was pouring through Trimble's Egyptian cotton shirt and droplets of it rolled off his thick top lip. Jack gestured towards the two men.

"Trimble tried tactics A and B and they failed, so he tried C, and now that's tanked as well."

Carmen's eyes widened and eagerness tinged her voice. Jack smiled inwardly; so the girl had some enthusiasm left after all.

"What's tactic C?"

"Do you remember when the Super looked exasperated

earlier?"

"Yes."

"Well, that was him pretending that C was working. C's a tactic that players use to exasperate the police. Stonewall every question and refuse to answer. Not a word. The gifted ones can keep it up for hours, just saying nothing or 'no comment'. They gaze around the room, look bored, lounge back in their seats, fold their arms…"

Carmen grinned, thinking of her older brother's behaviour when they were kids. "You mean they behave like a teenager?"

Jack laughed loudly, thanking goodness that the microphone was off. Craig had Trimble on the ropes and he wouldn't thank him for breaking his flow.

"That's exactly what they do, but you'd be surprised how effective it is. They can stonewall for hours until a police officer makes a mistake and says or does something that they shouldn't." He gestured through the glass. "Or until they meet their match and come up against someone who can play as hard as them."

As Jack said the words Craig smiled, as if he'd heard their conversation. He closed the file in front of him and rose to his feet. They watched as James Trimble glanced away in disgust and then reached for his mobile phone. Craig didn't stop him using it; there was no need, he'd obviously won. One minute later Craig was beside them in the viewing room, watching Trimble's perspiration soak through more of his shirt.

Jack turned to the younger man and smiled. "Quite the performance."

Craig grinned. "Trimble's a player, Jack, you know that. So we just played the game until he gave up." He turned to Carmen. "You probably heard but he's admitted he's the solicitor for both UKUF and SNI, although he's still denying any links between the two."

"Is UKUF proscribed under the 2000 Terrorism Act?"

Craig shook his head. "Sadly not, if it was then we'd have

more leverage. But I've put a shot across Mr Trimble's bow. If he's benefiting from the proceeds of crime and we can prove it then his own possessions could be forfeit."

"It would be hell to prove."

Craig nodded at Jack. "It would, but it was enough to get him worried. He doesn't want to lose his nice house. He's probably transferring his assets to his wife as we speak."

Jack gave a loud laugh and just then an even louder man entered the room. Jack saw Liam first.

"Ach, it's the boul Liam. What are you doing here?"

Craig turned to see his deputy squeezing himself through the door. "Yes, what are you doing here, Liam?"

"Lovely to see you too, boss."

Liam caught Carmen's eye and nodded curtly and she felt a moment's embarrassment about how badly their acquaintance had begun. Liam waved in the direction of reception.

"It was getting a bit crowded at UKUF central so I've brought Zac Greer in for a chat. Well, actually a chat and to tell him about his Mum. He definitely doesn't know, boss."

Craig swore under his breath. John had spoken to the Robinson, Delaney and McGovern families but he hadn't got round to Sharon Greer's.

"Damn. That's my fault, Liam. I'll tell him."

Liam shook his head. "Never worry yourself, I'll do it. The lad and I have formed a rapport."

Craig looked sceptical but Liam obviously had his own reasons for wanting to do the deed. Liam nodded through the two-way glass.

"I see Trimble's still here. That's handy. Zac just gave him a call." He turned to Craig. "Did you get anything from him? Anything useful that is. You're bound to have got a headache."

Craig nodded. "I'll update you at the briefing. When you've had your chat with the boy, take him to the mortuary if he wants to go. There's nothing left to see of his Mum but he might want to ask John something."

Craig suddenly noticed how crammed the room was and ushered Liam into the corridor. The others followed and they headed for the staff-room and five minutes of coffee and chat.

"Jack, I'm going to leave Liam and Carmen in your capable hands." He gestured at Liam. "And if he gets out of line you deal with him."

"Aye, you and whose army, Harris?"

As Carmen went to the sink to wash her cup Liam shot Craig a pleading look and attempted a whisper. "Do you not think it would be better if she went back to the ranch with you, boss?"

Craig shook his head firmly. Carmen was prickly but not half as much as Liam implied; it was six of one as far as he could see. He dropped his voice to match Liam's and Jack leaned in conspiratorially. "Suck it up and deal with her, Liam. It's one of the joys of rank."

Craig leaned back and raised his voice again. "Captain Smith has joined us, so we'll have a full team at the briefing except for Jake."

Jack gave Craig a puzzled look.

"He's army liaison. The case started with a bomb."

"Not more of that rubbish. I had enough of that for thirty years."

Jack had been station sergeant at High Street all through the Troubles in Belfast. If he hadn't seen it then it probably hadn't occurred.

"Different reason for the bomb this time."

Just then the staff-room door opened hesitantly and the smiling face of Constable Sandi Masters appeared. "Sorry to disturb you, Sarge, but that wee lad in reception is making an awful lot of noise."

Liam sighed heavily, drained his mug and grabbed a handful of Rich Tea before he rose to his feet. He beckoned Carmen to join him.

"It's time to watch the youth of today in action and Jimmy

Trimble doing his Rottweiler impersonation."

Craig stifled a smile. "I'll see both of you back at Pilot Street, no later than four o'clock. We're starting on time."

With a wave Liam and Carmen disappeared and Jack put on the kettle for another pot of tea.

Chapter Sixteen

Annette parked her small saloon on Linenhall Street and glanced up at the building that was marked on her map. It looked normal enough; seven stories of concrete façade, periodically interrupted by glass. Why couldn't architects come up with something more original? That particular look had been around since the sixties, not that she was old enough to recall.

Annette made a face, remembering just how long she had been around. She would be forty-five on her next birthday, time to start counting backwards. One of her friends had perfected the use of some ancient calendar, telling everyone her age by that; thirty-one. And people actually believed her! Not only because she looked considerably younger than her years, aided by her thin, blond looks, but also because no-one wanted to show their ignorance of ancient counting techniques, so they nodded as if they understood. Annette stared in the mirror and pulled a face, counting the wrinkles beneath her eyes. She got to five and gave up. At least she could do something with her hair. She'd worn the same brown bob since she was seventeen and she badly needed a restyle.

She glanced at the clock and climbed out of the car, crossing the street sensibly at the lights. In less than a minute she was in Regis House, being shown to a fifth floor waiting room. As Annette waited she gazed around her, taking in the expensive beige carpet and the elegant beige and white logo of SNI. Her interior design review was interrupted by an impossibly slim woman entering the room, impossible not just by Annette's standards but by anyone's who had ever eaten a meal. The woman was around forty years old and so blond and pale that she almost blended into the décor. She smiled and when she did so her skin stretched tightly across her face.

"Inspector McElroy?"

A thin hand touched Annette's own for a second then the woman turned, leading the way into an office. Annette walked behind her wishing that she was slim, not as slim as this woman, she would blow away in a breeze, but much slimmer than her hefty ten stone. Her determination to have a makeover grew stronger until her reverie was broken by the woman's next words.

"Tea or coffee?"

"Tea please."

After some whispered words into an intercom the drinks miraculously appeared. In a moment Annette was ready to begin.

"Mrs...?"

It was Mrs, if the woman's heavily decorated ring finger was anything to go by.

"Stenson. Hilary Stenson."

"Well Mrs Stenson, as I told your secretary on the phone, your company's name has come up in our enquiries so I need to ask you a few routine questions." Annette was sincerely hoping that the answers would be anything but routine, but it never did to reveal your dreams.

Hilary Stenson smiled gracefully and Annette imagined that she did everything that way. It must make cleaning the oven a real performance.

"First of all, your company name; SNI. Could you tell me what that stands for?"

Hilary Stenson looked shocked and glanced at the business cards beside her as if she was surprised by what was written there. It would soon become obvious that shocked was her default expression.

"Oh, I am sorry, Inspector. Of course. SNI stands for Saudi Northern Ireland."

It was Annette's turn to be shocked. She wasn't even aware that Northern Ireland had a Saudi population.

"Are there many Saudi people here?"

Hilary Stenson looked shocked again and then she laughed; a tinkling melody of a laugh that rose and fell for far too long. When she'd finished her song she explained.

"The Saudis don't live here, they invest here. Let me explain. The Saudis have owned property in England, principally London, for many years, but they wish to expand to other areas of the UK. Northern Ireland is one of those areas."

"So they're here to develop?"

Stenson smiled beatifically. Annette wanted to wipe the smile off her face for no other reason than that it irritated her, so she parked her planned questions about Belfast developments in general and went straight in for the kill.

"Why do they wish to develop in Smithfield? It's hardly the most elegant area of Belfast."

Stenson's default shocked expression reappeared but this time Annette saw something real behind it. Anxiety? No, the emotion in her eyes was too strong. It was fear. Fear of what? She watched as Stenson scrambled frantically for words to hide behind and decided not to give her the time.

"Why Smithfield, Mrs Stenson?"

"Well… because… well… it's up and coming."

Annette raised an eyebrow, remembering her mother's, a Maghera farmer's wife, verdict on the area; 'It might be up and coming but it's still too low for my daughter'.

"What were you going to build there? What was the development?"

Annette continued with a rat-a-tat-tat of questions as Hilary Stenson opened and shut her mouth like a fish. Finally when Stenson was stressed in the way Annette wanted her, she paused and sipped her tea, waiting for the fading debutante to answer.

"It… it was, is, a condominium. Apartments, but very high end. Swimming pool, gymnasium…"

Exactly as Sadie Robinson had said.

"And you needed the land cleared of local businesses so you offered to buy them out."

Stenson nodded so hard that she almost dislodged her hair-sprayed bob. "It's all quite legal. We offered them a lot of money to move."

Annette set down her cup with a bang and lurched forward, closing the gap between them.

"But some of them didn't want to sell, did they, Mrs Stenson? Some of them were preventing you from getting what you wanted." Stenson's eyes widened and she reached for the phone. Annette continued relentlessly. "Did you employ people to put pressure on them, Mrs Stenson? The same people who had been running protection in the area? Did they go too far without your permission, or did you tell them to do whatever had to be done?" Her voice rose for the most important question. "Did SNI cause the explosion in Gresham Street last week?"

Annette paused for breath, watching as a faint flush tinged the woman's porcelain cheeks. She was enjoying working alone, even though she knew that she would get told off by Craig. He'd told her specifically not to go unaccompanied but when she'd tried to get Liam to come he'd said she would have to wait until after five. Besides, if Liam had been there he'd have asked the questions, and if she'd had Jake in tow she would have had to be more polite.

Hilary Stenson's shocked expression became one of full-blown fear. She let the phone fall back into its cradle and stared at Annette. Then, to Annette's complete surprise, she started to cry. It was the last thing she'd expected from the prim exec, and if she'd thought about it she'd have expected a ladylike sob, but Hilary Stenson's tears were like a banshee's howl.

"I told them not to have anything to do with those thugs,

but they wouldn't listen. They said they had too much invested in surveys and costs already to let two small shops stand in their way."

Annett jumped in. "What were the shops' names?"

Stenson shook her head vaguely. "I don't know. All I know is that they were at either end of a terrace and they wouldn't budge. They were holding up the builders and costing the company money, so they brought those common thugs in."

"UKUF?"

Stenson nodded and howled again. "I think that was their name. They ran protection in the area, some woman called Greer. They already knew the shopkeepers so they were asked to pressure them to leave."

"For a big payment?"

"Yes." Stenson sniffed and quietened for long enough to lift a handkerchief from her bag and give her nose an elegant blow. "SNI offered them ninety thousand pounds to pressure the last two shops to close. One of the shops agreed to take our settlement figure quickly after that." She gazed at Annette, pleading to be understood. "They were generous offers, honestly. The shopkeepers got one hundred and fifty thousand pounds each." She shook her head, remembering something. "But the last shop's…the bookshop's owner still refused to leave. We raised the offer to two hundred thousand but the old man still wouldn't take it; he said that the shop was like his child, so…"

"So you told UKUF to go ahead and do their worst."

"The company Board did. But they only meant to rough him up; intimidate him a bit until he would sell. They didn't mean to blow the place up!"

Hilary Stenson's look of horror said that she was telling the truth. Annette sat back and softened her voice.

"When did you hear about the explosion?"

"On Thursday's six o'clock news. I couldn't believe that UKUF had gone that far. They must have known that the

Board wouldn't sanction it and they'd never get paid."

Annette's ears pricked up. "The company hadn't already paid UKUF the ninety thousand?"

"They got thirty in advance and thirty when each shop owner agreed to sell."

Annette shook her head; it didn't make any sense. Why would UKUF blow the shop up when they knew it would prevent them getting their last thirty thousand? But then why blow it up at all with Sharon Greer inside? Annette nodded to herself as Hilary Stenson watched, wondering what sort of trouble she was in. But Annette wasn't nodding because UKUF and SNI were responsible for the explosion; she was nodding because it was becoming clearer that they weren't.

Annette straightened up. "You realise that intimidation is a crime, Mrs Stenson?"

Stenson nodded.

"I need to know exactly who in SNI sanctioned such a tactic."

Annette watched as Stenson considered obfuscation and then thought better of it. Her shoulders slumped and her voice fell to such a low whisper that Annette could barely hear. She made out one word. "Board."

"The whole Board sanctioned the intimidation of the shopkeepers?"

"Yes."

"And whose idea was it to blow up the shop and kill the people inside?"

Annette already knew that SNI hadn't but she wanted to shake the tree and see what fell out. Stenson flew to her company's defence.

"No-one's! No-one ever agreed to that. It must have been those thugs' own idea."

Annette stood up. "I'm going to read you your rights and call for back-up now, Mrs Stenson. Then you're going to give me the names of SNI's Board members and Chair. You'll all be brought in for questioning."

Thirty minutes later Annette was on her way back to Docklands and Hilary Stenson was on her way to meet James Trimble at High Street. Annette called Jack Harris on the carphone.

"Jack. You're getting a new prisoner; Hilary Stenson. If Trimble wants to arrange bail, let him. She's cooperating and she's not a flight risk. I'll interview her tomorrow at some point."

"Same case as the Super's?"

"Yes, another branch of it. The uniforms have sealed off her office and I have a C.S.I heading over there to secure the papers. We'll deal with the rest centrally."

Jack smiled at her efficiency. "Grand. I'll see you tomorrow around two, if that suits?"

"Put the kettle on."

***

Banque de Paris, Rue des Lilas d'Espagne. La Défense district, Paris. 4 p.m. local time

Alain Berger waited while the bank manager made a show of opening the basement security vault and then another show of checking his fingerprints and the number he'd given him for the fifth time, glancing suspiciously at him between each check. Berger shrugged. His faded windcheater and tatty attaché case weren't what they normally saw in a place like this. He gazed around the high-ceilinged, marble-floored vault and then at the gleaming wall of safes, and smiled as he imagined what was in each one. Precious jewels and family heirlooms, and stolen treasures belonging to other, less fortunate families, long dead at the hands of their conquerors in the last world war.

The safes were larger than the security boxes beloved by writers of crime, inevitably used to hold fresh passports, currency or guns. But the principle was the same; absolute discretion for an obscenely high price. It was why everyone came there.

When the manager thought that he'd checked the number often enough he lifted his hands wide in a Gallic gesture of defeat. It wasn't his problem if someone owned something that they shouldn't or even if they'd liberated it from another theft. Berger had the verification required to open the safe so he could take what was inside, or climb into it himself for all he cared; he had done his job.

With a final glance at Berger's scruffy appearance that Berger knew was subtitled 'mon Dieu!' the manager turned on his heel and left the vault, closing the security grille. He gestured at a telephone on the wall.

"Call when you wish to leave. Just press zero."

Then he was gone. A pinstriped ghost who wandered the vaults then faded back into his own dull world. When Berger heard the man's footsteps enter the lift he turned swiftly to his task. He rotated the dial on the safe's steel door nine times this way and that, until, with a final fall of levers, a satisfying click said the safe was ready to reveal whatever lay inside.

Berger pulled the heavy grey door towards him and stared at the object. It was small, barely occupying one thousandth of the safe's large space, but it was heavy, so heavy that he struggled to carry it by himself. Whether it was heavy or not he had to see it again so he hefted it slowly from its box and set it on a steel trolley nearby, then he stood back to marvel. Its colours were sombre, aged with years of sun and sweat, making the once-bright leather rigid and its gold lettering fade. Berger smiled. No matter how it looked now, it had been a thing of beauty in medieval times. No wonder it had been hidden away, look what happened when such things became known.

He marvelled for a moment longer then he closed the safe quickly, spinning the tumblers to lock it tight. Once the buyers were content with the paperwork and transferred his money, he would tell them where to collect their prize. Until then it would sleep undisturbed.

***

Docklands. 4 p.m.

"OK, settle down everyone. John and Des are joining us and they'll be here in a moment, so meantime grab a coffee and one of the cakes that Nicky has so generously supplied."

Everyone knew that Nicky had purchased them on Craig's orders but it seemed redundant to point it out and detract from his compliment to his P.A. Craig set his chair against a desk at the front of the squad and the others formed a loose arc on either side. As the last two helped themselves to cakes the doors slid open and the familiar shapes of John Winter and Des Marsham crossed the floor.

"Hello. Nicky will sort you out with drinks then I'd like to start. We've a fair bit to cover." Craig scanned the room. "Anyone seen Annette?"

A moment later she dashed in, with a pleased look on her face that made Liam sit up and take note.

"OK. I'm going to update you on the bomb, Fintan Delaney and my interview with James Trimble, then John, Des and Davy on the forensics, Annette on the developers, Liam on UKUF and so on. Everyone chip in, as and when."

Craig was just about to start when a quiet cough from Nicky made him turn. She gazed pointedly at Carmen and Ken and Craig realised that they didn't know everyone else.

"Sorry, I forgot to introduce everyone." He waved his hand towards the two newcomers, noting briefly that they were sitting side by side. For security? A glance at Nicky said that she thought it was something else. Craig brushed past his P.A.'s romantic machinations and continued.

"This is Detective Constable Carmen McGregor, seconded to

us from Vice for two weeks. Beside her is Captain Ken Smith, from army bomb disposal based out at Craigantlet. He's acting as liaison on the case for the same period."

Des' cheerful voice cut through the introductions. "Both here to make sure that we get John to the church on time."

John blushed and Craig turned to the secondees. "Carmen, Ken, the hairy biker who just spoke is Dr Des Marsham, Head of Forensic Science for Northern Ireland; appearances can be deceptive." Des gazed down at his T-shirt and heavy boots with mock indignation. "The soon-to–be married man beside him is Dr John Winter. Believe it or not they have a combined IQ of over three hundred." Craig rolled his eyes. "God help us all."

A chorus of hellos followed then Craig nodded the group into silence and began to report. He covered the bomb-blast and then stopped, turning to Smith.

"Can you tell us anything more about the bomb?"

Smith's clear English accent rang across the room. "Actually yes. We may have had a breakthrough. We knew that the device was basically Semtex and a timer, but we've managed to source the Semtex. Well, when I say source, we've got the chemical composition. But it leaves us with a slight problem."

Des leaned forward eagerly. He'd missed all but the last few years of the Troubles and explosives fascinated him. "What's the problem?"

Smith made a face. "The Semtex was military grade."

"That's not good."

"No, it's not. Don't ask me which army owned it; we don't have tags that will tell us that."

Craig interjected. "But you're saying the explosion wasn't organised by amateurs."

Smith nodded. "It's either military or well-organised paramilitaries from somewhere. It's nearly impossible to get hold of otherwise."

Craig nodded. It made sense. But whose military? He waved Smith on.

"Every bomb maker has a unique signature. For example, they crimp wires exactly the same way in every bomb they make or they utilise fragmentation in a similar way. Our forensic team is looking at all that." Smith sipped his tea and then carried on. "It's also harder than it sounds to actually get a device to work. It's easy enough to put these things together. I mean, there's practically a 'how to' guide on the internet, but to be able to explode them when you want to is much harder than it sounds."

Des cut in. "You have a database of signatures."

Smith nodded. "Yes, and we're almost ready to start the wider search. It took a bit longer than we thought to get the info. We'll start running it tomorrow."

Craig interrupted. "Major James was going to run it against the past fifty year's bombs here."

"Yes."

"Did you get the message that I'd like the search to include international devices?"

Smith nodded and gave Craig a quizzical look. Craig shook his head.

"I can't say much more at the moment but can you do it?"

Smith nodded. "I've asked for it, but I'd rather you didn't mention it to the old man or he'll find some reason to block it."

"Fine. What about the photo-frame?"

Smith warmed to his subject.

"The frame's interesting. The metal was titanium and the scrollwork was decorative. That and the shape lead us to believe that someone put a photograph in the bomb, but what of is in the lap of the Gods."

Des shook his head. "It's in the lap of forensics. Your team found scraps of photograph?"

Smith nodded. "Yes, but very little. They're trying to reconstruct it now."

Des leaned forward so quickly that Craig thought he was going to topple his chair. "Send it over. They were supposed to send it to me days ago. We have state-of-the-art laser technology. It can pull an image off anything."

Craig interjected angrily. "The remains of the watch they used as a timer as well. Why hasn't it happened, Ken?"

Smith looked sheepish. "Major James being obstructive again, sorry. I've been chasing them, honestly. I promise I'll get them both to you after the briefing, but frankly there isn't much on the photo to see."

"I'll make you a bet that we can get more than your labs."

Smith nodded. Craig waited for him to continue but there wasn't anything more to say; they were at the mercy of the bomb database and forensics. Craig continued reporting until he reached Fintan Delaney's cause of death then he turned to hand over to John. John was just wondering whether to have another cup of tea when he vaguely heard Craig call his name.

"Preoccupied with bigger things, John?"

"Yes, namely that I'd love another cup of tea but the pot's empty."

Nicky took the hint.

"OK, Fintan Delaney. Well…he was murdered, no question of it. Everything about his P.M. showed a young, fit man recovering from a mild head injury, nothing that would have caused his death. But the tox-screen is interesting, more in what it doesn't show that what it does."

Craig frowned. "What do you mean?"

"Well… there are some poisons, because that's the likeliest cause of death given that we've ruled everything else out, there are some poisons that defy measurement. You can't simply say 'oh look, there's so much of X or Y in the blood', like you can measure insulin or potassium levels. You can only tell that the poisons have been given by their effect on particular organs or electrolytes."

"And Delaney was killed with one of those?"

John nodded. "Yes, I'm pretty sure that he was. They're quite rare so I want to be sure I'm right. I should have an answer for you tomorrow."

"OK, thanks. Anything on the unidentified victim in Papyrus?"

John's face lit up. "Now there I can help you. We withdrew DNA from the scaphoid bones and other tissue in the debris and by eliminating McGovern, Robinson, Greer and Delaney that left us with a fifth DNA; male. The database kicked out a name this afternoon."

Craig didn't want to spoil John's big reveal but they were pressed for time. "And?"

"And it belonged to a Saudi national called Ibrahim Kouri. Davy's running the checks on him now."

A squeak that passed for Annette's voice cut across the room. "Saudi? Are you sure?"

All eyes turned to her.

"Yes. He was listed as Saudi. Why?"

Annette's eyes were wide with shock; not at John's discovery but at the way things were falling into place. "SNI stands for Saudi Northern Ireland."

Craig's eyes widened as well. "What the hell are the Saudis doing developing in Belfast?"

Annette was about to answer when Des asked an even simpler question. "Who the heck are SNI?"

Craig suddenly realised that some people in the room knew nothing about the developers so he gave them a crash course. "The bookshop owner was being extorted by paramilitaries running a protection racket. UKUF; the UK Ulster Force."

Des shot Craig a sceptical look. "The what?"

"They were the UKF but they renamed themselves after the flag protests at the end of 2012."

Des snorted. "Acronyms are us."

Craig pushed through the laughter that followed. "Yep. Anyway, one of the bomb victims was Sharon 'Sharpy' Greer, the head of UKUF since her husband David died."

"Caught in her own bomb?"

Craig shook his head. "I don't think so. Even they're not that stupid, although there is some word of the son wanting his mother to step aside and let him take over."

Liam leaned forward to interrupt but Craig waved him back.

"Liam will tell us about that in a moment. Anyway, as well as the UKUF protection racket there was a firm of developers interested in Smithfield and they wanted to clear the terrace of shops that Papyrus was in. All the shop owners had agreed to sell except for Jules Robinson."

Des interjected. "And the developers are called SNI."

Craig nodded. "It's only this afternoon that we'd found out what the S stood for. John, let me come back to you in a minute. I'd like Annette to tell us what she found out."

Annette flicked open her notebook and started to report about Hilary Stenson. "SNI was putting serious pressure on the final two shopkeepers to sell and they were working with UKUF to achieve it. They'd paid them thirty thousand up front with another thirty when each shop was closed."

"Compensation for UKUF losing the protection money from the shops?

Annette nodded. "And a little on top. But Stenson denies that SNI authorised a bomb."

Liam smiled. "Well she would, wouldn't she? To paraphrase Mandy Rice-Davies."

Davy had been sitting quietly during the briefing, alternately doodling on his notepad and chewing on his nails. Now he spoke. "Mandy Rice w…who?"

Liam nodded knowingly. "Before your time, son. Back when women were women."

Craig shook his head in disbelief at Liam's ever-permanent foot in mouth. He considered giving him a lecture on sexism but he couldn't be bothered. Liam knew exactly what not to say, he just enjoyed saying it anyway.

"Carry on, Annette."

"There wasn't much more, sir. I believe Stenson that she

191

knows nothing about the bomb but we'll have to check out the rest of the Board."

"And check that none of the Saudi members have disappeared, given what John just said about the DNA."

Craig thought for a moment. The Saudis had bought up or developed most of London, was Northern Ireland their next port of call? Annette read his mind.

"Hilary Stenson said that SNI was interested in property everywhere in the UK. I've had a quick look and their developments look legitimate, even if their land clearance tactics aren't."

John sipped his fresh tea and leapt into a natural break in the exchange.

"OK, so UKUF was running protection, but unless Zac Greer wanted his mother dead, why blow up the shop with her in it? SNI wanted the building cleared but Stenson said that they wouldn't have blown it up, and if they were going to, why do it with a Saudi national inside?"

Craig nodded. UKUF and SNI weren't responsible for the explosion. He had his own theory about who was but he was keeping it quiet until the evidence pointed that way. Craig turned to Liam, who was still chortling over his earlier joke, then just as quickly he turned back to Annette, narrowing his eyes.

"Who went with you to SNI, Annette?"

Annette blushed. "Well Liam was busy so…"

"So you thought you'd disregard my direct order and go alone, with all the risk that entailed?"

The whole group fell silent as Craig glared at her. Annette gazed down at her feet and said nothing. After a moment Craig shook his head.

"I'll speak to you later. Liam, carry on."

Nicky gazed sympathetically at Annette but Craig was right. Her encounter with Hilary Stenson could easily have turned nasty.

"Aye, well, UKUF. I paid them a wee visit and Zac Greer's in High Street now, waiting for me to give the word to let him go."

Craig's eyes widened. "What are you holding him on?"

"I'm not. I brought him in to answer a few questions which he did willingly, enough to convince me that he hasn't a Scooby-Doo about the bomb. He just moaned about the fact they'd lost the protection income from the bookshop."

"So his mother hadn't told him about the deal with SNI?"

"Seems not, and for a man who's the solicitor for both UKUF and SNI, Trimble was keeping his mouth firmly shut." Liam nodded at Craig. "Did you get anything from Trimble?"

Craig shrugged. "He admitted that he'd been working for both groups, which we already knew, but said that UKUF only ran legitimate businesses."

"Aye, if you call drugs and girls legitimate."

"Precisely. Trimble's worried because he knows that we're looking at him now. I'll be getting Fraud to take a look at everyone's books once we wrap our case up. As far as SNI's concerned Trimble pretty much echoed what Hilary Stenson told Annette. That they're interested in developing land across the UK and will pay a lot to get what they want."

"But not plant bombs."

Craig nodded. "Not that."

Annette interrupted quietly. "That still doesn't explain why Zac Greer's still at High Street."

Liam's cheerful face clouded and his voice took on a solemn tone. "Because it became clear while I was talking to him that the lad had no idea that his mother was dead."

John's jaw dropped. He'd forgotten to contact Sharon Greer's next of kin! It was an unforgivable error. "Oh crap! Crap, crap, crap."

Nicky gawped at him. John rarely swore, unlike Liam who swore enough for ten men. John was gabbling.

"This is my fault. As soon as I identified Greer's DNA I

should have contacted the family. It's unforgivable of me."

Craig shook his head. It was a lapse but an understandable one. They'd only found out it was Sharon Greer's DNA two days before and they still didn't know if her son had ordered her hit.

"Liam, did you tell the boy about his mother?"

Liam shook his head. "He was conferring with Trimble. I'll go back and do it after this."

"How sure are you that he didn't order her death?"

"If he did then he's the best liar I've ever seen. My gut says he knew nothing about it."

Craig's heart sank; Liam's gut instinct was rarely wrong and his own was in agreement. He snapped out instructions.

"OK, Liam, take Annette to High Street with you. Ask the boy leading questions and when there's an opening, talk about the explosion and the victims before leading into his mother's death. Trimble's going to ask when we knew. Don't lie but say that we wanted to be sure before we caused any distress. Annette, help with the soft stuff here please and have another word with Hilary Stenson if she's still there. Especially ask her about any Saudi members on the Board, I want their whereabouts checked ASAP. And run the name Ibrahim Kouri past her."

He turned towards John. He was frowning and shaking his head.

"There's no point in the boy coming to the mortuary, Marc, there's nothing left to I.D. It's going to be a closed coffin."

Annette cut in. "We'll have to involve social services, sir. I don't care if Zac heads up a criminal empire now, he's under sixteen and both his parents are dead. Unless he has another relative, he'll…"

End up in care. Liam groaned. They all knew what that meant; Zac might learn even worse habits than he already had. Even worse, with Sharpy gone and Zac still only a kid, internal rivalries would surface within UKUF. Liam vocalised his thoughts.

"There'll be a leadership race and that'll mean gang warfare."

Craig nodded heavily. "I'll notify Geoff Hamill in Gang Crime and get uniform to keep a presence around the headquarters. There's nothing else we can do. Annette's right, the boy's welfare has to come first."

The rest of the briefing passed in a flurry of reporting and conjecture until at five-past-five Craig was almost ready to wind up. He turned to the quiet man of the group and smiled. Davy was always quiet but never more so than when he had something surprising to report.

"Davy?"

The lanky Emo roused himself from his semi-recumbent position and lifted a set of hand-outs at his feet, passing them around the group. Craig flicked through the pages.

"What are we looking at?"

Davy smiled. "Images from the s…street cameras and CCTV around Papyrus. The back sheet is Fintan Delaney's phone logs for the last six months. I'm still working on his computer."

They peered at the grainy images, but even John's extra strong glasses couldn't see what Davy was looking so pleased about. Carmen caught his eye and smiled. She'd seen it.

Davy adopted a patient tone and started to talk through the shots. "In the first image you can see Gresham S…Street outside Papyrus at ten-past-five last Thursday morning, the day of the explosion. There's a dark-coloured car parked up. Image two w…was taken at five-forty, thirty minutes later. The car has gone. Image three was taken at five-thirty-five, just before it left and s…shows two men climbing into the car. Yes?"

Everyone peered harder at the images and nodded, taking Davy's word for the fact that the dark blobs were what he said.

"OK. Turn the page. You'll see three more images that w… were taken in the alley at the back of the shop. They show two men walking down the alley towards Papyrus, then opening the back door and entering. They reappear twenty minutes later.

They're wearing balaclavas, s...so it's impossible to see their faces."

Liam cut in. "The back door was shut during the explosion. So how did they get in?"

Davy shook his head. "Des and I are s...still working on that, but it's obvious that they did."

Liam was about to ask something else when Craig glared him down.

"Go ahead, Davy."

"OK. Now turn to your third sheet. It s...shows images taken inside the shop."

It was Craig's turn to interrupt. "How did you get these? Surely the CCTV in the shop was blown up with everything else?"

Davy smiled. "It w...was, but for some reason Jules Robinson had his CCTV on a back-up. It uploaded images to the Cloud every thirty minutes. W...We have everything from the moment the men entered the shop till the next day at two p.m. They're not great images and I've only got as far as this first set but I'll have the other images analysed for you s...soon."

Annette leaned in. "Do you think Robinson was trying to compile evidence on his extortion by UKUF, sir?"

"Either that or he was very security minded."

"He was a cop for thirty years, boss."

"True, but I'm more inclined to go with Annette's theory, Liam. Ask his wife what she knows about it, please." He waved Davy on.

"OK, look at the images. The two men appear inside the s... shop at five-twelve a.m. on Thursday morning and stay at the back of the shop, in the area we know the bomb was planted."

Carmen interrupted cautiously. "Can we back to the image of them breaking in, Davy? Is one of them carrying something?"

Craig scrutinized the picture for a moment then gave a triumphant yell. "Yes, you're right. Look. There!"

Everyone looked where he was pointing. Carmen was right, while one man opened the shop's back door the second one withdrew a package from a dark bag across his shoulder, so dark that no-one had noticed it before. The image inside the shop showed him depositing it beneath a tall bookshelf at the rear.

Davy smiled. His slow reveal had been blown by Carmen's eagle eye. He moved quickly to his computers and tapped on his central screen, fast forwarding Papyrus' CCTV tape and then beckoning everyone to gather round. The video started with a man kneeling behind a tall bookshelf and setting something down, obviously the bomb. As he started to rise, he banged his head hard against a shelf. There was no sound with the image but the blow was so hard that they could almost hear it, and the expletives that followed.

But it was the next image that really shocked the group. The man rubbed furiously at his head and then, in a moment of pain and frustration, he ripped-off his balaclava, revealing his face. He covered his mistake quickly, pulling it back on, but not quickly enough to stop them all recognising him. It was Fintan Delaney! Delaney had planted the bomb in the shop!

But why had he returned the next day and risked his own death? And why was he later killed? Had he been supposed to die in the explosion and changed his mind? Craig sat silent amidst the noisy debate that followed, letting everyone speculate while he gathered his thoughts. Eventually he smiled and turned back to his analyst.

"Brilliant work, Davy. I presume Delaney's phone logs confirm it?"

"Yes and no. From w…what we know so far we'd expect to see calls from Delaney to S…Saudi or SNI, if Delaney was taking money from them to plant the bomb."

Craig shook his head. If he was sure of one thing it was that Fintan Delaney hadn't planted the bomb for money or for SNI. Davy was still talking.

"But his only unusual calls were to Pakistan. S…So I'm

confused."

Craig caught Liam's eye and they exchanged a smile. "OK, this is great work, everyone. Davy, that was outstanding, but we could sit here and speculate all night and learn nothing more. I have a theory but I'm not ready to share it just yet. Keep following the leads and let's see where we get to."

Liam went to say something just as Craig glanced at the clock.

"It's almost five-thirty and Liam and Annette need to get to High Street. Des, thanks for coming; let me know what you get from the photograph. John, could you join me for a moment. Everyone else go home; we're back in bright and early at eight a.m."

Before Liam could voice his objection Craig was on his way to his office with John, and Nicky was clearing away cups and plates with deliberate noise. Liam harrumphed and shot Annette a look that said the discussion wasn't over, but as the group dispersed he knew he'd have to continue it another day.

Craig entered his office and went straight for his ever-full percolator, flicking it on before he sat down. John walked past him to the wall of windows that gave the room a panoramic view of the Lagan and Belfast's docks. The docks were busy and getting busier by the week as the powers that be finally realised that Bronze Age man had built Belfast by the sea for a reason, and that people had made their homes on either side of the Lagan for one as well. Rivers brought trade, travel and a sense of possibility. They could be thoroughfares or recreational venues, encourage movement and throw a city's arms open to the world, saying come and see. The docks in Belfast had been buzzing once and now they were starting to buzz again. Cruise ships disgorged their visitors between March and October, ships and oil rigs came for repair and fitting out, using skills honed over centuries to make short work of the jobs. Even wind farms had their turbines built in Belfast nowadays and Craig had a window on it all.

"I'd kill for this view, Marc. My office is so closed in."

Craig gave a rueful smile. "I think there's been enough murder this week. Coffee?"

"Only if you've got some milk. Your coffee's strong enough to give me lock-jaw."

Craig pointed to a small carton behind the filing cabinet, the coolest place in the room.

"For the wimps."

When they'd sipped their coffee for a moment John spoke. "Natalie's being very secretive. I think she's finally found her dress."

Craig shook his head, knowing that his friend was fishing and that it was more than his life was worth to disclose what Katy had told him. "I'm saying nothing."

John leaned forward eagerly. "Ah ha! That means you know something."

Craig raised an eyebrow. "Or maybe it means I'm saying nothing because I've got nothing to say."

"Huh! You know all right. Katy's been with Natalie every step of the way. They have it all planned. Well, them and Natalie's mum. Anyone would think I had nothing to do with this wedding!"

The increased height of Craig's eyebrow said he was surprised that John had ever thought he had. Natalie's mother Isabel was a force of nature. A tiny, dark-haired clone of her daughter, or vice versa to be more accurate. They had the same voice, the same mannerisms and the same dynamic approach to life. Together they could create a force of hurricane magnitude and it would be a very brave man who stood in their way.

Craig smiled as he thought of them together, organising the wedding down to the smallest detail, while Natalie's father, the quiet, academic Bernard, clung on for dear life like Dorothy caught in the tornado. Out of control, powerless and never knowing where he was going to land. John was more like Bernard Ingrams than he knew, and just like Bernard he was signing on for the ride of his life.

John tried another few questions to get Craig to reveal what he knew, but if Marc Craig was anything, he wasn't a fool. Disclosing details of Natalie's wedding dress would carry a penalty worse that committing any crime; hours of earache from Katy. At least if he was arrested for a real crime he'd be locked up in peace. Craig changed the subject to something that would interest them both.

"I have a theory about this crime, John."

John knew the subject was being changed and stared past Craig huffily. He held the pose for thirty seconds before caving in.

"What?"

"Well, that's just it. It's so far-fetched I don't want to discuss it until I'm surer of my ground."

"Now you're just being irritating, Marc. You can't bring something up and then be mysterious about it."

It was on the tip of Craig's tongue to say "can't I?" Then he realised John was right. Playing word games was irritating.

"OK. I think that Jules Robinson had something in his shop that someone wanted destroyed."

John rolled his eyes. "Well that's obvious; otherwise they wouldn't have blown the place up!"

Craig sighed. John was still huffing but he was right. So far all he'd stated was the obvious.

"OK, I mean beyond the building and the people inside."

John leaned forward, showing that his interest was piqued.

"So you're saying that none of the five people in the shop was the target and the fact that the building was destroyed, something that SNI had wanted for quite a while, was pure coincidence."

Craig nodded. "Yes. Well, no, not entirely. The shop and people may have been a target, we can't rule that out yet, but they were secondary. What if the real target was something in the shop and the rest was window-dressing?"

"To cover up the real reason they blew the place up?"

"Yes."

John shook his head quickly then the movement slowed, as if he wasn't as certain of his ground. Craig watched his formidable brain kick into action, all of his earlier chagrin gone.

"So there was something in the building that people, let's call them group A, wanted destroyed. Fintan Delaney belonged to, or was acting for that group. Whatever the thing was, it was something important and something they couldn't easily identify and get hold of, or Delaney would just have stolen it that night. Yes?"

Craig nodded. It made sense. If they'd known exactly what their target looked like and where it was then Delaney could just have removed it that night rather than plant a bomb. Unless...

"Unless they also wanted to punish Jules Robinson for even possessing it in the first place?"

John nodded uncertainly. "Maybe... but it seems a fairly drastic thing to do. Blow up a shop when they knew there would be other people inside, including Delaney himself. They could have taken Robinson out at any time; when he was alone in the shop."

He was right. If they'd just been after an individual they'd have killed them somewhere quiet, not blown the place apart. Or would they? Craig leaned forward eagerly.

"OK, let's say I agree with that, and I'm not saying that I do. There are some nutters out there who would have wanted a public execution, even if it did attract attention..."

John interjected. "Sorry, but I have to say this, Marc. Why Jules Robinson?"

"What do you mean?"

"Well, just because it happened in his shop that doesn't mean he was the primary target. They could have planted the bomb to destroy something, yes, but they could also have done it to kill someone that they knew was going to visit the bookshop that day. It mightn't have been something in the shop at all; it might have been someone, like Sharpy Greer."

Craig frowned and John hurried on.

"OK, let's say that I'm someone who, for whatever reason, hates Sharon Greer. Perhaps her drug dealing killed someone I loved or perhaps her thugs had killed someone. Say I'd been waiting for a chance to kill her for a long time, but if I killed her in an obvious way like a shooting or stabbing, it would have been obvious that she was the target and traced back to me. So I pick a way to kill her where she's just one of a crowd." John's voice rose in excitement. "Think about it. She's just one body amongst five. It's enough ambiguity to stop UKUF running off half-cocked to blame any particular group for her death."

Craig went to disagree then stopped himself. John was right. Perhaps he'd been making it too complex; perhaps it really was about someone in the shop being a target. But if Sharon Greer was the one they'd wanted to kill then that made their suspect pool huge.

"Greer had a lot of enemies, so did her husband."

"You have to look at the possibility. Surely your sources can help?"

"Well, we know Delaney was one of the bombers, so we can start from there. If he had terrorist connections we could follow the trail."

"Maybe that's why Delaney was killed? To stop him leading you back to whoever ordered the killing."

Craig drained his mug and poured a refill. "Maybe, except so far we can't find any gang connections for Delaney or his family. Maybe Barry McGovern will suddenly turn out to be something. Davy's digging into all the backgrounds now." Craig paused, lost in thought for a moment, then he shook his head. "I know your idea's logical, John, and we'll follow up all the leads, but I still can't shake this feeling that there's something more to this."

John smiled. "Well, your instinct has been right before, even when the evidence led elsewhere." He raised his cup. "Here's to logic and instinct, at least one of them will turn out to be right."

Chapter Seventeen

Paris. 5.30 p.m. local time

Berger topped up his red wine from a carafe and waited patiently while Claude Augustin took payment from his last lunch customer and wished them 'Bon Chance', then closed the café's door until he had to re-open for the evening rush. Augustin lifted a fresh glass from behind the counter and brought it to Berger's small table. The two men drank in silence for a moment, Augustin watching the wax melting on a candle and Berger carefully watching his host. Finally Alain Berger could wait no longer.

"Well? What did they say?"

Augustin didn't answer, merely swilled some wine around his mouth before swallowing it in a gulp. Berger repeated the question impatiently, as Augustin stared at him through the flickering candle flame like he could read his mind. Eventually, when whatever he'd read there had satisfied him, he spoke, for the first time since Berger had entered an hour before.

"They would like to know more."

Berger smiled. It was the wrong move. Augustin's voice, normally a mid-tenor, became a growl.

"Do you think this is a game?"

The smaller man recoiled, knowing a threat when he heard one. His shock gave the café owner a frisson of satisfaction, but he knew that to show he was pleased would temper the other man's response. He growled again. "Well?"

"No, no. T…There is no game; I know it is no game. I was

smiling because I was pleased they wish to know more."

Augustin gave a dismissive wave. "It means nothing. They often wish to know more, but seldom buy."

His satisfaction grew as Berger's face fell.

"What do they need?"

"Sight of the item."

Berger shook his head firmly. "That cannot be until the exchange."

Augustin stood immediately and lifted the carafe. "Then it cannot be and we are done. "

Berger's voice was desperate. "No, we cannot be done. It is real, it is what they want."

"Then they must see it."

Augustin's tone left no room for compromise and Berger nodded in defeat. The volume of his voice dropped with his confidence.

"I cannot bring it here; it is secure. They must come to see it where it is."

Augustin set the carafe on the café's counter and started to wash his glass. After a moment's ritual he said.

"Very well. One of them will come and if they wish it we will arrange the exchange." He nodded sharply at the door. "Now, go. I must rest." He waved dismissively. "Remain close by; I will be in touch."

***

High Street Station. 6 p.m.

Questioning Zac Greer about UKUF's protection rackets was like interviewing someone from a silent religious order. James Trimble, on the other hand, wouldn't shut up, citing this legal right or that. Liam sighed heavily. He needed to know if Zac was culpable in Sharpy's death before he broke the bad news, so he asked his question again.

"Do you know where your mother is, Mr Greer?"

Liam thought that he saw a minuscule shrug, a shrug that in any other teenage boy would have said 'Who am I? Her keeper?' but in a kid brought up around killing could have meant 'she's six feet under and you'll never find her'. James Trimble interrupted the exchange.

"You've already asked my client that question…oh, five times. Why don't you just speak to Mrs Greer yourself?"

Liam squinted at the dodgy solicitor, testing his bullshit detector, but as far as he could tell Trimble's question was sincere.

"I'm directing the question at your client, Mr Trimble, not you."

"Yes, for the sixth time!"

Trimble leaned forward and stared Liam straight in the eye. "There's something fishy going on here and I'm going to find out what. Either tell me or I'll start digging."

Liam sighed again, this time in semi-defeat. He had to tell the boy about his mother, but he'd wanted to rule him out as a suspect first. It looked like that wasn't going to be possible. Not only was Zac not talking and Trimble beginning to smell a rat, but any minute now a woman from social services was going to bang on the door and tell him that he had to let Zac go.

Liam pictured a virago and the lecture that he was going to get from her. He nodded James Trimble to accompany him outside. When they were far enough away for Zac not to hear when he inevitably pressed his ear against the interview room door, Liam stared down at the faintly grubby man.

"I have some bad news for your client, but…" Liam searched for a reasonable explanation why he hadn't already told Zac about his mother's death. "We've only been sure for a short time and social services have to be present when I tell him."

Trimble's eyes widened slightly then he caught himself, knowing that the gesture looked naïve. He squinted meaningfully. "What have you done?"

Now it was Liam's eyes that widened. "Done? We haven't done anything. I think you're confusing us with the crooks you defend, Mr Trimble. We're the good guys; remember?"

Trimble snorted then realised that a pissing contest wasn't what Zac needed from his brief so he nodded Liam on. In less than a minute Liam had outlined the explosion at Jules Robinson's bookshop and the people who had died, finishing with Sharon Greer's I.D.

"It took forensics days to I.D. her."

Trimble shook his head, genuinely stunned. "You're sure?"

Liam nodded. "Informants have told us about UKUF's protection racket in Smithfield and we know Sharpy was working with SNI to pressure the bookshop's owner to sell, so the explosion was pretty convenient."

Trimble's expression altered with each word Liam said and the effect of the words 'protection racket' and 'pressure' were particularly telling. Liam gawped at the solicitor. The crooked bastard had known all about what SNI and Sharpy were up to! The officer of the court was as bent as a nine-bob-note! He roared in outrage.

"You knew what Sharpy was doing! It's written all over your face."

"Sharon. Her name was Sharon."

Trimble's sad expression and even sadder tone of voice told Liam something completely new. Trimble had fancied Sharpy Greer! Whether he'd done anything about it was another thing, but given the fact her husband had been one of the biggest thugs in Northern Ireland and he wasn't long in his grave, he somehow doubted it. The wimpy solicitor wouldn't have lasted five minutes with Davy Greer. Liam's sympathy didn't run to bent solicitors so he allowed a note of sarcasm to slip in.

"Sharon or Sharpy, she's dead and the boy needs to be told."

Trimble gathered himself quickly and nodded, turning back towards the room. Liam stopped him with a loud whisper. "Not until the social worker gets here. He's underage."

Trimble turned sharply. "They'll take him away from everyone that he knows."

"If there's no relative to care for him then that's their call." Liam smiled coldly. "I can't see them declaring any of you lot a suitable guardian."

"It'll destroy the boy! The gang is all he's ever known."

"Then he needs to get out more. He deserves a chance at a decent life, not one spent running drug dealers and pimps!"

It was on the tip of Trimble's tongue to say "prove it" when Jack Harris appeared, escorting a young woman dressed in T-shirt and jeans.

"I could hear you two in reception. Pipe down, will you? You're disturbing my customers."

Jack remembered the manners that he kept for special occasions and turned towards the girl.

"This is Ms Penny Murphy. She's the social worker here to see Zac Greer."

Liam gazed down at the woman, surprised by her perky prettiness. He sat firmly on the attraction that threatened to appear; he had enough problems with his secretary and nurse fantasies, he didn't need to add social workers to the list.

He nodded hello, "D.C.I. Cullen", then gestured dismissively at Trimble. "And this is James Trimble, Zac's family solicitor. I've just told him about Mrs Greer's death."

Murphy scanned the two men's faces astutely, turning back to Liam with narrowed eyes. She could sense they didn't like each other, and that something had happened before she'd arrived, but unless it affected the boy she didn't care.

"Does Zac have any idea that his mother's dead?"

Liam and Trimble shook their heads in unison.

"Are there any living relatives?"

Another shake then Trimble reconsidered. "There might be an uncle in Glasgow."

Murphy nodded. "Right, I'll check that out. I'll go in with Mr Trimble and break the news, skimming over the matter of his mother's I.D."

Liam was about to ask how she knew when Jack leapt in. "I explained about the remains and the thumbprint being the only means of identification."

Liam nodded gratefully; always glad when he didn't have to deal with emotional things. Penny Murphy was still talking.

"If you could wait for me, D.C.I. Cullen, I'd like to have a quick word afterwards."

Liam nodded. Annette was interviewing Hilary Stenson in the other room. Stenson had waved her right to a solicitor, probably knowing Trimble would inform the SNI Board that she was telling Annette everything she knew. He'd go and watch that for a while.

"I'll be in interview room two when you need me."

He headed down the corridor and knocked the door, entering on Annette's "come in." She looked surprised to see him but not as surprised as Hilary Stenson, who'd probably never met someone else as pale as her. Liam beckoned Annette outside.

As soon as she entered the corridor Annette hissed. "I was on a roll. Why are you interrupting?"

"Oh that's lovely, when I came to lend a hand."

"I've already got two."

Liam laughed at the retort and parked it for future use then he updated her on Zac Greer and the social worker who'd just arrived. He nodded at the door.

"Is she singing?"

"Like a bird. She's willing to give us details of everything; every corrupt deal and back-hander that SNI have ever done. That's why she didn't want Trimble there; he would have tried to gag her."

"Aye, I'm sure he would. So might UKUF and not metaphorically either. She'll need to be guarded."

Annette's face fell. She'd been so excited about the information Hilary Stenson was giving her that she'd forgotten she was a human being who might get hurt. Liam knew what she was thinking; that she'd started behaving like him. It was a blow for a woman who prided herself on her caring side. Annette's shame made her go on the attack.

"You were supposed to call me when you were telling Zac about his Mum. The chief said I was to be included."

Liam raised his hands in mock defence. "Whoa, girl. I didn't tell him. I was just about to call you when the social worker arrived. She's telling him now." His tone hardened slightly. "And don't go lashing out at me 'cos you forgot about Stenson's human rights. It's not my fault."

Annette went to retort then decided to be practical instead. "Who can we get to protect her and for how long?"

Liam furrowed his brow. "It'll have to be close protection and until this gets to trial. UKUF won't want her giving evidence on their protection racket, and SNI won't want her shopping their company Board."

Annette nodded then gave Liam a thoughtful look. "You know what this means, of course. If Zac knew nothing about his Mum's death, then either UKUF did it without his knowledge or someone else did, and Stenson's saying it definitely wasn't SNI."

"Then let's hope forensics comes up with something soon that points the way."

***

Pakistan. Tuesday 9 a.m. local time

The parched grass crunched beneath Jenny's boots as she walked and she grabbed for her near empty water bottle, gulping down its remaining few drops. The sand stretched endlessly ahead and she stared at it, until its yellow glare burnt her pale western eyes and not even the tears she was crying could cool them. A cough at her back made her turn, her finger reaching for the trigger of her Steyr. The man standing there smiled and cast an admiring glance at her curves, barely concealed by the fatigues she wore.

"I am not the enemy, Jenny." The way he said her name made it sound sensuous. The 'J' became a soft 'Jhush' and the 'y' an 'i' that made the syllables sound like poetry. "You are home now."

As Fareed said it Jenny questioned his words. How could a white-bread blond from Newtownards have ended up here, five hundred miles from the nearest city, and even then not one where anyone spoke the way she did? She answered her own question. Ideology; religion to be more precise. Five years ago she'd been a normal student, studying by day and partying at night. The theory of religion had been just that; theory. It hadn't meant anything in her modern western world, except as a topic to be debated at dinner parties or intellectualised during summer tutorials on the grass. And then she'd met Fareed. Dark-eyed Fareed, genius IQ Fareed, Fareed who could debate and deal with every query with good humour, his sensual voice and liquid eyes making even the most radical of ideas seem true.

When had she fallen in love with him? At the first lecture; the first debate? Or was it when he'd quoted the poetry of Nizar Qabbani and likened her blue eyes to a clear desert sky? Whenever it was it had swept her along like a river; no, like a storm, too strong to fight and no way to go but ahead. In his hands she'd become a woman and a warrior for Islam. She'd recruited others like Fintan and she'd killed brutally, yet still Fareed's arms felt like home.

Yes, she was home now. Jenny dropped her gun by her side and caressed the smooth olive skin of the man she was addicted to, knowing that his love would kill her someday and totally powerless to save them both.

***

211

Tuesday. 9 a.m.

"Thanks for seeing me at short notice, Geoff."

Geoff Hamill smiled graciously and continued pouring Craig's coffee. Not, as usually happened in C.C.U. offices, from a glass percolator whose brown-stained base contained weeks' old dregs of never washed out and continually topped up caffeine, but from a spotless stainless-steel cafetière that Craig knew he probably sterilised each night before he went home. When Hamill was satisfied that the perfect bone-china cup was filled not too high and not too low, he moved the milk and sugar towards Craig and took his seat.

Craig observed the ritual, amused, and wondered what Nicky would say if he requested the same, instead of his usual wham-bam-thank-you-Ma'am, can't get caffeine into me quick enough approach to life. As Craig mused Geoff Hamill thanked God that Craig hadn't sent his deputy to the meeting. He liked Liam Cullen well enough but there were only so many cracks that a man could take about his short stature without feeling inadequate, and Liam never missed the chance to make one. Even if he hadn't done, just standing beside the Jolly White Giant was enough to make a man feel like he wasn't enough.

Hamill sipped at his milk and two sugars coffee then steepled his fingers and leaned back in his chair. "What can I help you with, Marc?"

"Information. And I can give you a head's-up in return."

"Shoot."

Craig drained his small cup and poured another as he talked.

"Sharon Greer is dead."

The effect on Geoff Hamill was surprising. Instead of the nonchalant, 'ah well, if you live by the sword you die by it' expression Craig had expected, Hamill's jaw dropped and he looked like he was genuinely shocked. He stammered out a "H…How?" and its tone told Craig that Hamill had had the same relationship with Sharpy Greer that he had with Tommy

Hill; hatred of their crimes and the suffering that they'd caused, but a reluctant fondness for the old lag.

"Bomb blast."

Hamill leaned forward urgently. "The one in Smithfield?"

It was Craig's turn to look shocked. "Yes. Why? Have you heard something?"

Hamill shook his head so vaguely that Craig wasn't sure if it was in denial, mourning or disbelief. It was the first.

"Just what was on the news." He shook his head again. "I can't believe it. Of all the ways I thought Sharpy would go a bomb was the last." Hamill sat back in his chair. "I thought maybe some poor sod whose business they'd ruined would kill her, or one of her girls who was fed-up with the percentage she took, but not a bomb."

Craig lounged back, echoing Hamill's stance. "So she was definitely running extortion and prostitutes?"

"And drugs and counterfeiting, and probably some other shit that we know nothing about. We never managed to prove any of it; no-one would testify. You can ask Vice and Fraud; they've been banging their heads against the UKF's wall of silence for years."

"UKF; they've changed their name. According to our source anyway."

Hamill looked surprised and Craig was surprised that he hadn't known. Maybe Tommy had been winding Liam up about the new acronym. Craig elaborated.

"It stands for UK Ulster Force. Seems they felt emphasis was needed after the flag decision at the end of 2012."

Hamill shrugged, as if the name change carried all the importance of a twelve-year-old telling their parents that they wanted to be called Moonbeam or Stormbird in future instead of Ann. Hamill's next words said Craig had got it in one.

"Adolescent angst. It's a sort of puberty gangs go through, when they think they're not being paid enough attention. If the UKF have changed their name to UKUF then it's had so little impact on the gang world that it's passed everyone by." His forehead creased in a frown. "Sharpy's death is much more worrying." He glanced at Craig hopefully. "I don't suppose the I.D. could be wrong?"

"Nope. The fingerprint was unambiguous."

Hamill's round eyes widened. "Fingerprint singular?"

"Yep."

"Was that all…?"

Craig nodded. "Everything. We think she was standing near the bomb when it went off."

Craig sipped his cooling drink and watched as Hamill stared into space, picturing Sharpy Greer's ignominious end. When he thought the D.C.I. had had time to process the image Craig spoke again.

"I wanted to discuss the ramifications of her death and pick your brains."

Hamill nodded, pulling himself upright. "First, there'll be an internal battle for leadership. Zac is heir apparent, but he's underage so with both parents gone social services will step in."

"Already happened. There may be an uncle in Glasgow."

Hamill looked glum. "I bet he's as bad as the parents were. The kid has no hope." He rallied briskly. "OK, the in-fighting within UKF or UKUF; whatever it's called. There'll be a few weeks of beatings and maybe even a death of two before that settles down. Then, depending on which scrote takes over we'll have years more of business as usual, or worse."

Craig cut in. "What about challenges from other gangs? Won't someone try to take over from the outside? Or get rid of UKUF entirely and take over all their scams?"

Hamill made a face. "Now why did you have to go and ruin my day? I just settled an eastern European gang war last week near Portadown, the last thing I need is an inter-gang conflict in the loyalist camp."

Craig pushed him. "If there were to be one, who would it involve?"

Hamill's eyes narrowed. "You think a member of UKUF took Sharpy out."

Craig shook his head. "Maybe a few days ago, but not now."

Hamill opened his mouth to ask the question but Craig shook his head. "I can't release any information, sorry. But I'd still like to know who a loyalist gang war would involve."

Hamill rose to turn on the kettle, pondering as it re-boiled. As he placed the fresh cafetière on his desk he gave Craig two names. "The URF; the Ulster Royal Force. And the LDL; the Loyalist Defence League. They're my best bet. They're a shower of shits, all of them, on both sides, but if UKUF don't replace Sharon Greer quickly and show they're solid, one or both of those will try to move in. And by quickly I mean within a couple of days. These boys don't let the grass grow under them when there's money to be made."

Craig filed the names away for the briefing and then ten minutes of banter, mostly about Liam, commenced. Craig left the fifth floor without promising to update Hamill on the source of the explosion. If it ever leaked that the Saudis might be involved in Sharpy's death, UKUF would start targeting every brown-skinned person in Northern Ireland and they'd have a race war on their hands. No-one would thank him for that.

***

12 p.m.

Nicky glanced covertly at the pair of desks belonging to their two new recruits, wondering if anyone else had noticed what she'd done. She'd inched the veneered desks closer, so that now they were sitting directly facing each other instead of at a diagonal as they'd been the day before. She'd seen the way Ken glanced at Carmen even if Carmen hadn't, and she was going to do her level best to grow those glances into something more.

215

Nicky felt Davy watching her and she turned defiantly to him with a look that said 'what?'

"I didn't s…say a word."

"You didn't need to."

She walked sedately to his desk, hobbled by her pencil skirt. Her love affair with the 1950s was waning rapidly; she couldn't do anything even vaguely energetic dressed like this.

"Do you have something to say, David?"

Davy's eyebrows shot up. 'David'? No-one called him David except his granny. He wondered if it was Nicky's way of showing her disapproval or just a fifties throwback like the rest. He decided on the former and counterattacked.

"No, Mrs Morris. I don't. Except…" He leaned forward conspiratorially, dropping his voice to a whisper. "I'm running a book on Ken and Carmen."

Nicky widened her eyes in faux-disgust. "Don't you dare! It's so unromantic."

"Think of it as an incentive. I already have ten quid from Annette and a fiver from Dr Marsham. Do you w…want in on the action?"

Nicky thought for a moment, torn between her belief in the purity of love and her desire for a new pair of shoes. She rushed back to her desk and returned clutching a five pound note. "OK, I bet a fiver that I get them together by the end of this case."

Davy squinted. That might mean waiting until they got a court date and he wasn't waiting for his money for months. "Define end."

"No later than when we leave for the wedding. The 30th."

Davy extended his hand. "Done. Although I have to tell you it isn't looking good for you. The odds are five to one against at the moment."

Neither of them had noticed Craig re-enter the floor, so his words caught them completely unawares.

"Five to one against what?"

216

Nicky gawped at Craig then glanced quickly across at Ken and Carmen chatting about a report. When she was satisfied that they hadn't heard she dropped her voice. "We're betting that they get together by the 30th. I'm positive they will and Davy's running a book against it."

Instead of the frown or sceptical look they expected a boss to display Craig nodded as if he was deep in thought. "Five to one against, you said?"

Davy smiled. "Yeh. There's no hope."

"I disagree." Craig reached into his wallet and handed Davy a twenty pound note.

Nicky smiled adoringly at him and then shot Davy a triumphant look as Craig explained his bet.

"They're both single and he obviously likes her. My money says that she'll weaken and go on a date before the end of next week. I hope she does. He's a nice lad and she's lonely."

Before Nicky could gloat further Craig turned on his heel and walked across to Smith's desk, leaving them wondering if he was going to expose their bet. He wasn't.

"Any word on that bomb signature yet, Ken?"

Smith made a face. "Yes and no, sir. I was just going to tell you. The database search found something but Major James won't release it. He's insisting on speaking to you."

Craig glared at nobody in particular. "He won't release it! Who the hell does he think he is?"

"An army major. Sorry, but this is par for the course. I love the army but they invented obstacle courses and I think he wants you to run one."

Craig's glare changed to a look of fury. "I'll run all over him." He yelled "Nicky" and swung round just in time to see Nicky sit down at her desk. "Get me Major James on the phone. Let's see who's better at this game."

He disappeared into his office and the sound of a phone ringing and his voice rising followed. Five minutes of shouting later the phone was slammed down to be followed by another minute of Craig shouting at no-one in particular. Finally his office door banged open and he re-emerged, his normally calm demeanour distinctly ruffled. Four pairs of eyes turned hastily back to their work.

"Nicky, get Des on the phone and ask him to meet me at the base in thirty minutes. He won't object; he loves getting out of the lab." He turned to Smith. "Captain Smith, I want you to come with me, Your C.O. is being bloody minded and he's about to find out that two can play at that game." With that Craig was heading for the exit shouting instructions, with Smith hurrying in his wake.

"Nicky, brief Des when you call him. You heard everything I just said to the Major. Davy, work up anything that you have on the bomb and the time when it was planted. I'll give you a call from the base."

Davy waved him to slow down.

"Before you leave, chief, I s…spoke to Mrs McGovern. Her husband didn't have a regular day to visit bookshops; he rarely had any free time what w…with work and the kids."

Craig nodded. He'd pretty much ruled Barry McGovern out as a target, but it was good to have it confirmed. At the lift he turned to Ken. "Major James is going to play on your loyalty to him and I'm asking you not to let him. The only thing to focus on is the case."

Smith nodded, knowing he would be torn and glad of Craig's order to focus. But it wasn't loyalty to Stephen James that would divide him; his loyalty was to his regiment and much higher ideals.

***

2.30 p.m.

It took Craig and Smith thirty minutes to reach the base and when they'd passed all the security checks and driven onto the

218

Mess' gravelled forecourt Craig spotted Des Marsham standing by the front door. A uniformed private so tiny he looked as if Des could have eaten him was standing guard. Craig parked the car carelessly and they strode across to join them. Des spoke first.

"Nicky briefed me, Marc. They've got the bomb signature and they're withholding it? Whose bloody case does James think this is?"

Smith interjected. "The army's." Des went to object and Smith raised a hand in peace, his expression saying that there was no love lost between him and his boss. "That's not my view, but I know the army and I know Major James. To put it bluntly, he's a prick. He's got something that you need and he intends to make you wait for it as long as he can."

Des' normally genial expression soured. "What the hell for?"

Smith shrugged. "Because he's a power-mad megalomaniac who has no life outside his job, so he vents his frustration on his men and anyone else he can."

A snigger reminded them of the private's presence. Craig checked to see if Smith was annoyed but he merely slapped the young man on the back. "This is Floody; Private Ian Flood. Don't worry; he's heard me rant about James before."

Floody grinned. "Most Friday nights on your way back from the Mess, sir. And you'll get no argument from anyone on the base."

Craig raked his hair. "Well, megalomaniac Major James may be, but he's not above the law. He has information relevant to a multiple murder and he's withholding it; that's obstruction. If need be I'll lock him up until he gives me what I want and it won't be in some comfortable room in the Officers' Mess."

That put a smile on everyone's face and Smith led the way down the Mess' main corridor with a spring in his step. At the end of the polished conduit he halted in front of a door and waved Craig forward. With a sharp knock and an even sharper "come in" they were on the other side and standing in an office so plush that Craig knew he was in the wrong job.

A deep-pile carpet covered a wide floor set between walls of cherry-brown wood, so highly polished that they could see their reflections. Above them hung a brass chandelier that Craig imagined cast a more forgiving light than the fluorescent strips that gave him a headache at the C.C.U., and at one end of the room sat a desk, so old that Craig wished that it could speak.

The whole effect was regal and the stance of the man behind the desk even more so. Stephen James set down his fountain pen and stared at the men with no welcome in his eyes. Instead he did what he did best. He barked.

"Smith. Explain this intrusion."

Ken Smith stepped forward and snapped into a salute. He was just about to speak when Craig did so instead.

"You know perfectly well why we're here, Major."

Des was startled by the steel in Craig's voice. Not because he hadn't known it was there but because Craig rarely found it necessary to use it. Marc Craig achieved his goals by intelligence, impeccable manners and relentlessness, not the blunt force management style employed by less talented men. But Des could see blunt force emerging now and he was rooted to the spot.

Without being invited Craig pulled up a chair, motioning the others to join him. Des did so gratefully; he stood all day in the lab. Smith took his seat in stunned shock, knowing the action was a breach of etiquette that he would pay dearly for another time. Craig's actions were rude, deliberately so. James was a stickler for good manners and Craig was pushing his buttons. He intended to push every shiny button on James' uniform until he got what he wanted.

Stephen James stared at Craig, fading out the men on either side. Craig thought he looked like a sniper lining up his sights. The analogy was more accurate than he knew; James had served in Iraq during Operation Telic and he hadn't spent his tour locked inside a tank.

"Superintendent Craig. How nice to see you again."

James' drawl was deliberately Debrett's, designed to put the local yokel in his place. Craig could have matched it, if he could've been bothered, drawing on his mother's Italian minor royal ancestry to set the pecking order. If Major James wanted to play a game of 'who's better bred?' then they'd play and James would lose, but Craig had no truck with snobbery.

However Craig's thoughts manifested themselves on his face; Stephen James read them and recoiled. The movement was slight but it was there and it was a big enough crack for Craig to slip through.

"It's not nice at all and you know it, Major. So let's just cut the bullshit, shall we? I want the name on that bomb."

Des couldn't move anything but his eyes and they darted back and forth between the men as if he was watching a Wimbledon match. He'd never seen Craig use swearing as a tactic and he couldn't wait to tell John. Stephen James leaned forward, tightening the hands that he'd locked together until his knuckles were white. His voice had tightened just as much.

"The bomb signature is a matter of national security and the Ministry of Defence has ordered me not to release it."

"That's rubbish and you know it. You're deliberately obstructing my investigation and I could arrest you. If necessary I'll go over your head to the M.O.D. The Chief Constable knows the Chief of the Defence Staff very well."

James bristled at the mention of the C.D.S. and Craig knew how he'd feel if someone threatened to go straight to his C.C. But that was just tough. If Major James wanted to play hard ball then he should have practiced more. James decided to call Craig's bluff.

"Go ahead, I'm quite sure your Chief Constable has better things to do, and I doubt if he'll just take your word for it."

Craig smiled as if he was glad that James had challenged him, then he slipped out his mobile phone, pressing dial. The call was answered quickly. "Donna? Hello, it's Marc Craig here.

Is the Chief Con around?"

No-one got time to hear the reply. James folded like a bad hand of poker and waved Craig to put the phone away. "Very well, Superintendent. I'll give you the information. But if there are any leaks it will be a breach of national security. I was serious about that."

He leaned into his intercom and barked. "Corporal Crean, bring in the bookshop file." As he did so Craig glanced at the others. Smith had one fist clenched and Craig knew he was desperate to punch the air in triumph. As Craig glanced at Des he saw the beginnings of a smile form amidst his facial hair. Des gazed pointedly at Craig's mobile and Craig shot him a warning look; he hadn't phoned the C.C.'s office at all, he'd pressed the number for the squad. If he'd just had a conversation with anyone it was with Nicky. Craig allowed himself a small smile as the corporal entered with a file then left in a flurry of salutes.

Stephen James read the document in silence for a moment, eyes wide as though he'd never seen it before. More bullshit, but Craig let him play it out. He'd stripped the man of enough dignity for one day. Finally James pushed the file across the desk. Craig scanned it quickly then passed it to Des as his mind raced, trying to work out how it fitted with their case. When all three men had read it, Stephen James reclaimed the file.

"Do you understand now, Superintendent?"

"I understand that it's sensitive information, but I also trust my team. We'll need copies of the file."

James shook his head. "Out of the question. Military personnel are named."

"Of the forensic report then. Dr Marsham needs it to continue his work."

James thought for a moment then nodded tersely and stood, making it clear that they could wait elsewhere for their photocopies. As he motioned them out of his office, Craig saw the threat in James' eyes as he glared at Ken Smith. He planned to make Ken's life hell when he returned to the base. Well, not if Craig had anything to do with it.

Ten minutes later the men were standing by their cars, each holding a copy of the report.

"Work with Davy to get what you can from this please, Des. I need it tomorrow at the latest."

Des nodded then gave a small smile and shook his head. "James didn't have a clue."

Craig grinned and Smith glanced at each of their faces in turn.

"About what?"

Des laughed, frustrating the captain even further.

"Oh, come on, guys, let me in on the joke."

Craig slipped out his phone and pulled up his last call, to Docklands.

Smith gawped. "You bluffed him? Oh my God, you bluffed old James! Brilliant! Who did you call?"

"Nicky. She played along. We've done it before."

"I can't wait to tell the others in the Mess. James will never live it down."

Craig shook his head. "Leave him his dignity, Ken. Like you said, this place is his world."

Stephen James had made Smith's life hell in the past so Craig knew that he was asking a lot. Smith went to object then he shrugged reluctantly and Craig was glad that he did. He had plans for Ken Smith and they didn't include him going back to an army base in two weeks' time.

***

The men stopped for a very late lunch and by the time they arrived back at the squad it was time for the briefing. Craig needed more information before they met so he deferred it till the next morning and retreated into his office to think. It was the gap that Nicky had been looking for.

Carmen had been working on something for Liam for hours

and she'd barely lifted her head, not even when Ken had returned, despite him making a lot of noise. Nicky watched as he banged a file on his desk deliberately loudly then glanced hopefully at Carmen for some acknowledgement. She barely blinked, just tutted at the noise and curled even further into her screen. Nicky couldn't stand it any longer so she wandered over to Davy and started to chat, loudly enough so that everyone could overhear.

"The chief looked pleased with himself. I wonder what he found out at the base."

Davy was about to answer when he saw Nicky's warning glance and read his cue to play dumb.

"I don't know. Did you ask him?"

Ken overheard, just as he'd been meant to do. He leapt up and joined them, speaking in an eager tone. "You should have seen Superintendent Craig. He played old James like an expert. It was brilliant. At one point he even called Nicky, pretending that she was the Chief Constable, to scare James."

Nicky nodded. "He's done it before and it always works."

Liam and Annette lifted their heads then wandered across to join the chat. The only one who didn't was Carmen. Nicky tuned out the other's laughter, thinking. What made Carmen tick? She'd been lippy to Liam, but that seemed to have stopped for the moment; now she said nothing at all. Was she scared to speak? Somehow Nicky doubted it. It was more as if the life had gone out of the girl long before today. And as for not noticing that Ken liked her, or not caring more like, Nicky just couldn't work it out. Ken was handsome, in the healthy, outdoorsy Matt Damon mould and even she, happily married as she was, had given him a second glance. Carmen sat facing him all day, how could she not have noticed?

An idea hit her. Maybe Carmen was gay and she'd been trying to match-make her with the wrong sex? She dismissed the idea as soon as it came; her street sense was pretty good and besides, Carmen's body language was more wounded and lonely than disinterested. She'd been hurt badly by someone in the past, she was sure of it. So badly that she'd completely switched off. There couldn't be any other explanation for a pretty girl wearing such dowdy clothes. Nicky's analysis was interrupted by a loud guffaw from Liam.

"That's nothing. Do you remember the time…?"

Just then Craig's office door opened and he strolled over to the group. He joined in the banter for a minute before beckoning Davy to join him in his room.

"I need your help with something on my computer, Davy."

He nodded Davy towards his chair and unlocked his screen.

"W…What are you looking for?"

"I'm trying to access some chat-rooms that specialise in rare books. Not the mainstream ones, the ones with the real gossip. I'm not positive but I think Jules Robinson might have acquired something very rare recently. Maria McGovern remembered her husband saying as much."

Davy's eyes widened. "You think it got everyone killed?"

Craig gave a puzzled smile. "I'm not sure yet, that's what I want to find out."

"Do you w…want me to check for you?"

Craig shook his head. "No. I'll do the first sweep; you're needed on other things. Besides, this is just a shot in the dark. It might turn out to be nothing."

Davy typed for a full minute and then beckoned Craig to look at the screen.

"OK. This is a list of book-collectors' s…sites. At the bottom are the chat-rooms for real fans. McGovern might have heard something in one of those. I can check his computer to see w… what URLs he used."

"Great."

Davy hadn't finished. He clicked onto another window. Craig peered at it, not recognising the URL.

"What's that?"

Davy grinned. "Do you remember the Dark Web? We

accessed it during the Carragher case."

The Dark Web was a shadow internet, with sites accessible by those in the know. Many dealt in dubious activities. One of the sites, Silk Road, had been closed down by the FBI in 2013. Silk Road 2.0 started one month later.

"Yes. Is that a Dark Web chat-room?"

"Yes. Underground trades in books and other stuff."

Craig smiled. "By underground I take it you mean illegal?"

Davy nodded, throwing his hair across his face. "Very illegal. S...Stolen art changing hands, and all sorts of other things." Davy caught Craig's uncertain look. "Don't w...worry, chief. The fraud and cyber-crime boys know all about it. They monitor all these s...sites."

Craig made a face. "Oh, great. So they'll be knocking on my door."

Davy laughed. "I'll tell them you're doing it as part of a case." He stared at Craig curiously. "You really think a rare book could have been the bomb's target?"

Craig shrugged. "It's just a hunch. We have solid leads to follow and I need you focused on those, so I'll do the legwork on this. If I get anywhere you'll be the first to know."

"Second, but w...who's counting."

With that Davy returned to his desk, leaving Craig to explore the murky backstreets of the web.

Chapter Eighteen

Stix and Stones Restaurant, Belfast. 9 p.m.

Craig picked at his beautifully prepared steak and smiled vaguely at Katy. She looked lovely as usual and he knew he wasn't giving her the attention she deserved. Katy smiled back and then shook her head, as if she'd read his mind. It was something she was good at and Craig often wondered whether he was an open book or she had second sight. Her next words took him by surprise.

"Yes, I usually know what you're thinking. And no, it doesn't mean that I'm a witch, although I do come from a long line of strange women." She laughed at her own joke, making him laugh as well. "There's no trick to it. We're taught to read people in medical school, and years as a doctor teaches you how to interpret even the most fleeting facial expressions."

She reached for her glass of wine. "So I know you're preoccupied with your case this evening but I don't mind. You're not neglecting me, Marc. I'm not a child who needs constant attention. You're busy." She grimaced. "Trust me; I'll be just as bad as you when I've a complex case."

Craig nodded, comparing her grown-up approach to life to Camille's; her self-importance and drama had meant she'd needed to be the centre of every room. Even Julia, who'd understood his work, had sulked at his lack of attention; although in her case not out of self-importance but from insecurity that she was somehow never enough. He felt guilty about her for a moment and hoped that she was sitting somewhere with someone that she really liked.

Really liked. Yes, he really liked Katy, but he also knew that it was much, much more, something that he wasn't willing to put a name on just yet. Craig glanced away before she read that thought as well and sipped his wine, savouring the smooth red liquid as it slid down his throat. Then he smiled and attacked his steak with renewed vigour, packing his thoughts about their relationship away for a while longer, until they were lying under a Caribbean sun.

***

Wednesday. 8 a.m.

Craig perched on a desk and grinned at the bleary-eyed group.

"OK, we've a lot to get through, so let's start."

His bright-eyed enthusiasm earned him a jaundiced glance from more than one of his team, who knew exactly what it meant. At around the halfway mark in an investigation, when the rest of them were flagging and ready for a break, Craig always got his second wind. He was like a long distance runner who'd been pacing himself until the final leg of the race to fool his opponents, only to streak past them to the finish line. To those in the slow lane it was tantamount to taunting.

Only Ken perked up at the words. Liam shook his head ruefully; Craig and Smith were both sporty, Smith more so nowadays since Craig rarely managed to escape work to hit the gym. Maybe it gave them a stamina that the rest of the team lacked. Liam stared down glumly at his paunch, wondering where his six-pack was hiding. He used to have muscles like Craig; perhaps he was just getting old. He gazed at the younger yawning team members and shook his head. It wasn't him getting old; they were all wrecked. Craig and Smith were the odd ones. Craig's voice cut through his thoughts, beckoning them all to gather round.

"OK. I'll give a quick update then hand over to Davy for the forensics. Everyone chip in as and when." He took a swig of espresso and started.

"There are some outstanding bits of information that we're expecting today. The poison that killed Fintan Delaney, more details on the owner of the newly I.D.ed body, and hopefully more on Jennifer Weston's whereabouts as well. But first I'll tell you why we went haring off to the base yesterday afternoon." He paused for a moment and then turned to Ken. "Actually, no. Ken can tell you."

Craig nodded Smith on and took another sip of his drink. Liam had often wondered how he managed to drink so much coffee without getting a headache; he'd have had a migraine on half the amount. He'd always put it down to Craig's Italian lineage but today he wondered if coffee was actually the source of Craig's energy and resolved to drink more himself.

His attention was grabbed by Ken looking unfeasibly pleased about something. As Liam watched Ken glanced to see if Carmen was paying attention. She wasn't returning his glances; just scribbling quickly in her notebook. Ken's voice pulled him back to the case.

"We went to the base yesterday afternoon and met with Major James. To cut a long story short, he was reluctant to help and took a bit of persuasion, but eventually he gave us information on the bomb signature."

Annette raised her pencil to interrupt. "Sorry, I'm sure I should remember this, but how do you define a bomb signature again?"

Ken nodded.

"OK. A bomb's signature is its unique identifier, like the way you sign your name is unique to you. It's hard to fake and it basically tells us who made the device. Often the uniqueness comes from habit, the bomber simply doing what they do in the usual way they do it. Sometimes it's vanity; they do something deliberately because they want people to recognise their work. They take pride in it. I mentioned crimping wires and fragmenting the bomb in a specific way the other day, but whatever it is it's often so distinctive that we can I.D. the maker, and fortunately in this case that's what we've found. The signature belongs to an Arab national called Ibrahim Kouri. He's a member of a splinter Islamic radical group called the Militant Islamic Foundation."

The shock that ran through the group was exactly what Craig had expected. Davy and Nicky gawped at each other and Liam's jaw dropped open and hung there, until Annette recovered her composure enough to reach over and tip it shut. Even Carmen set down her pen to listen. Craig nodded Ken on.

"The M.I.F. has been active since 9/11. And despite God knows how many attempts to find out where they're based, so far both we and the Americans have drawn a blank. We knew of possible links with Iraq, Pakistan and Afghanistan but not that they were active here, or anywhere in Europe to be frank."

Liam gathered himself enough to ask a question. "How accurate are these signatures? I mean, don't lots of people make bombs in the same way?"

Smith nodded. "Well… yes and no. They could in theory; although it would be like me trying to copy your signature, there would always be small errors that a good graphologist would spot. Think of our bomb forensic team as expert graphologists. They've seen thousands of these things over the years, what with the Middle East…"

Craig interjected. "And here. You don't need to be tactful, Ken. We all know how many bombs the army defused here during the Troubles.

Smith nodded. "OK. And here. So they know their stuff. It's unlikely that this is a copycat and why would any bomb maker in Belfast want to copy the signature of an Islamic radical anyway? My knowledge of the terrorist groups here is that they usually want people to know when they've planted devices."

Liam conceded. "Aye, you're right. They'd sell T-shirts if they could get away with it. OK, so the bomb was the real deal made by this M.I.P bunch."

"M.I.F. Yes, that's what our lads are saying. But how it fits with the case goodness only knows."

Craig cut in. "OK, that's where we come in. We know the last victim of the bombing was a Saudi national called Ibrahim Kouri."

Smith gawped. "He was your victim? Ibrahim Kouri? When did you find out?"

Craig smiled. "John told us at the briefing on Monday." He saw Smith's quick glance at Carmen and flush of embarrassment and knew that his mind had been on other things during John's report. He brushed past the error and continued.

"OK. A man called Ibrahim Kouri was our fifth victim, but we don't know yet that he was our bomb maker. Tempting as it is to make that link, I don't want any assumptions. Kouri could be a common name in the Middle East."

Annette cut in. "So the man we saw on the CCTV planting the bomb with Delaney was Middle Eastern?"

Craig shook his head. "No. Again don't assume things. The victim of the explosion was Middle Eastern but we have nothing yet to say that he was the bomber. The bomber may not have returned to the shop with Delaney the following day. He could be hallway around the world by now."

Annette wasn't letting it go. "But it would make sense."

Of course it made sense that the man who'd planted the bomb with Delaney had returned to Papyrus with him the following day and died in the explosion. And that Ibrahim Kouri their dead bomb victim and the Kouri the bomb maker were the same man, but until they had things completely sewn up, saying so would make people narrow their focus and Craig wasn't having that. Craig's voice was firm.

"Just as it would make sense that the dead man was someone Middle Eastern from SNI who'd accompanied Sharon Greer to the shop to take a look around their future development site."

Annette was undeterred. "Except that Hilary Stenson is adamant that no-one from SNI is missing. I'm following up on that today, but she was sure."

Craig sipped at his now cold espresso, making a face. The others chatted until he had a fresh coffee in his hand and re-started.

"OK, Annette, did Mrs Stenson have anything else to say?"

Annette flicked open her notebook and read for a second, then she shook her head. "Basically just what we already know. SNI wanted Jules Robinson out of the shop and they were paying UKUF to lean on him. But Stenson denies vehemently that SNI authorised the bombing and she says that it was never a tactic that SNI used. There are obviously Saudi members of the Board but Stenson is certain none of them are missing. I'll keep checking."

Craig nodded. "OK, good. I'm inclined to agree with Annette; I think SNI are a dead end." He had a thought. "Ken, check with John to see if the Ibrahim Kouri's DNA he found matches your bomb maker's, if there's a record of his anywhere. Davy, was there anything more on the cameras outside the shop?"

Davy glanced up from the pages he had on his knee. "Like?"

"Like a car with a rough looking driver. Sharon Greer was head of a paramilitary gang; she didn't go anywhere without a bodyguard."

Davy rifled through his papers and pulled out a page triumphantly, handing it to Craig. "I w…was going to wait till my turn to tell you, but…"

Craig scanned the image and nodded, giving it to Liam to pass around. "What time was that taken?"

"One o'clock on the day of the explosion. It's from the s… street camera outside Castle Court shopping centre. A Ford Granada dropped Sharon Greer off and she w…went inside. The Ford drove off immediately afterwards."

Annette stared at the image, muttering to herself. "She must have walked through the centre, left by the door nearest Smithfield and walked to Papyrus. I wonder why she didn't just get dropped off there?"

Liam sniffed. "Didn't trust her driver? Or maybe she was meeting someone in Castle Court?"

Davy continued. "I've got a later one that shows more, chief. W…When we get to my bit, I'll show you on my s…screen. It's better than s…stills."

"We'll come back to you in a moment, Davy. I want to cover a couple of other things." Craig turned back to Ken. "Any more on the bomb?"

Smith nodded. "Yes. What we thought was a photograph frame attached to the bomb actually was. It held someone's photograph. Our forensics managed to reconstruct it partially, but unfortunately not enough to get a face. I can tell you that it was a woman."

It was Craig's turn to gawp. He'd pictured the frame holding some sort of rebel icon or symbol, but a woman's photograph? "How do you know?"

"Forensics pulled up the lower part of the image. It was a woman's feet in sandals and she was wearing a long skirt. That was all they could get."

Liam cut in. "What sort of sandals?"

Smith glanced quickly at Carmen and then back at Liam, with a faint blush lighting his cheeks. "What would I know about women's sandals?"

Liam gave him a martyred look. "You'd soon learn if you had a wife. The shoes could tell us something, boss. Were they high heeled or flat? If they're flat summer sandals then the photo might have been taken somewhere hot. Maybe on holiday. There might even be something about the shoes' design that could help us…"

Nicky interjected. "Does she have varnished toenails, and if so what colour? That could tell you when the photo was taken.

Popular nail varnish colours change all the time."

Everyone chipped in. "What sort of light was in the photo? It could tell you the time of day." And "If there's something in the background it could help with geography…"

After a minute's discussion Craig waved them down and turned back to Smith. "Go back and ask army forensics the questions please, and Des Marsham. I'm presuming he has a copy of it now?"

Smith nodded.

"What about the watch?"

Smith shook his head. "It was centuries old and made of solid silver; a serious antique. But that's all we know. It was in bits. There were no markings left to see."

"Why use an old, potentially unreliable watch as a timer instead of a digital switch? It has to mean something."

Nicky's husky voice cut across Craig's words. "Is no-one going to ask the most obvious question?"

Annette took the bait. "What?"

"Why the heck attach a photograph of a woman to a bomb in the first place!"

Craig laughed loudly. Nicky was right, and it was something he'd thought about a few days before. Davy answered before anyone else.

"That's easy. Either they loved her or hated her."

Nicky was undeterred. "Yes, smarty-pants, we already know it's a symbol of love. If it was some woman they hated they'd have blown her up, not her photo. But did they love her specifically, or was she just a symbol of something they loved, like country or family, or freedom?"

Davy opened his mouth then closed it again, thinking about what she'd said. Craig smiled. He'd long thought that Nicky would have been an asset as a police officer, but she liked her glamour too much to ever wear a uniform and the force didn't issue shoes with five-inch heels.

"Good, Nicky. We'll follow up on that. I think the use of an antique watch means something as well, but what I've no idea what yet." Craig turned to Liam. "Liam, anything more on Zac Greer before I hand over to Davy?"

Liam shook his head slowly, his mind still on Nicky's words. He had a hunch about something but he was keeping quiet about it until he'd checked it out.

"Nope. He didn't know anything about his Mum's death, I'm sure of that, and he definitely didn't order her hit. He was gutted when he found out she was dead. There's an uncle in Glasgow, Sharpy's brother, but until social services make contact the lad's been taken into care." He turned to Annette and his voice took on a slightly grudging tone. "You were right, cutty. He couldn't stay on his own at fifteen. He just seemed older because of the life he'd led."

Annette nodded. "It's a hard call because he's spent his life around UKUF; they're his family. But he can go back to them in a few months when he reaches sixteen."

"If he wants to. Who knows, a few months in a normal family might show him a better life."

Annette gave a sceptical sniff. "That's always supposing Sharon Greer's brother isn't just as bad as she was."

Craig nodded. What were the odds of that?

Liam continued. "With the whole Greer clan out of the way that means there'll be a battle for the crown, so watch this space."

Craig nodded. "I spoke to Geoff Hamill in Gang Crime, so they've been warned that it's coming."

Liam had finished so Craig turned back to Davy. He was scribbling a line of programme on the back of a page. Eventually he noticed the silence and looked up.

"S...Sorry, chief, I was writing a programme for shoe identification, but it can w...wait. OK..." Davy loped over to his desk and took a seat, beckoning them all to follow. A moment later his horseshoe of screens filled with images of Gresham Street.

"Right. This is last Thursday, the afternoon of the bomb." He pointed to his left-hand screen. "This one s…shows the street outside Papyrus and the right-hand one is the shop's interior. W…Watch the street film from one-forty-five."

They watched as a dark Mercedes pulled up on Gresham Street. It held three figures. The rear passenger door opened and a woman stepped out. She leaned back in and said something to a figure on the back seat, then crossed the street to Papyrus and entered the shop.

"That was S…Sharon Greer. The next five minutes are boring, so I'll fast-forward."

At one-fifty Davy slowed the tape again, just as a man walked down the pavement opposite the Mercedes and entered the shop. "You can't see his face from this angle, but take my word for it, that's Barry McGovern. I've had a good look at the enlarged s…stills. Now, w…watch the car driver."

Sure enough, as soon as McGovern entered the shop the driver stepped out and scanned the street, then he relaxed slightly and lit a cigarette. He looked just like a chauffeur waiting for his passenger, except that his steroid-bulked shape and the bulge in his jacket said he hadn't attended a nice training school.

"No-one entered the shop after that."

Liam cut in. "So that means Delaney, Robinson and Kouri were already inside before one-forty-five."

"Yes, w…which made me think; how could anyone have known that S…Sharon Greer was coming to the shop that day, or Barry McGovern? I haven't found connections to either of them on Delaney's laptop or phone."

Craig shook his head. "Delaney didn't know, because Greer and McGovern weren't the targets."

Annette nodded. "I checked with McGovern's wife. He just dropped into Papyrus the odd time. He didn't go regularly on a Thursday afternoon."

Craig sighed. A completely innocent victim. Liam

interrupted his thoughts.

"Which just leaves the shop itself, Jules Robinson or unlucky Mr Kouri as possible targets, boss. That's if Kouri wasn't the second bomber."

"Or something inside the shop was the target, Liam. We've stayed away from that possibility until now, but I'm not so sure." Craig ignored Liam's questioning look and waved Davy on.

"OK, now w...watch the right-hand screen. It shows the CCTV views from inside the s...shop."

The screen was split into two CCTV views, covering the front and back of the shop. The tall book shelves hid the centre entirely.

"Where were the interior cameras positioned, Davy?"

"There w...were only two, above the doors."

"So these are our only views?"

Davy nodded and Craig motioned him to carry on. The film fast-forwarded from one-forty and at one-forty-six Sharpy Greer entered the shop. She browsed for a moment and then headed towards the back, where they could just make-out Jules Robinson stacking shelves. They spoke for a while until at one-fifty-four; Robinson stormed angrily towards the front of the shop. Had they been discussing his protection payments or had Sharpy been telling Robinson he had to vacate the shop so that SNI could have the land?

They watched as Barry McGovern entered the shop just after one-fifty and browsed the shelves towards the front, his face lighting up as he flicked through the books. Just a book-lover, there for a relaxing afternoon. McGovern asked Jules Robinson something about a book and they started to chat pleasantly. Fintan Delaney was standing near the front door, ostensibly reading a book and then playing with his phone. Davy pressed pause and re-started the street screen. As the time reached one-fifty-eight they saw what he'd wanted to show them. The shop's 'open' sign was suddenly turned to 'closed' and the front door blind came down.

Craig exclaimed loudly. "Damn. Damn. Damn."

All eyes turned to him and Liam nodded slowly, understanding what Craig was swearing about.

"That's why Delaney stood by the door! To make sure no-one else came in. He knew the bomb was about to explode and he was trying to limit the number of deaths."

Annette shook her head. "But why not close the door earlier and save more lives, if we're sure that it wasn't Sharpy or McGovern the bomb was aimed at?"

Craig shook his head. "Any earlier and someone inside might have got suspicious and called the police. Delaney had to wait until the last minute."

Davy stared at Craig, waiting for permission to continue. Craig nodded him on.

"OK. W…Watch what the Mercedes driver does at two o'clock."

From one-fifty-eight, when Papyrus' front door closed, Davy played the street screen in slow time. The Mercedes' chauffeur lit a fresh cigarette and scanned Gresham Street, bored. At two p.m. precisely he jerked his head towards the shop and reached inside his jacket, withdrawing a gun. He ran towards the shop then stopped halfway as if he'd thought better of it or been called back, then he jumped into the car and screeched off in the direction of town.

"He heard the explosion and you saw his reaction. He went towards the shop to check on S…Sharon Greer, but w… whoever was in the Mercedes wanted out of there fast."

Davy tapped the screen again and the team saw the greys of the shop's exterior façade disappear in a ball of white at two p.m. It enveloped the street, depositing shards of glass and wood on the road and opposite pavement. They grew more visible as the white glow gradually disappeared.

Annette was the first to speak. "Who was in the car?"

"What?"

"Who was in the car Sharon Greer arrived in? Her men dropped her off at Castle Court nearly an hour earlier, so who owned the Mercedes?"

Craig paused; surprised by the question and by the fact that he hadn't considered it. Liam chanced an answer.

"SNI? If Sharpy was meeting them at Castle Court they might have driven her round to the shop. They could afford a decent car and chauffeur."

Annette nodded. "Maybe. That means it must have been someone from SNI in the back seat."

Craig nodded. "Good pick-up, Annette. Run the plates and confirm it, please." He motioned Davy to continue playing the film from inside the shop.

Davy cast a nervous look around the group, as if warning them what was to come. Craig took the hint.

"We're about to see the interior of the shop at the moment of explosion. Anyone who doesn't wish to see this, it's fine to go back to work."

Nicky took Craig up on his offer but everyone else stayed put. Liam's face set in a grim mask and Craig knew he was thinking of the friends he'd lost in bomb blasts, and that Ken must be thinking the same about Iraq. Davy tapped on the screen and ran the shop tape again from one-fifty-five. They watched as Jules Robinson chatted happily to Barry McGovern, about a book from the shop's wall shelves.

"That w…was the ancient history section." Davy paused the tape again and tapped up the shop's floor plan on his centre screen. "History was along the side w…wall, politics on the high bookshelf nearest the front, literature and religion towards the back."

Liam interjected. "The place sounds like a barrel of laughs; I'm surprised they sold anything."

At one-fifty-five Fintan Delaney set down the book he was perusing and made a show of playing with his phone. Liam waved Davy to stop the tape and turned to Smith.

"Could the bomb have been detonated by a phone?"

Smith shook his head. "Could have been but wasn't. The watch was the timer. I think Delaney was just playing with his phone to look busy."

Craig nodded. "Were there any outgoing calls or texts from Delaney's phone during the time of this tape?"

Davy shook his head. "None. I think Captain Smith is right. The phone was just a displacement activity."

He pressed start again and they watched as at one-fifty-eight, Fintan Delaney locked the shop's front door, set the sign to 'closed' and then slowly drew down the blind. The tape ran forward slowly as McGovern and Robinson chatted happily, oblivious to what was about to occur. Delaney moved nervously from foot to foot and then at two o'clock precisely the screen whited-out. Craig signalled to freeze the tape. He was frowning, but not for the same reason the rest of them were. He signalled Davy to reverse the tape.

"Oh, sir, do we really have to see it again?"

"I'm sorry Annette, but yes. I saw something. Davy, take it back to one-fifty-eight please." Craig leaned in, peering at the screen intently as it ran from Delaney shutting the front door to the moment of the blast. He nodded emphatically.

"Yes! Davy, print me out an enlarged still of Delaney at one-fifty-nine."

One minute later Craig was pointing at the page and the others were wondering what they were supposed to see. Smith saw it first. "My God! He's bowing. Delaney bowed to his right-hand-side just before the blast!"

"Yes. And my money says he was bowing towards the South-East. Davy, check which direction that side of the shop faces."

Liam rubbed his chin, half-seeing but not convinced. "Maybe he was just bowing to the people he knew he was about to kill."

Craig raised his eyebrow sceptically. "Except that they were at the back or left side of the shop from where he stood. No-one was on his right-hand-side."

Davy stared at his screen and gasped. "It's South-East! You were right."

Craig nodded. "He was bowing towards Mecca." He wasn't finished. "Delaney said something, Davy, just before he bowed, he definitely said something. I want a lip-reading expert to tell us what it was."

Smith whispered the words that he'd heard every day in Iraq. "Allah Hu Akbar." He shook his head sadly and then repeated them aloud. "It was Allah Hu Akbar. God is great."

If they were right then Fintan Delaney had left the God of his youth and his parents far behind and died for a completely different way of life.

***

1.30 p.m.

Determination was one of Nicky's virtues, or faults if you were her son Jonny and the topic was his homework. Nicky's determination to see her son graduate from university someday, preferably as a doctor or nuclear physicist, was a driving force in his life, manifesting itself in evenings spent doing homework and extra tutoring some weekends. Jonny's determination to kick a ball around the garden with his mates was just as strong. It resulted in frequent stand-offs which Nicky inevitably won, because she was his mother and he loved her. But also because Nicky could be Machiavellian when she had to be and she considered no tactic too low when she wanted something, including tears.

Nicky's current problem was that being in an office instead of at home, and her target being a stubborn thirty-something woman instead of a twelve-year-old boy who loved her, things weren't likely to go so smoothly. Her cajoling, orders and tears were unlikely to have an effect on Carmen McGregor.

As Nicky sat plotting how to get Carmen together with the obviously adoring Ken, Liam caught her eye. He raised an eyebrow slowly to say that he knew exactly what she was up to, then lifted a file as if it contained something of portent and loped noisily across to her desk. He perched on its edge and gave her a sceptical look. After a full minute of ignoring him Nicky made a fatal mistake; she glanced up. It was only a microsecond's glance, barely visible to the naked eye, but it was enough to tell Liam two things; A, he'd won the stalemate and B, she looked as sneaky as hell. He leaned in and spoke in his quietest voice, which meant that only Davy and Annette could overhear.

"What are you up to?"

Nicky sniffed indignantly. "I don't know what you mean!"

"Don't kid a kidder. You're trying to match-make McGregor and Smith, poor sod. What did he ever do to you?"

"Carmen's nice. She's just lonely."

Liam snorted. "Nice? And I suppose you think Hitler was just misunderstood!"

Davy strolled over to join them. "I'm running a book on them getting together. Do you fancy a bet, Liam?"

Liam gave a look of faux-shock, like a parent pretending to surprised when his child suggested that he might ever have got drunk.

"Tut, tut, gambling in the work-place. What would the boss say?"

"He put down twenty quid."

Nicky glanced over at the contenders. They seemed absorbed in their work. Or rather Carmen seemed absorbed in her work; Ken just seemed absorbed in her.

"Look at that; he really likes her."

Liam gawped at the pair. Nicky was right. "I need to get that lad drunk and find him a woman."

"Liam!"

Liam ducked backwards, expecting a frontal assault from

242

Nicky. As a smack hit him on the back of the head he realised too late that his name had been called by Annette. She'd joined the group without him noticing.

"Ow! I was only saying."

Liam's bellowed 'Ow' wouldn't have gone unnoticed anywhere and Smith glanced over, to be greeted by a series of innocent smiles. He smiled in return and turned to gaze dreamily at Carmen again.

Nicky sighed romantically. "You see. He really likes her. Now I just have to work out how to convince Carmen. Ideas anyone?"

She was answered by shrugs, a muttered "not a baldy clue" and a dispersing crowd. She realised that Liam hadn't gone and gazed hopefully at him, waiting for pearls of wisdom to fall. All she got was.

"Can I have a photocopy of that woman's feet?"

"What?"

"The picture in the frame at the explosion."

"I don't have it. Ask Ken."

Liam did as he was told and Smith logged into the army forensic database and printed out what they had, handing it to Liam absentmindedly. Liam shook his head. The lad had it bad; maybe he should consider a bet. Still, he should be grateful. At least it had stopped any cracks about him having a foot fetish. His thoughts were interrupted by Craig appearing from his office. He had a satisfied look on his face.

"I'm heading out. John's I.D.ed the poison. Before I go, does anyone have an update?"

Annette piped up and Nicky noticed for the first time that day that she'd done something different with her hair. She wasn't sure what it was but it looked good.

"I've checked every member of the SNI Board and they're all alive. I'm interviewing the Chair and Chief Executive at High Street later and checking other SNI employees based here. If SNI admit to paying UKUF to harass Jules Robinson to sell, can I charge them?"

Craig thought for a moment then nodded. "If they cough to it; but link in with the serious and organised crime lads. The next step will be to charge UKUF. Make sure Liam's with you on that trip."

Liam cut in. "Who at UKUF, boss? The Greers Senior are both dead."

"Find out who the biggest players are now that they've gone, and liaise with Aidan Hughes in Vice. They can get them on running the girls and drugs at least. Share whatever we have with them. The more they have the more likely they can get UKUF's main players off the street before the fight for the crown begins."

Craig scanned the room and his eye fell on Davy. He strode over to his desk. "Anything more on anything yet?"

Davy nodded. "There's a pattern in Delaney's phone calls. From March until last week he phoned s...someone in Pakistan every few days."

"That's where he went on his charity trip. Where in Pakistan?"

Davy shook his head. "I'm w...working on that. Whoever he called was using a s...satellite phone and their locations are tricky to pinpoint."

"Anything in his e-mails to shed light?"

"I'm s...sifting through them now. So far it's mostly s... student stuff. Asking for lecture notes, arranging tutorials etc. I searched for other accounts and he had a C-mail address. I'm waiting for the internet provider to unlock it."

Craig nodded. "OK, keep doing what you're doing and we'll brief at four. Until then I'll be at Botanic Gardens and then the lab."

Liam shot him a questioning look. Botanic Gardens? Before he could vocalise the question Craig had gone. Liam glanced at the photocopy in his hand and decided to play his hunch.

"I'll be on the mobile if anyone wants me. I'm off to St

Mary's to see a woman about a shoe."

***

Paris. 2.30 p.m. local time

Alain Berger gazed through the window of his pension room, his only view the business skyline of La Défense and the dusty streets below. Once the deal was done he would take a suite at the Hôtel de Crillon and have champagne and women all day long. Then he would retire to the Côte d'Azur. He glanced impatiently at the phone. That was if that bastard Augustin ever got in touch.

Another hour of frustration didn't make Berger feel any better so at three-thirty he lifted his attaché case and headed down stairs to get some sun on his sallow skin. As he reached the bottom step he heard the phone in his bedroom ring. He scrambled frantically back up two flights, reaching the receiver just as it stopped.

"Merde!"

His flow of expletives was broken by the buzz of the mobile in his pocket. He grabbed at it, almost dropping it in his haste.

"Yes?"

"Where were you? I told you to stay close by."

"I was on the stairs. Well?"

It was on the tip of Claude Augustin's tongue to tease him by saying "patience", but he didn't like Berger enough for that. Instead he said "Tomorrow morning, nine o'clock. At the bank. I will come too."

The phone clicked off and Berger was left staring at the closed-in skyline, for what he fervently hoped was the final day.

***

Craig pushed his way through the doors of John's outer office and called out "John? Are you here?" to no reply. He was on the verge of heading for the dissection room when a slight movement behind John's glass door caught his eye. For some reason it made Craig's hackles rise.

Call it instinct but he knew instantly that it wasn't just John pottering around his office and not hearing his yell; something or someone was preventing him. Craig's mind flew back to the near fatal attack on his friend three months earlier and he reached instinctively for his Glock, crossing to the office door without making a sound.

He pressed himself back against the wall and reached for the handle, turning it quietly. In one smooth movement he was inside with his Glock drawn and ready to shoot. "Armed police."

In a split second it took him to say the words Craig registered three men, one of them his friend. The other two were dressed too fashionably for pathologists and had guns drawn to match his own. After a moment's face-off the shorter of the men smiled and set down his gun, producing his I.D. The acronym emblazoned on it was one that Craig had seen in London many times, but he'd never encountered on the streets of Belfast before. What the hell was the CIA doing in Northern Ireland?

John spoke first. He smiled nervously and then introduced Craig as if they were at a cocktail party.

"Superintendent Marc Craig, these are Agents Ross and Mulhearn of the CIA. They'd like a chat."

Craig kept his gun cocked for a moment longer, then he nodded and put it back in its rarely disturbed resting place, thankful that Liam hadn't been with him. Liam was quicker on the draw than anyone he knew; God knows what might have happened. As the second agent re-holstered his gun Craig extended his hand.

"Marc Craig."

The shorter man shook hands first. "Owen Ross and this is

246

Mike Mulhearn." Mulhearn nodded a very large head that perched on a matching neck.

John urged them to sit and poured fresh coffees. "The agents arrived ten minutes ago."

Craig stared questioningly at them. "From where? Since when has the CIA had a presence in Northern Ireland?"

Ross answered. "Since we got wind you were researching the DNA of a terrorist combatant."

John nodded in confirmation. Their bomb victim was the known terrorist, Ibrahim Kouri.

Craig decided that caution was the order of the day. He had nothing against the CIA but this was Belfast business. "We've had terrorists here for years. What's so exciting about this one?"

As Ross answered again Craig realised that the bulky Mulhearn was the muscle and Ross was the brains; a neat allocation of duties.

"This isn't a republican terrorist; it's a terrorist who killed Americans in the Middle East. A member of the Militant Islamic Army."

He paused as if he'd asked a question but Craig said nothing.

Ross continued. "What's your interest in Ibrahim Kouri?"

Craig avoided the question by turning to John. "What do you have on the poison?" He knew he was being rude but something about Ross' high-handedness was pissing him off.

The agent went to object but Craig stilled him with a glare. "You might think that your countrymen's lives are more important than ours, but we have families here who would disagree." He nodded John on. "The poison please, John."

"I'll show you later."

Craig nodded. John wasn't giving the CIA anything that they didn't already have.

Ross persisted. "What's your interest in Kouri?"

Craig went on the attack. "What the hell was he doing in Belfast planting a bomb? Do you know?"

Ross snapped back. "We have no idea! All we were told was

there'd been a hit on the database and to get here fast. We're based in London."

Craig read the truth in the man's eyes and nodded, winding his neck in. "OK. So we have an Islamic radical working with a university student to blow up a bookshop in Belfast."

Ross' eyes narrowed. "A student? Who is he? We need to speak to him."

"You'll need a séance. He's dead."

"In the explosion?"

"No."

Craig gave John a look that said not to volunteer anything and stood up. "It's kind of you to visit, gentlemen, and I hope you enjoy the local sights, but this is our investigation so we'll take it from here."

Ross sprang to his feet and barely reached Craig's chin. If he wanted to have a pissing contest he was going to lose.

"We have instructions to stay and assist you."

Craig shook his head. "We don't need your assistance; this is local business. I can't stop you staying in Northern Ireland, unless you obstruct me, in which case you'll be on a plane faster than you can blink. Enjoy your visit but stay out of my way. If there's anything we need your help with then I'll give you a call."

Craig opened the office door pointedly. "Goodbye Agent Ross, Agent Mulhearn."

After a moment's glaring, Ross nodded to his companion and they exited the lab. Once Craig was certain they'd gone he gave a loud laugh.

"You don't see that every day."

John looked flustered. "No, you do not. I thought they were going to haul me off to Guantanamo."

"You've seen too many episodes of '24'." Craig nodded at the percolator. "Is there any chance of coffee?" He kept talking as John put a fresh batch on. "You know they're going nowhere, don't you? They'll be tailing me from now until the end of this case."

John grinned gleefully. "It's just like that time in NCIS when…"

They indulged in five minutes of banter and then Craig pulled them back to the case, updating John on what they'd seen on the CCTV. John nodded thoughtfully.

"That fits with Sharon Greer, Jules Robinson and Barry McGovern being innocent victims and Delaney and Kouri planting the bomb the night before. But if the bomb was on a timer why did Delaney and Kouri bother returning the next day to die? I know there are Islamic suicide bombers, but isn't it usually only done that way if it's necessary to get the bomb in the right place? Surely they'd already achieved that."

Craig shook his head thoughtfully. "Unless they believed the reason they were bombing the shop made it an honour to die."

John removed his glasses and rubbed them on his sleeve. "What reason? To destroy a small book shop in a business area of Bel…" He stopped abruptly, suddenly following Craig's train of thought. "You think there was something in the shop offensive to Islam? What?"

Craig raised his hands in semi-denial. "It's only a hunch at the moment."

John's eyes widened. "A book! You think one of the books in the shop was the target!"

Craig shook his head. "Yes and no. The book part is right, but I think they also wanted Jules Robinson and the shop destroyed. If Robinson had bought a book that was blasphemous to Islam then they might have issued a Fatwā on him, even if the book was very old. I've just been up at Botanic Gardens at the Museum. I had an interesting discussion with the Curator of Antiquities on the subject."

John slumped back in his chair. "This was all about Robinson and a book. The other victims were just collateral damage."

"I think so, but it's still speculation at the moment. I've been

249

scanning the legitimate book collectors' forums online but there's nothing concrete. Davy's hooked me into the Dark Web, so I'm trying that now."

"The illegal book trade? Is there one?"

Craig nodded. "You'd be surprised. Some of these collectors are fanatics; I wouldn't put it past them to kill for what they wanted. There's a big trade in stealing to order." Craig set his cup down. "Like I said, it's all just speculation. It might be nothing to do with a book. For all we know someone who was killed could have said something anti-Islamic in public, or harmed a Muslim in some way. God knows UKUF have been indiscriminate in who they've robbed and assaulted amongst the immigrant populations here."

John shook his head, puzzled. "So why kill Delaney afterwards? If he was a mujahedeen, then surely it was a good thing that he didn't die in the bomb. He could have lived to fight again."

Craig shrugged. "Perhaps they thought he might talk and give something away."

John nodded then reached into his desk drawer and withdrew a blue headered toxicology report.

"Delaney's?"

"Yes. I was puzzled by the choice of poison at first but now it's starting to make sense." He turned the report towards Craig. He read for a moment and then whistled.

"My God these guys are inventive. Saxitoxin. That's a new one on me."

"It's a neurotoxin and one of the most potent natural poisons known. Some shellfish like butter clams can store it for up to two years." John nodded at the door. "In fact the CIA made an assassination method from it during the Cold War. Look up Gary Powers and the U-2 spy plane."

"So Jennifer Weston killed Delaney by injecting this into his I.V.?"

John nodded. "Des found traces on the tubing. It's normally

given orally so injecting even a tiny dose would have caused instant death by respiratory failure. She killed him then recorded his seven a.m. observations as normal to play for·time, in case someone checked him before the nine o'clock ones. Delaney was dead before she left the room. If Weston wanted to keep him quiet she has to be part of the Islamic movement as well." John shook his head. "Who'd have thought it; here in Belfast."

"It's in the mainland so why not here as well? Just because we have home-grown terrorists doesn't mean we can't get tourists too. Speaking of tourists, did our American friends ask you anything else?"

John smiled. "They asked me everything, but I didn't answer. The Hippocratic oath teaches you to keep your mouth shut."

Craig rose to leave. "Can you come to the briefing?"

John stood up with an eager smile. "Wouldn't miss it. I've got a taste for freedom after Des' jaunt to the base."

Craig turned to leave but he was halted by John's solemn next words.

"Good luck, Marc."

"Why so sad?"

"Because you're entering murky waters and if you get yourself killed, I'll murder you. I need my best man in two weeks."

***

St Mary's.

Liam checked his watch; three o'clock. If Sister McHenry didn't appear soon he'd have to get back to the ranch. He repositioned himself on the hard ward chair and watched the staff and patients walking to and fro. His eyes fell on a student nurse. She looked like a school-kid and he tried to picture Annette at that age in training. It was young to have

251

responsibility, but he'd had it then too. Neither of them compared to his great-grandfather fighting in the Somme at sixteen. His daydream was interrupted by the ward clerk pointing towards the sister's room.

"She's just gone in. Knock on the door."

Liam hesitated. Not at the idea of door knocking, God knows he'd knocked down more than one of them in his time. No, his hesitation was at what he was about to ask. It sounded stupid, even to him. It was more than a long shot, it was way out in orbit, but if you don't ask you don't get. He would risk looking stupid for a moment.

He knocked firmly on the small white door. A soft "come in" followed and Liam contrasted the sister's dulcet tones with the virago they'd met on a previous case; Sister Laurie Johns. He wondered whether they'd known each other but thought it was better not to ask; Johns had met a very sticky end.

Liam opened the door and entered, smiling at the pleasant-looking woman. He smiled even more at her blue uniform. It reminded him of parties in the nurse's home and his extremely misspent youth.

"Sister McHenry, I'm D.C.I. Cullen; part of the investigation into Mr Delaney's death."

She nodded him to sit and gestured towards a kettle. "Tea, Chief Inspector?"

"I never say no to a brew."

They laughed together for a moment then Mary McHenry returned to the reason Liam had come. "It was a terrible business, and to think that Jenny Weston might have been involved." She shuddered. "She was a lovely girl and a really good nurse. It's so sad."

Liam took the proffered cup and perused the luxurious chocolate biscuits on the tray, limiting himself to one for the sake of good manners. "That's what I've come to speak to you about, Sister. How well did you know Jennifer Weston?"

McHenry's expression saddened. "Obviously not as well as I

thought. She had a degree before she entered nursing and when I met her in 2013 she wasn't long qualified. She was an instinctive nurse, which is very rare. Most people can learn how to care for people, but few have a truly caring nature. Jenny did. She was passionate about her patients."

If Craig was right her passion had extended to other things as well.

"You told the superintendent that Jenny had gone abroad and that you hadn't known she was back until you saw her on the tape?"

"Yes. We use a nursing agency and we never know who they're going to send us, just their level of qualification. I didn't even know she was back in Ireland." Liam eyed up a second biscuit and the sister smiled. "Take another, Mr Cullen. They'll only go stale. I rarely eat chocolate."

Liam took the biscuit gratefully and noticed how slim she was, and how attractive. He realised that he was enjoying their chat just a little too much and attempted a more official approach.

"Do you have any idea where Nurse Weston travelled to abroad?"

"I didn't, but after Mr Delaney's death I asked around. Jennifer went to work with the poor in Pakistan." She shook her head sadly. "She seemed like such a nice girl."

Pakistan. It was the third time that week he'd heard the word. Fintan Delaney had taken a trip there and he phoned there once a week; what were the odds that Weston had been in the same place? Liam reached into his pocket, withdrawing the piece of paper that Ken had printed off for him. He went to unfold it and then hesitated. He might have avoided anyone in the office thinking he had a foot fetish but for some reason it bothered him that the sister might think he was weird. He decided to lead into the conversation slowly.

"Sister."

"Mary."

Liam smiled and preened himself; she liked him as well. "Mary. Is there anything that you can remember about Jennifer Weston physically? Anything that stood out in any way?"

McHenry wrinkled her brow in thought. "Well...she was a pretty girl, but then they all are at that age." She laughed and Liam smiled; not only at that age.

"She was forever dying her hair different colours. They all suited her but I had to draw a line at blue. Some of the patients complained." She gave Liam a sad look. "A wasted life."

He urged her on, trying desperately not to lead her.

"I remember that she always painted her fingernails jet-black. It looked like she had gangrene. I know it was the fashion but it made her hands look dirty, so I asked her to stop wearing it on the ward."

Liam leaned forward, trying not to look too eager. "Did she ever paint them other colours?"

The sister thought for a moment and then shook her head. "No. It was some expensive varnish that she'd bought and she was determined to use the whole bottle." She laughed. "She painted her toenails as well, but that didn't matter because the patients never saw those."

"Was there anything else you remember about her appearance? Think hard. Clothes, shoes, bags?"

"Only that she never wore high heels. She said that she couldn't walk in them." She halted and gave Liam a quizzical look. "I don't mean to be rude, but why is this relevant, Mr Cullen? You've got Jenny on CCTV. You already know that she killed poor Mr Delaney."

It was a valid question and Liam decided that it was time to unfold the page. He smoothed out the print and set it on the desk. The sister peered at it and then at him.

"It's a pair of women's feet in sandals."

"Yes, it is. But look more closely." Liam pointed at the woman's toes. "Is that the shade of nail-varnish that Jenny Weston wore?"

"Well, yes. Yes, she wore that shade. Black." She peered more closely. "And she had a pair of jewelled sandals just like that! I saw her wear them on a staff night out. But what…"

Liam lifted the page and slipped it back inside his pocket then he smiled and gestured at the tea-pot. "It's probably nothing. I just wanted to ask. Now, is there any more of that delicious tea?"

***

Pakistan was a beautiful country. More than that; it was stunning, in a way that few others were. The landscape didn't need man-made icons to grab attention; nature's own were striking enough. Jenny Weston gazed around her. Thirty-metre high sand dunes tinted lemon-red and shades of ochre stretched for miles on either side of the camp. Set in the middle, like pure yellow stone, lay the hard desert floor; smooth and unmarked as if it alone had been there since time began. Polished by winds and bleached by the sun; with a resolve that said it would remain long after they had all gone.

It wouldn't be long now until she was gone and Jenny knew it. Just as Fintan had been dispensable so they all were now. All destined to die in the service of a higher cause; warriors; mujahedeen. At least it was their choice to die, unlike the thousands slaughtered by foreign drones. She was prepared for whatever came next. She'd said goodbye to her family long before and what personal love she felt now was in snatched moments with Fareed, a man who secretly thought she was a western whore.

Fintan had never thought of her like that. As she remembered the eager young man she'd met two years earlier and how she'd lured him to certain death, a tear rolled down Jenny Weston's cheek. She dashed it away. What did one death matter or one hundred if it was in the name of the cause? If she wasn't next she would be the one after. She was at peace with it.

Where and when she died was unimportant, what mattered was how and what it achieved. There was only one thing worth achieving now, and tomorrow it would lead her to France.

***

4 p.m.

Thirty seconds of rearranging chairs and clattering cups occurred, until finally there was peace and Craig made a start.

"OK. I'm going to update you on an encounter that John and I had this afternoon with our friends from across the Atlantic. Two CIA agents turned up at John's lab when the DNA from Ibrahim Kouri got a hit." He turned to see John squeezing the cream from a bourbon biscuit and licking the edges, just as he'd done when they were at school. "John?"

John set down his biscuit hastily and began to speak. "As you know we got a hit on our Saudi national. Well, earlier today two CIA agents turned up at my lab; Agents Ross and Mulhearn, over from their office in London."

Liam gawped. "They flew over just for this? Have they never heard of a phone?"

Annette joined in. "Or video conferencing?" She shook her head. "Talk about overkill."

Only Davy was excited by the mention of the CIA. John spotted his audience and continued eagerly. "They had the badges and guns, like you see on TV, and you should have seen their suits. Talk about sharp." He gestured towards Craig. "There was almost a gunfight. They all had their revolvers out."

Craig smiled, not at the guns being drawn but at John's schoolboy excitement. They wouldn't hear the end of this for weeks. Davy was interested in what the DNA had shown.

"What was so special about the Saudi, Dr Winter?"

"What?" John looked puzzled for a moment and then remembered why he was there. "Oh, yes, yes, of course. Well

256

apparently our Saudi national, Ibrahim Kouri, was Ken's bomber. The DNA matched. He'd been on the American's list of Middle Eastern combatants for years, but they'd lost his trail."

"Islamic radical then, you were right, boss."

Annette was puzzled. She'd just found that an SNI employee was missing. "Do you have a physical description of Kouri, Dr Winter?"

"Not yet, Annette. Why?"

"Because one of SNI's senior employees has gone missing." Annette produced a photograph from the papers on her lap. "Mohammed GhamdiAl. Aged thirty-five, six feet and one hundred and seventy pounds. He's a director, functioning just below Board level." She glanced at Craig. "What are the chances this is the same man, sir?"

"Kouri posed as an SNI employee for cover?"

Annette shrugged. "It would have got him a visa into the country."

Craig raked his hair. "SNI might know nothing about it, or they do and GhamdiAl not being at Board level could have given the company deniability. It's unlikely but the whole purchase of the bookshop could have been set up to get nearer the target, whatever it was. Davy, check GhamdiAl out, please, especially his DNA if you can find it. Annette, go back to Hilary Stenson and find out whose idea it was for SNI to invest in Northern Ireland, and in Smithfield in particular. Do it face-to-face, I don't want the CIA hacking into our systems."

"I've confirmed the Mercedes belonged to SNI as well."

Craig nodded at her then scanned the row of faces. "What I said about to Annette about the CIA hacking goes for everyone. Keep of the internet as much as possible for the next few days, and Davy, tighten everyone's firewalls please. The CIA will want anything they can get on the explosion and their equipment is advanced. It's back to old-fashioned policing for a while I'm afraid. Face-to-face interviews rather than phone calls,

257

preferably not taped unless you think it will be necessary in court, and no-one except Davy is allowed on the Net." He turned to Nicky. "Issue everyone with new pre-paid phones please, Nick."

Smith interrupted. "I might need to access the army database."

Craig shook his head. "Then go to headquarters. I know it will be time consuming but better that than an information breach." He sighed heavily. "And you'd better tell Major James that we may be under surveillance; he'll need to notify GCHQ."

Smith groaned. "I feel another 'you should never work with civvies' lecture coming on."

Craig gave a tight smile and turned back to John. "Before I forget, John, make sure the lab's firewalls are reinforced and ask Des to do as I've just said on anything to do with this case. I'll give the CIA what we have when I'm ready and not before."

Liam grinned and Craig felt a joke coming. "You'd better be a good boy for the next few days, boss."

"OK, I'll ask, even though I know I'll regret it. Why?"

"Because they'll be tailing you and listening to everything you say and do. I'd treat them to a chat with your Mum, just for a laugh."

Craig nodded, knowing that Liam was right. His apartment was probably already bugged. He'd be staying at Katy's for a few days, although there was no guarantee that they hadn't got to her place as well.

"Liam's right, and the rest of you might be targets too, especially you John. Look on the bright side everyone; you'll be the safest you've ever been with the CIA on guard."

He motioned John on.

"OK, so we know who Kouri was and we'll check Annette's description of GhamdiAl against whatever's known about him. I had to I.D. Kouri from a bone, so I'd say he was right beside the bomb when it went off." He held up a USB. "Des sent this over. Davy, can you do the honours?"

A moment later they were crowding round Davy's desk, gazing at a schematic of Jules Robinson's shop, as it had been when it was intact. John tapped a key and two body outlines appeared. One by the shop's left-hand wall looking in from the street, and the second two feet away from it towards the back.

"These were our two intact bodies. Barry McGovern and Jules Robinson. They were shielded from the main blast by the book shelves."

Smith glanced sharply at him. "The main blast?"

"Yes. Des is certain a secondary charge went off a few seconds later, most likely triggered by the force of the initial blast. It probably used a tilt switch that reacted to the shock wave. Seems they were determined that there'd be no survivors."

Smith looked puzzled. "Major James said nothing about that."

"Your forensics guys agree with Des. He met with them this morning." John brushed past Smith's surprise and carried on, knowing James had probably withheld the detail deliberately, to assert his power. He sounded like a complete dickhead.

"OK, it's neither here nor there except that it shows their determination to completely destroy the shop." He smiled at Craig. "Or whatever was inside."

John pressed another key and Fintan Delaney appeared by the front door and the bomb appeared under the bookshelves at the back of the shop. Another key added red crosses, to mark the likely positions of Sharon Greer and Ibrahim Kouri at the time of the blast.

John gestured at the screen. "You can see exactly where everyone was when the bomb exploded, the only reason Delaney survived was because he was by the front door, but the secondary device makes me think he was supposed to die in the blast as well."

Annette cut in. "He and Kouri both were. That's why they returned to the shop after planting the bomb."

John raised a note of caution. "If Kouri definitely was the man who planted the bomb with Delaney the night before. It seems logical, but we still can't be sure. There could be a third man involved. Remember that we didn't see the face of the second bomber, only Delaney's"

Craig cut into the debate. "I think Annette's right, John. I think there were only two bombers and they were meant to be martyrs for Islam. Whatever they knew about the movement was supposed to die with them. That's why Delaney was murdered. They couldn't risk him living to tell their secrets."

Liam interrupted. "And Jennifer Weston killed him because she was part of the cell." He updated them on his trip to St Mary's, ending with "She went to Pakistan last year, that's already too much coincidence for me. And what are the odds that the feet in the photo don't belong to her? Same sandals and same black nail varnish."

Craig frowned in thought. It was possible but they needed to dig deeper.

"OK, Liam, it was a good thought but we need this water-tight to be sure. Find out who made those sandals and how many pairs were sold." Liam went to object but Craig's glance said that he'd better not. He sweetened the task with his next words. "Nicky, you're our fashion guru, help Liam with that please." Liam's objection evaporated instantly and Craig carried on.

"OK, so if Jenny Weston was tasked with finishing Delaney off, she was most likely part of the same radical cell. But why trust a woman with the mission? Their status wouldn't be judged as high. Unless…What was her relationship with Delaney?"

Annette was the first to answer. "She recruited him?"

Craig nodded. "Anyone else?"

Davy chipped in. "She was his handler? He w…was her responsibility?"

"Yes to both of you. I think Weston recruited Delaney and

260

trained him so it was her job to finish him off."

Davy nodded eagerly. "I was going to tell you. I finally found a connection between Delaney and W…Weston. They met at Queen's."

"I thought you said she'd left university before Delaney started."

"S…She had. But some of her nurse training was at the M.P.E. in Elmwood Avenue, just down from the student's union. I checked with the nurse tutor and the nurses often went to the union coffee shop for lunch."

Craig's eyes widened excitedly then he shook his head. "It's thin, Davy. That only proves they could have met, not that they did."

Davy smiled smugly and tapped his left-hand screen, pulling up a double column of names. He scrolled down until he reached the pair he wanted. There, printed so clearly that no-one could argue, were two names side by side; Fintan Delaney and Jennifer Weston. Craig leaned in, excited.

"Where is this from?"

Davy considered dragging out his explanation to impress the crowd but his eagerness wouldn't let him. "I remembered that W…Weston had studied religion and we know that Delaney was religious. S…So I figured that if she was recruiting for a religious group, w…where better to find possible converts than amongst people already interested in religion and then just look for the floating voters! The table is a list of volunteers at a church near Queen's in 2012. Delaney had helped out there since s…school and Weston joined when she was a s…student nurse; they paired-up the new and experienced volunteers."

Craig wanted to shake the young analyst's hand, but it might have been overkill in the middle of a meeting, so instead he slapped him on the back, making Davy cough. "Excellent work, Davy. OK, so we have Delaney and Weston meeting two years ago, we have Delaney and possibly, probably, Ibrahim Kouri planting the bomb last Thursday morning, a bomb designed to destroy Papyrus and everything in it. And we have Weston returning to tie up the loose ends by killing Delaney."

John interrupted. "By injecting him with poison."

Craig waved him on.

"The poison was an unusual one, not normally administered I.V. but even more effective that way. Saxitoxin."

"Fugu?"

"Very good, Liam, you're almost right. Fugu is made from blowfish, not clams, and it contains Tetrodotoxin not Saxitoxin, but they're very similar poisons. Have you tried it?"

Liam made a face. "Have I, hell! If I want fish I'll go to the local chippie. Why anyone would want to risk death for a meal beats the hell out of me."

John smiled, envisaging Liam in Barbados searching for the nearest Irish pub.

"Saxitoxin blocks the sodium channels of nerve cells, preventing normal cell function and leading to paralysis. The usual cause of death is respiratory failure, as in Mr Delaney's case. It's virtually undetectable once it's in the body. Our friends in the CIA know all about it; they employed it as a suicide method during the Cold War. They issued agents with a needle dipped in it concealed inside a fake silver dollar."

A few minutes discussion followed about everyone's riskiest meals until Craig returned them to the case.

"I think that's most of what we need to cover on Weston and Delaney, except, Davy, you were looking into Weston's travel after the event."

"Yes. There w…was no-one travelling under that name anywhere, but we found a few likely matches and I'm running the images through facial recognition software now."

A loud cough made everyone turn to see Nicky shaking her head. Craig smiled; opening the door to what he knew would be something good.

"You're so busy looking at evidence and forensics that you've missed the most obvious thing." She smiled graciously at Liam.

"Liam came the closest." Liam puffed himself up as Nicky gazed at the others' blank faces. "Think, for goodness sake." She turned to Craig. "Sir? Surely you've seen it?"

Craig hadn't a clue what she was talking about and he said so. Nicky sighed exaggeratedly.

"Jennifer Weston has gone to Pakistan. Check the flights, Davy. Does one of your images link to a long haul flight from Dublin?"

Davy scrolled down his screen and nodded. "Dublin to Karachi on Sunday."

"That was her flight then."

Nicky stared at them all expectantly, to be greeted with total silence. She shook her head like a tolerant mother. "Jennifer Weston and Fintan Delaney weren't just colleagues, they were lovers. It's a clear as the nose on my face."

Craig looked sceptical. "Where did you get that from?"

Liam quipped. "She spends her life reading romantic novels."

Nicky was indignant. "I do not! I just listen to the bits between the facts. They met two years ago, they both went to Pakistan. Fintan Delaney called a satellite phone there every week."

"They could have been arranging the job."

"The phone calls maybe, but you said he had a second e-mail account. It won't have been for the job - who would risk wrecking a covert operation by communicating by C-mail? Any details of the job would have been discussed in an untraceable way. My bet is there was another side to Delaney's relationship with Weston and it was personal." She turned to Davy. "Have you read his C-mails yet?"

Davy shook his head. With everything else happening it had slipped his mind. Craig nodded him to pull them up as Nicky continued.

"The framed photograph attached to the bomb. If Liam's right it was of Jennifer Weston."

Annette interrupted. "So Delaney attached it to the bomb

because he was doing it for her? He'd given his life for her and it was his way of being close to her when he died."

Nicky nodded vigorously, seeing that Annette had got it. "And when Delaney didn't die, she probably volunteered to be the one to kill him, because she loved him and wanted to see him again."

Liam guffawed loudly, breaking the romantic mood. "God save me from women who love me if that's how they show it."

Nicky squinted at him. "Trust me, Liam; most women would want to kill you. Love has nothing to do with it."

Davy tapped his keyboard and began to read. "Dearest, Jenny. I can't bear to be apart from you..." He read Weston's reply and they quickly got the gist.

Craig motioned Davy to stop and Nicky gave a smug grin. She was right; Fintan Delaney had joined a radical group for love! Who knew if he'd ever come to believe in their ideals, but he'd killed for them anyway.

"Well done, Nicky. Liam, forget the great sandal hunt; I think we can take it the photograph was of Jennifer Weston and that she's gone back to somewhere in Pakistan. The question is where?"

Annette nodded thoughtfully. "I have an idea, sir. Delaney went to Pakistan last summer to do some charity work and the ward sister's confirmed that Weston went there as well. The odds are that they were together. Surely between travel itineraries and the C-mail address Delaney wrote to we should be able to pinpoint an area of Pakistan at least?"

Craig smiled. "Brilliant. Davy, get onto that please. But detach your system from the police net or the CIA will find out."

"I'll do it on my own laptop. I have firewalls on there that no government could crack. Give me till tomorrow morning."

"Good. OK, we have why Delaney did it and probably who he did it with, now we just have the simple task of finding out why Islamic radicals targeted a small bookshop in Belfast!"

Chapter Nineteen

Banque de Paris. Paris. Thursday 9 a.m. local time

Berger waited outside the stone building on the corner of Rue des Lilas d'Espagne, shifting nervously from foot to foot. He scanned the two streets leading from the junction, watching as suited men and women scurried along them, then disappeared through doors to be swallowed up by stone and glass. He'd never wanted an office job but he almost envied them now.

He checked his watch again, and again a few seconds later, stepping into the shade and gazing at the rooftops overhead. Anyone could shoot him and steal his number for the vault; they might even sever his hand for fingerprints. The manager wouldn't notice that they weren't him. He must see a thousand faces each week and Berger didn't fool himself there was anything memorable about his.

As he stood imagining his horrific death at the hands of a faceless man or group, two men appeared beside him. Berger stepped back so quickly that he almost fell. He hadn't heard their footsteps or seen them appear; that was how easily he could meet his death. One of the men spoke, shaking Berger from his terror; it was Augustin. He didn't even like the man but right now he could have kissed him on both cheeks! Claude Augustin repeated his words impatiently.

"Well? Do you want to stand here all day?"

Berger turned questioningly towards the second man, expecting an introduction. He was short, even shorter than him, but his mohair coat and perfectly plumped tie screamed wealth and power. Berger's questioning look went unanswered as Augustin pushed at the bank's revolving door and in a moment they were inside the cool building, striding across its marble hall. Five minutes later they stood in the echoing vault as the bank manager reversed obsequiously from the room, leaving them alone. Augustin gestured towards the safe and waited for Berger to open it.

Berger shielded the dial from his audience and began to input the digits, twisting it this way and that. His fingerprints and the numbers were the only things preventing Augustin killing him and stealing what he possessed, and he wasn't about to give them up. Finally the last lever dropped and he pulled at the steel door handle, revealing the safe's contents to the two men. He gawped as the wealthy man abandoned his dignified façade and grabbed hungrily at what lay inside.

"Careful! It mustn't be damaged."

The man stared at his hands as if they'd committed an assault then he breathed deeply and touched the safe's precious contents again. He stroked the object like the body of a woman he loved. Augustin felt like a voyeur and turned away, but Berger watched every touch as if the man would suddenly dematerialise his possession and disappear. After five minutes of close examination the man nodded then he uttered his first words since they'd met in the street.

"The figure?"

Not 'how much?' or 'what's the cost?' They would both have been too vulgar. Instead he merely asked for Berger's number. How much would it take for Berger to part with the most valuable thing he possessed, when they all knew he would never own its like again? How much would it take to pay for the life Berger wanted to live, the one that he had never had? Too low and Berger would kick himself forever, especially if he ran out of funds on the Côte d'Azur. Too high and he risked his buyer walking out the door, and with him the chance of a warm old age. Alain Berger smiled, confident for the first time in his struggle of a life that he had the upper hand. He'd done his research and he knew exactly what his prize was worth.

"Nine million euros."

The vault was silent and Augustin and the man even more silent than that. Berger watched the wall clock that he was certain contained a camera and bit on his tongue, tasting blood. Outwardly he stayed calm; to show doubt could lose him the deal. The rich man's silent stillness was a good sign. If he'd said yes too quickly the price would have been too low, if too high he would simply have walked away. He had to hold his nerve.

After a full minute the well-dressed man nodded and Berger exhaled, not realising until then that he'd held his breath. It was his turn to ask a question. "When?"

The man turned on his heel, leaving Augustin to answer. "Tomorrow. I will bring the cash here, again at nine. We will not meet again after that."

Alain Berger was satisfied. He waited for both men to leave then he replaced his fortune inside the safe, securing it for the night. If Augustin discovered the safe's combination he could try to steal the item for himself. He needed somewhere so safe to hide until the next morning that not even Claude Augustin could reach him there.

***

2 p.m.

Craig spent Thursday fending off calls from the Chief Constable and Stephen James, asking him why they were getting queries from the American Embassy and Ministry of Defence. Craig took the line he'd decided on as soon as the CIA had appeared in John's office; feigned ignorance, subtext 'I know nothing'. If the CIA wanted to know why Ibrahim Kouri had been in a bookshop in Belfast intent on blowing it up, then they'd have to wait until the case was solved like everyone else.

Craig wondered if they were still parked outside in Pilot Street like they had been that morning. Well, if they wanted to waste their time sitting in a car that was their prerogative.

Davy's cursory search of the internet had yielded nothing exciting in the book chat-rooms, but his own time on the Dark Web was beginning to bear fruit. Cyber mutterings about two books and a 'pair of something very rare' came and went, with recurring references to Paris. Craig toyed with the idea of contacting the Gendarmes and then thought better of it. That was all they needed right now, another enforcement agency to add to the already involved British Army and CIA. How many law officers can you get in a phone-box? Guinness World Records probably already knew.

Besides, all he had at the moment was conjecture, so what could he tell the Gendarmes? "Bonjour. We've had an explosion in a bookshop. We think it might be something to do with a special book, so special that someone killed five people to get rid of it. What was the book's name? Oh, we don't know that, but we think it's one of a pair and the second one might be somewhere in Paris. Just thought we'd alert you anyway so you could scour Paris' thousands of bookshops on a wild book chase." Nope, it wouldn't work. But as soon as they got the book's title he would give them a call.

Craig gazed out his office window, contrasting the bright July sky-line with the murkiness of the Dark Web. The river shone like mercury, only disturbed by the birds swooping through its surface in search of their next meal, and the occasional small eddies caused by the warden's patrolling boat. He longed to dive in and wash off the mental grime of the past week. He smiled to himself. The waters of the Lagan were many things; cooling, increasingly busy and a conduit to the Irish Sea, but they definitely weren't for swimming in.

God, he needed a holiday. If John's wedding hadn't been about to provide one he would have planned a getaway for Katy and himself. Sun, sleep and wine; the perfect recuperation package.

As Craig returned to the alternately esoteric and criminal chatter on the Dark Web, Jennifer Weston disembarked a flight at Paris Charles de Gaulle airport with everything she needed to complete her task. It wouldn't be long before she'd finished what had started in Belfast.

***

"Yes! The border with Iran."

The shouted words made Liam glance up from the file he was reading, just in time to see Davy racing towards Craig's office. He saw him knock and enter then heard Craig murmur something. They emerged together from the room and Craig glanced quickly at the clock. It was three-thirty, a bit early but they might as well brief now. It was going to be short and sweet. He beckoned everyone over, motioning Davy to start.

"I've traced the C-mail's recipient to Pakistan, a desert region near the Iran border. It also fits the s...satellite phone signal."

Ken cut in. "Do you mean actually in the desert, Davy, or in a town nearby?"

Davy shook his head. "In the desert itself, although the e-mail provider w...would only guarantee accuracy to within one hundred miles. I took the radius they gave me and crossed it with the phone s...signals and the area of overlap is here." He loped back to his desk and pointed at his central screen, prompting them all to join him. It was a map showing the Kharan Desert in Pakistan, sandwiched between Iran and Afghanistan; nine hundred miles from the Arabian Sea.

Liam was the first to state the obvious. "Who the hell lives in the desert? The heat must be dire."

Ken answered him. "Nomadic tribes, camels and..."

He didn't need to finish the sentence; the answer was obvious. People who didn't want to be found lived in the middle of the desert. And if Jennifer Weston and Fintan

269

Delaney were anything to go by, some of them weren't indigenous to Pakistan.

Craig nodded; it made sense. A radical Islamic group had to live off the radar. Was it a terrorist training camp? He shrugged; the answer to that lay with people who had much more powerful equipment than theirs. Damn! That meant sooner or later he'd have to return some calls.

"OK, thanks, Davy. Take it as far as you can."

Davy gave him a sceptical look then nodded. He'd already taken it to the limits of their equipment and legality and the boss knew it. This was his way of playing for time before the nerds from GCHQ started to interfere.

"Liam, what's happening with UKUF?"

Liam saw the exchange between Craig and Davy and smiled; the boss didn't want the CIA poking through their files until they absolutely had to. He tapped the folder in his hand.

"I've just been reading Shorty Hamill's report on them. We were right. With Sharpy and David Greer dead and the boy wonder in Glasgow with his uncle, the ructions have started inside UKUF."

"Who's the main contender for leadership?"

"A nasty bit of work called Derek Copeland. Hamill and his lads are keeping a close eye, but I thought I might ask Tommy what he thought."

Craig nodded. Tommy had a huge reason to be grateful to Liam, and he hated being in debt. "OK, good. Annette, what's the latest with SNI?"

Annette tidied the pages on her knee and read from the top one. "The director, Mohammed GhamdiAl, was our bomber Kouri, but I'm convinced that SNI didn't know anything of his plans. Kouri was in deep cover so they hired him and brought him into the country innocently. As far as I can see SNI is in the clear on the bomb. But they're guilty of working with UKUF to pressure shopkeepers to sell."

"Then let's get them on that. Ask the fraud boys to take a

good look at their books as well." Craig paused for a moment, lost in thought. When he restarted he said what was on the tip of Ken Smith's tongue.

"Ibrahim Kouri was one of the CIA's most wanted and a founder member of the M.I.F. He was important to his movement. He must have had plenty of raw recruits willing to die, so he wouldn't have sacrificed his own life unless he'd thought something really warranted it." Craig turned to Smith. "Ken, you've been in Iraq and Afghanistan fighting against the radicals. What would warrant Kouri sacrificing himself?"

Smith thought for a moment before answering and Nicky smiled as Carmen gave him a covert glance. It was the most interest she'd shown since he'd arrived.

"Two things. To hit a high value target; either military or propaganda. Or to destroy something that had major significance in the religious war."

It was what Craig had thought. "OK. The bookshop wasn't high value, so they were after something that had major religious significance."

Annette interjected. "It must have been something really offensive to Islam, if not positively anti-Islamic. They wouldn't destroy something just because it wasn't an Islamic text, or they'd have to blow up the whole Judeo-Christian world."

Craig nodded at her logic. "OK, something that was deemed very offensive to Islam. There was nothing about the bookshop itself that fitted that bill, or any of the occupants, so that brings us back to the idea of a book."

Craig asked Nicky to hand out the pages she'd printed before the briefing.

"This is text from some collector's chat-rooms on the Dark Web. Does everyone know what that is?" Craig already knew that his team did so he gazed pointedly at Carmen and Ken. Carmen nodded but Smith looked blank. "OK, Carmen, give Ken more detail after the meeting, please, but briefly, the Dark Web is a shadow internet. There's a lot of illegal activity going

271

on there and as soon as cyber-crime gets one site shut down another one sets up. Anyway, there are some rare book collectors around who it seems would do pretty much anything to get their hands on what they want. There's big money involved, millions in fact, and the chatter at the moment is about a book or pair of books linked to Paris in some way."

Liam interrupted. "Was Belfast mentioned?"

Craig nodded. "On one of the conversation threads but it passed pretty quickly. All the others mention Paris and they aren't speaking in the past tense; the latest chat was ten minutes ago." Craig turned to Davy. "Davy, if I give you the thread that mentioned Belfast, can you dig into its archives for the past couple of weeks? I want to see if Belfast was mentioned more before the explosion."

"S…Sure."

"Good. For now let's concentrate on Paris."

"What're they saying on it, boss?"

"That there's a bidding war for a book that has something to do with the Crusades."

Smith gawped at him. "The Crusades from the 11th to 15th Centuries?"

Carmen's mouth opened before she could stop herself. "Were there any others?" She bit back the word 'idiot' and smiled to soften her words' impact, but Nicky had seen the flash of sarcasm in her eyes. Thankfully Ken hadn't. Liam shot Carmen a warning look and she glanced away. He thought that she'd managed to be nice for too long.

Ken smiled cheerfully at her. "No, you're right of course. We're taught about the Crusades in military history. Their stated goal was the restoration of Christian access to holy places in and near Jerusalem, but some historians see them as part of a defensive war against the expansion of Islam. The Crusaders' belief in the absolute 'rightness' of Christianity meant that they didn't always behave well."

Craig nodded. "If fear of Islamic expansion was prevalent at the time then there must have been scholars whose opinions backed it up. Perhaps they went one step further and actually blasphemed against Islam."

Annette and Davy glanced at each other; it was starting to make sense. Fatwās had been launched against modern writers for blasphemy, so it made sense that if a medieval anti-Islamic text existed, it would be considered blasphemous as well. Perhaps even more offensive because the modern world valued it so highly. Annette asked the question.

"What's the value to the collectors, sir? The book's age, its rarity or the right to hold an anti-Islamic and basically racist opinion and think they can get away with it because it's written in a historical text?"

"Good question and the answer is I don't know. I'll go back and read the threads again. The books would be very old and very likely beautifully worked, and their rarity wouldn't be in doubt; how many artefacts of any sort survive from that period? All of that would contribute to their value, but the reason behind wanting to destroy them must be the text. Except… it can't only be that, because there must be other examples of anti-Islamic sentiment in old writings. I think the monetary value placed on the books by the collectors was probably the final straw. Imagine if something that we found grossly offensive was valued even more highly by someone because of that; we'd be angry too."

Smith nodded. "I think you've nailed it, and I think using an antique watch as a timer was them telling us the bombing was about something old."

Davy cut in. "Des drew a blank on finding more details on the pocket w…watch. It was too badly damaged. All he could say was it was probably 18th Century."

"Not as old as the Crusades but definitely pointing us to the past."

Craig decided to play a hunch. He raced into his office and reappeared a minute later, holding a fresh printout and reading

273

aloud. "During the 15th and 16th Centuries clock making flourished. In 1504, the first portable timepiece was invented in Nuremberg, Germany by Peter Henlein."

Ken gawped at him. "1504! So that's why they used it as the timer. The last crusade ended just before then; the watch was pointing us to medieval times…Very clever."

Craig nodded. "There was no way they could have acquired a pocket watch old enough, so the 18th Century one had to do, plus it was more reliable."

Ken shook his head. "It was symbolic. My guess is if it hadn't worked Delaney or Kouri would have detonated it by hand anyway. That's what the tilt switch was for."

Liam was still thinking about the books. "But who was going to buy the Belfast book? If Jules Robinson brought something that valuable into his shop, he must have had a local buyer lined up."

Craig nodded. "Good point, Liam. I doubt it was anyone in Papyrus that day so we need to dig deeper. But there's something more urgent. The chat-rooms mentioned a pair of books, let's call them volumes one and two, so the real question is, if volume one was destroyed at Papyrus and there's a volume two in Paris, then who's buying it? Is it the same buyer or a new one? We need to find out because whatever we may think of them they're a target as well."

***

5.30 p.m.

Craig was peering at his computer screen when the knock came on his office door. He said "come in", certain that it would be Nicky saying goodnight. Instead he was surprised when Carmen appeared. She opened the door slowly, as if afraid of what might lie behind it, and stood in the doorway like a pupil who'd been summoned by the Headmaster.

Craig smiled vaguely and glanced behind her, expecting to see Nicky.

"Nicky's gone home. She said it was OK to knock."

Craig shook himself free of the web he'd been stuck in for the previous hour and beckoned her to sit.

"Of course it is. We haven't had a chance to say hello properly. I'm sorry, that's my fault, as you'll have seen the case has rather taken over."

He held up the percolator, pouring a single cup at the shake of Carmen's head.

"The case is the reason I knocked. I'd like to offer my help."

Craig noticed two things. One, that Carmen was pretty but there was none of the warmth that was usually attractive to men; whether that was deliberate he could only guess. He corrected himself. It was obviously attractive to at least one man on the team, if Ken Smith's longing gaze and blushes were anything to go by. And two, that she never called him 'sir'. Not that he minded, he'd got used to chief or whatever the cool term of the day was from Davy, and Liam had never called him anything but boss. He didn't mind how Carmen addressed him, but the fact that she didn't address him or come to think of it, any of her senior officers by a title, was slightly strange.

As the thoughts ran through Craig's mind, other thoughts were occupying Carmen's. Old Giant Cullen had been right; Craig liked to run a happy ship and, much as she hated the word nice because it was so insipid, he was nice. But he was very far from insipid.

He was also very attractive in a film star sort of way; well that was what her granny would have said. A rugged Cary Grant. Eat your heart out girls. Except that she couldn't imagine Craig even looking in the mirror, judging by the usually vertical position of his hair.

Their mutual assessment completed, Craig smiled warmly.

"You're already helping the investigation, Carmen. It's great to have you and Ken here for a few weeks. You've been working

275

on things for Liam and Annette, haven't you?"

She nodded impatiently. "Yes, but I can do more. I didn't want to say in front of the others but my degree was in computer science and since I left Uni I've taken a lot of courses. I write programmes in my spare time."

Craig's ears perked up. He knew why she hadn't said it in the briefing. Computers were seen as Davy's terrain and he could just hear what Liam would have said about her hobby; sad, geeky girl, then he'd have used the revelation to explain all her character flaws. But he was interested in computers himself and would love to have more time to explore them so he leaned forward, interested.

"Go on."

Carmen blushed a faint pink. "I've even hacked a few sites that I shouldn't have."

Craig rolled his eyes. That was all he needed; cyber-crime bursting through the door to arrest one of his staff. Carmen was still talking. "Nothing major but… what I'm trying to say is I know my way around the Dark Web, and if Davy and you are busy with other things…"

Craig nodded furiously. "Yes. Thank-you. That would be great."

She was taken aback by the speed of his acceptance, but what she didn't know was that Craig had spent almost twelve hours over the previous two days navigating the firewalls and hidden doorways savvy programmers had created in their sites. He would cheer if he could hand the task over to someone else.

Craig turned his screen towards Carmen then pulled a chair beside her, spending the next thirty minutes outlining how far he'd got in the various fora, and the avatar and profile he'd created in that world.

"I think it's best if you stick with the I.D. I've created. I've been posing as a very amateur book collector to gain people's confidence. They're less likely to see me as competition for any significant steals or buys and tell me the gossip."

Carmen nodded; good ploy.

"There seem to be four main chat-rooms and three big auction sites, not to mention the private instant message chats that are going on all the time. My guess is that's where the really useful information is, but I've no idea how to hack into them."

Carmen glanced up from the screen and smiled. It was the happiest Craig had seen her look. "I have. I can get in and out without them seeing me."

As Craig looked on she navigated herself in and out of chat-rooms and websites, finding cyber backdoors and alleyways that he'd completely missed. She was just about to eavesdrop on a private exchange when Craig noticed the time. It was almost seven o'clock.

"It's getting late, Carmen."

She didn't hear him, absorbed in her cyber-world. Craig stood in front of her and smiled, then gestured pointedly at the clock.

"Tomorrow, Carmen."

She shook her head furiously. "No. Tonight. These people won't wait. With one book gone the value of the other will rocket. If it hasn't already been sold and gone underground it easily could do by morning." She gazed up at Craig, almost pleading him to let her stay. "I'll keep going until I've found them. If you could just tell security downstairs that I'll be here late."

Craig hesitated. It felt like a cop-out by him, even though she'd got deeper into the Net in ten minutes than he had all day. He came up with a compromise.

"Only if you have something to eat with me at The James first. You can't stay here all night without food."

Carmen glanced at the screen then felt her stomach rumble and agreed. She shot Craig's computer a longing look as they left. She couldn't wait to see what was lurking in its various worlds, and get paid overtime to dig deeper than she'd gone before.

***

Paris. 11 p.m. local time

The small café stood in near-darkness. Only one candle flickered on the final cleared table and once he'd finished cleaning the coffee machine Augustin would snuff that out, using the brass douter his father had used before him. He loved his café. It had been his life since birth. Running across the polished boards of the living quarters upstairs with his sister, and sneaking downstairs when Maman wasn't looking, to steal a Pain Au Chocolat from the window display. How he'd loved that display; to his child's eyes Éclairs had vied with Mille-feuilles for 'King of the Window'. He was always sad that they'd be eaten by coffee-drinking customers later that day.

When his parents had died his sister had handed the keys to him, strangely happy to tie herself to the mechanic from five streets away and start producing babies of her own. He already had his child; the café's polished wood and shining glasses were more beautiful to him than any enfant. Now he was getting old and had no son to leave his empire to, and the wet Paris winters and humid summers had taken their toll on his bones. It was time to sell and move to the Dordogne and by tomorrow he would have the money to fund his dream.

Augustin set the last dried glass on the aging marble counter and whistled softly beneath his breath. He didn't hear the front door open or see the woman till it was too late. Not until he felt her gun's silencer against his neck, forcing him out from behind the safety of his counter to sit by the last candle's fading light. She sat down opposite, shifting the gun to press its silencer hard against his throat, so that his voice tightened as he spoke.

"I have only what is in the till. Take it, take it."

As he squeezed out the words Augustin stared frantically at the girl, for that's what she was, a girl no older than twenty-five. Her clothes were good and she looked well-fed, so why was she

278

stealing? He answered his own question. She wasn't stealing; she was here for something more and he knew immediately what it was.

Jenny Weston's French was good and she hissed out her words in a perfect accent.

"How much?"

Augustin's eyes widened in fear at her tone. He knew exactly what she meant; he also knew that his only hope lay in bluff. "What?"

She pressed the gun harder against his Adam's apple, making him recoil in pain. "How much?"

Claude Augustin closed his eyes in defeat and optimistic faith; if he couldn't see her perhaps she would cease to exist. The pressure reminded him otherwise. Finally he croaked.

"Nine million euros."

"When and for whom?"

Augustin shook his head in reflex, some childhood code of honour making him reluctant to tell tales. A sharp reminder of his predicament swiftly changed his mind.

"Tomorrow morning at nine o'clock. Banque de Paris, Rue des Lilas d'Espagne. The seller will be there. Alain Berger."

Jenny was getting bored dragging each fact from him, and quite enjoying the power to frighten a grown man; it was a rare sensation. The camp had a strict pecking order and women definitely came last. She pulled back the gun's slide, loading the chamber with a round, and smiled maliciously as beads of sweat rolled down the Frenchman's flabby cheeks.

"Who is the buyer?"

Augustin's eyes widened further, in cartoon-like panic. If he gave her the buyer's name he was a dead man. There would be nowhere he could hide; Troy Keaton had people everywhere. The illogical nature of his thoughts completely escaped him but the pressure of the barrel focused his mind.

"Their name. Now!"

"He will kill me. He is a very powerful man."

Jenny smiled inwardly, half-sickened by how much she was enjoying her task. Killing wasn't meant to be a pleasure, but it became one when there was no other happiness left in life and Fintan had been her last real source of that. Her voice became persuasive.

"I can help you if you tell me. I have many friends."

Augustin weighed his options rapidly, coming down on what he thought was the best side to save his life. He didn't know that chance was already lost.

"Troy Keaton. He lives in Geneva. He is from a wealthy family in New York. They're in business in…"

Claude Augustin never finished his sentence because Jennifer Weston already knew what their business was; the name Keaton was well known in the terrorist world. As her finger squeezed off a silenced shot she made plans to get the information to Fareed. She watched dispassionately as the plump man fell sideways off his wooden café chair, and lay face pressed against his polished floor. Then she snuffed out the final candle and turned the door sign to 'Fermé', leaving the same way that she came.

***

Paris. Friday 9 a.m. local time

Alain Berger stared at the young woman with an untrusting expression on his face. Where was Augustin? He didn't like doing business at the best of times, but doing it with a complete stranger who said she'd been sent by the buyer attracted him even less.

"Why should I believe you? I've been dealing with Augustin and I'm going to continue with him to the end."

Jenny Weston smiled seductively then let her eyes roam across Berger's body; they held a clear message. Her mouth said "Augustin's part in the transaction is over. My boss wants me to handle it now." But her eyes said 'if you play ball there could be more than money in this for you'.

Every fibre in her shuddered and she wanted to turn and run away; anything rather than flirt with this shrivelled little man. But she would do anything for the cause. She teased a tendril of blond hair around one finger and thanked goodness she'd painted her face with a bedroom look. She had no intention of sleeping with the rat-like Berger, but if the offer of sexual favours gained her access to his safe then she would do whatever worked.

Berger hesitated for a moment and then glanced behind him through the bank's revolving door. This woman knew about the transaction and that Augustin was supposed to meet him there. How could she unless she was part of it? But where was Augustin? Jenny saw his vacillation and revealed the clincher.

"You met my boss Troy Keaton here yesterday with Claude Augustin, and you showed them the merchandise. Augustin was coming here to meet you today at 9 a.m."

Even if Augustin hadn't already told her everything in an attempt to buy his life, it was a fair guess. Nine o'clock was when the bank opened and Augustin wouldn't have wanted to wait longer than he had to. Seeing Berger teetering, she added.

"I know what the merchandise is."

Berger's eyes narrowed as he calculated the odds that she wasn't who she said she was. No-one but Keaton and Augustin knew what they were buying so she must work for them, mustn't she? His eyes narrowed further as the second possibility, the one that he'd feared for weeks, filled his mind. What if she was a radical? Someone who wanted to destroy both the item and him? As quickly as the truth entered Berger's mind he dismissed it, gazing at Jenny's blond hair and blue eyes. There was nothing Arabic about her, nothing to suggest Islamic beliefs; she looked as Northern European as it was possible to be. He knew it was impossible to guess someone's politics by looking at them, but...

As Alain Berger calculated, Jennifer Weston relaxed, knowing that she had already won. He was a man ready to be seduced and her Aryan good looks were doing their part. She laughed inwardly, knowing that he was attaching significance to her fair skin and dismissing any possibility that she belonged to Islam. Why were people so stupid? Why did she care? If pale skin and make-up persuaded him, who was she to complain?

Their trains of thoughts converged in a single word as Berger turned towards the bank's front door. "Allons." Jennifer gave an outwardly seductive and inwardly triumphant smile, knowing that Alain Berger had just sealed both their fates.

***

Docklands. Friday 8.am.

"OK. There's a lot to get on with so this will be quick. You need to know that after this briefing I'll be involving the Chief Con and our friends from the CIA. It's time to hand over some things."

Craig looked as if he hadn't slept all night, and he hadn't. Instead of counting sheep he'd been running theories, all of which hit a dead end. He turned to Carmen to see that she hadn't slept either; he just hoped that her insomnia had been more productive than his.

"Carmen?"

All eyes turned to the small red-head and all of them looked curious, not least of all Liam's. His were glaring as well. He'd left Carmen the evening before with instructions to work up the membership list for UKUF, what had that got to do with the boss?

Carmen couldn't resist a smug smile, knowing that what she was about to say was impressive. Her smile deepened when she saw Liam's scowl.

"I asked the Super if I could help with the cyber-chat side of things. I've been hacking for years."

On the word 'hacking', Davy looked up from his nails. "You're a hacker?" It was said excitedly and incredulously, as if he'd met someone who liked the same obscure rock band while walking along the Great Wall of China. Liam would have asked the same question in a very different tone.

Carmen nodded, hearing Davy's genuine interest. "I did computer science at Uni and writing programmes became a hobby. I can find a back-door into pretty much any site."

Before they started speaking in Java Craig motioned Carmen on, explaining. "I wasn't getting very far in the Dark Web so Carmen offered to help. What did you find, Carmen?"

"I found the exact reason for the explosion. There was a lot of chatter about a collector called Troy Keaton who collects old religious texts."

Liam interrupted with a guffaw. "I have a truckload of those; they hand them out every day outside the City Hall."

Craig glared at him, scenting sour grapes. Liam may have brought Carmen in but that didn't mean that she was his slave. "They're tracts, Liam, not texts. Let Carmen speak, please."

Liam's grin changed to a frown and he clammed up, but before Carmen could restart Ken cut in. "Did you say Troy Keaton?"

She raised an eyebrow at his interruption and then nodded. Craig leaned forward. "Do you know the name?"

Ken nodded vaguely. "I'm not sure… it might not be the same man. Leave it with me."

Craig nodded Carmen on again.

"OK. There's a thriving market in antiquities on the web and an even more thriving illegal one on the Dark. People put out a request for something and there's always someone who knows where to find it, or steal it to order if required. It seems Keaton heard of a pair of 15th Century Crusade texts written by Paul of Salerno, one of the best known writers of the period."

Annette cut in. "What were they about?"

"They were essentially opinion pieces on the Crusades written from the Christian side. From what I could gather by following the threads, Salerno was pretty scathing about Muslim beliefs and essentially about their God. He basically debunked the whole of Islam."

Liam whistled. "Well I'll be damned."

Davy came back like lightning. "Probably, but not because of a book."

Craig let the laughter that erupted carry on for a moment and then nodded Carmen to restart. She smiled, enjoying herself for the first time in days. An excited tone tinged her Scottish burr.

"We're all aware what one careless word about Islam by a celebrity can lead to nowadays, well Paul of Salerno had no filter. Back then Christianity ruled the roost and he thought he could say whatever he liked. The cyber-chat says the books are rough stuff."

Craig nodded; he had a fair idea what they'd said. He shook his head in despair. "But still, some idiot was prepared to pay a lot for them."

Carmen nodded. "Twenty million euros for the pair or nine million each. A thief was commissioned to steal the books and the rumour was that a book antiquarian in Belfast had got his hands on one of them and was preparing to sell it to someone in Ireland."

"Jules Robinson."

"Yes. There's chatter about the bomb all over the Dark Web. Some praising the bomber, most talking about the financial loss of the book. You won't be surprised to know that no-one gives a damn about the victims. The Dark Web isn't filled with altruists."

Craig interrupted urgently. "Any speculation about who planted it?"

Carmen nodded. "The name Kouri came up. And another name; the M.I.A."

Liam groaned. "That's all we need. A new acronym."

Carmen continued, ignoring him. "I think it stands for Militant Islamic Army. From what I can find on the web they're a small but very feared force, even within the Muslim population."

Craig nodded. "The CIA mentioned them. They must be the military wing of the M.I.F."

"That makes sense. Anyway, on the second book in the pair, it seems that Keaton had agents trying to locate it. That's where Paris comes in. The second book is there. The collector viewed it yesterday and the transaction is taking place today."

Craig interrupted. "Any idea where and when, Carmen?"

Carmen nodded. "There are two venues mentioned. One is a café in the Marais. The owner Claude Augustin seems to be involved somehow."

Craig shook his head. There was no way they would keep a book that valuable in a café, sitting between the coffee and cognac; especially not after what had happened at Papyrus. Carmen was still talking.

"The second venue is a bank somewhere in Paris."

Craig nodded. "That's it. My guess is the book's being kept in a vault. Whoever's selling it heard about what happened here and isn't taking any chances."

"You're right. The seller's a guy called Berger. He's been stealing to order for years. Word has it that he's got it secured at the bank, readying to exchange today."

Craig stood up with a speed that surprised them all and yelled across the floor. "Nicky, get the Gendarmes on the phone for me." He turned back to the group. "Take five minutes everyone. Carmen, come with me."

Five minutes later Craig had briefed the Parisian Gendarmes what was happening then he handed the phone to Carmen for the details. It might turn out to be nothing, but God only knew what the M.I.A. was planning to disrupt the exchange so they needed to keep their eyes peeled. They re-joined the group.

"OK, Carmen, anything else on that?"

"Only what I just told the Gendarmes. There's chatter about a blond western woman being involved with the M.I.A. Not only her, it seems they have quite a few recruits from the West; they target universities in particular."

Annette sighed. Hire a teenager now, while they know everything. Universities were hothouses for altruistic and frustrated teens who thought they could save the world. Didn't they realise that their parents' generation had already tried?

Davy nodded at Carmen's words. "That's w…where they got to Delaney."

"And God knows who else."

Liam laughed loudly, breaking the sombre mood. "Here, do you remember that sect who used the 'flirty fishers'? What were they called?"

Craig nodded, picturing 1970s America and young women handing out flowers. "The Children of God. They were a religious sect that used pretty young women to seduce people to join. It was called evangelical prostitution. They promised peace, love and sexual favours."

Liam was about to say something rude when Carmen cut in. "Jennifer Weston! That must have been her job. To go out there and recruit young men for the cause."

Liam shook his head. "Delaney. Poor sod."

Annette smacked Liam on the arm. "Poor sod nothing. Fintan Delaney made his choice, and if he'd kept his mind where it should have been instead of in his trousers he'd still be alive now!"

Liam grinned and so did everyone else. Annette realised what she'd said and blushed. "Well, you know what I mean."

Craig laughed. "Everyone knows exactly what you meant, Annette, and you're probably right. Young men don't always think."

Nicky offered an opinion from her desk. "They do think but very rarely about the right things. And it's not just the young ones."

A laugh ran through the group then Craig nodded Carmen on. "I gave Weston's description to the Gendarmes, on the off-chance that she's heading to Paris to do her worse. "

"Good idea." Craig turned to Davy. "Send her picture across now, Davy, before we carry on."

It only took Davy a few seconds and when he re-joined the group, Craig asked. "Is that everything, Carmen?"

"Yes, for now. I'll have another try after the meeting to see if I can get anything on the time of the exchange."

"Thank-you, that's great work. Davy, anything more on possible locations in Pakistan?"

Davy nodded, then he realised that no-one could read his mind and started to speak.

"W…We've, Ken and I, managed to narrow it to a strip of desert west of Karachi. It's the western edge of the Kharan Desert, bordering on Iran."

Craig groaned. "Iran? As if this wasn't bad enough."

Ken echoed Craig's sentiment. "My thoughts exactly. I was hoping for Iraqi or Afghan connections; better the enemy you know sort of thing. Iran's impenetrable."

Davy smiled, more upbeat than the others. "Maybe they've s…stayed on the Pakistan side and Iran isn't even aware that the camp is there."

"Optimist."

"Anyway, w…whether they know it's there or not, the Kharan Desert fits with the origins of the romantic e-mails between W…Weston and Delaney and the radius of the s… satellite calls." He stared directly at Craig. "It's also only five hundred miles from the village where Delaney went to help build houses."

Craig nodded; it all made sense. Jennifer Weston had targeted Delaney, knowing that he was interested in religion and charitable works, and as part of their relationship she'd convinced him to come to Pakistan to help build a village. It was only a short trip from there to a terrorist training camp in the desert.

"Nicky, get Tweedledum and Tweedledee in here."

Nicky stared at him blankly.

"The CIA. They've been tailing me for days. They're parked outside the Rotterdam Bar."

She headed for the lift and two minutes later Agents Ross and Mulhearn were installed in Craig's office. Craig and Davy were with them, sharing everything they had on the location of a possible terrorist camp.

"You can stay in here and use my phone; ask Nicky if you want to send anything securely to your people."

Craig and Davy re-joined the group, knowing that in less time than it would take them to order lunch the CIA would have turned their satellites towards the Kharan desert to search for the camp.

Davy carried on briefing, handing out copies of a photograph. It was Jennifer Weston. Liam was the first to comment.

"Here, is that a trolley dolly's uniform she's wearing?"

"If you mean w…was she a member of the air-crew, then yes."

Craig stifled at smile at Davy's droll tone.

"She was working for Asia-Nimbus Air. That's how s…she travelled so freely."

"With her nurse training any airline would have snapped her up."

Craig sighed. Annette was right. Jennifer Weston had planned ahead; it made sense of why a theology graduate had suddenly changed tack and trained as a nurse. Weston and her handlers must have been planning for years how to make her mobile in a way that avoided suspicion. It was the perfect cover for an international terrorist; be pale skinned and western so that no-one suspected your sympathies and join an airline to get free travel anywhere in the world. Craig asked his next question in a tired voice, already knowing the answer.

"Does Asia-Nimbus fly from Karachi to Dublin by any chance?"

"Yes. I'm following the trail now, but it looks clear that s… she flew Karachi-Dublin when she came to kill Delaney and…"

Craig finished Davy's sentence. "And now she's probably flown to Paris."

"Possibly connecting through Istanbul. I've alerted the airports."

"Thanks, Davy, but my guess is that she's already in Paris and I doubt she's planning a return flight."

***

Paris 9.15 a.m. local time

No-one looked twice at the small dark man who'd just entered the bank foyer, although they certainly looked at his companion. Jenny Weston was used to admiring glances, but the appreciation of beauty in France was something else. Men smiled and stood back for women in the streets and every little girl seemed to see adoration as her right. Jenny played to her audience and smiled back, then she turned her megawatt charm on the suited man who approached them.

"Ah, Monsieur Berger. You wish to access your safe?"

Berger nodded and watched as the manager's eyes travelled slowly up and down his companion. "Your charming guest, she will accompany you?"

Jenny smiled and extended her hand, watching as the manager bent at the waist and took it almost lovingly between his own. If she'd believed in reincarnation she would ask to come back as a beautiful woman born in gay Paree. She glanced seductively at Berger and giggled, artfully playing the game.

"Yes, I can't wait to see what Alain has been raving about."

The manager gestured her forward like a showman,

indicating the way to the vaults. "Then Madame shall have her wish."

The security checks went faster than Berger had ever known them and in less than a minute they were standing in front of the open safe. Berger removed the hide-bound volume as Jenny gazed at it, entranced and disgusted in turn. This was it; a faded mahogany-coloured volume four feet square, embossed in gold letters that declared it was the Holy Christian Word.

She slipped on the gloves that lay inside the safe and turned over the cover gingerly. The religious scholar in her was fascinated. The book was art, each letter lovingly inscribed in ink that had survived for centuries and each page embellished with columns of brightly illuminated Christian symbols on either side of the text. The paper was thick, parchment that had probably cost a fortune even back then, and the words were medieval, some barely recognisable from the versions used nowadays. But she could make out others and they were unambiguous. The Crusades had been God's work, the unbelievers justifiably killed and their God debunked. Even if she hadn't converted to Islam years before, she would find the words offensive. They couldn't, wouldn't be published nowadays; to do so would be a hate crime. But back then…

Jenny inhaled the scent of age and ink and longed to touch the pages with her bare hands. Why didn't she? She had no fear of damaging the book; she already knew what fate it had in store. As Alain Berger watched open-mouthed she removed first one glove and then the other and stroked the illuminated designs gently with her fingertip.

Berger gawped at her. "What are you doing? You will damage it. Keaton will be furious!"

She ignored him and his pathetic attempts to pull the book away, pressing down harder on the page and beginning to read aloud from the text. Her voice rose and soared, echoing around the small vault and as she reached the words of blasphemy that she could never say, she also reached for something else.

This was a bank not an airport, and there were no security scanners or female guards to pat her down. Pretty women were rarely questioned and even more rarely searched, but if she had been they would have found the improvised device that Jenny Weston was wearing beneath her fashionably loose summer dress, and they would have found the control switch that she had strapped against her waist. But no-one had searched her and as she gazed down at the blasphemous words and then at Berger's aghast, uncomprehending face Jenny said the words of praise that she had come to say and did what she had come to do. She pressed the switch hard, shouting "Allah Hu Akbar"; words immediately drowned out by Alain Berger's screams and the shattering sound and silence of the blast.

***

Docklands. 9 a.m.

"Liam, bring us up to date on UKUF."

Liam had waited patiently, well, as patiently as a man who was constantly dragging his fingers through his scrub-like hair and tapping his pen irritatingly against the back of Annette's chair could ever seem. Now he acknowledged Craig's request with a beatific smile that said 'I forgive you for letting others report first, even though I am your second in command.' Liam's exaggerated show of tolerance didn't pass Craig by. He rolled his eyes and poured more coffee as Liam's deep bass filled the room.

"Aye, well. We were right. With Sharpy and Davy both gone the illustrious members of the UK Ulster Force have been running around like headless chicks."

Craig re-took his seat. "How have they been behaving on the street?"

"Badly. There've been fights in the betting shop, and two of them got into it on Donegall Street last night outside a club. Uniform lifted them and let them cool off overnight at High

291

Street, conveniently getting two of the main contenders out of the way for a while. I've spoken to Jack this morning and he's requested permission to detain them for forty-eight hours."

Craig stared at him sceptically. "On what grounds? A drunk and disorderly won't warrant that."

"On the grounds that someone seized the throne overnight and if Jack lets them out right now there'll be a blood bath."

Davy leaned forward, interested. "The King is dead, long live the King. S...So who is it?"

"Take a guess"

"Tommy Hill?"

Liam guffawed so loudly that Annette clamped her hands over her ears.

"Nope, Tommy's moving to Antrim to be near Ella."

It was Annette's turn to gawp. "How did that happen?"

Craig answered her. "We put in a word with the housing exec and got him a transfer. That was what Liam gave him when they met a few days ago."

Davy was undeterred. "So Tommy's living out his days in small town bliss. W...Who's the new UKUF boss then?"

Liam rubbed his chin. "You weren't far off, lad. It's one of Tommy's old gang; Rory McCrae."

Annette looked surprised. "I thought he was in Maghaberry until later this year?"

"Time off for good behaviour. Seems McCrae excelled at everything from crocheting to helping old cons across the recreation ground. He played the game inside. Now he's out and planning to play a different one."

Craig gave a low whistle. "I though Derek Copeland was the front runner?"

Liam shook his head. "He's one of the ones locked up in High Street. Seems he thought he had it in the bag but he was too radical even for UKUF. Maybe it's no bad thing; McCrae's a bad boy but he's not a killer as far as we know. He'll knock some shape into the rabble, even if they only do it because he scares the crap out of them. They know he ran with Tommy for years and Tommy's reputation should be enough to keep them in line." Liam laughed. "McCrae can always call him in for advice."

Annette laughed. "Tommy Hill the management consultant."

Liam tried to look wise. "Reggie and the lads in East Belfast say they're happy enough as long as UKUF calm down and it's business as usual. At least they've avoided a gang war."

Davy cut in. "W…Was one likely?"

Liam nodded. "It was guaranteed. Geoff Hamill had already heard rumblings from the URF and LDL about taking over the Greer's turf. With McCrae in charge they'll get back in their boxes."

"So all's well in the w…world of acronyms again."

Craig had been watching Ken Smith's face during the exchange. He looked fascinated. Even Carmen had noticed his boyish glee and Nicky watched as she stared just a little too long at his profile then glanced away when she caught her gaze.

Craig motioned Smith to speak. "Something you'd like to say, Ken?"

Smith stumbled over his words. "It's… it's just that there's so much going on. As soon as you get one plate spinning there's another one about to fall."

Craig smiled. "And it isn't like that in the army?"

"No, absolutely not. Things are pretty straight forward except when we're on an operation. About the most excitement we get at the base is the odd problem recruit, but they'd be put on a charge as soon as they stepped out of line."

Liam interjected. "Discipline; good stuff. Unfortunately democracy has ruined the real world. People get up to all sorts and even when we manage to catch them some bleeding heart lawyer bangs on about their Human Rights." He gazed wistfully into the distance. "Bring back national service; that would tighten them."

Craig cut in. "Great as it sounds to be able to lock them all up and throw away the key, we're stuck with the system we have. Liam, ask Reggie to give me a call, would you? And go and have a word in McCrae's ear. Tell him that we're watching, Vice is watching and Fraud will be checking his books at regular intervals. Hopefully he'll get the message."

Just then Nicky let out a squeal and all eyes turned towards her. She was staring at her screen as if a giant spider had just appeared. Craig raced over to her desk and when he saw what she'd squealed at he swore under his breath.

"Bugger."

A second later they were all looking at the same thing. A report on the news about an explosion in central Paris. The Banque de Paris had been blown up. Annette was the first to speak.

"It might be nothing to do with the case, sir."

Liam snorted. "Aye and pigs might fly. It's too much of a coincidence."

Craig wheeled round to find Carmen. "Carmen, you and Davy get onto the web immediately and see what you can find out. The rest of us will continue the briefing."

Five minutes later Carmen and Davy re-joined the group. Davy shook his head and Craig's heart sank.

"The w...word's already out there, chief. Someone's even uploaded the bank's internal CCTV from five minutes before the blast." Davy tapped on the tablet he was holding and turned it so that everyone could see. "It must have been backed-up on the Cloud, like the bookshop's was."

As they watched a small man and a blond woman entered the bank's foyer. The woman's I.D. was clear. It was Jennifer Weston. A well-dressed bank manager greeted them then led the way to a lift that descended to what must have been the vaults. Two more minutes of the foyer tape ran, with customers entering and leaving the bank, and then the manager reappeared alone.

"He took them to the vaults."

They watched for another minute until the screen was suddenly filled with white and the image abruptly cut out. The blast had blown the foyer camera or electrics out, hopefully just the latter or everyone in the bank's foyer was dead.

"It was Jenny Weston. She must have found the location of the second book."

"And the mug with her must have thought she was going to buy it. There's no way he'd have gone to the vault with her otherwise."

Craig nodded. Liam was right. The small man was Berger the book dealer and he'd been keeping the book protected in a safe. The way the manager spoke to him said that he'd been at the bank before. There must have been security tests to pass and Weston had needed the man there to complete them, so that she could get close enough to the book to fulfil her aim.

After a long pause Craig shrugged. There was nothing they could have done. As soon as Carmen had given them Berger's name they'd told the Gendarmes and passed Weston's photo along, but without the name of the bank it was too late.

"The time difference."

Craig turned Ken and he elaborated. "France is one hour ahead of us. It's after ten there now. The bank was open for business over an hour ago."

Craig nodded. "Even if it hadn't been it was like looking for a needle in a haystack. All we had from the chatter was a bank in Paris. The Gendarmes would have needed an enormous operation to have prevented this."

Annette had been quiet since they'd viewed the blast but now she spoke. "Our murder cases are solved, sir. We know who blew up Papyrus and now we know why. Jennifer Weston killed her fellow terrorist, Delaney and now she's killed herself. Surely that's it, apart from the court reports?"

Craig almost nodded. Almost but not quite. Then he realised why he hadn't.

"She wasn't acting alone. Weston and Delaney took their orders from someone and my money says they're on that strip of land in Pakistan."

"But surely that's CIA business now? If there's a training camp then won't they deal with it?"

"Yes and probably today. But the radicalisation of Weston and Delaney tells us that there's been recruitment going on in Northern Ireland for some time so they won't be the only pair." Craig turned to Liam. "Get onto the terrorism team and pass on everything we have about the recruitment aspect of this case. They can start chasing. Carmen, help Liam with that please; you have a lot from the Dark Web. Annette, I want SNI charged with anything that fits, you lead on that and Ken can help you. Davy, liaise with the CIA and find out what their plans are for that training camp."

"Delta Force or Predator drones. That's the usual."

He was right. Either the CIA would send in Delta Force, their equivalent of the British S.A.S., or they'd bomb the camp to buggery with an unmanned drone, except...

Craig shook his head. "Maybe so, but not yet. They'll want every last piece of information they can get from this and they won't be able to do that if they destroy the camp and everyone in it." Something occurred to him. "MI6 will want it all as well, Davy, so make sure they get copies of everything we gave the CIA. These bombings happened in Europe. That means that even if the CIA thinks they have dibs on everything, MI6 and Interpol should be taking the lead. Are you OK doing that?"

Davy nodded gleefully. He was going to get to work with the spies.

"If they insist on speaking to me I'll be around." From the glint in Craig's eyes it was clear that he planned to follow up another lead.

"What are you up to, boss?"

Craig smiled, wondering whether to be enigmatic. He decided he couldn't be bothered.

"The CIA is only interested in the terrorists and…" He glanced at Ken. "With all due respect, the army are just interested in the bomb. Everyone seems to have forgotten why this all started."

Annette interjected. "Because some fat cat wanted a pair of rare books."

"Exactly. Those books were stolen to order and we need to know more about them. Who owned them originally and did they steal them in the first place? Carmen, what was the thief's name being mentioned on the web?"

"Larry Benner."

"OK, I'll find out what I can about him. Was there any mention of where the books were to be stolen from and who the middle-man was who brokered one of them to Jules Robinson? And what about the man in Paris? Berger."

"Not so far, but if I had a bit more time…"

"You've got it. Focus on that after you've given Liam everything he needs."

"You mean ten pints of beer and a lads' mag?"

It was the first joke Carmen had cracked since she'd joined them and everyone laughed, even Liam who tried for an offended frown then gave up and joined in.

"After that. You know where all the internet chat-rooms and back doors are. I want names; the original owner or owners of the books, the thief or thieves who stole them and details of all the middle-men in Belfast and Paris. Also, chase up the new buyer here."

Annette gave a puzzled frown. "But why do we care, sir? Isn't this work for cyber-crime?"

"Yes and no, Annette. We'll hand over everything at close of play today, but my instinct says that the M.I.A won't be content with just killing the people they've already killed and destroying the books. They'll want everyone linked to the books they can find. They've only managed to kill two middle-men as far as we know; Jules Robinson and the man in Paris with Jennifer

Weston. He was probably Berger but we need that confirmed. A café in the Marais was also mentioned, so was there another man there? If we know that these other people exist then so do the radicals and they'll want them all dead. Davy, you know about rare books. A serious buyer would have put the word out that he wanted the books, yes?"

"Yes. That w...would have set people running to find them. Auctioneers, booksellers like Jules Robinson and all-out thieves."

Craig nodded excitedly. "We have two locations; Belfast and Paris. That means the books were most likely owned by people in Europe somewhere, possibly two different owners, and stolen by European thieves. If the books were in Europe it's probable that the buyers are as well. All of those people are sitting ducks just waiting to be killed."

Annette nodded slowly, not entirely convinced. "We're trying to prevent all these murders?"

"Yes."

"Apart from the fact that it's a nice thing to do, sir, surely it's not our job? Unless…"

"We have a week left before we go on leave and I don't like loose ends."

Annette burst out laughing. "At least you're honest about it. OK, let's see what we can get. I just hope that in the process we don't become targets as well."

***

3 p.m.

Between Carmen and Davy working on the Ethernet, Liam squeezing every contact he had in Belfast, Craig doing the same in London and the Fraud Squad reluctantly opening their books to Annette, by three p.m. the trail had led them to two names and one of them was more familiar than Liam would have liked.

"What the hell is Tommy doing getting involved in this crap?"

Craig shook his head tiredly and swung his chair round to gaze out his window, trying to make sense of this latest twist. Liam hadn't finished his rant.

"The stupid wee get. I thought he was going clean for the baby's sake. And to think we got him a new house."

Craig held up a hand to still his rant. It had been going on for five minutes and looked as if the steam Liam was generating was going to propel it for five more.

"Once a thief… anyway, we can debate Tommy's ingratitude once we have him safely in an interview room. Get Reggie to lift him, Liam. Just say I want a chat. We need to find out what part he had in all this."

"We know what part! He stole at least one of the books to order for Jules Robinson. An ex-cop in bed with Tommy Hill!"

The note of indignation in Liam's voice almost made Craig laugh. He wasn't offended by Tommy still walking a crooked path; he was offended that a cop had been working with him.

"Robinson may not have known that the book was stolen."

Liam pointed out the window. "There goes that flying pig again…"

"Point taken. But either way, we're not going to prosecute Jules Robinson's corpse and all we have on Tommy is rumour, virtual rumour at that. I want who Tommy got the book from; they'd already stolen it from someone else. This isn't about theft; it's about preventing these fanatics from killing more people."

He waved Liam out. "Tommy in High Street by four o'clock and we're interviewing him together. I'll meet you there."

"What are you doing till then?"

"Trying to work out how to prevent the CIA putting him on a plane to Guantanamo."

***

The name of the second book's buyer was unfamiliar to Craig but it wasn't to Ken Smith.

"I was right. It is the same Troy Keaton. Keaton's one of the biggest illegal arms dealers in Europe; the bane of the legitimate military's life. Every time we thought we had the guns off the streets in Kabul more would appear. He had a sales technique. He'd give the freedom fighters the first dozen guns free; so that everyone would see them and want one, then he'd make his profit off the next thousand they ordered. After that he'd introduce more sophisticated weapons so they would buy those and discard the old ones."

"Smart marketing. Newer flashier versions to make people discard the old; just like mobile phone companies."

Smith nodded at the analogy. Craig was making a list in his head, now he grabbed a flip chart and put it down.

"These are the names we have so far. Troy Keaton, the man lined up to buy the book in Paris." He swung to check where Davy was. He was tapping furiously at one of his screens. "Davy. Do we know where Keaton is now?"

Davy thought for a moment then gave a half-nod.

"Why the hesitation?"

"W…We know where he was this morning. At home in Geneva. But he left for the International Airport thirty minutes ago."

"On the run."

"Probably. He must have heard about the explosion and put two and two together."

"OK. It's time to get him off the street, if only for his own safety."

Craig turned to find Annette. She was nowhere to be seen.

"Nicky, where's Annette?"

"She said she was following up a hunch."

Craig smiled. He liked people to follow their hunches, even if they didn't pan out.

"OK. Nicky, get onto the Cantonal police in Geneva and ask

them to hold Troy Keaton at the airport until I get in touch. Tell them it's on the basis of suspected theft and for his own protection."

He turned back to Ken. "Liam's gone to lift someone else for me, which leaves us with the local buyer Jules Robinson had lined-up for the first book; someone called Neeson according to what Carmen found on the web. That's right Carmen, isn't it?"

Carmen glanced up from the sandwich she was examining suspiciously. She was vegetarian and the pink substance inside had a distinctly carnivorous tinge. "His name is Jack Neeson. I have more on him if you'd like."

"Please." Craig waved her to take the floor.

"Jack Neeson, sixty-three years old. Retired banker who made his money in the City of London and started acquiring antiques when he was in his thirties. It's rumoured that he has quite a collection of paintings and books."

Craig raised a hand to stop her. "That reminds me; get onto the Antiquities' Squad please. It's time they got involved. Carry on."

"The word is Neeson's turned more to rare books in the past few years and he was definitely the name mentioned in association with Jules Robinson's book."

"Where is he living now?"

"Hillsborough. Near the castle."

It was one of the wealthiest areas of Northern Ireland.

"How sure are we that he's the Neeson mentioned on the web?"

Carmen smiled, not at the fact she knew the answer but at the trust in Craig's voice. He'd trusted her opinion quickly; it made a refreshing change from the second guessing in Vice.

"One hundred percent. He's the only one that ticks all the boxes."

Craig nodded to himself, imagining Jack Neeson in some rural idyll playing golf, totally unaware that his steal-to-order request was about to disrupt his life.

"OK, Carmen contact C District and explain what's happening. Neeson needs to be brought to High Street for questioning."

He turned back to the flip chart but not before he saw Carmen's excited smile. She'd handled the web side of things well, there was no reason she shouldn't do the same with this, although he knew Liam wouldn't be pleased by her autonomy.

"OK, so we know both buyers: Keaton and Neeson, and the likely thief Larry Benner. Carmen, get him lifted as well, please, wherever he is. We know that two of the middle-men are dead; the man in the bank who we think was Alain Berger, and Jules Robinson. Ken, until Annette comes back I want you to work with Davy on confirming Berger was the man at the Banque de Paris and finding the previous owner or owners of the books. When Annette returns track them down and do the same as we have with the buyers. The longer they're out there unprotected the likelier it is that they'll be killed."

Craig glanced at his watch. "Right, it's three-fifty. I'm heading to High Street to interview someone with Liam. We'll reconvene at five for an update. Can I have a one page summary from each of you then please, ready to be handed over to the CIA."

Carmen groaned. "Do we have to give it to them? They'll wreck everything."

"Yes, we do. They're good at what they do and the special relationship has to be maintained. Ken, get onto Agents Ross and Mulhearn please and tell them I want them here at five, with an update on the location we gave them in Pakistan."

Smith looked puzzled. "How will I contact them, sir? Through the American Embassy?"

"You could do. Alternatively you could just look out the window. They've been sitting outside in their car again for hours."

***

High Street Station. 4 p.m.

By the time Craig reached High Street Liam had his feet up in the staff-room and was munching on a custard cream. Craig smiled hello to Jack Harris and deliberately knocked Liam's feet off the coffee table as he walked by.

"We need to start; we have to be back by five. Where's Tommy?"

Jack answered him. "Having tea and biccies in interview room one and ranting about the injustice of it all."

"Injustice my foot. The only injustice here is that we ever believed he was going straight."

Craig poured himself a coffee and headed for the door while Liam slipped some biscuits into his pocket for later. One minute later they were sitting opposite an unrepentant Tommy Hill who was munching noisily on a Rich Tea.

"Do you know why you're here, Tommy?"

Tommy squinted at Craig, trying to muster up his animosity of a year before but failing. Craig and the ghost had done all right by him; they'd done for the scrote who'd killed Evie and now he'd got a nice new house in a posh area where he could live out his remaining days. So instead of his customary scowl, Tommy grinned at them. It wasn't a sarcastic smirk or a pitying smile, he actually grinned, happily, like a normal person. Liam gawped at the old lag and then at Craig, who shook his head in disbelief.

"Tommy, are you taking this seriously? I repeat; do you know why you're here?"

Hill maintained his sunny demeanour and gave an amused shrug. "'Cos you've nathin' better tee do?"

Tommy was going to play the denial game and they didn't have the time. Craig had come prepared. He took something from his pocket and set it on the desk so Hill could see. It was a photograph of Jules Robinson. They both saw the glimmer of recognition in Hill's small eyes.

"Don't bother denying that you know him, Tommy. How?"

Hill yawned and reached into his pocket for a cigarette, putting it un-lit into his mouth. The silence that followed said he was going to play games, so Liam did what he did best. He roared.

"We know you were working with him, Tommy. When did you two meet?" Liam slammed his palm down hard for emphasis making Hill jump back.

"Here, don't be starting all that. I've dun nathin'"

Craig cut in. "You've done enough for us to take your new house away, so talk if you want any hope of holding onto it."

Craig had no intention of blocking Hill's house move but he needed answers and fear seemed like the quickest route.

Hill's affability switched to a familiar scowl and he hissed at them under his breath. "I'll kill both of ye if you try. See if I don't."

Craig rarely raised his voice but he did now. He rose to his feet and loomed over the small man.

"You stupid bastard, we're trying to save your life here. Just answer the question. How do you know this man?"

Hill reared up so that his face was six inches from Craig's and Liam watched as they stared each other out. Tommy blinked first and sat back heavily in his chair.

"He nicked me a few times, back in the day."

Craig retook his seat. That may have been true but it was a more recent acquaintance he cared about. "Recently. What contact did you have with him recently?"

Hill considered for a moment, thinking about his new council house. His shoulders dropped, signalling concession. "He contacted me about some aul books he wanted."

"And asked you to do what?"

"Well he didn't ask me to buy them for him in Waterstones, did he?"

Liam leaned forward. "You stole them?"

Hill shook his head, surprising both men. "Nah. They was in

304

England. I got a mate of mine tee nick them. He brought one over on the Liverpool–Belfast last week. I paid him and Robinson paid me."

"Was your mate's name Larry Benner by any chance?"

A quick creasing of Tommy's forehead said yes.

"Did you meet him while enjoying Her Majesty's hospitality?"

Still no answer but Craig was undeterred. He tried a different tack. "What happened to the second book, Tommy?"

Hill shrugged. "Benner got a better offer from some bloke in Paris. I only got one of them."

They'd confirmed that the two books had had one owner and Davy had just called through with a name; Gareth Holmes. Now they had the owner, Gareth Holmes, the thief, Larry Benner, two buyers, Neeson and Keaton, and three middle men that they knew of; Tommy, Jules Robinson and Alain Berger in Paris.

Craig cut in. "How much?"

Tommy answered in an incongruously prim voice. "I don't think that's any of yer business."

"Dealing in stolen goods is. How much did Robinson pay you, Tommy?"

Tommy shrugged. He'd already spent most of it; good luck to the cops trying to get it back.

"Five grand. I paid Benner one."

Craig almost laughed at the pettiness of the amount. Jules Robinson had had Jack Neeson lined up to pay millions. Robinson had crossed the line between law and disorder; probably fed up with years of watching crooks making a fortune while he'd struggled by on an average wage. But there was a reason why people instinctively chose one side or another; they usually didn't have what it took to cross the floor. Trying to be a criminal had killed Jules Robinson.

Craig thought for a moment and then decided that Tommy deserved to know how much at risk he was. In a few minutes

Craig outlined the trail of book theft and trafficking across Europe, then he came to the piéce de resistance.

"Did you hear about the bomb in Smithfield last week, Tommy?"

Hill nodded and waved a hand at Liam. "Aye, sure Ghost here was asking me about protection rackets." His face lit up suddenly. "Here, guess who's the new boss of UKUF? Only McCrae." His voice took on a note of pride. "I alays knew that boy wud do well."

Craig shook his head at Tommy's definition of 'well' and got back to the point. "The bomb was planted at Jules Robinson's bookshop and we believe that it was set specifically to destroy the book that you obtained for him."

"What? What the hell for? It was only an aul book. Mouldy looking thing too."

"The book was considered blasphemous by some people, Tommy and they want anyone who had anything to do with its sale dead."

Craig paused to let the words sink in then watched as surprise morphed into incredulity and then horror on Hill's thin face. The aging criminal jumped to his feet in shock.

"Ye mean they… I only got the book for Robinson, I didn't steal it!"

Craig shook his head. "They don't care, Tommy. As far as they're concerned anyone who was involved is fair game, so we need to keep you safe till this blows over." Craig waited a moment before continuing. "The American authorities will want to speak to you as well. The group who planted the bomb is wanted by them and others."

Tommy shook his head furiously. "I'm not goin' to the States. They lock people up fer life fer jaywalking." He added "Ella…" pathetically and Craig nodded.

"We won't allow that to happen. You're an idiot, Tommy, but you're our idiot. We'll charge you with dealing in stolen goods and you can explain it all to a judge."

Craig stood up and gazed at the subdued man. "For God's sake go straight, Tommy. Or if not for God's sake for Ella's, please."

***

Docklands. 5 p.m.

As Craig and Liam re-entered the squad-room they were treated to the sight of Nicky flirting with Agents Ross and Mulhearn, in a way that had them leaning back in their chairs, more afraid than if they'd been faced with any terrorist. Craig nodded at her in gratitude and slipped into his office with Liam loping behind.

Once there he phoned Carmen at her desk. "Anything on Neeson?"

"Yes, sir. Chief Inspector Duncan had him lifted and he's in custody now."

"Good work. When he comes down to High Street you can interview him with Annette. Is Ken there?"

A moment later Smith came on the phone.

"Ken, Nicky's keeping the CIA busy. Tell me about our friend in Geneva."

Smith grinned, more pleased at the arms dealer's arrest than by anything in a long time.

"They're holding Keaton at their headquarters. It's brilliant, sir, we've been after this guy for years for arms dealing and now we get him because of a book!"

"Ted Bundy was caught during a routine traffic stop. OK, good. Alert MI6 and Major James now please."

"Already done."

Craig smiled.

"Just one thing, sir. Keaton's an American citizen. That means the CIA will want to be involved."

"Interpol and MI6 will get a crack at him first then the CIA can have their turn. OK, we've got the name of the perp who stole the books and the name of their original owner in England. Get onto the English forces to lift them and get them both down to the Met; a Chief Inspector Idowu will be expecting them. Then join us at the briefing. I'll delay it for five minutes."

By ten-past-five everyone pretty much knew everything, including the name of the books' original owner Gareth Holmes, who lived in Cookham Rise in London's wealthy commuter belt. The Met could find out who he'd got the books from.

Craig kept Tommy Hill's name until last, giving the two agents a challenging look as he spoke.

"He's under arrest and going nowhere, so if you want to question him then you'll have to do it here."

Ross was about to object when a sudden buzz in his pocket made him take out his phone and exchange a look with Mulhearn. They stood up abruptly. "We need to take a call. Is there..."

"Use my office."

The two men strode into Craig's office and a few murmured words were quickly followed by whoops of delight.

Liam gestured towards the noise. "Inhibited pair, aren't they?"

An even less inhibited series of air-punches followed and when the men re-emerged they looked unfeasibly pleased.

"Anything you can share with us?"

Ross grinned. "We sure can." He gestured to Davy's screens. "If your boy could turn on his screen, they're just sending the images through."

The boy did as he was bid and they crowded round Davy's tech horseshoe, watching as grainy black and white images appeared on his central screen. Ross explained in his southern drawl.

"They're streaming it through from the Pentagon. It's on a

five minute delay."

Craig squinted at the image. "What are we looking at?"

"The Kharan Desert at night." Mulhearn glanced at his watch. "It's after nine p.m. there."

As they watched the screen, several white shapes moved in the darkness. One or two in the open and the rest inside makeshift tents. There were approximately twenty in all, spread out in a circle four hundred metres across. It was a camp! As soon as the word entered Craig's mind he knew what was coming. At the periphery of the camp were more white shapes, moving swiftly and on foot. They entered the tents one by one, shooting anyone who resisted in a shower of white gun-fire. In less than a minute there were only three from the twenty shapes still moving and they were being herded forward at the point of a gun. The screen flickered off in a hail of static and they all knew what the agents had been whooping about.

No-one said anything until Craig broke the silence. "How many?"

Mulhearn answered cheerfully. "We got three. They're on their way back home now."

Craig's face was solemn. "I meant how many did you kill?"

He didn't wait for an answer. Disgusted as he was at the terrorists' behaviour he couldn't feel much better about what he'd just seen. He pitied the men in custody in Geneva and London and hoped that MI6 got to them first. In that moment he made a decision.

Craig beckoned Carmen and Ken to follow him to his office, leaving the others still gawping at the blacked-out screen. As they entered he spoke quickly.

"I want you two on a plane to Geneva via London tonight. Check on Benner and Holmes in London first. Question them thoroughly and make sure they're not likely to be extradited to the States, then get to Geneva and do the same for Troy Keaton. Ken, liaise with the military over Keaton's arms dealing please, and Davy will give you his contacts at MI6 and Interpol. The

CIA will want to interrogate everyone who had anything to do with this case, even though it happened on European soil; that's fine but it's your job to make sure that only happens under supervision. OK? I want these people to be tried where their crimes were committed. What the European courts decide to do with them is another thing."

Smith nodded. No-one liked terrorists and thieves, but everything had happened in Europe so they should be tried in its courts. Keaton would be their hardest sell; he was a US citizen.

"Carmen, are you OK to go?"

Carmen nodded excitedly, flattered to be trusted with the police side of the task. Craig smiled, wondering what the odds on their romance would stand at once Davy knew about this. They would have to wait till they got back from John's wedding to see whether Switzerland's beauty had had a romantic effect.

"Get ready to leave and call me with regular updates. We're all on leave from Monday but I'm contactable by phone."

They slipped out and Craig re-joined the group just as Annette arrived. She was brought up to speed quickly by an awe-struck Davy.

"You s…should have seen it, Annette. They went in and shot…"

Craig beckoned her quickly to one side.

"Nicky said you were following up a hunch?"

Annette dragged her eyes away from the agents and tried to look less shocked than she felt.

"Yes, sir. It may be nothing but something that Hilary Stenson said rang a bell."

"What bell?"

"Well, I thought that if SNI had worked with a gang like UKUF to get the land they wanted over here, then how many other times had they done it? So I checked the land registry throughout the British Isles."

"And?"

Annette nodded. "There was always a delay between SNI exploring planning permission on a site and actually buying the land, but they put a huge amount of money into preliminary searches, not only about the land but about its current occupants."

"They'd been banking on getting the land, whatever it took."

"Yes. So I contacted the serious crime lads in each city and asked if the areas in question had gangs or protection rackets running in them. And if there'd been any suspicion of pressure being exerted to obtain the land. It's early days but the facts seem to point to yes, so I thought we should build a case against SNI UK wide, before showing our hand?"

Craig smiled. If Annette was right the case could crack SNI's racket wide open.

"Do you want to be seconded to Serious Crime until it's done?"

Annette shook her head. "I can do it in my down time, if that's OK. SNI have no idea that we're onto them and they're going nowhere."

Craig smiled again, relieved. He didn't want to lose Annette from the team, but he hadn't wanted to stand in her way. He had a second thought; how would she fit in all the extra work around her marriage? He decided that she'd probably already made her choice.

He ushered Annette back to the group, marvelling at how what had started as an explosion in a small bookshop had turned into an international case. He was reluctant to allow the agents any more access to his squad-room than they already had so he made an executive decision.

"Anyone for dinner at The James?"

As Carmen and Ken packed up their desks, he nodded them to join the group for dinner, with a subtext to keep quiet about their task. As everyone filtered off the floor Craig put a call through to the lab, inviting John and Des to join the group. Tonight they would celebrate cracking the case and cement the special relationship over a beer. Tomorrow they would get to the serious business of sealing things off.

Chapter Twenty

Barbados. Friday, 1st August. 11 p.m. local time

"You're certain you've got the ring?"

Craig nodded and took another sip of wine. "Why only one?"

John shrugged. "I offered to wear one but Natalie doesn't like jewellery on men, thank goodness. My hands are in and out of gloves so often I'd have lost it within a week." He glanced at Craig anxiously. "You're not going to say anything too embarrassing in your speech, are you?"

Craig raised an eyebrow and held his glass up to the light in the hotel bar, smiling as John panicked at his silence.

"Promise me you won't mention that time in the student's union?"

"Which particular time are you referring to? The time when you brought a book into a disco to read and then wondered why everyone stared at you? Or the time when you got so drunk you attempted the routine from Flashdance, including all the leaps?"

John's eyes widened; he'd forgotten about both occasions. "No, I meant the time we laid a bet on how many women we could snog in one hour."

Craig grinned, remembering. John added. "But you're not to mention the others either."

Craig shook his head. "I can't make any promises. Best man's speeches have free licence. Think of it as a rite of passage."

"It'll be right to the loony bin if Natalie's parents hear any of those."

Craig tutted exaggeratedly at John's non-P.C. words and then smiled again. "All I can promise you is that your in-laws will still be speaking to you when I've finished, even if they do look at you in a slightly different way."

John groaned and put his head in his hands. "Am I doing the right thing, Marc? Being married to one woman for the rest of my life? What if I meet someone else?"

Craig rolled his eyes. John's track record with women was a mixture of two-week catastrophes and celibacy. Natalie was the only woman he'd ever been seriously interested in.

"I'll make you a deal. If you ever get the urge to release your inner Casanova, give me a call and I'll talk you out of it. OK?"

John nodded solemnly and Craig realised he thought he'd been serious. He laughed loudly.

"I was joking. Natalie's all you've talked about for two years. She's perfect for you and you're going to be very happy together. Now, finish your wine and get some sleep. You're the star turn tomorrow."

As John loped off to his bedroom, Craig poured himself another glass of wine and thought about the case. Ken and Carmen had been successful in blocking the CIA's attempts at extradition so far, but he knew he'd have an argument on his hands when he returned. Just then Katy entered the bar, providing a welcome diversion from his thoughts. Craig smiled as she approached, marvelling how brown she'd turned in only two days.

"How's the blushing bride?"

She plonked herself down at the small table. "Raring to go. How's John?"

"Wondering if he's being fair on womankind, taking himself off the market."

They laughed simultaneously.

"Since when was John a lothario?"

"Forever, in his dreams. He's fine, just worried about my

speech. He thinks I'm going to embarrass him."

"Are you?"

Craig nodded. "I sincerely hope so. But not half as much as Liam intends to later on."

Katy smiled then turned to gaze across the veranda at the white sand beach. Craig watched her, thinking again how much he liked her. He caught himself, pushing the thoughts away. Weddings had a romantic effect on people and it wasn't helped by everyone saying that they would be next. Kind wishes or misery loves company? He was split on marriage as an institution but he didn't know why; his parents had been happy for decades. As an abstract concept marriage seemed fine, someday and for some people, he just wasn't sure that he was one of them. He'd been with Camille for nine years and engaged. That had failed, so who was to say that actually tying the knot was any guarantee.

Katy turned to him and smiled again and Craig felt his heart flip, throwing all his logical arguments into disarray. Falling in love was one thing, but falling in love with a woman you liked so much was something else entirely and it was his first time. He made himself a promise not to get carried away by the romance of the Caribbean, no matter what the pressure from everyone else, and just thanked God that his mother wasn't there. She'd have spent the whole two weeks pursuing Katy with a questionnaire!

John had invited his parents to the wedding; they'd basically adopted him when his own parents had died leaving him with only one living relative, a ninety-year-old aunt. They'd declined reluctantly but the flight was too long for his father. John's aunt hadn't been fit to travel either, so John had promised a wedding dinner for all of them when he and Natalie returned home. It meant if you looked at the wedding in the traditional 'his side/her side' way then the only people on John's side of the church were Lucia, Craig and the pathology and murder teams. It didn't matter; they were his family now.

315

Craig turned his thoughts back to Katy. Whatever was going to happen between them would happen in Ireland or it wouldn't happen at all. He would think about things when he got home. He startled, remembering that he'd promised himself the opposite the week before. He knew he kept shifting the romantic goal-posts but he wasn't quite sure why. Did it mean that Katy wasn't right for him? Or, more likely, that she was. Really was, in a marriage and not just a girlfriend way. The thought frightened him so he pushed it away with a smile and another glass of wine. This was John and Natalie's wedding and his, if it ever came, was going to be a long, long time away.

***

Saturday, 2nd August. 10 a.m.

"Ready, Natalie?"

Katy gazed at her petite friend and caught her breath. Natalie looked stunning. She'd paired her white-silk dress with island flowers threaded through her dark hair and she carried a matching posy in her hand. Katy caught a glimpse of herself in the mirror and smiled. Her lemon bridesmaid's dress looked lovely. No taffeta blancmanges today.

Natalie lifted her small bouquet demurely to her waist and then nodded, not trusting herself to speak. If she did she would cry with happiness and water-proof mascara only worked so far. Katy led the way from the beach-front room where Natalie had slept the night before, observing the age-old tradition of not seeing the groom until the big day. She'd slept with Craig to make sure Natalie had had the room to herself, well, that was her excuse and she was sticking to it.

As they crossed the sand, accompanied by Liam's four-year-old daughter Erin and Des' toddler Rafferty, Katy watched as Natalie's worries seemed to fall away. It was as if all life's tribulations were unimportant now that she was going to be with John.

They reached the small chapel on the sand, set with rows of chairs facing the sea and the altar where John and Craig stood, wearing pale grey tails. As the string quartet began Bach's 'Sheep may safely graze' Katy fell in behind Natalie with the children. Then Bernard Ingrams took his daughter's arm and led her slowly to the man who would love her for the rest of her days.

***

3 p.m.

Craig tapped his glass until everyone in the marquee fell silent then he rose and turned towards Natalie and John, grinning so hard that he thought his face would crack. He normally hated weddings because they were full of strangers, but everyone knew each other today and everyone was smiling. Best of all they knew the craic was going to continue for two weeks.

"It's my honour to be John's best man today and, as such, I'd like to propose a toast to the bride and groom. Please be upstanding for Natalie and John."

Everyone stood and toasted and after the cheers and comments had died down and Craig had formally thanked the bridesmaids and parents, he tapped the glass again.

"It's also my job, as best man and as someone who has known the groom since he was twelve, to embarrass him as much as possible."

John groaned and put his head in his hands and Natalie began to laugh.

"Now, there are plenty of stories I could tell you about John, many of them amusing and most of them embarrassing, but I thought the best way to make you feel as if you were actually there watching him put his foot in it, would be to play you a little tape."

At that Craig nodded towards the back of the marquee and the lights dimmed as much as they could in the sunshine. Liam appeared carrying a projector pressed a button to play a fanfare, the signal for the show to begin. Twenty minutes of photographs and video clips of John from the age of three played, with Craig providing a commentary to them, including a video of John performing Flashdance in the student's union bar. He wrapped up with "John will be performing his dance routine later this evening and all donations will go to charity" and then led a round of applause for the groom's misspent youth.

As the show ended John turned to Craig, laughing.

"Where did you get all those photos?"

Craig smiled. "As soon as you asked me to be best man I wrote to everyone I could remember from school and Queen's, and your aunt. They were more than happy to dig up clips for me, particularly embarrassing ones."

Natalie laughed. "I'm just glad you haven't known me that long."

Four hours later the formal photographs were all taken, the main players had changed into something more relaxed and the marquee was laid out for the evening dance. Craig wandered across to the circle his team and their other halves had formed, smiling at the sight of them all dressed up.

Nicky had kept to her fifties theme, in a blue ballerina-length dress. Her husband Gary had been forced into a colour-coordinated suit, with Jonny, their twelve-year-old dressed like his mini-me and pulling his collar loose as soon as his mother's back was turned. Liam was wearing a cream linen suit, with a matching fedora to protect his fair skin from the sun. It made him look like a mobster from a Humphrey Bogart classic but Craig had to admit that he carried it well. Davy and Maggie were the picture of Hilfiger cool and looked like they belonged on the cover of Harper's Bazaar, but the biggest shock of all was Annette.

In the week since the end of the case she'd managed to lose half-a-stone and it suited her. Her hair had been professionally done in a style that Katy later told Craig was called 'messy cool' and in her low-backed turquoise dress and matching high heels, she looked ten years younger than her age. Craig cast a look around for Pete but Annette shook her head.

"He couldn't get the time off. The school signed him up for some summer camp. I only found last weekend."

She looked sad but not as sad as Craig had expected and he saw another nail go into the coffin of her marriage then and there. He smiled kindly.

"Well you look lovely, Annette. Save me a dance later on."

Annette smiled and then glanced over his shoulder. Craig turned to see where her gaze led and saw Mike Augustus, John's deputy pathologist, pouring himself a drink. Craig read the signs and he couldn't say that he was altogether surprised. Pete McElroy had wrecked their marriage with his affair twelve months before, and after a year of trying to make things work it looked as if Annette had finally had enough.

Liam's deep voice broke through his reverie. "Nice party. Mind you, that vicar went on a bit."

Craig agreed but decided to wind Liam up. "That vicar, as you call him, is Natalie's uncle. So I'd be careful who you said that to."

Liam back-pedalled furiously. "Aye, well. I suppose he wasn't that bad… I was only saying…"

Craig laughed. "He's not her uncle at all and you're right, he did go on. But I suppose it's only once in a lifetime."

Liam glanced pointedly at Annette and raised an eyebrow, saying nothing.

A ripple of applause behind them made Craig turn to see Natalie and Katy entering the marquee. Natalie was wearing a shorter version of her wedding dress and her dark curly hair was in a high pony-tail; if Craig hadn't known she was in her thirties he would have thought she was about eighteen. But it was Katy who really caught his eye. Her bridesmaid's dress had been replaced by a short red halter-neck with five-inch heels to match. She looked stunning, and sexier than Craig had ever seen her look.

A sudden shove from Liam almost landed Craig flat on the floor. "I'd run away now, boss, otherwise you'll never want to run again."

His words were drowned out as the music started and the crowd clapped for John to perform his Flashdance routine, but they were already lost on Craig. He walked across to Katy and kissed her gently, knowing they were about to have the best two weeks they'd ever had.

THE END

Fantastic Books
Great Authors

Meet our authors and discover our exciting range:

- Gripping Thrillers
- Cosy Mysteries
- Romantic Chick-Lit
- Fascinating Historicals
- Exciting Fantasy
- Young Adult and Children's Adventures

Visit us at:
www.crookedcatbooks.com

Join us on facebook:
www.facebook.com/crookedcatpublishing

PLJ

P Hay.

CPSIA information can be obtained at www.ICGtesting.com
Printed in the USA
LVOW08s0258041214

417105LV00007B/299/P

9 781910 510124